THE CENTER OF
EXCELLENCE

ISBN: 978-0-9890713-1-4

THE CENTER OF
EXCELLENCE

A NOVEL

By

MICHAEL BANAS

CHAPTER ONE

GRADUATION DAY

PHIL DRUMMER FOUND it impossible to believe that it was the last day of his surgical internship. While methodically scrubbing his hands at the surgical sink his gaze peered through a glass window into operating room number five. A teenage boy admitted to the hospital with acute appendicitis was on the table. The anesthesiologist had just completed placing a breathing tube down the young man's trachea and the scrub nurse was prepping out the abdomen. Phil was amazed as to how skinny the boy was while motionless in the supine position. Standing next to Phil was chief resident Peter Larson, who also had difficulty believing that it was his last day at the Philadelphia General Hospital.

"This one is all yours," said Larson while finishing up his hand scrub with a toss of the brush into the sink. "Don't screw it up."

"I won't," said Phil somewhat confidently. He had seen several appendectomies over the past few months and was comfortable with the procedure. "Where is Doc Johnson?" was his question directed at the chief resident who rapidly turned the corner into the operating room without responding.

As Phil quickly finished his preoperative scrub a rush of adrenaline pulsated through his body. Finally, after one harsh year of training it was his turn to perform a surgical procedure. While entering the room a nervous bravado overtook him as nurse Ella Frey greeted him with a smile.

"Ready doctor?" was her simple question.

"Yes," said Phil, "But where is Doctor Johnson?"

"He is on his way," said Larson as he began to place sterile drapes over the patient's abdomen. "Let's go before this appendix ruptures! The sooner we start the better."

Phil responded to the urgent command and quickly joined the chief resident at the patient's side. In a flurry of activity the team began to set up the equipment in preparation for a laparoscopic appendectomy. The last step of the preoperative process involved Dr. Larson drawing out three small incisions with a skin marker that would allow the minimally invasive procedure to be done. Nurse Frey then handed Phil the scalpel.

Phil looked up at the clock and said, "Start time 1312 hours," and then began to bring the knife down to the young patient's skin. His first surgical case was about to begin and he thought of how proud his parents would be.

"Stop!" said an elderly voice from behind the team. "What's going on here?" asked Doctor Francis Johnson who had just walked into the room with a slow plodding gait. Dr. Johnson was the most senior attending surgeon on the hospital staff, having spent the last thirty-two years at the PGH. He was holding an untied surgical mask up to his face as he approached the table. The surgical scrub outfit that he wore sagged on his bony frame. "What the hell is going on?"

"Acute appendix, in a sixteen year old male," said Larson.

"I'm not asking you Larson," said Dr. Johnson sarcastically. "Next week you will be in Los Angeles wasting your talents doing face lifts and implanting artificial breasts. I'm asking the intern here to update me on the case."

Phil continued to hold the scalpel in his hands while turning backwards to speak. "Acute appendix Doctor Johnson. Sixteen year old male with a classic presentation, symptoms started last night."

"Why don't you put down the knife young man and turn around to face me," said Johnson. "Then as concisely as possible tell me what your definition of a classic acute appendix presentation is."

Phil turned about to face the attending surgeon and began to present the case in detail. It was obvious to him that this was the first time Dr. Johnson had heard of the case, since he had been operating for the last six hours in the adjacent room. Phil noticed that his shoes still had blotches of blood on them from the prior patient. Over the next three minutes he concisely summarized the patient's presenting symptoms, exam findings and blood work. This was followed by a detailed description of the preoperative CAT scan. Upon completion of the dissertation Phil was confident in the diagnosis and plan.

"What's all this crap on the table?" said Dr. Johnson with a wave of a crooked and arthritic index finger. "I mean what's with all the television monitors and screens around the table? Are we at a goddamn movie theatre?"

"We consented the procedure as a laparoscopic appendectomy," said Larson who was quite aware as to where the old time surgeon was headed. The laparoscopic procedure utilized a small digital camera inserted through a quarter inch incision, allowing the physician to perform the state of the art procedure while viewing an overhead screen.

"Don't worry about what the consent says in an abdomen case Larson," blurted Johnson in response. "Just remember to put the phrase "sound surgical judgment" in your operative report and let me talk to the parents after the procedure." The elder surgeon then returned his gaze to intern Drummer.

"Why are you doing this simple procedure through tiny incisions that requires more technology than the Space Shuttle launch?" asked Johnson. "Why make a simple task complex?"

"Ah, sir the benefits of laparoscopic…"

"I mean this procedure has been done successfully through a several inch open incision for centuries. Why mess with something that works?" said Johnson calmly but with a disturbed look in his eyes.

Phil then tried to speak saying, "Doctor Johnson I have only seen the procedure done through a laparoscope, I've never…"

"Get all the cameras off the table!" screamed Johnson. "For Christ's sake you are not going to leave this program without knowing how to do a simple, goddamn open appendectomy. That laparoscope is the instrument of the devil!"

The surgical team immediately responded by rapidly removing the laparoscope and multiple connecting video cords from the field. As they feverishly cleared the field of modern technology the salty old surgeon continued his tirade while pushing the overhead monitor screens away from the table with a vengeance.

"What happens when the mom and pop community hospital you're working at five years from now tells you the single laparoscope they have is out for repairs?" yelled Johnson. "Or how about the fact that the surgeon next door is using the primary laparoscope and the backup one has a large scratch on the lens that doesn't allow a clear picture. What then Dr. Drummer! What happens when you put the scope into the patient and the appendix has already ruptured, what then doctor? I'll tell you what," said the elderly physician whose face was now turning beet red, "You stand there with your thumb up your ass wondering why no attending surgeon at the great PGH taught you how to do a simple open appendectomy."

As the rant continued Phil noticed that Pete Larson took the surgical marker and drew out a short oblique line over the proposed incision site. In disgust he motioned at nurse Frey to pass the scalpel back to Phil. The knife again ended up in Phil's hands as he slowly brought it towards the skin.

"What are you doing intern Drummer?" said Johnson with an incredulous tone. "What is God's name are you doing? Put the lancet down and turn around to face me young man."

Phil responded rapidly and turned about to again face the elder surgeon. His frame towered over the slight body of his mentor. Out of the corner of his eye he saw the anesthesiologist's head surface above the surgical sheet, a harbinger of a pending calamity. Phil then gazed into the bloodshot eyes of the aging physician suddenly realizing that he may not be allowed to perform the surgery. He noticed a series of thick melanotic nevi around his nape, with long curly hairs emanating from each mole.

Over the next five minutes the senior surgeon pimped Phil Drummer on his knowledge of the appendix and surgical care of the vestigial organ. He demanded exact anatomic answers regarding arteries and organs that needed to be protected during the surgical approach. He requested rapid answers to scenarios involving possible intraoperative complications. Only after Drummer answered each question fully and correctly did the surgical attending motion to Nurse Frey to place the scalpel in the hand of Dr. Drummer.

"Never forget the time that old Doc Johnson taught you how to do an open appendectomy son," said the crotchety professor as he turned and began a slow walk towards the door. "You will thank me some day," was his trailing line as he exited the operating room, never to be seen throughout the remainder of the case.

Phil Drummer then performed his first surgical procedure under the watchful eye of chief resident Pete Larson. The case proceeded from start to finish without complications. After Phil passed the swollen appendix off the table he noticed that Larson extended a bloody handshake to him from across the surgical field.

"Good job kid," was his line with a firm shake. "Close up and always remember, keep the faith," said Larson as he stepped back and peeled off his surgical gloves and gown. Larson then nodded towards nurse Frey saying, "So long Ella, it has been a true pleasure knowing you."

"We will miss you," replied the scrub nurse. "Don't forget us."

"I won't. So long Philadelphia," said the chief resident as he briskly walked away. "California here I come!" was his final line as he bolted out the door, never to be seen again.

Upon completion of the case Phil Drummer walked out of the surgical suite. Upon passing the waiting room he saw Dr. Johnson speaking to the parents of the young boy that he had just operated on. His tone was professorial and compassionate as he spoke into a gaze of awe and reverence. Blood stains still speckled his shoes in an eerie pattern that complemented his aura. Heartfelt thanks were extended towards the senior surgeon, who then smugly retreated back into his occupational fortress, which was off limits to the common man.

Phil then made his way down to the Polk Lounge to gather his belongings. Awaiting his arrival was Rick Polk who sat alone with a packed duffle bag next to him. No other house staff was present in the room. Phil noticed that the ever-blaring television was turned off, signifying the end.

"Where have you been?" asked Polk. "I've been up all night worrying sick about you young man."

"It's over," said Phil. "Can you believe it's over?"

"Don't get too excited," said Polk as he arose and tossed the bag containing all of his worldly goods over his shoulder. "We still have four more years to go before being board certified surgeons."

Phil smiled as he rapidly gathered up a few personal belongings in the Polk Lounge. He realized the departure from the room was difficult for Polk, who appropriately called the place home.

"What about your throne?" asked Phil while pointing to the oversized lounge chair that Polk occupied exclusively.

"I'm leaving it," was the reply. "Time to pass on the torch to a new generation." Polk then paused and looked around at the stark walls while attempting to hold back some crocodile tears. "I'm going to miss the old place," was his line muffled with a few sniffles. "So many memories. It was our first home together."

The two interns then laughed heartily while exiting the call room facility. Upon closing the door Rick Polk reached up and peeled off a strip of duct tape with the name "The Polk Lounge" written upon it in black marker.

"The official abdication of the king," said Phil sadly. The duo then turned right and began to slowly walk together down a long hallway, towards an emergency door exit.

"Wait," yelled Polk as he turned about and sprinted back into the room. He quickly exited again while holding the DVD box set of Seinfeld episodes that he so coveted. "Almost forgot," was his pant as he rejoined Phil in their exodus from the great Philadelphia General Hospital.

The interns then abandoned the hospital onto University Avenue in an unceremonious graduation from surgical internship. As the steel door behind them slammed shut, they became junior residents, reaching yet another rung on the ladder of surgical training. Sweltering heat engulfed their frames as they turned west towards the Greycliff apartments. As the sun began to set in the West, the contrasting silhouettes of the two residents began to disappear into the steamy horizon in mirage like fashion.

It was then that a pedestrian passing by heard junior resident Polk saying, "Saint Michael's Hospital, here we come!"

CHAPTER TWO

SAINT MICHAEL'S HOSPITAL

RICK POLK SPENT the night at the Greycliff Apartments with Phil and Jennifer Ranier. Unfortunately a somber pall hung over the trio and smothered Polk's trademark levity in grim fashion. It was apparent to Rick that Jennifer was distraught over the pending departure of her beau. Her words were depressive and her actions drained, as she tried to unsuccessfully mask her sadness.

Phil and Rick were about to begin their second year of residency at Saint Michael's hospital, which was located in central Pennsylvania, being three hours away. Their rotation would encompass six total months, during which they would reside with fellow PGH trainees in an adjacent housing complex. The Saint Michael's rotation was a mainstay in PGH training, having existed for over fifty years. It represented a resident's initiation to community medicine, which was a stark contrast to that of a major medical center.

The only semblance of laughter that evening occurred after dinner when Jenna handed Phil a small package with excitement in her eyes.

"What's this?" asked Phil. "A parting gift?"

"Oh, a little something I put together to remind you of me," was her coy response. "Open it," said Jenna with a smile upon her face.

Phil reached forward to pick up the neatly packaged box and opened it. Inside was a small, framed photograph of himself and

Jenna taken on their first date together, some nine months ago. Phil recalled Jenna taking the picture with her cell phone as they slid close to each other that memorable night. He was immediately impressed by the energy and excitement in their eyes as seen through the picture frame.

"Do you remember it?" asked Jennifer.

"Of course," said Phil. "That's me at my high school senior prom, but I can't remember the name of the stunning date sitting next to me."

"Hah-hah," said Jenna with a smirk. "You better remember me. I have an exact duplicate and plan on keeping it on my night table during your absence."

"Nice selfie," said Polk while looking at the small photograph. "Do you know that the word "selfie" was recently deemed the international word of the year?"

"Thanks Jen," said Phil with a hug. "I'll keep it on my table too."

His words were then followed by a prolonged silence that signified their impending physical breakup. While sleeping on the couch that night Rick Polk appreciated a constant low-level discussion between the two in the adjacent room. A tone of perpetual consolation emanated from Phil's mouth, in an unsuccessful attempt to calm the emotions running amok in Jennifer's mind throughout the night. All involved parties suffered through a fitful sleep that hot summer night.

Sunrise found Rick Polk snoring on the couch in his underwear, oblivious to Phil and Jenna's excited actions. Jenna was preparing to leave for work while Phil was finishing up packing his clothing. Five minutes prior to their planned departure, Jennifer shook her guest's shoulder in an attempt to arouse him. After several attempts he arose and wandered into the kitchen, where she poured him some coffee.

"Why thank you Jennifer," was his remark while sitting down and looking at the morning newspaper. "Is the master of the house, or should I say the master of his own domain in?"

"Yea," yelled Phil as he walked out of the bedroom stuffing some clothes into a duffle bag. "Just about ready. Five minutes to departure."

"Ms. Ranier, may I say that you look absolutely beautiful as usual," said Polk. He noticed that Jennifer was dressed sharply and ready to report to work at the PGH.

"Enough of the sweet talk," said Jenna. "Listen up Polk, I want you to keep the nursing students away from old Dr. Drummer here, do you understand?"

"But of course," said Polk. "I will make it a priority of mine."

"I am holding you personally responsible for his well being," was her next line.

"You can always count on me," said Polk with a smirk. "Why I didn't even know that there was a nursing school attached to St. Mike's with an average of 75 female students per class."

"Don't make me strangle you," said Jennifer in jest as she lunged forward to put her hands around Rick's neck. "I'm a girl on the edge."

"Let's go," said Phil as he deftly stepped between the two in order to give Jenna a tremendous hug. Phil made the hug quick as he didn't want any emotions to burst out in front of Rick.

Within one minute Polk ate a muffin, got dressed and freshened up in the bathroom. He picked up his duffle bag and quickly swung it over his shoulder, like a sailor heading off to sea.

"Good luck," said Jenna in reply realizing that brevity was the key to the final goodbye. "Good luck to both of you."

"Don't forget to write," said Polk as he shoved Phil out the door. "It's lonely at sea."

The two doctors then bolted out of the apartment and quickly made their way down to Polk's vehicle double parked on a side street. It was a beat up Toyota with more miles on it than Polk cared to discuss, having been purchased at a police auction just three months ago. Rick assured his classmate that the vehicle was safe and would make it, despite not having any functioning air conditioning. He nonchalantly took a fake parking ticket off the front windshield and placed it inside the vehicle. Phil then lowered his six foot five inch frame into the cramped front seat and with a concerning engine back fire, the two comrades began their three-hour trek to the middle of the state. The second year of their surgical residency had just begun amid no fanfare whatsoever.

The ride took them an hour west and then two hours north into the gut of Pennsylvania. Rumor had it that Saint Mike's was equally inaccessible from all points throughout the state, which appeared to be true. During the three-hour trek the occupants discussed every possible topic that two young men care about at such a stage in their life. Women and relationships dominated the discussion as Phil learned that Polk had struck up a romance with one of the young nurses at the PGH. The relationship was in its infancy but Phil was immediately stricken by Polk's description of his girlfriend as "a lot like me." Despite multiple efforts a visual image of Mrs. X could not be accurately generated within Phil's mind. Regardless, the thought of Rick leaving behind a significant other in Philadelphia brought some solace to Phil, as the two plotted rides back and forth to the city over the next six months.

Also discussed with the resignation of Dr. Barnes and CEO Rineman from their positions at the Philadelphia General. Both men were criticized for their delayed action in notifying the authorities of perceived wrongdoings. Barnes was struggling to make a living as a general surgeon in a suburban Philadelphia hospital, while Rineman was rumored to be out West, sulking in a mid level HMO position.

Good conversation continued that morning as the two residents forged their way through the Keystone State. Then, as the soon to overheat vehicle navigated around yet another mountainous turn, the majesty of Saint Mike's Hospital appeared below them, obvious in the midst of a valley that was bisected by a slow moving river.

"There she blows," yelled Polk out the open window as he blew the horn in celebration.

"Wow, who put this city out here?" asked Phil as he scanned the valley from east to west.

"God only knows," replied Polk. "But it's home sweet home for the next six months."

"All I see is one big hospital surrounded by a bunch of church steeples," said Phil.

Saint Michael's Hospital was built in 1870, and like most hospitals was an original tuberculosis sanatorium. At the turn of the century it developed into a full-fledged hospital that then cared for a bustling lumber trade in the area. Once the old growth forests were depleted along the mountainsides, the coal barons stepped in to further rape the land. The industrial revolution of the early 1900s fueled fortune and fame for Saint Mike's and the surrounding community. As the population boomed in the area, so did the size of the hospital that was funded by wealthy industrial mavens. However, like every great financial boom an even greater financial bust followed, rendering the valley and Saint Mike's nearly obsolete. As more cleaner and efficient energy means evolved, the 1960s marked the low point of the valley and surrounding communities. Saint Michael's fell into disrepair and financial red ink, only to exist by the generosity of government run Medicare and medical assistance programs that provided monetary funding to the rural institution. At the turn of the century the area was making a slow but steady recovery thanks to the efforts of a proactive mayor and city council. Slowly but surely a series of clean industries relocated to the area, centering their business upon the internet and all its riches. Suddenly the old mansions lining the river began to sprout young families and Bed and Breakfast Inns. Schools began to fill up with energetic and aspiring white-collar offspring and the valley became a trendy weekend destination for the well to do. A rebirth occurred in the valley and St. Mike's came along for the ride, with a little help from a for profit company from Kansas City.

Americana Medical Group or AMG was a mega corporation from the Midwest that made a fortune in buying up small rural hospitals. Over the past twenty years AMG had developed a formula to turn around financially struggling hospitals by incorporating them under one large umbrella that by sheer volume, garnered beneficial contracts with national vendors. Over the past 10 years they had bought twenty hospitals along the east coast, with St. Mike's being the first. Within five years of purchasing St. Mike's, AMG poured in over 100 million dollars of capital improvement towards the facility and surrounding valley, thus making it the flagship of their Northeastern thrust.

It was this revitalized Saint Michael's Hospital parking garage that Phil and Rick Polk pulled into that sunny morning. The two residents then made their way to the medical education office to receive their working orders. Behind the reception desk was an elderly, polite and fastidious secretary who happily welcomed each physician. Within five minutes each resident was oriented to place and time, and given a manila envelope that contained their housing and rotation schedule. The secretary then directed Phil and Rick towards resident housing, which was a short three blocks away from the hospital campus. She recommended they walk while noting that hospital parking was free for the length of their six month stay.

Both interns made their way out to the hospital lobby and exited the hospital. The usual buzz of activity occurred just outside the front hospital doors, as patients arrived and departed with loved ones at their side. While turning left they passed the hospital's Emergency Department, which appeared miniscule in comparison to the Philadelphia General's E.R. Then at the end of the city block both residents crossed a street that lacked traffic and stepped into a quiet, inviting neighborhood.

"Wow, what a nice town," said Phil as he scanned the homes on each side of the block. "Reminds me of home."

"Quiet," said Polk in a tone of agreement. "Where are all the city buses, traffic and smog?"

The neighborhood they were in was characteristic of the town that surrounded St. Mike's. Simple homes with a small patch of front yard grass lined the street. Lawns were well manicured and roses bloomed alongside peonies, offering a pleasing scent to the passerby. Some homes had full front porches adorned with a swing, while others had quaint entrances covered by a peaked roof. Homes were small and basic, yet welcoming and pleasing to the eye. Occasionally a dog could be heard barking amongst the song of birds chirping. Cats of all breeds now and then appeared as they slept off a night of roaming, curled up in a favorite patch of sun. Sidewalks were old and uneven as overgrown oaks lifted their slabs in characteristic fashion. The occasional remnant of a child's chalk artistry graced the walkway below. Ubiquitous throughout the block was the United States flag, each jutting outwards in a slanted fashion towards the sidewalk. A soft breeze gently furled and unfurled each flag in haphazard fashion, which in harmony with the surrounding environment, created a celestial scene.

"Toto, I've a feeling we're not in Kansas any more," said Polk as the two continued their walk down the lane.

"I think you are right Dorothy," said Phil in agreement. "What a beautiful town."

The second block that each resident traversed was just as captivating as the first. Rick was sure that Norman Rockwell had to have lived on the block at one time. Then per their instructions the team turned left, heading past a series of majestic churches that adorned Main Street. Resident housing sat at the end of this block and as Phil and Rick approached, the housing complex was obvious.

The compound consisted of five two-story barracks type structures that sat atop a subtle knoll on Main Street. The housing was originally constructed and used to shelter overflow patients from an adjacent psychiatric hospital in the early 1950s. However with the advent of antipsychotic drugs and outpatient treatment, both the hospital and housing complex fell vacant for two decades. St. Mike's eventually bought the buildings thirty years ago and turned them into a lucrative short term rehabilitation center. They also transferred their well respected School of Nursing into the facility, while making the row of barracks affordable housing for the students. Ultimately, visiting surgical residents from the Philadelphia General Hospital program began to call the stark brick buildings home, affectionately referring to them collectively as "Skid Row."

"Block B, cell number five," said Phil as he looked down on his manila envelope. "Sounds like a jailhouse."

They then entered the Block B complex and headed down the first floor hallway towards cell number five. Both residents were immediately impressed with the cleanliness of the facility. Even more impressive to Rick was the obvious presence of female nursing students, who happily walked by in the coed dormitory. Then as the two approached cell number five which sat at the end of the long hallway, a dull thumping sound could be heard. The blare of the noise increased as the duo approached the door marked "Cell Five." It became apparent that rap music was being blasted by someone within the cell prompting Phil to cock his eyebrow toward Rick, while inserting a key into the doorknob lock.

Upon opening the door the blast of music shook the inner soul of the two as they tentatively walked into the common space of the apartment.

"I'm the last of three, in North End it's always free. Bangin' with the General, Hondo and Joe B," shrilled the lyrics of the song.

"Hello?" said Phil looking around carefully. In the middle of the living room sat a bench press with a tremendous amount of weights upon it, teetering on the verge of collapse. A massive stereo system was apparently on, blasting the music. Phil thought he smelled the subtle but lingering remnant of marijuana. "Hello, anybody home?"

Phil's voice was drowned out by the unabated lyrics of the song as it proclaimed, *"I'll tell you one more time, cause it ain't no crime. It's the D-O-C, T-O-R, X-dot-L-dot gonna be a star. Keep it on me can't you see, even the ladies cry D-O-C."*

"What the heck is going on?" asked Rick as he proceeded forward into the apartment, heading for an obvious kitchen area. He held his hands to each ear in an attempt to muffle the clamor.

Just then a shirtless man of similar age to Rick and Phil, turned the corner wearing only surgical scrub pants. He was holding a milkshake concoction laced with whey, protein and creatine supplements. The appearance of Rick and Phil in front of him caused no hesitation whatsoever in his stride. On his right arm was an amateurish appearing tattoo that said "J.R." It was readily apparent that weightlifting was a passion of the young man, whose upper torso was cut and lean.

"When I cruise with the crew I cruise with my nation. Chillin with pops at the fillin station," screamed the overhead song.

"My brothers from another mother!" screamed the unknown denizen of cell number five as he approached the two. "Como se llama homeboys?"

Phil tried to speak but winced at the continued noise above him proclaiming, *"As a little scrapper I went by el pequeno, now as a rapper X.L. is my lingo."* His body language suggested a distinct offensive displeasure from the ongoing lyrics.

The unknown resident then quickly swerved to the right towards a stereo system on the shelf. He quickly turned down the rap to a tolerable level and spun energetically back towards the two saying, "Sorry about the volume, but I can't get enough of Doc X.L."

Phil composed himself for a second as the ringing in his ears settled down. He then stepped forward and extended his hand saying, "Hi, I'm Phil Drummer and this is Rick Polk. I think we are your new apartment mates."

"Check that, I agree," said the man with a rapid tone while extending his hand to shake Phil's. "I've been waiting for you. Jackson Rhimes here, got into town two nights ago," was the response. He then shook Phil's hand and pulled him towards his bare upper body in chest bump fashion. "Just call me Jack or Jackie."

"Temple boy?" asked Rick well aware that the replacement for Fred Riles was a transplant from the Temple surgical program.

"Yea, yea" said Rhimes. "North Philly product. Born and raised," was the reply amidst another chest bump now applied to Rick. "Saint Joe's Prep," was his next line that alerted every one to his Philadelphia High School roots despite no obvious question in that regard.

The three junior residents then exchanged some more superficial information amongst themselves while Jack pointed out the two remaining rooms that were available in the apartment. Both Phil and Rick noticed that Jackson Rhimes frequently stroked his biceps and pectoralis muscles while talking to them, and occasionally looked at a mirror reflecting his physique nearby.

"Why the jump from Temple to the Philadelphia General?" asked Rick Polk.

"Temple wasn't ready for Jackie Rhimes," said their new roommate emphatically. "Hey, check it out," said Rhimes. "Some fine looking ladies live across the hall. Met them last night. One is a named Kendra." He pronounced Kendra very slowly and then spelled it out for effect, "K-E-N-D-R-A, a Philly girl."

Phil and Rick just stared at each other in an attempt to respond to the disconnection of thought. Phil spoke first while asking, "Are they nursing students?"

"Yea, yea," said Jackie as he worked his body under the weights sitting on top of the work out bench. Then, while beginning a series of bench press repetitions he continued saying, "Third year students who are about to get on the Jackie Rhimes express." His comment was followed by a loud cackle and then another slow pronunciation of the nursing student's name across the hall, "Kendra. K-E-N-D-R-A."

Phil and Rick again just stared at each other in somewhat disbelief as they picked up their bags and chose rooms. Phil then headed into the clean but stark room that would be his home over the next six months. A single window looked out upon a short stretch of grass that ultimately ran into Block C. Phil noticed a rabbit sitting in the grass casually eating a piece of clover. It was strange to him that the first floor windows did not have metal security bars across them, ala West Philadelphia. Suddenly he realized how far away from Philadelphia and Jennifer he was. Upon unpacking his clothes he took out Jennifer's picture frame and placed it carefully, per her instructions, on his nightstand. At that very moment the music from the adjacent room roared back to life, shaking the wall that separated the two.

"As the chillin grip ya, fever dip ya, and the tummy go rip, rip, rip ya. Lookin for the cure, page me anytime, gots to get to know me while I'm in my prime. Swaggin with the cutter."

Phil then took a deep breath and collapsed back upon a single bed that sat adjacent to an outside wall. His body sank into an old and soft mattress that moaned under his weight. The deep bass sound of the rap music gently shook the adjacent window. Suddenly it became coldly apparent to him as to how long the next six months may actually be. He took a deep breath and slowly pronounced the name Jenna, while then spelling it in his mind.

"Spell it, D-O-C, T-O-R, X-dot-L-dot- gonna be a star..."

CHAPTER THREE

THE TUCKETT INSTITUTE

ALL THREE RESIDENTS left cell number five the following morning to attend an orientation at the hospital. They walked in tandem through the three city blocks that separated skid row from the hospital complex. They blended into the stream of fellow residents and nursing students making the trek to work that morning.

"The locals call our complex the white coat ghetto," said Jack Rhimes to the group, referring to the long white coats worn by the residents.

"Skid row is what I've heard," said Polk while chomping on a banana.

"Nice walk when the weather is nice," said Phil. "I wouldn't want to do it every day in the winter, must get nasty in this part of the state."

The trio soon arrived at St. Mike's and located the conference room hosting the orientation. The meeting was a requirement for all residents and nurses beginning their rotations that month. All in all about forty young men and women congregated in the auditorium where fresh coffee and pastries were available. At exactly seven o'clock that morning a short middle-aged balding man wearing an ill-fitting suit approached the podium from a side door. Emblazoned on the front of the podium was the logo of St. Michael's Hospital with the terminology "An AMG Affiliate" beneath it.

"Good morning everyone," said the COO of the facility. "My name is Mr. Barry Reynolds and I am the hospital's Chief Operations Officer. Welcome to Saint Michael's."

"Nice suit," said Rick to Phil, "He should be fined for wearing that."

"Saint Michael's Hospital is a full service facility that serves as a tertiary care center for other hospitals within a two hour radius," said the COO. "It recently has obtained certification as a Level II Trauma center in the state of Pennsylvania. A small round of applause followed this announcement from the few administration lackeys that graced the front row.

"Check it," said Jackie to Phil with an elbow to his gut. "K-E-N-D-R-A." He gestured to a group of nursing students sitting in the row in front of them, just to the right.

"Which one?" asked Polk.

"On the end, the dirty blonde," said Jackie with a smile. "Now that's a fine Philly girl."

Phil craned his neck just slightly to the right in order to catch a glimpse of the object of Dr. Rhimes' affection. His immediate impression was that of a stunning young women who was quite cognizant of her appearance in public. Kendra Mason had slightly highlighted blonde hair, held in a short ponytail that morning. A perfect tan adorned her face, which was slightly scarred by two chicken pox souvenirs. This enhanced her beauty. Although seated it was apparent that her stature was slim and of average height. She held a pen ever so gently up to her pursed lips while listening to the speaker. Her fingertips were manicured to perfection as they slowly rotated the pen back and forth. There was a tad of glitter on her lips.

"Saint Michaels has recently been honored by the Joint Committee of Hospital Accreditation's highest ranking," said COO Reynolds with a broad smile. "This A+ ranking places us in the upper ten percent of hospitals throughout the nation." Again, a round of obligatory applause followed the crowing remarks of Mr. Reynolds.

Then, as the three residents stared to the right, Kendra Mason slowly turned to look back towards them, with a slight smile on her face. Her gaze was well calculated and although in the direction of the three, fixated upon Phil. He noticed a cute, celestial nose that sat between a set of soft blue eyes. Her lips immediately reminded Phil of Jenna. She gently smiled at the three and then turned slowly back towards the drone at the podium, while continuing to twirl the pen in front of her.

"She was looking at me," said Rhimes and Polk in unison.

"Welcome, welcome and welcome," said COO Reynolds with a pretentious smile and extended arms. "We hope your stay at Saint Michael's is enjoyable and educational, and remember, my door is always open."

Following another round of applause Mr. Reynolds then introduced the Residency Coordinator who made a few quick comments about each resident's rotation schedule, which was listed in a packet to be picked up at the end of the orientation. She then made note that all residents were invited to the hospital's July 4th pool party that upcoming weekend at a local country club. Information and directions regarding the gala event were contained within the information packet. The meeting then ended, sending all auditorium occupants to a series of tables to gather their rotation packets. The nursing students headed to the right while the junior surgical residents headed to the left.

Upon opening his packet Phil discovered his first two months would be spent in Orthopedics. He knew ahead of time that each resident would be spending two of their six months in orthopedics, and the other four in general surgery. He also discovered that the first weekend of call belonged to him, that being the upcoming July 4th holiday. A pitiful feeling overtook him as he realized the disappointment this news would bring to Jennifer. She was desperately anticipating his return back to Philadelphia. Phil knew she had social commitments that weekend that would not allow her to travel out to St. Mike's.

Then, after receiving their marching orders, each resident headed off in separate directions, finding their way to their assigned attending surgeons. Phil was assigned to a Dr. Ian Tuckett, chairman of the Department of Orthopedics at St. Michael's hospital. A smiling hospital representative just outside the auditorium directed him to the Tuckett Orthopedic Institute, while reassuring him of the privilege to have drawn such a coveted resident rotation. As Phil left the auditorium foyer he noticed a troop of nursing students across the way excitedly discussing their upcoming rotation schedules. Then while peering at the group a gap occurred ever so slightly in their midst, suddenly exposing an excited Kendra Mason, who briefly made eye contact again with Phil with a subtle smile. The connection was ever so brief, yet left a lasting impression on Phil throughout the day.

Phil then worked his way through a series of hospital wings and an above ground walkway connecting one hospital ward to an even older one. Signs placed at every corridor intersection directed him towards the hospital's orthopedic wing. Soon Phil noticed at the end of another hallway a large overhead sign gracing the top of several shiny double doors announcing his destination, the Tuckett Orthopedic Institute.

The lobby of the Tuckett Institute smelled of opulence and wealth. Upon entering Phil initially thought he had walked outside of the hospital boundary and entered the foyer of a five star hotel. Large white pillars surrounded an oval floor made of marble, graced by a three story high rotunda. In the center of the lobby was an inlay floor logo with the capital letters of T.O.I. emblazoned together in a pleasing pattern.

Scattered throughout the foyer were plush chairs and sofas well positioned for polite conversation and relaxation. Lamps sat atop adjacent tables that created a warm and welcoming ambience as classical music graced the airwaves above. Live trees were well situated to accept sunlight entering several large windows just shy of the rotunda's curving arch. Phil wondered who the several well dressed people were, sitting amid the furniture.

Immediately to his right was a large reception desk similar to those in a hotel, where two sharply dressed attendants awaited with a smile. Upon making eye contact one of the two asked Phil, "May I help you?"

"Yes," was his response while heading towards the man and woman. He noticed they wore uniforms with the T.O.I. logo upon their chest. "I am looking for Dr. Tuckett."

"Ah you must be Dr. Philip Drummer," was the quick response from the male attendant. "We have been awaiting your arrival. My name is James."

"Why thank you," said Phil, impressed by the welcome. In front of each of them sat an orderly, black pearled granite counter, with a computer screen and telephone. Behind them hung two sixty-inch sleek flat screen television monitors that welcomed everyone electronically to the Tuckett Orthopedic Institute.

"Welcome to the Tuckett Orthopedic Institute," said the woman with a professional smile. "My name is Madison. Today you will be meeting Emily Reyes who is Dr. Tuckett's personal assistant. May I interest you in a beverage Dr. Drummer? A coffee or latte perhaps?"

"No thank you," said Phil, who was then politely escorted by the male receptionist around a corner into a short but sparkling clean hallway towards a set of elevators. The aroma of freshly brewed coffee beans permeated this airspace. Phil observed James to be fastidiously dressed and well perfumed. While walking down the hallway Phil noticed several framed national newspapers and magazines upon the walls, with the words Tuckett Institute intermittently peppered throughout each article's headlines. An elevator car awaited the two. Phil was then escorted into the car as the receptionist hit the third floor button.

"Ms. Reyes will be awaiting your arrival sir. Have a wonderful day," said James. "Enjoy your stay at the Tuckett Institute."

The elevator car was not a standard issue hospital transport. Brass encircled the space with mirrors surrounding the rider in all directions from the waist level upwards. Along the back wall of the car hung a framed poster that proclaimed the Tuckett Institute a proud recipient of the Joint Commission's Gold Seal of Approval for Joint Replacement Centers. While reading the poster a soft overhead voiced informed Phil that he was arriving on floor three of the Tuckett Institute. He then turned around to exit the car as the doors slowly opened.

Awaiting Phil was an attractive female in her mid thirties who wore the now pervasive uniform of the Tuckett Institute.

Her hair was black and held in a short, tight bun behind a pair of thick-framed fashionable glasses. She wore a well pressed skirt down to her knees followed by nylon stockings that ended with a pair of shoes with a thick, slightly raised heel, all exuding a professional appearance. Standing ten feet back from the door, she smiled warmly while holding a clipboard across her chest.

"Good morning Dr. Drummer, I am Ms. Emily Reyes," was her opening line as she confidently stepped forward with an extended hand. "Welcome to the Tuckett Institute," was her follow-up with a firm handshake.

"Thanks," said Phil with a smile, again noticing the Tuckett Institute logo upon the floor. "Nice place you have here."

"Why thank you Dr. Drummer," said Ms. Reyes with a smile. "We are all proud of the Institute and what it represents." Ms. Reyes then escorted Phil down a hallway towards a double door marked "Pre-Operative Consultation Room" aside the entrance. Phil appreciated the smell of expensive perfume emanating from his host's bodily pores.

"The Institute is closed this morning since Dr. Tuckett is out of town," said Reyes. "That will give us a good opportunity to introduce you to the field of Orthopedics and what we do here."

"Great," said Phil while scanning the room, which appeared similar to a home entertainment center. Off to his left sat a plush leather black couch surrounded by several oversized chairs, all facing a large flat screen monitor set at eye level for the seated guests. Several coffee tables sat next to the seating area with fresh flowers adorning each. No one else was in the room except Phil and Emily Reyes.

"This is our preoperative consultation area," said Ms. Reyes. "It's where clients learn about the Tuckett Orthopedic Institute and view informative videos regarding pending surgical procedures." She then led Phil to the seating area where he proceeded to sit down to face the screen.

"Joint replacements?" asked Phil as he sunk down into a warm and expensive smelling leather sofa.

"Yes Dr. Drummer. Dr. Tuckett exclusively performs joint replacement or arthroplasty procedures involving the hip and knee."

Phil nodded while trying to recall his brief orthopedic surgery rotation in medical school. His mind recalled gory procedures that involved power tools, mallets and muscular surgeons overflowing with testosterone. He then recalled a common joke regarding orthopedic surgeons stating they were all "as strong as an ox and twice as smart."

"I have taken the opportunity to load three videos for your viewing pleasure Dr. Drummer," said Reyes who remained standing. "The first is an informative video of the Tuckett Orthopedic Institute and Dr. Tuckett himself. The second and third are in regards to the most common operations performed at the Institute, that being a total knee and total hip replacement. All clients who are about to undergo a joint replacement procedure review these informative videos preoperatively. Total running time for each video is approximately ten minutes. Do you have any questions?" asked the smiling host.

"No I'm O.K.," said Phil feeling quite at ease in the environment.

"Very well," said Reyes. "Enjoy the videos and I will see you immediately after they are completed." Then Ms. Reyes smiled and turned away as the lights in the room dimmed and the large screen in front of Phil came to life. Before him burst a Hollywood caliber production that introduced the viewer to Dr. Tuckett and his Orthopedic center of excellence called the Tuckett Institute.

Ian Tuckett was a local prodigy, having grown up in the town surrounding Saint Michael's hospital. His intelligence opened doors to the Ivy League where he attended undergraduate training at Cornell, graduating with degrees in biology and engineering. Medical school followed in New York City as did an Orthopedic residency at the prestigious Hospital for Exceptional Surgery. An additional year of fellowship training in joint replacement surgery then capped off the educational process, having been completed at New York's General Hospital. Over the next ten years Dr. Tuckett became one of the premier joint replacement surgeons in the New York City area. His accolades included multiple publications in peer reviewed literature regarding the mechanical design of implant materials. His engineering background led to a breakthrough design of a commonly used acetabular component for hip replacement surgery that was used world wide under the proprietary name of The Tuckett Cup™. Dr. Tuckett garnered international fame and courted a clientele from all continents. He became the proverbial "surgeon of the stars" as evidenced by several cameo appearances in the video of aging athletes with national recognition. Then, per the video, in an apparent act of gratitude and indebtedness, Doctor Ian Tuckett returned to the valley in order to establish the Tuckett Institute, a center devoted solely to the art of joint replacement surgery. The Institute was formed as a paragon for orthopedic centers, adhering to the well recognized fact that centers of excellence produced superior results, at least in the baby booming business of joint replacements. The propaganda show ended up with a tour of the Institute's facilities offering state of the art surgical theatres along with plush perioperative amenities. It was obvious to the viewer that the Tuckett Institute courted a national patient base, treating each "client" as a V.I.P. while providing avant-garde surgical techniques. The promo then ended with several marketing catch phrases of the center including "Big City Medicine, Hometown Care," and "Let Us Get You Back to the Human Race."

"Wow," thought Phil to himself after the first video. He heard stories of private surgeons with an entrepreneurial flare doing well in the community, but what appeared to be unfolding in front of him was beyond his expectations. The second and then third video clip of the series ran through, each showing the actual surgical procedures of a total knee and total hip replacement. These videos combined intraoperative footage and complementary anatomy diagrams that described the nuts and bolts of joint replacement surgery. Describing the action was a commanding voice that reminded Phil of watching old NFL highlight films with his dad as a young boy. Throughout the hip replacement infomercial the magnitude of the revolutionary Tuckett Cup was highlighted, along with its developmental team, led by Dr. Tuckett. Upon completion of the third video the overhead lights returned on and Ms. Reyes appeared behind Phil.

"Any questions on the information provided?" asked Ms. Reyes.

"No," said Phil getting up with a stretch. "Thank you very much, that was extremely informative."

"It is our pleasure Dr. Drummer," replied Reyes. "We look forward to working with you over the next two months. Dr. Tuckett enjoys being affiliated with a residency program. He has always been and continues to be an excellent mentor for young surgeons." Ms. Reyes then paused, smiling at Phil to allow time for any further questions.

"When do I start?" asked Phil. "I mean actually getting to the O.R.?"

"Tomorrow morning. Dr. Tuckett does two joint replacement surgeries every Monday, Tuesday and Thursday of the week. The other two days are usually spent seeing patients in clinical follow up downstairs."

"What time do I report for duty?"

"Operative procedures start at 7:30 sharp," said Emily Reyes. "Please be there by 6:45 to prepare for the case." Ms. Reyes paused and then said in a quiet but effective tone, "Dr. Tuckett runs on time, always on time. Please do not be late."

"Understood," said Phil, recalling how crazy Dr. Knight regarded his O. R. start times back at the PGH.

The orientation then wrapped up after Ms. Reyes reviewed a few other minor administration matters. One that caught Phil's attention was a Tuckett Institute policy regarding nationally known athletes or persona that may be treated at the Institute. No autographs, requests or public notoriety were allowed around such clientele who were to be protected by a strict confidentiality agreement. Phil acknowledged this fact and was given an Employee Education Pamphlet as the two then headed back towards the elevator. Ms. Reyes then politely said goodbye to Phil as she hit the Lobby button on the elevator, sending his car back down to the front desk.

The punctilious male attendant greeted Phil upon his arrival in the lobby. Phil at that point accepted his offer for coffee and a pastry, which was served to him in the swank lobby along with a copy of the *Philadelphia Chronicle*. Phil spent the next thirty minutes enjoying his mid morning treat and then stood up to exit. James immediately stepped forward to remove his eating utensils, as Madison escorted him to the door.

"Good day," said Madison. "Thank you for visiting the Tuckett Institute," was her last line uttered prior to Phil stepping through the heavy doors that placed him back into the hospital proper. Suddenly the drab and colorless hospital hallway struck out visually at Phil. Overhead was the drone of the hospital operator paging a physician, a voice not heard on the other side of the doors. A dirty carpet then led Phil back to the hospital proper as he suddenly wondered what to do with the rest of the day. He then thought of Jennifer and how she would like working at the Tuckett Institute, amidst its refined expertise. An aimless stroll took him out of the hospital and back to Skid Row, where he proceeded to read about the art of joint replacement surgery.

The boys from cell number five enjoyed a macaroni and cheese dinner that evening while discussing their upcoming rotations and attending surgeons. Rick Polk appeared to have drawn the short stick, with a frumpy middle-aged female surgeon, who did nothing but complain about her lifestyle. Jackie Rhimes was hyped after meeting his attending with a nickname "Fast Eddie" who operated to blaring disco music from the 1970s. Phil then described his orthopedic rotation and was dubbed "bone crusher" by his colleagues.

The highlight of the evening was a visit from Kendra Mason and her roommate. The two girls from across the hall spent about thirty minutes in cell five, excitedly discussing their upcoming hospital rotations. Each would be spending the next two months on the general surgery ward of St. Mike's while learning the nursing trade. The energy that emanated from Kendra's body captivated the trio of young men, who all agreed with her prediction of a fascinating six months ahead. Immediately after her departure a wrestling match broke out between Rick and Jackie with each vowing true love to Kendra. The match was short lived after a slightly injured and short of breath Rick Polk begged for mercy beneath the chiseled body of Jackie Rhimes.

Later that evening Phil called Jenna amid the wall shaking beat of Doctor X.L. in the background. The exchange started off well with a brief description of the day and each caller pining for the other. Phil sadly explained to Jennifer the call rotation and his need to stay at Saint Mike's over the upcoming weekend. As their conversation terminated, her disappointment was palpable over the cell line. Thankfully Phil failed to mention the nursing students across the hall, or the fact that Kendra Mason was also working that holiday weekend.

CHAPTER FOUR

A Total Joint

THE FOLLOWING MORNING Phil Drummer arrived at 6:30 AM in the lobby of the Tuckett Institute, remembering his dad's advise to always arrive ahead of schedule. Despite the early hour a flurry of activity was ongoing at the Institute between patients and staff. Phil noticed Ms. Reyes across the lobby as she rapidly approached him with a smile. She then escorted him to a private staff elevator that took him to the third floor, where the operative suite was located. Ms. Reyes then directed Phil to the locker room where an awaiting attendant escorted him in.

The locker room of the Tuckett Institute was unlike any other hospital locker room, and Phil was sure of this upon his immediate inspection. The facility was large, warm and welcoming. A clean, plush carpet anchored a row of large dressing stalls each complete with a series of shelves, hooks and hangers. Each stall was about five foot wide and five foot deep with a comfortable chair directly in front. Phil's stall was empty yet contained complimentary toiletries such as those found in a hotel, complete with a collection of facial and body towels. Situated inside Phil's locker was a set of surgical scrubs, starched with a crease and exact to his size. The room that morning was empty as he proceeded to put on his scrubs and head towards the operating room. A sign above the door exit read "No Cell Phones Allowed Within the Operating Room Proper." Phil immediately thought of Dr. Knight and a nostalgic smile came upon his face.

There were two operative theatres at the Tuckett Institute, which were completely separate from the other ten suites in Saint Mike's hospital. Both rooms were for the sole purpose of Orthopedic surgery, specifically that of Dr. Tuckett. Phil walked into Suite A and was immediately impressed by both the vastness and modernization of the room. Absent was old equipment, scuffed walls and crammed quarters. Present were multiple LCD video screens, sparkling clean overhead lights and spacious confines to appease any demanding surgeon.

"Good morning young man," said a nurse preparing equipment on several tables as Phil walked into the room.

"Good morning," was his response. "Dr. Drummer here."

"Hello Dr. Drummer. I'm Renee Brown one of the two nurses helping Dr. Tuckett today. Welcome to the Tuckett Institute," was her introduction while rapidly preparing a series of large sterile surgical trays containing a seemingly endless amount of instruments and surgical implants.

Nurse Brown then instructed Phil on the protocol of the O.R. in relation to total joint procedures. On that specific morning Dr. Tuckett had two total hip replacements scheduled, and was fully expecting to be done by eleven o'clock. Nurse Brown instructed Phil on his role as an assistant, asking him to stay alert and follow exact instructions from Dr. Tuckett. She warned him that Dr. Tuckett would instruct him once, maybe twice, but never a third time on his assistive requirements. She asked that Phil either follow her lead or that of Nurse Bryant who was yet to arrive. Lastly she warned Phil that the entire staff was insanely anal about surgical site infections and the avoidance of such a possibility. She reviewed with Phil exact sterile technique protocols that were mandatory at the Institute. Lastly she placed a surgical helmet system on Phil, similar to an astronaut's headset that all personal wore during a total hip replacement.

At that moment the door to the room swung open and in walked Dr. Tuckett with a male and female behind him, all dressed in surgical scrubs. Phil recognized Dr. Tuckett behind his surgical mask from the video he watched the prior day.

"Good morning Renee," said Dr. Tuckett with a commanding voice. While extending his hand he approached Phil saying, "This must be our resident for the summer, Dr. Drummer."

"Yes it is," said Phil. "Good morning Dr. Tuckett." Phil estimated Dr. Tuckett to be just over the six foot mark in height. He had a lean build and firm biceps that suggested a daily work out routine. His eyes were a dull brown yet emanated a commanding intensity. Authority exuberated from his persona, both in dress and mannerism. He possessed a firm handshake while staring directly at Phil who felt that his whole being was being sized up in a single moment.

"Welcome to the Tuckett Institute," said Dr. Tuckett proudly.

Phil noticed that the male who accompanied Tuckett into the room headed towards an x-ray view box and began to rapidly hang up some radiographs. The other female nurse accompanying him shot off through a side door to begin the scrubbing process. She wore tight scrubs and walked with a swagger in a manner of certain high profile nurses.

"It's a pleasure to have you here," said Dr. Tuckett. "Hopefully we can teach you some ortho, and who knows maybe turn you into an orthopedic surgeon." Dr. Tuckett then let go of Phil's hand saying, "Just follow the lead of myself and Nurse Bryant who will be scrubbing this case. Stay alert and keep up with us. O.K.?"

Phil answered in the affirmative as he watched Tuckett spin around and walk towards the other male in the room to review some radiographs. Phil was able to recognize a series of hip x-rays that were written upon with marking pen in preparation for the case. Suddenly the doors to the O.R. suite burst open with a bang and a surgical bed containing that morning's patient roared in, being pushed by an anesthesia team. A sedated male patient was then shifted over onto the surgical table at which time Phil appreciated a wave from Nurse Brown. She directed him to the scrub room where Nurse Bryant was already getting ready for the case. Phil quickly headed towards the surgical sink.

When Phil turned the corner to the surgical sink he walked directly into Nurse Nicole Bryant, who was completing her preoperative scrub.

"Good morning," said Phil politely.

"Good morning," was the impassive response from the personal scrub nurse of doctor Tuckett.

"Wow," said Phil in jest, "You're the first one here who hasn't said 'Welcome to the Tuckett Institute'."

"Forgive me," said nurse Bryant with a mock look. "But you will soon learn that I'm not one of his robots."

Phil then quickly scanned nurse Bryant from top to bottom after appreciating the sarcasm in her comment. She was your classic smoking hot scrub nurse, the kind that every operating room had. Tight scrubs adorned a body that was obviously enhanced by a plastic surgeon above the waistline. Manicured nails complemented long fingers that were connected to arms familiar with aerobic exercises. Obligatory clog shoes amplified her height and buttocks that commanded a second look by any male within the vicinity. Any exposed skin was deeply tanned and a surgical mask covered a face that had to be beautiful beneath. She smelled expensive yet somewhat trampy. Lastly and most importantly with regards to the operating room diva was her perceived personality, which had to be quick and biting, with a silvery sharp tongue.

"Ever seen a total hip before?" asked Bryant.

"No," was Phil's reply. "Looking forward to it."

"He's pretty fast," said Bryant as she finished her scrub and walked past Phil towards the operating room. "Just watch your fingers, you don't want to lose one."

Just as nurse Bryant left, Dr. Tuckett turned the corner to join Phil. Over the next four minutes he stressed the importance of sterile technique to Phil and the disastrous complication of an infected hip replacement. A brief tutorial was given on the mechanics of joint replacement surgery. Throughout the discussion Phil was able to peer through a large glass window looking into the operative room. He noticed that the anesthesia team had completed a spinal anesthetic and the patient was rolled onto his left side in preparation for a hip replacement. The nursing team was painting the patient's right hip with a generous supply of antiseptic scrub. Doctor Tuckett then tossed his scrub sponge into the sink and walked away towards the operating room. Phil quickly followed his new mentor's lead, suddenly anxious to see the Tuckett Institute's namesake replace a worn out hip that was well past its expiration date.

While Phil and Dr. Tuckett were placed into their sterile gowns by nurse Bryant an introduction was made to the gentleman standing in front of the x-ray view box. His name was Dr. Aran Lee and he was associated with the company that was providing the implants for the case. Phil was informed that Dr. Lee had a doctorate in biomedical engineering and was present for every case at the Tuckett Institute. His role was to have on hand a wide range of total joint implants that would fit the size of any patient on the table.

At exactly 7:25 A.M. the first case of the day began for Dr. Tuckett, who after announcing the time asked the circulating nurse to read him the surgical permit. This time out process was mandatory at the Tuckett Institute to avoid the not so rare wrong site surgery that could tarnish a surgeon's reputation.

"Are you aware as to how many orthopedic surgeons operate on the wrong body part by the time their career is over Dr. Drummer?" asked Tuckett.

"No sir," said Phil as he stood opposite the table from Tuckett.

"Twenty percent," said Dr. Tuckett while receiving a scalpel placed in his right hand by nurse Bryant. "That's one out of five," was Tuckett's next comment with a shake of his head. Phil noticed that nurse Bryant stood very close to Tuckett, in an apparent zone of comfort and familiarity.

Then Dr. Ian Tuckett made a slashing cut across the outside portion of the patient's hip, which was pointing directly upwards towards the ceiling. A stream of blood erupted from the wound as Phil was instructed to suction the bleeding.

Just then a state of the art speaker system gently piped in some overhead music that immediately sent a shutter down Phil's spine. The genre was again classical, although the volume and tone was instantly more pleasing than Dr. Knight's Borodin Symphony. "Anything but classical," Phil thought to himself.

"You don't mind if we play some Schubert do you Dr. Drummer?" asked Tuckett while continuing to look down in the wound.

"No. Not at all," said Phil looking up at Nurse Bryant who gently shook her head in a show of quiet disgust regarding the music selection.

"We start off every case with *The Piano Quintet in A, Opus 114*," said Tuckett.

"Better known as *The Trout*," piped in nurse Bryant as if knowing the next question that was about to be asked by the head surgeon.

"Thank you nurse Bryant," said Dr. Tuckett. "You are obviously a woman of art and culture. What an honor to have you here."

Phil looked at the two across the table and appreciated a laugh and show of joviality between them. It was apparent that they were comfortable with each other's presence.

"We spin down all this blood and give it back to the patient," said Tuckett as he continued to dissect deeper down into the hip. "It markedly reduces the need for post operative blood transfusions." Just below the skin arose the gluteal or buttock muscles, which were deftly split in line with the incision. Nurse Bryant then handed the surgeon a self-retaining retractor, which once in place, held back the skin and exposed the back capsule of the hip joint itself.

"An old orthopedic saying is 'Get down to bone and stay there'," said Tuckett without taking his eyes off the wound. He then incised the patient's joint capsule and instructed Phil to hold the patient's leg in an awkward, non-physiologic position. Tuckett then reached across the table and pushed Phil's arm in a rotating clockwise fashion, which placed a tremendous torque on the ball and socket hip joint. Suddenly a sharp sucking sound emanated from the wound, similar to a snug fitting drain cork being pulled from a tub of water. Phil looked down quickly into the wound only to see the hip joint completely dislocated with the eroded yet still glistening ball of the hip looking directly at him.

"Saw," said Tuckett to nurse Bryant before Phil could react from the disarticulation that just occurred in front of him.

Dr. Tuckett then made a power saw cut through the neck of the femur just below the ball. He handed the saw back to nurse

Bryant and then reached into the wound to pull out the now detached round femoral head.

"See that arthritis?" asked Tuckett only stopping for an instant to show the eroded head to Phil. "That's why we are here. Looks like we got here just in time."

Phil gazed down at the bone, which was about the size of a tennis ball and was littered by deep erosive changes that exposed raw bone beneath. Dr. Tuckett then handed the ball to nurse Bryant who put it in a metallic kidney basin destined for the pathology department. It was at that moment that Phil heard an unfamiliar voice from the head of the table.

"How's it going?" was the simple question.

"Very good Mr. Banks," said Dr. Tuckett as he continued with the procedure, now placing a series of retractors around the cup or acetabulum of the pelvis. "A lot of arthritis, just like the x-rays suggested," was Tuckett's next line to the patient lying on the table.

Phil suddenly recalled that the patient had a spinal anesthetic in place, which was not commonly used in general surgery procedures. He wondered how much the patient would remember from the case.

"The use of a spinal anesthetic significantly reduces the chance of a post operative blood clot in a patient's leg," said Tuckett. "Everything being done in this room this morning has a purpose. An exact purpose."

Dr. Tuckett then used a series of semicircular steel reamers attached to a drill in order to remove the arthritis from the acetabulum. The working end of each reamer had the rough consistency of a potato grater and each sequential reamer increased in size by increments of two millimeters.

"We are reaming the arthritis out of the acetabulum," said Tuckett. "The acetabulum is the cup of the socket joint which is replaced first in a total hip procedure." After about the fifth reamer Tuckett then stopped to visually inspect the fit of the reamer in the acetabulum.

"Looks good," was his line. "That was a size fifty-two so lets use a fifty-four millimeter," was his line directed towards Dr. Lee who was standing behind Phil throughout the case.

"Exactly what you thought," said Dr. Lee while looking at the x-rays on the view box. Phil noticed that he had a somewhat nasal voice behind the surgical mask. "Just happened to have that exact size in my hand," was Dr. Lee's next line.

Dr. Lee then held up a sealed box that fit easily within the grip of his right hand. Tuckett looked at the box and agreed with the predetermined size, which was printed boldly on the side of the box. Nurse Bryant was then shown the box and agreed that it was a size fifty-four millimeter acetabular cup implant. Aran Lee then cut a layer of tight plastic from around the box and opened three layers of airtight wraps, with the last being a molded plastic contoured to the acetabular cup's design. Nurse Bryant then reached into the mold while using sterile technique to grasp the cup, which had been irradiated during its packaging, thus rendering it fit to be implanted. She pulled out an acetabular cup which had the appearance of a tennis ball cut directly in half through its midsection, and then attached it to the end of a straight metal bar. Nurse Bryant then handed the device to Dr. Tuckett.

"Behold the Tuckett Cup," said Dr. Tuckett to Phil while holding the cup up in regal fashion towards him. Tuckett spun the cup back and forth in front of Phil in order to show him all sides of the semicircular component which if measured was exactly fifty-four millimeters across. The cup was perched securely atop the metal rod and reminded Phil of a wand that could be used by a wizard in order to cast a spell. "A state of the art marvel that is currently being used in twenty two states across this great nation of ours," said Tuckett in a salesman line tone.

"Actually as of this morning twenty three," said Dr. Lee proudly.

"The Tuckett Cup was developed by Dr. Lee and I over the past fifteen years," said Ian Tuckett as he took a large metal mallet from the hands of nurse Bryant. "It represents the end result of countless hours of research and development that has consumed a large part of our professional lives," said the head surgeon as he lowered the cup down into the patient's pelvis. "Dr. Drummer please watch as to how perfectly this cup fits into the reamed acetabulum of Mr. Banks here." Then with a series of exactly ten smashing blows from the mallet, he drove the Tuckett Cup into position with a smile beneath his mask. The driving bar was then disconnected from the cup leaving it within the pelvis.

"As you may have noticed the cup is two millimeters larger than the size of the final acetabular cup reamer that I used," said Tuckett as he inspected the fit of the cup. "Therefore, once driven into place it wedges down securely so no cement or screws are necessary."

"Final resting place?" asked Lee.

"Final resting place," said Tuckett while attempting to jostle the firmly placed cup. "Excellent fit as usual."

"Must be the design," said Dr. Lee in a self-aggrandizing tone.

Phil was impressed, as it appeared to him that the cup was expertly positioned and secure in place. A plastic liner was then locked into the cup with a few taps of a mallet and Dr. Tuckett then proceeded to turn his attention to the patient's thigh bone or femur. With fifteen minutes a metal component made of titanium was wedged into the femur, which had atop it a metal ball. Then with a quick maneuver the patient's hip was mechanically relocated to fit the ball into the awaiting Tuckett Cup.

"Tension good," said Dr. Tuckett to Dr. Lee as he moved the new ball and socket joint through a range of motion. He then held the legs downward in a fashion that placed one on top of the other while visually measuring their length. "Leg lengths perfect," was his next line.

"Another one in the books," said Dr. Lee to the surgeon upon hearing the news. "Another one in the books."

Phil looked up at the clock and suddenly realized that only about thirty-five minutes had gone by since the case started. Over the next five minutes Dr. Tuckett sutured together the muscles and soft tissue beneath the skin.

He then stepped back from the table with a satisfied look saying, "Franz always keeps us on time."

Phil noticed that *The Trout* was coming to an end at that very moment. He then realized that the smooth surgical moves of Tuckett had been apparently orchestrated over time with the work of Schubert.

"I can't get enough of *The Trout*," said Nurse Bryant as she slid up the table into the vacated spot of the head surgeon. "Just can't get enough."

Dr. Tuckett then asked Phil to close the skin layer and assist Mr. Banks to the recovery room, while he went to the adjacent surgical suite to begin the second case of the morning. Phil obliged and then watched both Dr. Tuckett and Lee bolt out of the room.

"He's the best," said the anesthesiologist while peering over the head sheet that separated him from the surgical field. "People from all over the United States come to the Tuckett Institute to have their joints replaced."

"I'm from New York City," said a sedate Mr. Banks from deep beneath the surgical sheets.

"Wow," said Phil as he looked up towards nurse Bryant in anticipation of another line of adoration. His visual contact with her was met with a sarcastic roll of the eyes and shake of the head as she firmly slapped the suture and needle driver into Phil's awaiting hand.

"Hurry up," was her snappy line. "I've got a hair appointment at one o'clock."

Phil smiled beneath his mask and obliged to her request, realizing that the next two months with this O.R. diva could be quite entertaining. He later rejoined the founders of the Tuckett Cup in O.R. number two to help send another acetabular implant to its final resting place, deep within the pelvis of a second out of town client. By eleven o'clock Phil's day was over at the Tuckett Institute after assisting in the two hip replacement procedures. Upon exiting the locker room he was met by Ms. Reyes and her never ending smile and exuding energy.

"Pretty amazing stuff," was her line to Phil as he exited the locker.

"You bet," said Phil with a smile. "It's one thing to see it on video, but much more striking to actually watch it from start to finish."

"They are the happiest patients in the end," said Reyes as she began to escort Phil to the private elevators. "Their arthritic pain will be completely gone allowing them to rejoin the human race."

"Hey didn't I hear that line before?" asked Phil in jest realizing it was one of the Institute's mottos.

"Indeed you have Dr. Drummer, indeed you have," said Reyes with a warm smile.

She then informed Phil on their ride down to the lobby that Dr. Tuckett was off that afternoon for administrative reasons. The schedule for the following day was reviewed in detail as she then handed over Phil to the lobby attendants. After declining an offer for lunch and a beverage, Phil was politely escorted out the doors of the Institute, which led him suddenly back into the comparative squalor of St. Mike's hospital. Again, he wondered what to do with his free time, which throughout his internship year had never existed.

Later that evening Phil and the boys from cell five gathered together after another dinner of macaroni and cheese. They discussed their rotations up until that point as Jackie helped Rick start a weight training program that he agreed to for unknown reasons. While straining under a minimal amount of weights Rick Polk moaned about his mentor, a Doctor Martha Brace, whom he described as a depressive woman possessing limited surgical skills. He reported that she had nothing good to say about a career in surgery and reported a professional life up until that point that sacrificed her role as both a wife and mother. Jackie Rhimes however glorified his mentor in being "Fast" Eddie O'Neil who was a bundle of energy and positive vibe, and operated to blasting music and sexual innuendos hurled at the nurses. More importantly he spoke of nurse Candice Adams who went by the moniker "Candy Apple" and was the reigning diva of the operating room in St. Mike's proper. Phil knew that Candice impressed Jack both by the tone in his voice and the fact that he spelled her name lyrically while lifting weights beneath the bench press.

Then Phil described to his housemates the utter affluence, exactness and greatness of the Tuckett Institute, along with a description of the revolutionary Tuckett Cup. Surprisingly his description of the orthopedic greatness was met with disdain by the bodybuilding duo in front of him.

"Fast Eddie said he is associated with the mob," said Jack who was short of breath from a repetition of weights. "He warned me not to snoop around the Institute or I might end up on the bottom of the river with a pair of cement shoes."

"Even Doc Brace mustered up enough energy today to bad mouth Tuckett and his Institute," said Polk while looking down at his sore forearm muscles. "She said that no surgeon could possibly work hard enough to pull in the money to fuel his so called Center of Excellence."

"Ah they are all cry babies," said Phil in defense. "He developed an implant that is being used across the country. Imagine the royalties from that product."

"The mob," said Polk to Phil. "You're dealing with the mob."

"The mob, give me a break," replied Phil with a laugh. "I'm reasonably confident that we are not in a hotbed of syndicated crime here in the valley."

"Swimming with the little fishes," said Rhimes jokingly as he approached the stereo system on the wall. Then with a turn of the dial he jacked up the volume on the music, sending the glassware dancing on the nearby coffee table. The workout session then kicked into high gear between the chiseled mentor and his corpulent student as they pimp rolled back and forth to the never-ending lyrics of the rap music.

That very night Phil had a most peculiar dream that took him to the edge of the river that ran next to St. Mike's hospital. He found himself perched upon a wooden dock edge dimly lit by the overhead light from a rusty lamppost. Next to him stood Ms. Reyes with a clipboard neatly tucked across her chest, with the Tuckett Institute logo behind it. Her energetic smile was somehow replaced by a stern look of resignation, in anticipation of pending action. She did not speak but was apparently awaiting the arrival of someone from beyond the dock's lit area. Then suddenly and slowly, two figures appeared from the edge of darkness and proceeded to walk towards Phil. While squinting his eyes it was apparent to Phil that the lead figure was Dr. Tuckett and the somewhat shorter Dr. Lee trailed two steps behind.

Tuckett then stepped coldly to within two feet of Phil's face and just shook his head in a pitiful manner. The namesake of the Tuckett Institute appeared deeply disappointed. Phil peered over his shoulder and noticed a smug smirk across the face of Dr. Lee who appeared somewhat impatient. He tried to speak but words failed to articulate from his mouth. Phil then tried to run but upon looking downward noticed that his feet where encased in a block of cement, just as Jack had predicted.

"Final resting place?" asked Dr. Lee slowly.

"Final resting place," said Dr. Tuckett without hesitation as he turned to walk away.

Dr. Lee then walked forward and stopped directly in front of him, while looking upward with a sinister smile. With an effortless push of his right foot he slid the cement block backwards sending Phil into the depths of the swirling river below. The water was pitch black and tasted of sulfuric pollution. The waning vibration of Ms. Reyes shoes signaled the departure of the trio from the abandoned dock above. Phil's decent downward was rapid and strangely quiet, allowing him to peacefully sink into the mud of the riverbed below.

CHAPTER FIVE
FOURTH OF JULY FIREWORKS

PHIL'S FIRST WEEK at the Tuckett Institute passed by quickly. Fortunately for all junior residents taking call, the obligatory overnight stay in the hospital no longer existed. All junior residents were responsible to carry a pager or cell phone and be available for emergency room or operative cases. This allowed Phil and his fellow residents to take call from the skid row complex, a true luxury when compared to the draconian days of internship.

The morning of July 4th was sunny and warm. Phil completed hospital rounds that morning and then helped assist in an appendectomy case that Fast Eddie O'Neil oversaw. Phil was shocked as to how much of the case Fast Eddie allowed him to do, as he chatted with a nurse about his holiday weekend plans. A second case soon followed which consumed Phil's time until two o'clock in the afternoon. Upon completion of the surgical cases Phil returned home to eat, shower and ready himself for the July 4th party at the country club. Throughout the week he had heard countless stories as to the magnificence of the party, which was sponsored by AMG and the Tuckett Institute, and not to be missed.

Phil arrived at the country club alone that mid afternoon. His cellmates had cancelled their weekend plans to attend the gala event, having arrived several hours earlier at the club. A hospital courtesy shuttle drove him through the gates of the country club and towards a large building that sat alone atop a hill, overlooking acres of manicured golf links. Once inside the private club a sense of wealth and good fortune overtook Phil as he looked upon a plush landscape brightly colored by nature's palette. An uncharacteristic sense of exclusionary privilege briefly overcame Phil as he approached the sacred knoll of The Brookside clubhouse. Once inside the hallowed halls of the building, Phil was immediately impressed by its old world beauty and grace.

The Brookside Golf Club was founded in 1920 and offered three championship courses to privileged members that in total occupied 950 acres of land. The complex also contained indoor and outdoor tennis courts along with three swimming pools, nestled among multiple outdoor eating venues. Originally built by local coal barons, the club was now fueled by several local industries, including AMG and the Tuckett Institute. The setting represented a popular venue for ritzy weddings and social gatherings, including the annual Fourth of July gala, complete with lobster tails, alcohol, and fireworks. Since no detail or expense was spared by the Brookside, it represented the ultimate locale for the upper crust of society to enjoy the benefits of their elite lives.

Once inside the lobby of the clubhouse Phil was met by representatives of AMG, including COO Barry Reynolds who was flaunting a vulgar Hawaiian shirt and hat in an apparent honor of the nation's birthday. Phil was given a nametag that he stuck onto his shirt above the outer left pocket.

"Ah Dr. Drummer, welcome," said COO Reynolds while gazing directly at Phil's nametag. "Welcome to the annual July 4th party at Brookside."

"Thank you," said Phil as he appreciated a mixture of cigar smoke and scotch upon Reynold's breath. Asymmetric rings of sweat drenched the COO's armpits despite the air-conditioned environment.

Barry Reynolds then introduced Phil to a series of upper management personnel from the Kansas City based company that owned St. Mike's. Despite the mid afternoon hour all members of the greeting line had an alcohol fueled look and persona upon them. Each member of the contingent offered an obligatory smile and handshake towards Phil, only then to look beyond him towards the next guest in line. Above all of the greeting chatter arose the voice of Reynolds who, like a barker at a carnival, offered grandiose promises of good food, swimming and fireworks that day. After being jettisoned from the end of the line Phil immediately walked into a waitress offering him a wide array of cocktails upon her tray. Since he was on call for the weekend he passed on her offer and headed through the clubhouse in search of the pool, where he knew Jackie and Rick would be encamped.

The Brookside's main pool sat about one hundreds yards off the rear of the clubhouse, nestled amongst stately oak trees that allowed overhead light to completely engulf the water. Surrounding the pool sat a series of gazebos, lounge chairs and bars, which appeared to be the sine qua non of the Brookside experience itself. The pool and surrounding environment was packed with jovial hospital employees and their guests. Within a minute Phil was able to make out the sculpted body of Jackie Rhimes as it soaked in the sun amongst a collection of young nursing students. Phil worked his way towards him and as he did, ran face to face into Emily Reyes.

"Dr. Drummer so good to see you," said Emily without a trace of alcohol on her breath. She wore a neat summer skirt and top that complemented her figure. Professionalism emanated from her body.

"Hello Ms. Reyes," said Phil while being bumped from behind by passing guests. "Good to see you here."

"Please, call me Emily. Welcome to the July 4th party, which as you know is partly sponsored by the Tuckett Institute."

"Of course, how could I forget?" said Phil with a smile. "On the ride over here I saw two billboards with the Tuckett Institute on it. Then a commercial came over the bus radio to again remind me of a possible return to the human race."

"Don't forget the Institute's welcoming sign in the Brookside's foyer," said Emily proudly.

"And the Tuckett Institute logo that was emblazoned upon the side of the shuttle bus," said Phil with a laugh.

The two then exchanged a few more niceties as it became apparent that Emily Reyes was working that holiday at the

Brookside. It was also obvious that she had a bona fide love for the Tuckett Institute and all it stood for. As he walked away Phil wondered about her overall social status and pedigree, knowing quite well that it would be ultimately divulged in due time.

Phil then neared the pool and gathered his composure as he laid eyes upon the trio of Jack Rhimes, Rick Polk and Kendra Mason. The overpowering whiteness of Polk's body somehow distorted the voluptuous beauty of Kendra's body, which was barely covered by a bikini that fit her ever so well.

Where's your bathing suit Phil?" asked Jack.

"Yea, we are having a cannonball contest shortly," said Rick with an inebriated smile. His gaze was half upon Phil and half upon Kendra.

"Just a social visit today," said Phil to the gang. "I'm on call this weekend. So you know, have to stay dry."

"Me too," said Kendra with a pout.

"But that's your second drink," said Jackie to the fellow Philadelphia product beside him.

"I know," said Kendra with a devious smile, "But I'm pacing myself."

"I wouldn't worry about it," said Rick to Phil. "I just saw Fast Eddie at the pool bar, it doesn't look like he will be operating any more today."

Then at that very moment a middle-aged female with a bright polka dot bikini came up behind Jack and put her hands across his eyes. She wore a set of high heel shoes that somehow complemented the swimwear and shouted, "Surprise, guess who?" to Jackie who immediately turned around with the correct response.

"Candy Apple, I've been looking for you!" screamed Jackie.

Candice "Candy Apple" Adams was thirty-six years old and had the skin of a seventy year old, the result of a never-ending addiction to both sun bathing and tobacco. Each habit was started in the ninth grade and continued nonstop over the next two decades. Outside of these two vices she however was a lean, mean physical specimen that filled out her swimsuit well. She was no stranger to the local gymnasium and working out was her passion. Her claim to fame was being a semi-finalist for a professional football cheerleading squad some fifteen years ago, an honor that still served her well amongst the provincial crowd in the valley. Folklore had it that a blonde gold-digger who was sleeping with the team's quarterback beat her out for the spot, a rejection that still simmered in her soul. Candice was the uncontested diva of the St. Mike's operating room, having climbed to that position both in words and actions. She knew absolutely everything about every surgeon, from their most peculiar operative quirks to their most intimate personal fascinations. After emerging from a vanishing hug amid Jackie's body she turned to the crew with a snappy crackle of gum in her mouth. In her right hand was a tall cocktail drink, with an umbrella on top. Fashionable sunglasses covered her eyes while bright red lipstick framed out a set of pearly white teeth.

"This must be your hottie roommate," said Candice to Jackie as she stepped towards Phil. "All the nurses at St. Mike's are awaiting your arrival young man."

"But I've been here for a week," said Phil. "I'm over at the Tuckett Institute."

"That doesn't count," said Candice with a smile while taking out a cigarette from her purse. "Only St. Mike's counts, not T.O.I." Phil noticed that she rolled her eyes and smirked with contempt while enunciating T.O.I. "T.O.I., oh say it again, I'm getting faint," was her final line before deftly lighting another one of her trademark Dunhill smokes.

"What's wrong with T.O.I.?" asked Phil with full anticipation of an informative and colorful response. He sensed that Candy Apple was the mother ship of gossip at St. Mike's and he soon found out that he was correct.

Prior to her response a waitress approached the group with a tray of hors d'oeuvres and drinks, prompting the troop to retreat into the cozy confines of a gazebo, nestled amongst the gathering crowd. It was within this milieu of alcohol, hormones and scantly clad women that Candice "Candy Apple" Adams began to divulge the inner secrets and quirks of the players that made up the Tuckett Institute. She began her tutorial at the top, with an overview of the kingpin himself, Dr. Ian Tuckett.

"I won't deny he is a gifted surgeon," was her opening line and last one of a complimentary nature. "But beyond that he is a controlling, neurotic and paranoid womanizer," was her next comment given with a nervous puff from her cigarette, as if she spoke from personal experience.

"Wow, this is going to be good," mumbled Polk as he gulped down an oyster from a tray seated upon the gazebo bench.

Candice then began to describe Dr. Tuckett as a local sensation who excelled in everything he did before going off to college. Then magically he reappeared out of thin air, twenty years later as a famous surgeon who left the glitter of New York City to return home to his roots. Rumors swirled as to the rationale of his return including the expected whispers of a jolted love and legal matters. However the exact reasoning for his return was never truly clarified, which only fueled the aura of this worldly surgeon amidst the valley locals. Soon he joined forces with the new kids on the block from AMG and the Tuckett Institute was born, arising majestically next to St. Mike's. An east coast advertising campaign soon began funneling in patients to the Tuckett Institute, with the promise of surgical excellence and V.I.P. service. The Institute instantly became a destination for the well to do who required a knee or joint replacement. To the local medical community it all seemed way too easy in a time of medical reimbursement uncertainty. Local physicians wondered how the former valedictorian from Valley High was able to buck the trend and expand his services in light of shrinking economics. Rumors again swirled as to where his funding came from and what was his relationship with AMG, and more importantly why were they all back in the valley.

"I hear he has his own jet, true or false?" asked Jackie to Candice.

"True," said Candice. "Absolutely true. He has told me on numerous occasions that he only works in the valley. He lives in New York, Washington, Miami and Los Angeles. Pick your city, it doesn't matter, wherever the famous congregate is where he is. It's rare for him to be here on a weekend. On Friday he just picks up with his nurse of the month and flies away from it all." Candice then paused to look into the bottom of her empty drink glass with a touch of remorse in her eyes. It was apparent to the group that she may have been that "nurse of the month" at one time, but that one time had now passed her by.

"I hear he is dating his scrub nurse," said Polk to the group.

"True again," said Candice with a sigh. "Believe me it's intoxicating when you are with him. Friday will take you to a Lakers game at courtside, then Saturday will find you in D.C. at a White House function. It's a magical ride that is difficult to fully describe, a ride that seems out of place here in the valley."

"What about Dr. Lee?" asked Phil. "He seems his opposite."

"Dr. Lee was his old college roommate at Cornell," said Candice. "They were both engineering majors and roomed together for four years. He went on to get his doctorate in biomedical engineering at Princeton. They have been inseparable since."

After another round of drinks were brought to the table, the weathered yet still enchanting Candy Apple proceeded to paint a picture regarding Dr. Aran Lee. He was indeed Dr. Tuckett's alter ego, rarely seen in public and living several miles out of town on a secluded ranch. Lee was instrumental in helping his former college roommate develop the Tuckett Cup and apparently was reaping the economic benefits along side him. Beyond that obvious connection, not much was known about him. Being of North Korean origin his ancestral tree was nonexistent. Lee was only seen in public in and around the Tuckett Institute, always at Tuckett's side. He rarely was seen about town, and by his own account, never traveled away from the local area. He had no vices or obvious skeletons in the closet. Candice couldn't even speak with authority on his sexual inclinations, which represented a thorny conundrum amongst all of the kibitzers who managed the local gossip stream.

"The odd couple," said Jackie.

"Yin and Yang," quipped Polk.

"Yea I guess so," said Candice as she sucked the olive off the swizzle stick of her martini in a sad tone. "The devil you know and the devil you don't."

Suddenly a women burst into the gazebo with a trailing party of young females following her, each carrying a gift basket loaded with goods including wine, cheese and condiments. The woman leading the charge was thin and tan and wore a sundress that sagged somewhat on her bony figure. Her face was fair and marked with freckles, each having the appearance of being present ever since her childhood. Atop her head sat shoulder length red hair that was being protected by a large sun hat, thwarting the rays from the sun above. Before she spoke Phil looked quickly at her nametag, which read 'Anastasia Tuckett, V.P. of Hospital Affairs'.

"Candice, just the person I'm looking for," said the V.P. of Hospital Affairs. "Some raffle tickets for a good cause? All proceeds benefit the children's ward at Saint Mike's."

"Of course Stacie," said Candice as she reached into her purse. "What can I win?"

"Wine, wine and more wine," said Anastasia with a gesture towards the baskets being held by the young hospital volunteers beside her. "What middle aged woman wouldn't want a basket of wine?"

Over the next few minutes Anastasia Tuckett sold tickets to all of the guests gathered under the gazebo that sunny afternoon. Phil noticed that she moved among the crowd with a confident grace and carefree manner. Upon seeing his nametag she did make reference to the Tuckett Institute and asked if his rotation was going well. He noticed her gaze and conversation to be more exact with himself as opposed to Rick and Jackie. Then after announcing that the winning tickets would be drawn after that evening's fireworks, she left the scene and proceeded to the next gazebo filled with guests.

"Who was that?" asked Phil to Candice immediately upon her departure.

"Anastasia Tuckett," said Candice with a hard emphasis on the last name of Tuckett. "A.K.A. Stacie."

"Stacie," said an inebriated Jackie Rhimes, "S-T-A-C-I-E."

Before Phil could respond a loud voice suddenly came over the crowd via a speaker system. Upon looking upwards Phil saw COO Reynolds at the head of a podium perched atop a plaza just outside of the clubhouse. Beside him was an entourage of upper management from AMG, spread out in a manner of rank and file consistent with their known corporate pecking order. Barry Reynolds proceeded to welcome the crowd to The Brookside and thank everyone for another great year of hard work and community service at Saint Michael's. He noted from a financial standpoint that Saint Mike's was doing well and continued to be the flagship of the AMG Corporation along the East Coast. Then, in a manner of all COOs with a microphone in their hand, he began to rattle off a litany of VIPs in the audience while touting their contribution to the well being of the hospital. It was during this portion of the speech that Phil began to scan the vast crowd in front of him, which he estimated to be at about seven hundred people.

The attentive crowd was staring upwards towards the podium, some with sunglasses on and others shielding the bright sun with their hands. They stood still and listened to every word of COO Reynolds as if he were a seer coming down from the mountain to speak. A few guests floated silently in the main pool while others sat upon the edge, with their feet cooling in the water. Every bench, lawn chair and gazebo was filled to capacity and the aroma of an awaiting clambake permeated the air. An occasional child would burst free in a short sprint only to be corralled in by a parent that was thankful to be on the invite list for the affair. Phil looked to his left and saw Jackie Rhimes sitting ever so close to Nurse Adams who nervously swayed a crossed leg up and down as the nicotine from her last cigarette soothed her addiction. To Jackie's left was Kendra Mason who sat erect and peered past Rick Polk as the two listened to the hospital COO. Phil then scanned beyond Rick's shoulder towards the adjacent gazebo, and his look was immediately met by the stare of Anastasia Tuckett, who stood out amongst the seated guests around her. Her fixed glare was locked onto Phil and a gentle breeze suddenly brushed some strands of red hair across her pale face. She then smiled a warm and friendly smile at Phil, which lingered before she turned attention back towards the babbling speaker. Phil however continued to stare at her, wondering what her relationship was with the Tuckett name and the Tuckett Institute. He appreciated a certain beauty in Anastasia that was not completely physical, yet seemed as if it were.

"I would now like to turn the microphone over to someone that we all know and respect," said Reynolds to the crowd. "A man that has brought orthopedic excellence to the valley and continues to set the standard across the nation for joint replacement surgery." Reynolds looked proudly behind the line of AMG flunkeys in anticipation of the next speaker stepping forward. "Please give a nice round of applause to another proud sponsor of this great Fourth of July tradition, Dr. Ian Tuckett."

A roar of applause lifted from the crowd as Dr. Tuckett approached the podium to address the throng before him. The good doctor wore a crisp seersucker suit that morning complete with a fashionable bright pink tie. A confident stride brought him to the microphone where he began to welcome the crowd and thank them for another fantastic year of work in regards to the Institute. The silence amongst the crowd was deafening as Tuckett spoke. During this time Phil noticed two distinct characters upon the stage.

The first was Dr. Lee, who stood behind Tuckett in a manner of strict attention. He wore a darker suit and tie that was formal and overpowering among the other dignitaries to his sides. No emotion transmitted from his face as he listened to the speech with a set of dark sunglasses protecting his eyes. Throughout the entire speech, he remained motionless.

The second was Emily Reyes who stood to the far right of Tuckett with a look of devotion upon her face. She swayed with emotion and clapped vigorously in approval of Dr. Tuckett's remarks. The contrast between her and Lee was quite noticeable to Phil as he took in the scene before him.

Suddenly Dr. Tuckett completed his speech with a toast lifted towards the crowd. A final applause broke out and handshakes were exchanged between Drs. Tuckett and Lee and the AMG bigwigs. Then as quickly as they appeared, both Tuckett and Lee disappeared from the stage, never to be seen again that joyous afternoon at Brookside.

The remainder of the day was everything it was anticipated to be, and then some. A massive lobster fest followed with a plethora of food and drinks. Children enjoyed hot dogs, hamburgers and animal rides operated by clowns with balloons and smiles. Two live bands rocked the crowd into the evening hours. A fireworks display then lit up the overhead sky and faces below, bringing the gala to a fitting end. Complimentary shuttle buses then took the satiated guests to multiple drop-off points throughout the valley, including the Skid Row complex, where Phil eventually ended up with his drunken cronies.

Despite Phil's sober objections the holiday party spilled into his apartment with Jackie Rhimes leading the charge. Among the cast of characters were Candy Apple Adams and a cohort of her fellow nurses. Kendra Mason and her roommate Stephanie jumped on board along with several other unidentified nursing students from the complex, both male and female. The heart stopping music of Doctor X.L. rattled the walls as the gathering of barely clad partiers danced into the midnight hour. Phil initially joined the gang but then retreated to his room in an attempt to break from the mob.

A knock on his door signified the futility of his effort. Upon opening the door Phil was not at all surprised to see Kendra Mason with her bikini on and a smile. Phil immediately knew that she was intoxicated as her tanned body swayed back and forth to the musical beat. Before a word could be said he heard a loud series of raps on the front door of the apartment. As Kendra Mason moved towards him he gently held her shoulders back and side stepped her to answer the front door.

Upon opening the door Phil was surprised to see Anastasia Tuckett standing in front of him with a large basket filled with wine bottles. She informed Phil that he had won the basket of cheer that evening but failed to pick it up after the fireworks. After inviting herself in Phil found himself sandwiched between the fetching Stacie Tuckett and steamy Kendra Mason. Reluctantly he agreed to a single celebratory glass of wine with the Vice President of Hospital Affairs. As the three toasted the birth of their great nation another knock rattled the front door.

Phil opened the door and was shocked to see Jennifer Ranier standing in front of him. An astonished look covered her face as she gazed upon the chaotic scene unfolding before her. Standing next to Phil was a stunning middle-aged woman and scantly clad young beauty, each with a glass of wine in their hands. Behind the trio roared a crowd of males and females wearing swimwear and chanting "Candy Apple" as a middle-aged female clad in a polka dot bikini performed a football cheer atop a table. Several new comers to the party then brushed beside Jennifer in an inward rush to join the fun.

The women exchanged awkward introductions as Phil attempted to explain the situation. Anastasia Tuckett thought it so sweet that Jennifer drove all the way up to the valley that holiday evening to surprise Phil. Kendra Mason politely said hello and then sulked her way back into the crowd, having just met her strikingly beautiful competition. Phil nervously put down his drink and described the country club experience to Jennifer while trying to downplay the regality of the spectacle. Despite his best efforts that night, the wrath of Jennifer Ranier crashed upon him with all its feminine might. Suddenly the newly appointed junior resident found himself struggling to survive his first weekend of surgical call at Saint Michael's hospital.

CHAPTER SIX

THE V.I.P. ROOM

IAN AND ANASTASIA Tuckett were married for a total of seventeen years, the first ten of which were happy. They had met at a fundraiser for the General Hospital in New York City, he being an orthopedic fellow and she the daughter of a wealthy benefactor. Their social backgrounds were quite dissimilar, yet they were married within one year of that fateful night. Their marriage paved the way for the young Doctor Tuckett to accept a coveted staff position at the Hospital for Exceptional Surgery, thanks in full part to Anastasia's father, who was a third generation New Yorker and powerful member of the hospital's board of trustees.

Their first five years together were everything a young couple with a dream hoped it would be. Anastasia busied herself with events that only an Upper East Side resident was privy to, including an endless list of social functions. She immersed herself in fund drives, hospital charities and projects for the underprivileged. Her face commonly graced the social section of the local newspapers along with her strikingly handsome husband, the gifted surgeon. Ian on the other hand spent every available moment of his young career plying his trade within the confines of the hospital. His combination of dexterity, intelligence and work ethic served him well as an associate professor, setting him apart in a city full of top-notch surgeons. By word of mouth he rapidly developed a following of patients who requested his services by name in time of need. His popularity seemingly bloomed overnight after performing surgery on a local sports hero, thereby solidifying his moniker as the "surgeon of the stars." Soon the floodgates opened and every retired athlete with a bad knee appeared at his doorstep, requesting a joint replacement.

The storybook marriage continued on schedule with two offspring appearing three years apart in their Manhattan apartment. Ian junior arrived first on a snowy February morning and possessed the blended good looks of his parents. Natasha arrived on the scene next, being an exact visual duplicate of her socialite mother. A predetermined path of fine schooling and entitlement then propelled the young Tucketts forward, under the watchful eye of their parents and grandfather. A tenth wedding anniversary cruise found the happy family touring the Mediterranean together, awash with sunshine and happiness. It appeared to their close friends that their union was surely one of divine perfection.

However every sailing ship will eventually hit rough seas in order to test its crew and inner core. Some survive the storm and emerge stronger, while others take on water, capsize and sink amid a scene of horror. The good Sailing Ship Tuckett was unfortunately unable to weather their personal storm, which over a several year period ultimately destroyed their vessel, sending it in an irreversible fashion to the ocean floor below. The disturbance that brought upon this calamity consisted of three common woes of life, that being money, alcohol and infidelity. Each alone will test a sailing ship, however when combined together they generate a tempest of famed and fatal proportion. It was this perfect storm that ultimately led to the demise of the Tuckett marriage.

The money matter occurred first and involved Anastasia's side of the family, specifically her father. For years he expertly managed the family's inherited wealth with a cocksure style, frequently bragging about returns that clobbered the market averages. With fantastic returns padding the family's already bloated coffers, he began to uncharacteristically pour an inordinate amount of savings into a prized investment vehicle, that being a stock fund run by a trusted friend and former college teammate. Harsh fiscal reality struck upon the arrest of the fund manager and exposure of his Ponzi Scheme, thus wiping out sixty percent of the family's net wealth overnight. A foreign word previously unknown to Anastasia's lexicon then suddenly dominated her family for years, with that word being "austerity".

The alcohol matter also involved Anastasia's side of the family, in Anastasia herself. A decade of fundraisers and social events generated a never-ending stream of cocktail parties that had one common thread among them, which was alcohol, and in Anastasia's case, wine. Her bout with alcoholism had no defining moment or entry point to mark the onset of an illness. Rather it was a slow and methodical slide into a rising physiologic tolerance and dependency that seemed to ultimately define and become a part of her social persona. Pleas to seek help from her husband were met with tender reassurance and personal promises that connected one failed intervention to another over time. With each passing year the demonic grip of alcohol held more tightly to Anastasia's thin and socially acceptable gaunt frame. She then became a well to do lush, capable of hiding her addiction behind the muse of a well-meaning socialite.

The infidelity factor however belonged exclusively to her husband. Spending so much time in a hospital setting has its risks and rewards, with one at times outweighing the other. In Dr. Tuckett's case his first illicit act outside the realm of his wedding vows occurred with a nursing administrator who was ten years his elder. They had been working on a research project together for approximately one year at which time her closeness and sensuality turned the relationship from professional to sordid in a matter of minutes. They carried out their uninhibited research together for another six months before bringing the memorable project to an end, thanks in part to a random variable better known as the nursing administrator's insanely jealous husband. Regardless of the outcome, the young and now sexually liberated surgeon considered further research in the field necessary in order to combat the negativity that was starting to ring aloud at home. His brazen attitude then proceeded to cut a swathe through the ripe female crop readily available throughout the hospital, despite constant warning signs of Anastasia's implicit awareness.

The unexpected dismissal of Ian Tuckett from the staff at Hospital for Exceptional Surgery marked the death knell of the Tuckett family existence in New York. Along with the loss of gross amounts of family money, Ian's father-in-law also lost his confidence and power amidst the Ponzi rubble. His weakness tilted the tables against him with regards to an ongoing feud among the hospital's board of trustees. Upon his father-in-law's expulsion from the board, the remaining members thought it appropriate to further sully the family name with a dismissal of Dr. Tuckett from the hospital staff. The dismissal was based upon a weak sexual harassment allegation levied by a young nurse against Dr. Tuckett that would have no chance in a courtroom. However the clearly defined threat of the complaint going public was enough to coax Dr. Tuckett into leaving the staff.

The couple's fifteenth wedding anniversary was celebrated quietly with a visit to an overpriced marriage counselor in New Jersey. A decision was made by the dysfunctional couple to strike out and start anew in a last ditch effort to save their marriage and family life. After a brief debate over a glass of wine, a unilateral decision was made to return to Ian's hometown, where an outside company was buying the local hospital. A deal was subsequently struck with Americana Medical Group and the Tuckett Institute was born. The Tuckett family then moved west, where over the next two years they attempted to unsuccessfully iron out their marriage difficulties. During the two hour exodus from Manhattan a gigantic chip developed upon Dr. Tuckett's shoulder that would energize his every action from that moment forward. The grudge was against both the social and orthopedic establishment in New York City. Dr. Tuckett made a commitment to himself to create a national center of orthopedic excellence that would rival any tertiary care hospital in a major metropolis. He vowed to exercise every waning moment of his orthopedic career to accomplish this goal, and prove to the establishment that they were wrong in their actions and perceptions. The exiled Dr. Tuckett soon found out that this anger was a powerful fuel that rocketed his dreams into reality amidst a sea of seeming underachievers.

With this backdrop in mind it was obvious why Dr. Tuckett and Dr. Lee vanished from The Brookside that sunny holiday afternoon. Despite the national day off for the common man, they had work to accomplish. Upon leaving the Brookside they proceeded to the local airport and left the valley in route to a more fashionable clambake in Martha's Vineyard, where bigger fish remained to be fried. Hosting the event was a powerful Washingtonian and senior board member of the Food and Drug Administration, who just so happened to steer the Tuckett Cup through the approval process five years ago. The good doctors enjoyed a spectacular meal overlooking the sea, as did the host who received a very generous donation towards his son's bid for congress. Accompanying the doctors was nurse Bryant who titillated the host with her beauty, energy and closeness. The New England clambake proved to be yet another boost for the Tuckett Institute, which at that point in time was firmly solidifying its national reputation as an Orthopedic Center of Excellence.

It was into this world of excellence that Phil Drummer continued to roll through after the Fourth of July fireworks. His following week on rotation was again set in a routine that went off like clockwork. Two joint replacements a day occurred three days a week, with the other two days spent seeing patients back in office follow up. It was the Wednesday of Phil's second week that he again met Mr. Banks from New York City, who was presenting for follow up with regards to his hip replacement. Mr. Banks had just been escorted to examination room number eight, having just had post operative x-rays taken of his hip.

"All the out of town clients are placed in exam room number eight," said the ever-present Ms. Reyes as she spoke to Phil that afternoon. "Mr. Banks just arrived in from New York this morning. We make it a point to never have a client wait for the doctor to see them. They appreciate this attention to detail and time," said Ms. Reyes.

"He flew in for this appointment?" asked Phil. "Couldn't he just be seen by someone in New York for follow up?"

"He could have," said Ms. Reyes. "But that's not the Tuckett Institute way. Dr. Tuckett did the surgery and will be the only physician to monitor the client's progress after the procedure. Again all clients appreciate this attention to detail. "

Ms. Reyes then instructed Phil to make his way into room eight to initially see the patient in follow-up. She instructed him not to touch the patient or offer any advice until Dr. Tuckett arrived in the room. She knew that patients appreciated youth and good looks around them, two physical attributes that Phil possessed about himself.

"Room eight is the so called V.I.P. room," said Ms. Reyes.

Upon entering room eight Phil immediately appreciated an environment unlike any other exam room he had seen. The walls were lined with stately oak beams and expensive leather hugged all the furniture. The room looked like the study from an old Tudor home along an English countryside. Soft classical music played overhead as a characteristic smell of opulence filled the room. A personal attendant stood at attention in the corner of the room, wearing the characteristic Tuckett Institute uniform with a T.O.I. logo in place. Phil immediately introduced himself to the client who was sitting on an exam table wearing a medical gown with wing tipped shoes and high black socks on, reading the Wall Street Journal. As their conversation continued Phil learned that Mr. Banks lived and worked in New York City, having heard of the Tuckett Institute from several good friends, who were happy with their experience there.

"Everything is going great," said Mr. Banks. "I am very glad to have had my surgery here. I truly feel like a person here, not like a number in those Manhattan joint centers, where they all claim to be the greatest. "

"It's quite a place," said Phil. "I would definitely have my family members come here for surgery."

Over the next few minutes Phil answered some generalized life questions from the appreciative client. He then found out that Mr. Banks was an investment banker from the city, having been born and raised there.

"I hope you are saving your money in a retirement vehicle," said Mr. Banks with a coy smile. "Age is a powerful advantage in the quest to obtain wealth."

"Most definitely," said Phil with a smile. "I'm using my dad's time proven plan that has served our family well for generations."

"Hmmm," said an amused Mr. Banks as he looked up from above reading glasses perched upon his nose. "What plan would that be young man?"

"Why it would be the Five B plan," said Phil with a smile.

"The Five B plan?" said Banks. "I've been in investments all my life and have never heard of that plan." Mr. Banks then put the newspaper down and turned his face upwards to look through his glasses and study Phil with a skeptical grin. "May I ask what is the Five B plan?"

"Its simple," said Phil. "It stands for the Big Bottle Behind the Boiler in the Basement. That's my dad's Five B plan. That's where he puts the family money."

A tremendously regal roar of laughter erupted from the New York investment banker upon completion of Phil's last syllable. Tears came to the client's eyes as he appreciated the self-deprecating humor from the surgical resident. Phil had used this joke many times before but never had it received such a grand response. The laughter between them continued onward for what seemed like a full minute. Phil even noticed the stoic attendant in the corner of the room to be laughing at the humor.

"The Five B plan," said Mr. Banks with joy. "I love it. Absolutely love it young man."

Dr. Tuckett then walked in to the room with an office nurse at his side and an inquisitive grin upon his face. Mr. Banks made Phil repeat the line again to the delight of himself and the audience. The investment banker then became serious as he opined to the staff that the Five B plan may not be that bad of an idea in the trending market of the day. Phil then stepped to the side to watch Dr. Tuckett apply his polished bedside manner and trade to the client. The visit itself lasted approximately fifteen minutes as Mr. Banks was notified that all looked well, including his x-rays and surgical wound. Plans were discussed as to the next several weeks of care, and an appointment was scheduled for one month later. Upon completion of the evaluation Phil received a hardy handshake from the banker as he prepared to depart. The V.I.P. then in jest politely asked Phil if he could share his comedic material. Phil consented to the request and the banker immediately thanked him and began to send out a text message regarding the joke that he found so appealing. Ms. Reyes then escorted the laughing and texting Mr. Banks out of the room to the lobby below, where a limousine drove him to the awaiting personal jet of Dr. Tuckett. He would be back home within an hour, still smiling from the well-timed joke and V.I.P. room care that he had just experienced.

By the Friday of Phil's second week at Saint Michael's he began to feel quite comfortable. His routine was quite predictable as compared to the absolute chaos of internship back at the PGH. The obvious key to Phil's comfort was the perk of taking call from home and not having to sleep in the hospital. Complementing this perk was the home environment of Skid Row, which was upbeat in the presence of Polk and Rhimes. Certainly the presence of a plethora of female nursing students helped matters, as did the rebounding warmth between Phil and Jenna. Ironically Phil felt more of an attraction from Jenna as she displayed an innate territorial prowess and affection previously unknown to him. With peaked anticipation he headed back to Skid Row that hot and sunny Friday afternoon with plans to drive back to Philadelphia. A fantastic reunion weekend was planned at the Greycliff Apartments that weekend, and Phil was the scheduled guest of honor.

Upon entering cell five Phil immediately came upon Rick who was sitting on the couch watching television. He appeared to be depressed and in a trance as Phil said hello to him.

"Let's go," said Phil. "Three hours to Philly."

"Change of plan," replied Rick. "I'm not going."

"What!" said Phil. "You're my ride. My ticket home."

"Nah, I'm just going to hang around this weekend. You go and have a good time," said Polk. "Here, take the car," and with a flick of his wrist he threw Phil the keys to his Toyota.

"What about your so called "squeeze" back at the PGH? Isn't she expecting the return of King Richard?" asked Phil.

"Oh that, it's over," said Rick with a wave of his hand. "And besides I've received word that my furniture was moved out of the Polk Lounge back at the PGH. The nerve of those interns, they have no sense of history."

Phil just stood still staring at Rick in disbelief. "So you have nowhere to go? Nowhere to stay now in Philly?" asked Phil with a sorrow in his heart.

A knock on the door then occurred, followed by the door suddenly opening. The inquisitive yet smiling head of nursing student Stephanie Thomas then appeared from behind the door.

"Ready to go?" asked Stephanie to Rick with a wide smile.

"You bet," said Polk with a quick hop up from the couch. "See you Philip, have a good weekend," said Rick with a sinister smirk on his face. He winked at Phil in passing as he headed out the door with nursing student Thomas.

Before Phil could register what had just happened the frenetic appearance of Jackie Rhimes appeared in his peripheral vision. Jackie was exiting his room with an energetic gait while singing a rap tune. Lacking was his characteristic set of surgical scrub pants and shirt. Jackson was dressed quite handsomely with a touch of gel in his hair.

"My boy," said Rhimes upon seeing Phil.

"Don't tell me, K-E-N-D-R-A, right?" said Phil.

"Kendra Mason wasn't ready for Jackie Rhimes," blurted Phil's friend as he quickly made way to the exit door.

"Where are you going?" said Phil now starting to feel left out.

"Where else but Candyland," said Jackson slowly with a mischievous smile on his face. "Ciao," was his final word prior to turning down the hall and quickly disappearing.

Suddenly all was quiet in Phil's apartment complex as he headed to his room to pack up for the weekend. Ten minutes later he was ready to go and heading to the kitchen for some nutrition. Then, while wondering whether or not Polk's car had any gas in it, a series of sudden knocks rattled the front door. Upon opening it Phil gazed upon a somewhat frazzled Anastasia Tuckett, who without saying anything, suddenly stepped into the apartment and closed the door.

"Hi," said Stacie Tuckett while staring up at Phil. She brushed back her hair while apparently trying to explain her presence. Phil noticed that she was somewhat disheveled in dress and harried in presentation.

"I guess you are wondering why I'm here," said Stacie with a nervous smile.

"Good guess," said Phil, "But I will say your presence is in keeping with a theme of surprise this afternoon."

Stacie smiled as she suddenly felt more at ease. "May I come in?"

"Sure," said Phil as he escorted the hospital's Vice President of Patient Affairs into the squalor of the living room. Stacie then sat down on a couch opposite Phil and took a deep breath prior to speaking.

She prefaced her comments in saying that it was important for Phil to understand how small the valley community was in comparison to a major city. Generations of families grew up next to each other, and gossip abounded. Everyone knew everyone else's business. With that in mind she then began to superficially describe the close relationship between the Tuckett Institute and St. Mike's Hospital. During this phase of the discussion she described an inordinate amount of wealth and power being generated from the business partnership. Wealth that in her opinion was starting to cloud the judgment of several parties involved. Phil noticed intermittent audible cracks in her voice and an infrequent quiver of her lower lip throughout the conversation. Her conversation left out exact names but rather used vague descriptions of "him" and "them." It was apparent that a lack of trust existed between her and the parties she was trying to describe. Towards the end of her ramblings it was apparent to Phil that Stacie Tuckett was expressing some inner sense of trepidation and uncertainty. She had divulged to him a good amount of information regarding her ex-husband's practice, yet left out any specifics that Phil would consider privileged information. She suddenly paused to look Phil directly in the eyes with a pleading gaze.

"Why are you telling me all of this?" said Phil.

"Right, good question," said Anastasia while seemingly reorienting herself. She paused and then said, "Because you are new to the area, fresh, an outsider. Someone who I could trust."

"Trust, I don't understand," said Phil. "Over the past two weeks I've gotten the feeling that you are quite popular around here."

"Please, Dr. Drummer, time is of the essence," said Anastasia as she slid forward on the couch coming closer to Phil. She reached out her hands close to his saying, "I'm going to be leaving town in an hour and have a simple favor to ask of you. A very simple favor."

Phil's heart began to beat more rapidly as the well-respected woman neared him. He appreciated her beauty and the subtle scent of chardonnay on her breath.

"I need someone I can trust to hold onto an item of extreme personal interest when I am gone," said Anastasia. She then quickly reached into her handbag and pulled out a small manila envelope, the size that normally would hold a set of keys. Phil noticed that it was sealed and unmarked. "Just for ten days, upon my return I'll pick it up and explain everything," was her plea.

"But, I...."

"Please Dr. Drummer. It's a simple favor, one that I will always be grateful for," said the former Mrs. Tuckett. "My home was unfortunately broken into six months ago and since then I can't rely on anything of importance being left behind." She then extended her hands and placed the envelope in Phil's hand, while pressing it firmly into his hand. "I will forever be indebted to you," was her final plea.

"But Mrs. Tuckett, I... "

"Dr. Drummer, please, this will all make perfect sense in ten days. This is a very private matter that I am in the midst of sorting out. Believe it or not I cannot trust anyone else with this envelope until I return," said Anastasia. "Again, everyone knows everyone else's business in this town."

Phil paused as he tried to gather his response realizing that he was about to submit to a strange but simple request. "Why me?" he again muttered.

"Because you are so young, pure and trustworthy," was the quick reply. "In thirty years you will understand the absolute beauty of that comment," said Anastasia as she stood up in a gesture to leave despite not receiving approval for the plan. She continued to hold the envelope in Phil's hand.

Phil stood up upon her movement and stared directly into her eyes. He noticed that she smiled ever so softy at him to seal the deal. He shook his head and then verbally consented to her apparent benign request. Anastasia then released the envelope into his hands, leaned forward and gently hugged him while softly kissing his cheek. Although the kiss was one of gratitude, Phil appreciated a subtle yet definite sensuality from her contact. She held her gaze upon him for several long seconds after which goodbyes were exchanged.

"Thank you very much doctor," said Anastasia. "I will never forget your kindness. Never."

As she approached the door to leave Phil said, "By the way, where are you going?"

"Out west to see some old friends," was her happy reply. "It's a trip that has been way overdue." Then with a gentle wave she disappeared down the hallway with an appreciative smile upon her face.

Phil suddenly looked at his watch realizing that he was now late and had a long road trip ahead of him. He quickly put the manila envelope in his weekend luggage bag and slung it over his shoulder. While walking to the car a rapid text was sent out to Jennifer notifying her of a delay. Within a few minutes he was driving away from St. Mike's and heading south, towards Philadelphia.

During the trek Phil had plenty of time to digest the events that occurred over the past two weeks. Questions abounded in his mind regarding so many different aspects of St. Michael's and the Tuckett Institute. Curiosity piqued his interest as to the contents of the manila envelope and what could possible be so important. Why had Anastasia Tuckett asked him not to discuss the matter with anyone? Suddenly a queer feeling overcame Phil as he physically distanced himself farther and farther away from the valley. A feeling that strangely pulled his attention and desires back to St. Michael's Hospital. Back to the quirky and pastoral environment where drama was brewing and excitement abounded. As the young surgeon approached the outskirts of Philadelphia he actually began looking forward to the end of the reunion weekend and his return trip back North.

CHAPTER SEVEN
THE NEWS BULLETIN

JENNIFER AND PHIL spent a late Friday night out on the town in West Philadelphia. There they found a corner booth in a popular bar that served the Penn community. Phil excitedly yet cautiously filled in Jennifer with the latest news from up north. She was somewhat saddened to hear that both Rick and Jackie Rhimes had already secured new girlfriends within a matter of two weeks. Jennifer's inquiries concerning Anastasia Tuckett were met with uninformative vague answers that thankfully calmed her emotions. Deep within Phil's mind he felt it paramount to provide as little information as possible regarding both Kendra Mason and Anastasia Tuckett. The unexpected meeting between the three females just one week ago still burned bright in his memory along with the wrathful scene that followed.

Phil then began to describe his first two weeks at the Tuckett Institute. He impressed Jennifer with details of affluence, exactness and professionalism. The term "Center of Excellence" was clarified with descriptions of personal attendants, limousines, and aircrafts. Jennifer then heard about the V.I.P. room and its tony clientele, along with the Five B joke. Lastly he described the impressive surgical skills and persona of Dr. Tuckett himself. A man who in Phil's mind seemed to have risen above the squalor of an uncertain medical community trying to survive in uncertain economical times. Just then a couple walked up to their booth with drinks in their hands. Looking upwards Phil was happy to see fellow junior resident Randy O'Keefe and his date for the night, nurse Heather Cruise.

"Randy!" yelled Phil over the crowd. "Have a seat."

"Don't mind if we do," said Randy as he slid into the seat next to Phil. Nurse Cruise then sat next to Jennifer and the two women immediately struck up a quiet conversation between themselves laden with local gossip.

"How's it going up North?" asked O'Keefe.

"Great," said Phil. "Working in the Tuckett Institute which I'm sure you know well."

"Of course," said Randy. "My favorite rotation at St. Mike's last year. We used to call the orthopedic wing the Taj Mahal."

"What a place," replied Phil. "It makes the PGH look like a run down warehouse."

"Cash is king up at the Institute," said O'Keefe. "The place is awash with money." O'Keefe then took a swig of his beer in a reminiscing fashion before asking, "Is Tuckett still flying around the country with that fox of a nurse? If I remember correctly her name was Nikki."

"Yea," said Phil. "Nicole Bryant. Some good looking arm candy."

Phil and Randy then exchanged some additional stories regarding the Tuckett Institute and the St. Mike's Valley. It was Randy that brought up Anastasia Tuckett.

"Have you met his ex-wife yet, Anastasia Tuckett?"

"Yes I have," said Phil. "Nice woman."

"Yea, but sad though," said Randy. "She stuck with him throughout all the years of training and hard times. Then when he hit it big he tossed her over the side like a sack of potatoes. I here she is a booze hound though."

"Who told you that?" asked Phil with a somewhat defensive tone.

"The gossip queen of St. Mike's," said Randy. A nurse whose name I can only remember as Candy Apple. Have you met her yet?"

"Yea, she is already dating my new roommate, Riles' replacement from Temple."

"Oh yea, how is our new fellow resident?" asked O'Keefe.

Phil then began to paint a picture of Jackson Rhimes in a positive light with adjectives describing a care free, sculpted and testosterone fueled young man. His weightlifting habits, street lingo and tendency to spell out names gave O'Keefe a colorful picture of a resident that sooner or later he would be working beside.

"Anyone is better than Fred Riles," said O'Keefe. "That kid was a bundle of nerves."

"I think he got a raw deal," said Phil "Too much pressure and pedigree to live up to."

"Well don't feel too bad," said Randy. "His old man is one of the two legitimate remaining candidates to become our new chairman."

"What!" said Phil. "I thought his name was on the list just as a formality. What about Knight? He wants that chair more than anything else in life."

"His health," said Randy. "Still not clear as to how he will stand up to the rigors of the job and still maintain a practice. Time will tell."

The two residents then shook their head and ordered another round of drinks. Phil noticed how great Jennifer looked, as did nurse Cruise. Heather Cruise obviously was several years younger than Jennifer and rumor had it that she had a killer crush on Dr. O'Keefe. A rumor that was apparently true. Their drinking and revelry went on well into the night before breaking up. Phil and Jennifer then headed back in an intoxicated state to the Greycliff Apartments.

Upon exiting the apartment's seventh floor elevator they turned right towards their corner apartment. Approaching them from the opposite hall was a single male, wearing surgical scrubs and walking with a spring in his gait, as if his Achilles tendons were too tight. Jennifer quickly whispered to Phil that the young man was the new occupant of Jim Turner's apartment from across the hall. He moved in yesterday and was apparently a first year surgical intern at the PGH named Troy. Phil noticed that his scrub pants were too short and he wore blazing white socks.

As the trio came face to face in the hallway Phil immediately said hello and introduced himself as did Jennifer.

"Hey, Troy Huckabee here," said the intern with a distinct and quirky southern drawl. "Everybody just calls me Skeeter though. So just call me that." Before Phil or Jenna could respond to the unusual nickname the young southern man continued by saying to Jennifer, "You are just too beautiful Jennifer. Are you my neighbor? I pray that you are my neighbor."

Jennifer blushed at the blunt yet strangely warm comment prior to telling the young intern that indeed both she and Phil lived across the hall. Troy was even more astonished by the fact that Phil was an upper level resident at the PGH.

"You know, somebody did tell me that another resident lived here in the Greycliff," was his comment with a particularly long drawn out emphasis on Greycliff. "What are the odds that I live across the hall from him?"

Brief information was exchanged between the group, including the reasoning for the late arrival of Troy into the Greycliff, being already into his second week of internship. It appears that he tried to take up residence in the vacated Polk Lounge but an executive order from above closed down the Lounge, thereby not permitting anyone to take up permanent residence in the hospital. Skeeter then excused himself from the group saying that he had to go grocery shopping at that late hour, since he was on call every other night that week. He then departed down the hall whistling a tune in a carefree manner.

The gala reunion weekend then continued well into the night as Phil and Jennifer caught up on intimate personal business. It was apparent to Phil that their relationship was stronger than ever despite the two-week separation. Jennifer exhibited an elevated level of affection that was not only physical, but deeply emotional. Her heightened sensuality both excited and slightly alarmed Phil as he knew their relationship was becoming all that more complex. Sleep did not come easy to Phil that night despite the combination of alcohol and personal attention just bestowed upon him. As the summer heat penetrated his senses he thought of Anastasia Tuckett that early Saturday morning while lying in bed.

Phil pictured her standing in the breeze with the wind slowly ruffling her dress during the July 4th picnic. He appreciated her gentle gaze that caught his eye while the rest of the country club guests stared straight ahead at the speakers. He then saw her smiling face delivering a basket of cheer to his apartment door, and then offering a toast. Lastly he felt the soft kiss upon his cheek that occurred just over a day prior. The kiss was so innocent yet so suggestive of things to come. Phil wondered where she was on the west coast and who she was visiting? What series of events could have possibly put her in a situation to apparently fear someone or something at St. Mike's? These were all questions that had no answer, yet seemed to generate more questions. Questions that remained unanswered but continued to torment Phil throughout the long night in Philadelphia.

The remainder of Phil's weekend with Jennifer was fantastic. A sunny Saturday afternoon found the couple picnicking in Fairmount Park, followed by a baseball game in South Philadelphia. Alcohol fueled another night out with Jennifer and her social work girlfriends in tow. Sunday morning found the twosome bleary eyed and eating breakfast in the kitchen nook of the cramped apartment. Phil was physically exhausted from the weekend joy ride as was Jennifer as they read the Sunday paper. Unfortunately for each of them the lead article in the *Philadelphia Chronicle* was a recap of the series of events that occurred at the PGH just seven months ago. The impetus for the story was the recent jury verdict just delivered in reference to Jim Turner. He had received a sentence of life without parole, having avoided the district attorney's sought after verdict of death by lethal injection.

"Poor Jim," said Phil in a depressed tone. "I still can't believe it."

"Poor Jim?" said Jennifer. "What about the four innocent people that he killed?"

"I know. I know," said Phil. "I'm not justifying his actions. I just still feel that somehow I was a part of it. An accomplice despite being completely unaware that it was occurring."

"Phil we've been through this before, the evil that occurred was solely from the actions of one man and one man only," said

Jennifer putting down the newspaper. "We were just pawns in his game."

Phil didn't respond, still feeling deep in his heart that Jim was a good person. A good person that was hurt badly as a child, who then as an adult had access to records that suggested his mother's death was a botch up rather than an accident. Thoughts of his deceased mother entered his mind as did a spark of anger. As Phil paged through the lengthy newspaper article he came upon a series of photographs regarding the case. The photos included one of Dr. Knight walking into the courtroom with his wife at his side. The photo was not complimentary to Knight or his wife, making each one look somewhat old and fatigued. Perhaps it was the black and white photo or the angle of the shot that explained this perception. Phil thought of asking Jennifer her comments but wisely said nothing, thus allowing the bleak morning to continue with the shadow of his pending departure looming.

Phil returned back to skid row that evening in an exhausted state. The three-hour drive alone was more difficult then he thought as his body continued to recover from the weekend. Upon walking down the hallway to cell number five Phil wondered whether or not his roommates would be home. As he opened the door the apartment was empty, looking the same as he left it forty-eight hours ago. Looking up to the wall he saw the time already eleven o'clock. Phil immediately headed to his room where he tossed his travel bag upon the bed and turned on his computer. At that moment he heard the main apartment door open and close, followed by the sound of Rick Polk singing a happy tune.

"How was your weekend?" asked Phil as he headed back into the living room proper.

"Great," said Polk as he went airborne onto the couch, landing on his back and grabbing the television remote control. "Couldn't have gone better as far as I am concerned."

"Since when did you and Stephanie become an item?" asked Phil as he sat down on a chair facing the television.

"She goes by the name "Steffie," said Polk as he began to scan the channels via the remote. "And her roommate is in love with you."

"Phfff," said Phil shaking his head. "That's all I need, another woman in the mix. I'm not sure what Jenna would do if she ever caught wind of Kendra and I hooking up, but I can guarantee you it wouldn't be pretty."

"I tell you what," said Polk as he machine-gunned through the T.V. stations in a manner that a male can only do. "She is one hot piece of…"

"Stop!" screamed Phil while looking at the television. "Go back, go back to the prior channel!"

"What?" said a frightened Rick Polk as he fumbled with the remote to hit the return channel button.

"No not that channel! One more back," yelled Phil as he stood up to approach the screen.

Rick then navigated backwards one more channel to pick up the area's local eleven o'clock newscast. On the screen was a serious looking middle-aged female newscaster who ten years ago rationalized that coming to the valley was an upward step to bigger and better markets. She held a series of papers in her hand and beneath her torso was the term "BREAKING NEWS" emblazoned in red print.

"Shhh," said Phil waving his arm in Polk's direction. "Turn it up. Turn it up."

"And again to recap our top story," said the news anchor. "The body of local socialite Anastasia Tuckett is now missing somewhere off the coast of San Diego, California."

Phil glanced at Polk with an incredulous stare before scanning back to the screen. A photograph of Anastasia again appeared on the screen as the anchor continued talking. Anastasia was smiling in the photo while hugging her two children.

"Preliminary reports have confirmed that she was involved in a boating accident some fifteen miles off the coast, with her body currently being lost at sea. An all out rescue effort is under-way by the local authorities and Coast Guard."

"What?" said Phil now with a pitiful feeling beginning to churn in his stomach. He looked over at a concerned Polk who was now sitting on the edge of the couch listening. The exact couch where he and Anastasia had sat just over forty-eight hours ago.

"No further details are currently available regarding the event," said the newswoman as her tired face returned to the screen. "However this channel will certainly keep the valley updated on any further information we receive regarding this ongoing search mission." The newsperson then swiveled her chair to the left and smiled at a separate camera, segueing to a lesser story with an ease that belied her current mid market position.

"Oh my god," said Phil in disbelief while looking back at Polk. "Missing at sea?"

"She won't last long in those waters," said Polk. "I used to be a lifeguard at Venice Beach. Hypothermia will send her to the promised land in about twelve hours."

Phil continued to stare at Rick not sure how to continue the conversation in light of the recent news and lifeguard comment from his portly roommate. He just continued to stare forward as a dark ominous thought began to enter his mind.

"The mob," said Polk as he began to rapidly fire through the channels with the remote control. "Don't mess with the mob. Jackie and I warned you. Lost at sea is their forte."

Phil then stood up and slowly walked away and returned to his room. An absolute numbness seized his body and mind as he zipped open the travel bag lying atop the bed. As he slowly ruffled through the bag full of dirty laundry a picture of Anastasia Tuckett saying goodbye with a smile entered his mind. Then, while reaching to the bottom right of the bag he felt the texture of the small manila envelope that she have given him two days prior. He pulled the envelope out of the bag and held it in his hand for several minutes while sitting on the side of his bed. His eyes began to scan the stark room in an attempt to find a secure spot for the envelope while the situation unfolded. Only then did Phil Drummer realize that his life once again was about to become much more complicated.

CHAPTER EIGHT

DR. IAN TUCKETT

DOCTOR IAN TUCKETT was driven by an inner desire to succeed. A desire that over time had made the Tuckett Institute a nationally recognized Center of Excellence. The Tuckett Institute was his glorious creation that garnered national attention and provided state of the art orthopedic care. Ian Tuckett was the Tuckett Institute, and his life was consumed by this brainchild.

The news of his ex-wife's disappearance was met with a certain concern and sadness. The concern centered about his two children who adored their mother. The sadness centered about the relationship that both he and Anastasia once had. Outside of these two factors there was no emotional turmoil with regards to the possible loss of his prior soul mate. He had stopped loving his wife years ago but always maintained a feeling that the reverse was not true. Anastasia frequently threatened to leave the valley with her two children, yet never did. She rationalized her physical permanency through her children, who were entrenched in excellent schools with good friends. Over the years the divorced couple developed a stable and respectful relationship primarily for the sake of their children. This respect was mutual and it was this regard that prompted Dr. Tuckett to board his jet and proceed immediately to the west coast upon hearing the news of his wife. Of course in tow was Nicole Bryant who adored southern California. She planned a self-proclaimed overdue spa visit to a posh La Jolla hotel that catered to those who needed catering.

Surely if Dr. Tuckett required any comforting during the trip, she would be the one to provide it.

The flight out west was uneventful. Dr. Tuckett took multiple phone calls during the trek, not wanting to waste any time in his pursuit of excellence. A call from Dr. Lee was taken over Kansas with notification that a new fellow would be joining the Tuckett Institute team for the rest of the academic year. This orthopedic fellow would spend a full year at the Institute to closely learn from the master himself. The fact that the pending fellow's father was a United States Senator from New England made all the difference in the selection process for the coveted spot. While over Las Vegas the couple enjoyed a bottle of wine with lunch and almost gave new meaning to the term "sin city" before the pilot announced their pending descent into the San Diego area. Upon arrival to the golden coast the jet setting couple parted ways, each getting into a waiting limo to be wisped away in opposite directions. Dr. Tuckett's destination was that of the Southern California Coast Guard station, five miles south of San Diego. There he would meet the team responsible for the ongoing search of his former wife and mother of two – Anastasia Tuckett.

The ride to the station took the surgeon through winding canyon roads that occasionally provided a commanding view out across the Pacific Ocean. As the doctor peered across the waters he shuttered upon seeing the brilliant horizon touch the ocean's surface so very far away. Certainly he thought, no one could survive for any prolonged period of time so far away from shore.

Upon arrival at the station he was escorted to a control center filled with screens and coast guard personnel. An officer close to Dr. Tuckett's age approached him upon arrival to the nerve center. The thirty-year veteran of the Coast Guard then reached out his hand to Dr. Tuckett, aware of the magnitude of the situation.

"Dr. Tuckett, welcome. My name is Commander Steve Wilson. I am in charge of this search and rescue mission."

Introductions were then exchanged between the surgeon and several other upper echelon officers that were under the charge of Commander Wilson. The commander then succinctly updated

Dr. Tuckett on the situation. Tuckett was impressed with his professionalism and disciplined attitude. He appreciated his tight crew cut hairstyle that somehow complemented a short, oblique scar above his left eyebrow. Every piece of metal on his uniform and body shined a bright polished look.

"The last radio contact with the vessel was approximately 1900 hours yesterday evening doctor. It was a distress signal from the ship's captain, saying they were taking on water fast."

"What was she doing out there?" asked Dr. Tuckett.

"Private whale watching excursion," said the Commander with a slight raise of his eyebrows. "At least that's the information we have from the shore crew who last saw them."

"Them? How many people were aboard the craft?" asked Tuckett, immediately aware of the Commander's peculiar emphasis on the word "them".

"That's were the information gets a bit sketchy," said the Commander with a direct look at Dr. Tuckett. "It wasn't a group of sightseers on the boat as one would suspect," said Wilson. "Maybe only one or two other non crew members. I can't be exact on that information but the local Police Department is in charge of the land portion of the investigation."

"Land investigation. What are you talking about Commander? There is a person, my ex-wife to be exact, who is lost out there somewhere at sea. This should be an all out rescue effort to find her," said Tuckett. "Not an investigation by a local police department on the shoreline."

"Doctor please, let me assure you that we have every available ship and plane out there as we speak looking for your wife. This is a drill that we unfortunately perform all too often during the year. If there are any survivors of this mishap our goal is to find them ASAP before it is too late."

Dr. Tuckett took a deep breath to gather his emotions in realizing that the United States Coast Guard was involved in an all out effort to find Anastasia. Certainly if anyone could find her it would be the Coast Guard. He then heard over the next twenty minutes facts that somewhat confused his orderly mind.

It was known that Anastasia rented a private sailing crew to take her and perhaps one or two others out to sea to search for whales. Then, two hours into the journey a brief series of distress signals were sent into the local communication center, which then forwarded the info immediately to the Coast Guard. At first a problem with the vessel's GPS signal was reported, and then corrected, only to provide a weak signal that couldn't be pinpointed for upwards of sixty minutes. Then, a hurried call came across the airwaves describing a vessel in severe distress with the crew and parties about to abandon ship, having perhaps no time to deploy their life rafts. No other communications were received after this call, which occurred with about one hour of sunlight remaining. An aircraft was immediately dispatched to the last known GPS contact, being unable to visualize any vessel or remains of a craft. The search was called off as night set in, only to be resumed that very morning at the break of dawn. Since then no reported sightings of the vessel or crew were reported.

"How long can someone survive in the water?" asked Tuckett.

"It depends," said the Commander. "We have to assume that the vessel did not carry wetsuits for passengers, that is not regulation for a tour boat. However the big question is whether or not the lifeboats deployed. If they did deploy and all persons were able to be quartered onto the craft, then they can survive for days."

"And if the lifeboats didn't deploy?" asked Dr. Tuckett. "How long can they survive in the water?"

"In the open water at this time of year," said Commander Wilson with an obvious measure of his words. "Approximately forty-eight hours before hypothermia sets in. Definitely no more than seventy-two hours in the open sea."

Doctor Tuckett then shook his head while looking around at all the personnel in the room, realizing that the sole purpose of all those involved was to find Anastasia. For some odd reason he thought of her father back east.

"Dr. Tuckett, may I please provide you with one more piece of information?" asked Wilson.

"Yes, Commander, please do," said Tuckett while calculating that Anastasia had already been lost at sea for nearly twenty-one hours.

"It's not whale watching season off our coast doctor," said Wilson. "I mean the peak season is from December thru April."

"What are you saying, or implying?" asked Tuckett.

"Nothing outside of that peculiar fact," said Wilson in all seriousness. "It just seems odd that a tourist, yet alone a boat's captain would head out to sea in July to search for whales."

Dr. Tuckett did not immediately reply. He fully understood the meaning of Commander Wilson's comment. He blinked his eyes rapidly while taking a deep breath. He was outside the cloistered environment of his Institute. He thought it best not to pursue this topic further.

"Thank you Commander, I will be staying in La Jolla tonight. I believe you have all of my contact information," said Tuckett.

"Yes we do doctor," said Wilson. "I will be here in the command center until this mission is complete. Do not hesitate to contact me and please, rest assured, that I will employ every available resource at my disposal to bring this mission to a successful ending."

Dr. Ian Tuckett spent a fitful evening at the luxury suite, which he shared with nurse Bryant that night. A phone call from Commander Wilson at nightfall brought the dreaded news that no craft or survivors had yet to be located. The massive search off the Pacific Ocean, some five to ten miles off shore failed to yield any information regarding the crew and sailing party. Adding to the misery was an exchange of anger between Tuckett and Bryant as to the seriousness of the matter. A defiant Nicole Bryant then stormed out of the room to head downstairs where she spent the next several hours running up a bar tab on the good doctor's name. Lastly, Dr. Tuckett made the decision to cancel the remainder of his office hours and surgery for the rest of the week. He was fully aware that the CEO of a prestigious Wall Street Investment firm was on the schedule that week, bringing only greater angst into the equation.

At one o'clock in the morning an inebriated and barely conscious Nikki Bryant stumbled back in to the Presidential Suite that was hosting the couple. She wobbled through a sitting room past a distraught Ian Tuckett en route to the king size bed that adorned the bedroom proper. Approximately five steps before the bed's edge she became unconscious and collapsed onto the floor, compliments of the massive quantities of liquor that she poured into her system. Dr. Tuckett did not respond to her self-imposed misery but he did allow her to lie, exactly where she dropped, throughout the long night.

For the next hour Dr. Tuckett sat alone, in a chair, collecting his thoughts. The recent series of events involving Anastasia deeply troubled him, as did thoughts of her body adrift at sea. At approximately two in the morning west coast time, he made a decision with the cool calculation of a surgeon about to place a scalpel upon a patient. Reaching to his left he picked up his cell phone and scrolled through a never-ending series of contact numbers. Without hesitation he settled on an east coast number and promptly hit the send button while raising the phone to his ear. He was sure that the voice on the other end of the line would be expecting his call.

"Hello," said the sleepy voice on the other end of the line. "Ian?"

"Eugene it's me," said Ian. "I'm in San Diego. We need to talk."

"Ian I heard the news. I'm so sorry," said the voice from the east coast. "Any word on her whereabouts?"

"No," said Tuckett followed by a long pause of silence on each end of the phone. "Nothing at all. The only known fact is that each hour brings us closer to this being a recovery effort as opposed to a rescue mission."

"Ian, I'm so sorry."

"Eugene, I need some advice," said Tuckett. "You have never steered me wrong in the past."

"Of course I haven't," said Eugene Adelman. "That's why I'm still your attorney after all these years, even at five o'clock in the morning."

"Eugene there have been some concerns raised by the Coast Guard about the events that led Anastasia out to sea," said Tuckett, now feeling a level of comfort from hearing a familiar voice.

"What are you talking about?" said the prominent attorney from his Manhattan high rise. He sat up in bed next to his wife who continued to snore, in anticipation of a prolonged phone conversation.

"A series of peculiarities and facts about only a few people being on board the vessel, a weak GPS signal, and it not being whale watching season. Stuff like that," mumbled Tuckett.

"Ian, don't tell me what I know I am about to hear," said Adelman. "Please do not tell me."

"Eugene, I'm afraid there are suspicions arising in regards to Anastasia's disappearance," blurted out Tuckett with a strange sense of relief. "Serious questions will be coming my way very shortly." A moment of silence followed.

"Well, do you have anything to be concerned about in relation to her disappearance?" asked his legal counsel slowly and politely.

Tuckett paused to gather his response. A rush of emotions churned through his stomach as the intoxicated body of his current lover lie muddled and prostrate on the floor in front of him. Thoughts raced through his mind as to how he, the world famous Ian Tuckett, namesake of the Tuckett Cup, had arrived at such a crossroad.

"Ian, I'm waiting for an answer," said Adelman politely. "We cannot proceed forward until I hear an answer to that exact question."

The uncomfortable pause continued as attorney Adelman's wife now stirred, appreciating his uneasiness.

"No, absolutely not," said Tuckett, feeling a burst of drive and passion that had rocketed his career to that very moment in time. "I had nothing to do with her disappearance."

"Good, that's always our first step," replied Adelman with an audible sigh of relief. "Now let's get down to discussing all possible scenarios and a measured response to each." The attorney then got out of his bed and headed to his adjacent library where the two spoke well into the morning hours, preparing for the inevitable questions about to arise.

CHAPTER NINE

A SURGEON'S SWITCH

ANASTASIA TUCKETT WAS never found off the coastline of California. Her rescue mission slowly evolved into a recovery mission that ultimately resulted in the conclusion that she was lost at sea. The finality of the event was marked by an appearance of Commander Wilson and his staff of advisors at the new hotel room of Ian Tuckett in downtown San Diego. Several days earlier Dr. Tuckett jettisoned the defiant Nurse Bryant back to the east coast via coach class aboard a second rate commercial airline carrier. Tuckett then relocated his quarters nearer to the Coast Guard command center in San Diego. There he kept a closer vigil upon the efforts of the search mission. During that time he admired and innately trusted the expertise of Commander Wilson, who was seemingly ever present at the controls of the mission. Tuckett greatly appreciated his professionalism and compassion exhibited throughout the ordeal. It was Commander Wilson who knocked that early morning, unannounced at Tuckett's hotel door with a contingent of personnel at his side. Upon opening the door Tuckett immediately knew that his former wife and mother of their two children would never be seen again.

What commander Wilson told Dr. Tuckett he already knew from daily briefings at the Coast Guard Station. When Wilson stoically told him that the mission was complete and a stand down order was given to all personnel, he accepted it with a firm conviction that everything had occurred per military protocol. After receiving condolences from Commander Wilson and the United States Coast Guard, Tuckett was then introduced to the second tier of dignitaries that made up the contingent. This portion of the combine was composed of detectives from the San Diego Police department, who were responsible for the land portion of the investigation.

Over the next thirty minutes, the SDPD disclosed new information to Tuckett. Most troubling was video footage of the presumed vessel that escorted Anastasia out to sea that fateful day. The video was captured by several security cameras atop the Coronado Bridge, which were operated by the police department. There, from afar, Ian Tuckett was able to make out the classic silhouette of Anastasia as she moved quickly from the rear of the vessel to the inner cabin, escorted by a single male. She wore her trademark wide brimmed hat, holding it tight against the wind of the open sea.

"We put a trace on the vessel's markings," said Detective Carmone who was leading the discussion. Carmone was born and raised in New York City prior to heading west some twenty years ago. His native New York City accent struck a harsh cord in Tuckett's gut. "The vessel was from Mexico, not uncommon in the harbor. Quick in and out before any harbor patrol could react."

"Who else was on board?" asked Tuckett.

"From what we can tell, no one," said Carmone with a shake of the head in a back and forth fashion. "Just the pilot, two apparent crew members and the female in question."

Tuckett held his ire with regards to the heartless description of his former wife as "the female in question." He only had one follow up question as the vessel carrying his wife out to sea disappeared from the edge of the screen. "Who were they? I mean, in your experience who was operating that vessel, that ultimately was lost at sea?"

"Miscreants, sea vagrants, pirates, illegals. You can call them what you want doctor, but from my experience they were goons who slipped in and out of the harbor for no good reason," said Carmone as he closed the laptop screen with a slow motion. "Remember we are only twenty nautical miles from the Mexican border. The coastal seas are lawless below that borderline."

Several seconds passed before Detective Carmone asked Tuckett if he had any further questions. His mind was jumbled as he tried to decipher the facts at hand. No other questions arose.

"Very good," said Carmone as he looked towards his partners in a manner suggesting their work was done. He then introduced the final line of the troop, which consisted of two attorneys representing the State of California.

Over the next thirty minutes they compassionately defined the term "missing at sea" as it related to legal matters. Terms such as "statute of limitations" and "maritime law" quickly confused Tuckett, who could only think of his children at home. A surreal aura overtook him as legal terminology assailed his cranium in an incomprehensible fashion. Lastly, the attorneys notified Tuckett, that several bureaucratic matters were in order before the case could be officially sealed, perhaps requiring several more months. Upon completion of the legal presentation, he thanked the attorneys for their time and understanding. He then gave them contact information for Attorney Adelman back east.

Then, as quickly as they came, the party departed. Tuckett was left alone in his hotel suite, wondering what to do next. He slowly made his way to an oversized ottoman chair next to the bed and sat down. For the next thirty minutes he tried to rationalize what had just transpired over the past week. His former wife was gone, lost at sea. His children were at home, praying and hoping for some good news that will never arrive. His institute was sitting dormant back east, cancelling surgeries and losing money in his absence. His life from that point forward was to be altered in a manner that he could not fully understand. Yet what troubled him mostly was the word "presumably" which was constantly attached to the phrase "lost at sea" by the State of California. Deep down inside, he held onto some odd glimmer of hope that she was still alive, despite the obvious finality of the situation at hand. While staring out the balcony window at a clear blue Southern California sky, he watched a small single engine airplane go by. It reminded him of Anastasia's life long desire to go skydiving with him, which he never did. Then for the next thirty minutes he recalled the wonderful times that they had together. He truly knew that Anastasia Tuckett was a beautiful woman, both physically and spiritually. She was much too good a person to meet such an apparent tragic demise, so far away from those that she loved. He inhaled a deep sigh of regret.

Then, suddenly and without prompting, a mental switch flipped inside the head of Ian Tuckett. Every surgeon had such a switch, which was both a blessing and a curse, allowing them to continue forward in a cerebral fashion of utter disregard. Disregard for their patient who had just unexpectedly died in order to continue on with the next complex surgical case. Disregard for the attorney lingering in their waiting room with a lawsuit subpoena, in order to skillfully treat thirty office patients in need. Disregard for the angry patient demanding release of all medical records, in order to rush to the emergency room and care for an acute injury. Lastly and most sadly, disregard for family members who always came in second, behind the constant demand of the masses. Loved ones who stoically celebrated birthdays and graduations with a smile, knowing that the empty chair at the ceremony represented a surgical emergency that could not wait, soon to be followed by yet another. Not all surgeons were born with this innate mindset, yet it ultimately evolved even within the most merciful ones, being the byproduct of a harsh training process. A process that was acerbic to the uninitiated yet bred an inner guile that was necessary for a surgeon to succeed. It was this inner mentality that led Ian Tuckett to pull out his cell phone and begin a series of calls.

His first call was to the pilot of his jet craft, standing by at the airport for instructions. The pilot was ordered to prepare for takeoff within the next hour. Destination was the Tuckett Institute where work awaited.

The second call was to Emily Reyes, notifying her of his pending arrival back home. He instructed her to reschedule all of his cancelled surgeries as soon as possible. The option of weekend surgery would be given to all the VIP cancellations, if their schedule warranted such a move. Tuckett was happy to hear the exuberant voice of Ms. Reyes as she excitedly took the call, knowing well that everything would be promptly taken care of and arranged to perfection by his personal assistant.

Next he phoned Dr. Lee, making him aware of the situation out west. Dr. Lee informed him that the new fellow arrived as scheduled and was standing by to assist. Tuckett asked Lee to work in coordination with Reyes to rearrange his schedule and get things back in forward motion.

The next to last phone call was to the nanny caring for his children. She notified him that his father-in-law was in town to help with the children. Tuckett instructed her to notify them all of his arrival, wanting to break the grim news to his family himself. He thought mostly of his daughter Natasha, who by nature was closest to Anastasia.

Lastly he called his attorney in New York. This phone call took the longest of all. Adelman informed him that he already received a call from the California state legal team, and a conference call was scheduled for the following morning. Tuckett then informed him of the suspicions regarding the gang of perceived pirates that took her out to sea. He promised to Adelman that he had no hand in the matter, with a conviction that was appreciated by his attorney. Plans to meet the following evening were made, along with a brief discussion of Anastasia's estate and the children's financial future.

Dr. Tuckett then called the front concierge requesting a limo for immediate departure to the airport. He packed his bags, freshened up and headed down to the lobby. It was only on the elevator ride down when his conscience tried to have a voice in the whole matter. Briefly it objected to the fact that his actions had no impact upon the events that just unfolded. Certainly spending the night with Anastasia on the eve of her departure could have altered her plans and subsequent doings. Perhaps thought Tuckett as he briefly listened to the speaker inside his head, but it was just another night of intimacy with his ex-wife, an impromptu event that occurred once or twice a year. He could not recall anything out of the ordinary that was discussed that night, despite the alcohol they shared together. Then with a forceful jolt his surgical switch muted the feeble squeak of his conscience, catapulting him into the lobby with a vigor befitting his persona. As he dipped into the cool confines of the waiting limousine, he felt comfortable in not having apprised Adelman of this recent liaison, which still stirred a fiery passion in his heart.

CHAPTER TEN

THE FELLOW'S ERROR

DR. ARAN LEE was a genius, by any definition of the word itself. He was the product of a strict Korean family, rooted in an Eastern discipline that commanded one to excel. An inordinately high I.Q. coupled with mandated self-discipline propelled him to the top of every class he attended. Fine boarding schools along the East Coast assisted him in obtaining a full academic scholarship to Cornell. There he continued to impress, obtaining a degree in engineering. It however was a random lottery drawing that brought he and Ian Tuckett together, in a run down freshman dorm one hot August day. From that awkward moment forward the unlikely duo formed a bond that only a collegiate atmosphere could forge, while they plotted grandiose dreams and aspirations. Tuckett was the athlete, at times struggling to stay on the path of academia. Lee was the brilliant geek, making school look easy and relishing his role in the odd couple relationship that benefited the two. Upon graduation Lee went on to Princeton while Tuckett attended medical school, yet the two kept in constant touch. It was this steely bond of kinship that prompted Tuckett to successfully recruit Lee to join his research staff in New York City, which ultimately developed and patented the Tuckett Cup. With Lee's background in engineering and chemistry, the duo invented a breakthrough design in press fit acetabular cups that went by Tuckett's name. However the cup's legal patent bore both Lee and Tuckett's name, thereby solidifying their relationship for the foreseeable future. Once Tuckett was exiled from New York City it was predictable that Lee would follow, hence defining their symbiotic relationship.

Dr. Lee was a student of economics, minoring in this field while at Princeton. A technophile to the extreme, he utilized data, numbers and computer systems to his financial advantage. His hobby was the stock market, where again he excelled. It was here that his brilliance and knowledge separated him from Tuckett. Ian Tuckett simply had no time to understand or master the intricacies of Wall Street, as his surgical schedule would not permit. However Tuckett entrusted Lee with vast sums of money, which his accounting team assured him was legal, in light of outlandish returns. When it came to the market, Dr. Aran Lee had the Midas touch. This touch allowed Lee complete access to the finances of the Tuckett Institute. Again, this was another clear separation point between Lee and Tuckett. Tuckett had limited knowledge regarding finances yet was quite comfortable with Lee's input, along with that of a chief financial officer, two accounting firms and a slew of lawyers that kept a close eye on the monies involved.

Dr. Lee's personal life was an enigma. He sparingly dated women in college and rarely socialized. His parents were deceased and no close relatives lived in the United States. He demanded to be addressed as "Doctor" in conversation. He was a bona fide germaphobe, who had a well-vetted cleaning service scrub his house from top to bottom on a weekly basis. Shaking hands was forbidden in his company. He never ate at local restaurants, mistrusting their utensil cleansing process. A personal chef prepared him balanced meals served to the utmost specifications on a daily basis. He dressed like a fusspot, with crisply starched shirts and the finest tailored suits. A hair was never out of place, and his shoes were always spit shined. He was precise regarding dates, times and details of all doings, being able to recall past occurrences with a remarkable veracity. His car was a jet black imported Mercedes, unavailable in the United States and exclusively owned by those with impeccable taste and wealth. Lastly and most specific to his DNA, was a characteristic stealth movement epitomized by a quick, soft gait.

He worked and moved quickly, seeming to never waste a second, being able to wisp from one project to another while leaving behind only success and the aroma of expensive cologne. It was this gait that seemed to be every present throughout the Tuckett Institute, moving in brilliance just a few paces away from Dr. Ian Tuckett.

The morning after arriving back East, Tuckett met Lee early in the surgical locker room, over one hour in advance of the first case.

"Two problems," said Lee. "The first is that this new fellow is no ball of fire." Lee was referring to the new orthopedic trainee who was about to spend a full year at the Institute.

"Doesn't matter," said Tuckett. "He is Franklin Stortz, son of Senator Ari Stortz from New England." Tuckett then smiled saying, "That is what really matters."

"I spoke to a few physicians at his residency program who are on the orthopedic staff. They were politely indifferent regarding his skill level," said Lee. "One attending however condemned him, saying he was all thumbs in the O.R. and a liability to any surgical team."

"You can't please everyone all the time," said Tuckett as he quickly got on surgical scrubs for the first case. He then closed his locker door and headed quickly towards the O.R. proper.

"The second is that you uncharacteristically logged onto your private computer last week," said Lee. "Just wanted to make sure there wasn't a problem."

Tuckett kept moving now diverting into the bathroom wash area to freshen up before the case. Unlike Lee his mind had no desire or free space to worry about computer systems. He delegated this to the legions of computer gurus who lurked around the complex on a constant basis.

"No problem," said Tuckett not even recalling the log in. "Must have been looking up some info for a case."

"The entry was at three o'clock in the morning," said Lee.

"My mind never stops working Dr. Lee," said Tuckett with a smile. "You should know that by now."

Then, before Dr. Lee could continue, the two colleagues sensed a massive presence behind them. They were startled by both a hulking shadow across the wall and an eerie respiratory pattern that seemingly belonged in a horror movie. They turned around to see the six foot eight, portly frame of Franklin Stortz, M.D., who was reporting for the first day of his fellowship. Stortz wore an extra large surgical scrub outfit that hugged his flabby extremities and protruding belly in a displeasing fashion. Curled patterns of chest hair extended above the outfit's neckline. He was raising his hands to put on a scrub hat atop a prematurely balding head while he entered the bathroom area. Despite having just put on the outfit, sweat marks soaked his armpits. He smiled and approached the two with a gait pattern that consumed a tremendous amount of energy with every step. He then went to speak with an inhalation of air that whined of an obvious respiratory condition.

"Good morning," came his labored line as he extended a hand towards Tuckett. "Franklin Stortz here, reporting for duty."

Tuckett reached out and shook his hand while saying, "Ah, Dr. Stortz a pleasure. Welcome to the Tuckett Institute, we have been awaiting your arrival." Tuckett then released the grasp of the fellow, sensing sweat across the palm of his hand.

Stortz then introduced himself to Dr. Lee who despite the offer, declined to shake the hand of the asthmatic fellow. During the conversation, Stortz reached into his back pocket and pulled out an inhaler to open the small airways of his lungs. As the trio exited the locker rooms Dr. Stortz expressed appreciation regarding the orientation program headed by Emily Reyes earlier in the week. Tuckett asked a few obligatory questions about Senator Stortz, who arranged the coveted fellowship for his son with a single phone call several months earlier. Dr. Lee then politely pointed to the sign in reference to cellular phones in the operating room, prompting Stortz to deposit his communication device in the basket.

The first two cases of the day went off without a glitch. Present at the table were Tuckett, Stortz, Phil and nurse Bryant. It was plainly obvious to Phil that nurse Bryant was not herself. She barely spoke throughout each case and her characteristic intimate stance adjacent to Dr. Tuckett was lacking. Most noticeable was the absence of her biting comments as she missed several glorious opportunities to ridicule persons of all ilk. Phil sensed a deep discord throughout the day between Bryant and Tuckett.

It was also obvious to all that Franklin Stortz was a klutz. His physical frame consumed precious space at the table, pushing Phil into a position jammed between the fellow and the patient's extended arm. His movements were slow and stumbling, even with the simplest of maneuvers such as cutting a tied suture for Dr. Tuckett. Despite his large frame he possessed short, stubby fingers that moved in a remarkably slow and unprofessional manner across the operative field, getting in the visual way of all other parties. His labored breathing pattern seemed to be worsened by the surgical mask that covered his face, accentuating the audible sucking of air with every breath. Lastly, to complement his entire persona, a body odor suffocated everyone within a ten foot diameter of his physical core. The odor itself sat heavy and oppressive, lingering long after he moved to another geographic area in the operative suite.

By the end of the second case the punishing physical presence of Stortz was starting to wear upon the team. By dropping a suture needle on the floor he caused a delay as the circulating nurse searched beneath his massive feet to find the needle. During the second case his head hit the frame of the overhead surgical lights, requiring him to sit down and regain his senses. Most disturbing was a tear in his surgical gloves spotted by Dr. Tuckett himself, thus exposing the patient to a higher infection risk. By the end of the second case Tuckett politely but sternly asked the fellow to observe from the end of the table, until he "learns the moves of the surgical team."

It was only between the second and third case that Phil was briefly treated to the brackish lip of nurse Bryant as they scrubbed for the final case.

"He stinks," said Bryant.

"I know," said Phil. "It's a peculiar odor too."

"He's farting too," whined Bryant with a rapid shake of her head. "For God's sake I'm sure you heard it too."

"Yea, I did," said Phil, hoping the repeated audible flatulence from Stortz's posterior hadn't traveled to the other side of the surgical table.

"Well we owe this to the esteemed dynamic duo for bringing this bozo to the Institute," said Bryant as she began to complete her preoperative scrub. The two were looking through the surgical glass into the O.R. suite where Tuckett and Lee were templating a preoperative x-ray for component fit. "Where they dug up Franklin-stein I have no idea," continued Bryant with a quick look at Phil. "Now he is our problem for a full year."

Phil couldn't respond as he nearly folded over in laughter in response to the Franklin-stein moniker. He knew that the cruel nametag coined by nurse Bryant was going to stick to the new fellow like glue, for once the reigning O.R. diva dubs you with a nickname, it stands. Without further words the two surgical team members completed their scrub, and headed into the final case of the day.

On the surgical table was Mr. Randolph Billington, whose hip replacement surgery was cancelled last week due to unforeseen personal issues in the life of his surgeon. Mr. Billington was the current CEO of a prestigious Wall Street investment firm called the Mayflower Group. The name matched his pedigree, which took him back to the original Pilgrims who landed in this country aboard the Mayflower. He inherited the CEO position that his grandfather held some eighty years ago. This lineage, together with a firm that controlled seventy billion dollars in investment money, garnered Mr. Billington V.I.P. status at the Institute. The prior evening he flew to the valley compliments of the Institute. An attentive Tuckett Institute staff catered to all his needs throughout the preoperative process. All in all, up until that point in time, the New York City socialite was quite impressed with his stay, as it lived up to the hype that his tight inner circle of advisors promised.

Tuckett was on his absolute A-game throughout the case, moving in a manner that impressed Phil. His every movement was well anticipated by the pouting nurse Bryant, who slapped instruments in his hands with a professional, yet borderline sadistic manner. In short order the surgeon reamed and measured the acetabulum, calling out the size to Dr. Lee, who was attentively waiting at his side, several feet behind the surgical zone. "Measures a fifty-four," said Tuckett to his sidekick. "Exactly what I templated," said Lee with a confident bob of his head. "I just happen to have that exact cup in my hand. May I open the fifty-four cup?" Per protocol Dr. Tuckett turned around to read the cup dimensions that were factory imprinted on the sealed box that contained the sterilized implant. The box size was approximately six by six inches wide with a depth of three inches, just enough to contain the Tuckett Cup securely. Dr. Lee held the cup up to Tuckett's eye level, allowing him to confirm the dimensions.

"Yes fifty-four millimeter press fit porous cup," said Tuckett to Lee while reading the box label. "Open the cup." His use of the word "porous" described the back end of the cup, which would sit adjacent to the patient's bone stock. The porous nature of the cup allowed natural bony ingrowth to secure the cup, thus avoiding the need for any cement. The porous coating itself was coarse with a microscopic honeycomb matrix, being composed of titanium.

Dr. Lee then quickly stepped towards the sterile instrument table at nurse Bryant's station. He deftly peeled off an identification sticker from the outside box cover and handed it to the circulating nurse in room, who then via an adhesive back, attached it to the patient's chart. This I.D. sticker contained a bar code and serial number for the cup, a standard process for any implantable device in an operating room. He then removed a clear outer wrap before taking the lid off the box. Reaching inside he pulled out the acetabular cup, which was sealed inside a sterile, airtight hard plastic wrap. Using two hands he then carefully peeled open this final wrap in a manner that exposed the sterile cup to nurse Bryant, who brought it onto the surgical field with a firm grasp. She deftly attached it to a metallic driving rod, which to Phil gave the cup the appearance of a magician's wand. Tuckett then reached out his hand while continuing to stare at the surgical field. Nurse Bryant then went to slap the driving rod into his awaiting hand. At that very moment, Franklin Stortz felt obligated to assist.

In an unanticipated and unnecessary manner he reached across the surgical table to aid nurse Bryant with the transfer. She was looking at the surgical field and Tuckett's extended hand, unaware of the massive forearm moving in her direction. In a split second his uncoordinated stubby fingers slammed into the cup, knocking it out of nurse Bryant's hand and sending it in a trajectory away from the field and onto the floor.

Dr. Lee was the first to notice the event and let out a short scream in absolute unison with nurse Bryant. Both Lee and Bryant made a reflexive move towards the falling cup, yet it hit the floor with a smack, knocking a piece of metal off the porous back coating.

"Oh my God!" screamed Tuckett as he quickly looked back on the cup hitting the floor.

"What are you doing?" yelled nurse Bryant at Stortz. She quickly looked at Tuckett saying, "He hit my…"

"You fool!" cried Dr. Lee as he quickly approached the cup lying on the unsterile floor. "You ruined the cup!"

"Oh my God," said Tuckett again shaking his head. "Franklin we have done this operation a million times, please we do not need your help." The whole team paused to gather their composure. "Please, until you know our moves keep your hands in front of you and try not to help us."

"I'm sorry," mumbled the senator's son. "I'm sorry. I understand."

"Is there a problem?" said the voice of Mr. Billington who was awake under the surgical sheets with a spinal anesthetic in place.

"No problem whatsoever Mr. Billington," said Tuckett. "Just routine discussion amongst us." Tuckett then looked quickly back at Dr. Lee saying quietly and firmly, "Another size fifty-four cup Dr. Lee, and quickly."

Dr. Lee then exited the room towards a large metallic industrial cart stationed just outside the operative door. The cart contained extra cups in every size possible, kept well stocked by Lee himself. He expertly pulled down a size fifty-four cup and bolted back into the room where Tuckett read the dimensions followed by a much faster delivery to nurse Bryant. Bryant then loaded the cup on a backup wand and handed it to Tuckett, who began driving it into place with smashing blows from a large mallet.

It was during this time that Phil observed the circulating nurse attempting to pick up the fallen cup. She was immediately signaled away by Dr. Lee who was dawning a pair of surgical gloves in approach. He picked up the cup, which had some blood on it from nurse Bryant's hands. He rapidly rotated the cup to inspect any damage, and then with a quick gaze looked back onto the floor to swiftly search the drop zone. With a quick dip of his knees he then bent downwards and picked up a portion of the cup that had cracked in shard like fashion. His eyes panned the drop zone for any other cup fragments. Confident that no other cup pieces remained on the floor, he arose and exited the room, holding the cup as if taking a mortally wounded colleague from the battlefield.

The case continued uneventfully. Within minutes Dr. Lee returned to the room with a cold sneer. His body language exuded anger towards the fellow and his role in the debacle. No further words were spoken to Dr. Stortz who exited the room in a dejected fashion upon completion of the case, a failure on his first day.

"We have to put up with him all year?" blurted an angry nurse Bryant immediately after the fellow left the room.

"Yes," retorted Tuckett. "We all do nurse Bryant, and I suggest you get used to it." Tuckett then paused to contain his anger before saying, "I expect absolute respect towards Dr. Stortz, he has committed a year of his life to study with us. We owe him that much." Then with a quick step Tuckett picked up Mr. Billington's chart and exited the room, with a still fuming Dr. Lee several steps behind him.

Phil kept quiet while looking at nurse Bryant in expectation of a fiery quip. However no words were spoken by the diva, whose face suddenly became troubled and sullen. The duo then helped Mr. Billington onto his hospital gurney, while he thanked them for their good work.

Later that evening Phil sat in his apartment, feeling uneasy about the day's events. He felt sorry for Franklin Stortz, and out of respect for the new fellow spoke nothing to Polk and Rhimes about the incident. It was Polk and Stephanie who were sitting next to him on the couch that evening. Rick Polk was watching a Seinfeld episode and constantly referring to Stephanie as "schmoopie" in a mushy way. Stephanie was ignorant to her beau's obsession with the series as she held a cell phone just inches from her face, in a sort of texting supernova. Both were in separate worlds, oblivious to his presence. He stood up and walked towards his room, thinking that a late evening jog through town would serve him well.

"I'm going for a run," said Phil.

Out of the corner of his eye he saw Polk quickly look towards Stephanie while jolting her with an elbow to the ribcage. Stephanie failed to acknowledge the gesture, yet continued to rapidly pound the keys on her cell phone. With five minutes Phil exited his room with a suspicious feeling, it was then that the doorbell rang. Polk and Stephanie failed to acknowledge the ring, as if knowing who was on the other side of the door.

Phil opened the door to see Kendra Mason standing in front of him in a tight, professional running outfit. Her legs were well toned and suggested a passion for running. She smiled at Phil as if he should have been expecting her at the door.

"Thanks for the invite," said Kendra to Phil with a perky smile. "I love running at night." Her stance pleaded innocence with a subtle tone of temptation.

Upon exiting the apartment with his new running mate, Phil gave a quick look back towards Polk who puckered his lips fully while silently mouthing "schmoopie." He hugged Stephanie in a manner of mock fashion. His partner in crime cracked a sinister smile of guilt, yet could not break her gaze from the small keypad in front of her.

Throughout the run Phil enjoyed the delightful view to his right as the firm frame of Kendra bounced in perfect harmony with each stride. The warmth of the summer day gave way to a slight chill that suggested autumn's arrival. He thought of Maria

Cruz back in Philadelphia and the ultimate end point of their shared running passion. As their four mile loop circled back past the hospital Phil failed to notice the completely lit upper research floor of the Tuckett Institute, despite the late hour. He failed to espy the slight silhouette of Dr. Lee moving feverishly behind the window frames, perfecting his trade. Phil's sole attention was on the enticing girl from Philadelphia at his side, who gazed back at him with a smile across her pretty face.

CHAPTER ELEVEN
THE CANDY APPLE AFFAIR

BARRY REYNOLDS SOMEWHAT enjoyed being the COO of St. Michael's Hospital. Having been born and raised in Des Moines, Iowa he was hard working, resourceful and polite to a fault. Upon graduating from his state's university cum laude with a degree in business, his first and only employer was AMG. Since then he worked for the Kansas City based firm in an admirable yet undistinguished fashion. His slow, plodding rise to the coveted COO rank was highlighted by a combination of mid management attrition and Midwestern patience. Over the past thirty years it was Barry Reynolds who had the intestinal fortitude to faithfully attend every corporate meeting on a seemingly hourly basis. It was Mr. Reynolds who toed the company line that rang out state of the art medical care, while keeping a close eye on profits. It was also Barry Reynolds who sadly watched his fellow colleagues plucked away one by one by competing companies, yet never received an offer of his own. Thus thirty years later it was Reynolds who rose in large by default to the Chief Operations Officer position of St. Michael's. From that moment forward the higher ups in Kansas City kept him locked in the system, confident of the company man they so carefully crafted over time.

Barry Reynolds served AMG or "corporate" as he liked to call it well. His smiling face was a fixture in the local newspaper as he attended every major local fundraiser in mandatory fashion. He happily gave away AMG money to the local needy that had been tagged as a charitable contribution by the Kansas City accountants. Dinner engagements clogged his schedule with guests that corporate flew into the area in hopes of funneling more business to St. Mike's. Most importantly, he never made a decision of any magnitude without first clearing it with the legal team back at the corporate office. Over the years he faithfully carried out the duties of his office, garnering him the prestigious title of "Co-Employee of the Year, Eastern Division" just two years ago.

COO Reynolds was also a devoted family man who loved his wife of twenty-five years. Together they raised two soft spoken and polite boys, one away at college in the Midwest, and the other a soon to be junior at Valley High. Their marriage was both boring and successful in a manner that many marriages are. The Reynolds lived in a modest turn of the last century home that sat along a riverbank some ten miles from the hospital. From within this humble dwelling they tried to enjoy living along the eastern seaboard. Barry Reynolds was able to accomplish this, but his wife could not. She was socially miserable living in the valley, and made it quite clear to her husband on a daily basis. In her mind relocating back West was mandatory, needing to be triggered upon the high school graduation of their second son in just two short years. She therefore applied a slow, subtle, almost unbearable pressure upon her husband in this regards, in a manner that most loving wives were quite capable of. Fortunately for each of them, Mr. Reynolds had grown accustomed to subtle abuse, thus allowing the couple to exist together and present themselves happily to the community.

Dealing with the Tuckett Orthopedic Institute was not one of COO Reynolds' strong points. The Institute represented an anomaly that even the financial gurus back at corporate had difficulty understanding and dealing with. Ever since Reynolds arrived at St. Michael's both he and corporate battled the Institute for not only bragging rights, but also monetary issues. The hospital struggled to survive in an era of poor Medicare reimbursement in rural areas, while the Institute thrived amid clientele that warranted jet transportation to the area. Reynolds was under constant pressure from his higher ups to leverage some money from the Institute, in turn for their services as an ancillary institution. Without a doubt the Institute could not survive without the hospital's ability to accept perioperative emergencies such as a myocardial infarction or pulmonary event. Reynolds constantly shouted this battle cry during discussions with Tuckett and Lee, however it fell upon deaf ears. Their response was that the Tuckett Institute was a nationally recognized Center of Excellence that brought fame, fortune and prestige to the Valley. Both Tuckett and Lee knew that the hospital certainly could not slam the door on an acutely ill patient that was emergently referred to their facility. Historically the Institute held the upper hand on St. Mike's in this regard, until relatively recently when a string of events leveled the playing field. It was with this newly found mandate that COO Reynolds welcomed both Tuckett and Lee to his office just one week after the body of Anastasia Tuckett was declared lost at sea.

"Doctors, welcome, welcome," said Reynolds to the duo that always seemed to travel in tandem. They entered his office, which had an interior décor that befitted his personality, drab and dated.

"Barry, a pleasure as usual," said Tuckett as the two sat down in front of Reynolds' desk. Dr. Lee did not speak but carefully checked the seat of the chair for any debris or concerns with regards to his expensive suit. The smell of a recent cheap cigar permeated the room.

"Ian, let me start off by offering my most sincere condolences regarding your ex-wife," said Reynolds. "Please accept the sympathies of the entire St. Michael's staff in this regard."

"Thank you," said Tuckett. "Thank you very much. I still can't believe she is gone." Tuckett shook his head slowly in a motion to gather some composure before saying, "I still expect her to walk through the door at any moment."

"She was a tremendous bellwether throughout the hospital and community," said Reynolds. "Her charitable work will never be forgotten."

"Thank you again," said Tuckett, already sensing from Dr. Lee that time was of the essence, and would not permit another offering of grief from the COO.

"Mr. Reynolds," said Lee in a nasal tone. "We received your letter regarding the new Presidential Wing that is about to be constructed. We are concerned as to the tone of the letter." His abrupt dismissal of the Anastasia Tuckett topic fazed no one in the room.

"Gentlemen, as you know the new hospital wing represents the continued emergence of AMG as a major player along the Eastern seaboard. It will contain fifteen floors of state of the art critical care units and over two hundred private patient rooms. One floor will host seven operating rooms, equipped with the most up to date technology on the market. In fact I dare say that the ambience of the facility may rival that of your beloved Institute." Upon completing the sentence the COO smiled smugly at the two men stationed in front of him, awaiting their customary direct response to any monetary issue.

"Why should the Institute donate a half a million dollars to your cause?" asked Lee, who routinely argued financial matters with the hospital. "Isn't it enough that we choose to exist in the valley, bringing jobs and accolades to your doorstep?"

"Dr. Lee, please never underestimate the deep gratitude that all of us here at St. Mike's have for your beloved Institute. It has been an honor to be affiliated with the Tuckett Orthopedic Institute in both a public and private manner." Barry Reynolds made sure to dictate the words "Tuckett Orthopedic Institute" in a phonetically slow manner, knowing quite well that it irked Dr. Lee.

"We believe your request for support is a bit steep Mr. Reynolds," whined Lee. "We, as usual will be supportive, but not to that level of monetary value."

"I'm sorry to hear that Dr. Lee. As you know St. Michael's is slowing becoming a major referral center for all smaller hospitals in a two hour radius." Reynolds then brushed some cigar ash off his lapel before continuing. "The board of trustees has even considered hiring some orthopedic surgeons to shoulder the load, I mean with all of the trauma cases that will soon be diverted here with the new beds available."

"Don't threaten us," fired back Lee. Both he and Tuckett knew that a skeleton crew of orthopedic surgeons manned the emergency room at St. Mike's, all borderline competent and none performing joint replacement surgery.

"We are thinking of even starting our own joint replacement program," said Reynolds to ice the cake. "I mean with the baby boomers coming of age certainly your Institute cannot shoulder the whole load of the valley."

"Barry, our relationship has always cordial," said Tuckett in an attempt to defuse the boiling situation. "Symbiotic in nature."

COO Reynolds just stared at Tuckett, pretending to understand the biological term of symbiotic. He did not speak but just shook his head in agreement while waiting for one of the other two to speak.

"Symbiotic," said Lee, aware of the COO's intelligence. "It means a close and quite often obligatory association of two organisms of different species that live together, often to their mutual benefit."

"Of course," said Reynolds. "Of course, symbiosis."

"I believe the emphasis of that definition should be 'mutual benefit'," said Tuckett.

"Yes, yes," said Reynolds. "I agree, however our corporate team in Kansas City believe that the benefit has been lopsided over the past five years. They asked me to secure a more significant benefit, say a half million dollars worth to assist the creation of the Presidential Tower."

"That's absurd," barked Lee.

"No, actually it isn't Dr. Lee. The tower construction will begin in six months and we expect a sizeable donation from your Institute." Reynolds then smiled and leaned back in his creaky faux leather chair. "A half a million will get you in the coveted Presidential Circle along with a plaque in your honor that will be displayed in the building's main foyer."

"One hundred thousand dollars," said Lee in a matter of fact fashion. "I have the check in my hand."

"Again gentlemen I am only the messenger," whimpered Reynolds with his hands held palm upwards in a pathetic fashion. "This is coming down directly from corporate back West." Both Tuckett and Lee knew from past experience that once Reynolds mentioned the word "corporate", no other new information or demands would be made. The word signaled the end to any further independent thought generated from the man sitting before them.

"No," said Tuckett with a shake of his head. "A bit too much to ask from us, I mean with reimbursements and health care going the way it is."

"Of course this dovetails into our whole "symbiotic" relationship together," said Reynolds while using his fingers to place quotation marks upon the term. "Symbiotic, I like that term."

"What do you mean by that?" asked Tuckett with an idea as to where Reynolds was heading.

"I mean we have history together," said Reynolds. "Some good and some bad." He smirked and shrugged his shoulders saying, "You know, history."

"Don't think you can bully us," said Lee. "Or better yet should I use the term blackmail us."

"I don't know what you mean?" said Reynolds.

"We are not idiots," said Lee. "If you want to discuss the Nurse Adams affair then discuss it, don't suggest it."

"Oh yes the Nurse Adams affair, or should I say the Nurse "Candy Apple" Adams affair," said Reynolds in jest. "Now may be a good time to bring everyone updated on that somewhat delicate situation."

The nurse Candice Adams affair occurred two years ago. Nurse Adams represented the first affair open to the public that Ian Tuckett had after his divorce from his popular wife. Candice Adams was the antithesis of the former Mrs. Tuckett. She was brash, overtly sexy and full of strut, the perfect fodder for Tuckett's backlash against the marriage establishment. Their intimate relationship stretched across the United States as the two lit up every major city and resort in the land. The only problem was that Candice Adams fell in love with Tuckett. She adored his persona, local flair and sense for adventure. In Tuckett she had her man, full of good looks, power and money. Unfortunately Tuckett did not fall in love with her. He lusted the trashy Candy Apple that appeared at his doorstep on weekends, but he did not love Candice Adams. This singular fact led to the ultimate demise of their relationship, along with the emergence of the younger and more refined nurse Nicole Bryant at the Institute.

The final six months of their relationship was similar to many couples experiencing emotional Armageddon. One moment was marked by a heightened passion that sensed the end, followed by another moment marred by anger and rejection. It was the final height of passion that got Tuckett in trouble with the former professional football runner up cheerleader. This incident, subsequently known as the "Candice Adams Affair" began one sultry hot summer night as nurse Adams came off her hospital moonlight shift. She asked Tuckett to pick her up, and he obliged in a newly leased Maserati together with animalistic thoughts on his mind. Nurse Adams exited the hospital into the poorly lit physician parking garage wearing her trademark tight scrubs and clog shoes. She walked with a gait that cried out for attention, which she was about to receive from her designated driver. Immediately upon entering the vehicle nurse Adams sensed her beau was on the prowl, and she playfully puckered her lipstick-laden lips out for a kiss. The instant coolness of the vehicle's air-conditioned heightened her female senses. Within one minute both the head nurse and orthopedic surgeon were manhandling each other in a fashion well known to each other. Within five minutes the namesake of the Tuckett Institute was introducing Candy Apple to the expensive leather of the Maserati's backseat, when a part time hospital security guard knocked on the door. The underpaid alcoholic sentry was concerned about the car being parked in an isolated corner of the garage yet somehow being in subtle motion. Upon peering into the front passenger window he was pleasantly amused at the scene and actually waited a few seconds before knocking. At first the occupants were oblivious to the polite knock, but Candice's visualization of his ruddy, creepy face peering into the window marked the abrupt end of the tryst. Her shrill scream damaged Tuckett's inner ear and was reportedly heard by another security guard on a separate floor of the garage. After refusing to accept a generous bribe from Tuckett, the rental cop reported the on site event to his supervisor, per hospital protocol. Within three weeks, Ian Tuckett was in front of the hospital's medical board trying to explain his actions that occurred with a hospital employee on hospital grounds. It was only the provincial aura of the valley along with some assistance from a hospital board of trustee member that saved his stellar reputation from ultimate public embarrassment.

Within four weeks of the event Tuckett made it clear to Candice Adams that their relationship was over. His abrupt termination of the torrid affair was met by wrath from the feminine soul of Adams. At first she directly confronted Tuckett hoping to change his mind, but he would not. She then made one visit to a well-known plaintiff attorney in the valley who loved to see his gigantic fifteen-foot head adorning local billboards in a plea for lucrative justice. For two hours the scorned lover and narcissistic counselor discussed the legality of terms such as assault, forceful entry and sexual harassment. Promises of unthinkable riches were made to the distraught nurse while legal papers securing her sixty percent of the harvest were delicately placed beneath her pen. As the proxy smiled and stared at nurse Adams, he smelled financial independence as gravity pulled her pen towards the final signature line. It was his lifelong dream to get a crack at the Tuckett Institute in hopes of taking their multiple insurance carriers to the cleaners. The dream was now about to become a stunning reality.

However nurse Adams truly loved Ian Tuckett and it was the mystical power of love that prevented her from sealing the attorney's membership into the Half a Billion-Dollar Roundtable Society. Her mind cried out for retribution, yet her heart still pined for her lost lover, causing her to put down the pen and take pause. Over the next thirty minutes she made it clear to her counsel that a public lawsuit seeking financial damages and causing irreversible harm to Tuckett's public image would be out of the question.

Although fiscally shaken her legal advocate remained in control of the situation. Options were discussed as he skillfully put together a plan that equally violated both legal and moral precepts in dramatic fashion. By the end of the meeting nurse Adams agreed to a diabolic plan that had more twists than a rollercoaster, thus benefitting everyone except Ian Tuckett. A verbal agreement was made between the two allowing the attorney to approach all parties involved. Nurse Adams then politely declined an invitation to dinner from the unhappily married attorney.

Unknown to nurse Adams was her attorney's position on the hospital board of trustees. Prior to the board's next meeting the legal eagle held an off the record discussion with several power brokers on the board. To avoid embarrassment to both Tuckett and the hospital a series of conditions had to be agreed upon quickly, or else the threat of legal action in the public eye was to be triggered. All of the agreements involved vast sums of money. First and most importantly the salary of nurse Adams was to be raised threefold, from fifty thousand dollars to one hundred and fifty thousand dollars a year. This would be the equivalent of a multi-million dollar jury verdict paid out over a lifetime, absent any prison time for Tuckett. The guise would include changing Adam's title to Vice President of Clinical Nursing in order to justify the raise. Of course Ian Tuckett and the Tuckett Institute would be responsible for the salary increase. Secondly the hospital would agree upon keeping Nurse Adams on staff, and away from the Tuckett Institute's daily operations. Thirdly, the lucrative food contract for the hospital would be transferred completely to the corporation in which the attorney owned fifty percent of, thus garnering him millions of dollars over time. Lastly, the deal would be kept secret and off paper, only known to Tuckett, Reynolds, Adams and her attorney. Reluctantly all parties agreed to the deal, thus saving the public humiliation of the whole incident. Tuckett was the last to agree, but the memory of his New York City indiscretions and ultimate dealings with an outraged hospital board prompted him to accept the bitter pill.

"Corporate has asked me to revisit this oh so delicate topic with you again Dr. Tuckett," said Reynolds. "Its seems like the legal team back in Kansas City is suggesting that we distance ourselves from this whole ugly situation."

"We are all involved," said Lee with authority.

"That's right Barry," said Tuckett. "If the ship sinks we all go down with it."

"Dr. Tuckett, we are a corporation employing over twenty thousand workers. We are a conglomerate having experience in dealing with the publicity of a sexual harassment suit." Reynolds then pulled out a cigar from the top drawer of his desk knowing that Dr. Lee would object to him smoking in the room. While lighting the cigar with a smirk he continued by saying, "Now you on the other hand Dr. Tuckett, are a singular person, who will be crushed by the avalanche of criticism from such a story."

"This meeting is over," shouted Dr. Lee as he stood and headed towards the door. "The Tuckett Institute respectfully declines from funding any portion of your white elephant."

Reynolds did not respond as he blew some smoke into the air. He tried to remain calm but his inners were trembling as he looked directly at Tuckett, knowing quite well that the hospital owned the upper hand.

"I have to agree with Dr. Lee," said Tuckett. "Spill the story if you like, we can handle the fall out." Tuckett then stood with a shake of his head. "Get back to us after you speak to corporate," was his final line before he and Lee walked out.

Reynolds sat alone in the room trying to calm his nerves. While bringing the cigar to his mouth he noticed an uncontrollable tremble in his hand. Playing hardball was not his strong suit, but the recent pressure from Kansas City to secure local funding had been intense. He paused for thirty more minutes to gather his thoughts prior to reporting back to the bigwigs in Kansas. During his conversation he tried to recall the term symbiosis but could not, as an avalanche of profanity was hurled upon him by the crotchety manager above him.

As Tuckett and Lee rode the elevator down to the lobby there was a pensive silence between them. Tuckett knew that financial matters always fell into the lap of Lee. A nervous energy caused Lee's body to sway back and forth as he formulated a plan.

"Well," said Tuckett. "What do you have in mind?"

Lee continued to face forward as his eyes peered to the left, looking directly at Tuckett. A confident smirk came across his face as if everything was going to be all right.

"Don't worry," said Lee with a sinister tone. "I've got it figured out already. By this time next week the Candy Apple Affair will be nothing more than a bad memory. "

Within minutes the two were back within the confines of the Institute, confident of the ingenious plan crafted by Lee.

CHAPTER TWELVE

THE MANILA ENVELOPE

PHIL'S HANDS SLIGHTLY trembled as he carefully opened the manila envelope that Anastasia Tuckett handed him just two weeks ago. Her lingering perfume was still apparent on the coarse paper as was her trust worthy description of a "matter of extreme personal interest." Keeping the envelope sealed at this point was not an option, as Phil realized the finality of her misfortune. By all news accounts she was killed in an accidental boating mishap, and no concern of foul play existed in his mind, or that of the local populace. Resonating in his mind was the pure confidence that she placed in him with regards to the envelope's content, and the suggestive kiss that sealed the deal.

The apartment was quiet as Phil sat alone at his desk, with the door closed. A single lamp lit the top of his desk, illuminating the object in his hand. After slowly releasing a metal clasp he flipped the envelope open with an upside down motion. Out slid a ruby red flash drive along with a note, written with magic marker on a file card. The note simply read, "Thank you. See you soon. – Anastasia." A heart was drawn behind her name.

Phil examined the flash drive and noted it to be unremarkable. He then flipped upon his lap top computer and thought of his options as the screen came to life. Without hesitation he inserted the drive into the side computer port and watched the icon soar up into the top corner of his screen. The icon read

"Banks" and again, without hesitation he double clicked to expose the flash drive's contents.

Onto his computer screen appeared thirty pages of single-spaced lines containing apparent abbreviated notations between separate parties. Short hand terminology immediately identified the communications as cell phone text messages. Phil scanned to the top of the list to read the initial transactions which read as:

> -surg went ok, no problems, how are u?
> -great. Get some sleep. Love u. I'll let everyone know.

The next set of communications read:

> -surgery went well. Any office news?
> -no. all well here. Glad u are doing ok.
> -how about the McCoy deal? Done?
> -done deal. Congrats. Everyone happy.
> -thanks. Tired. Signing off for the night.
> -get some rest, talk tomorrow.

Phil then proceeded to scan hundreds of text messages that recounted Mr. Banks' hospital stay after his hip replacement. The communications were intermixed with personal messages to his family and professional messages to his work staff. A sense of unease overtook him while superficially scanning the private messages of the big city banker. This unease caused him to rapidly come to the end of the list upon which he encountered an eerie communication that read:

> -waiting for the doc, posh office.
> -dinner time?
> -home by six, love u
> -great.

The final text exchange read as:

> -heard of the five B plan?
> -no.

No? What school did you go to?

-Stanford.

-The five B plan. Big bottle behind the

The final text was incomplete and Phil immediately recalled Mr. Bank's texting as he walked out of the V.I.P. room with Ms. Reyes. While staring back at the screen he tried to comprehend the magnitude of the information in front of him. Illegality surfaced, as did an uneasy feeling as to how the information was obtained. He wondered about the whereabouts of Mr. Banks' cell phone throughout his hospital stay and postoperative visit back to the Orthopedic Institute. Lastly he tried to understand Anastasia Tuckett's role in the whole matter, and why she would entrust him with material of such a private nature. Questions abounded, but answers did not. What was obvious was the apparent criminality of the information, causing Phil to ponder his next step.

Suddenly the shrill of his beeper shattered his concentration. He was on call that evening and the page summoned him to the operating room immediately. Dr. O'Neil had an emergency case and needed a set of hands to assist. Phil closed down the computer icon and removed the flash drive from his laptop, returning it to the manila envelope. He opened the bottom drawer of his desk and placed the envelope beneath a stack of papers, towards the back of the drawer. In his haste he failed to place Anastasia's note back into the envelope, leaving it upside down atop the somewhat cluttered desk. He then bolted out the door towards St. Mike's hospital.

"Fast" Eddie O'Neil was fast, very fast.

"There are good fast surgeons, and bad fast surgeons," said O'Neil who was on the other side of the operative table from Phil. "But there are no good slow surgeons," said O'Neil with a smile. "Knife!" was his command to the scrub nurse next to him.

Phil barely heard the advice from the attending surgeon as the overhead music blared out a song. He did manage to get his hands off the abdomen of the patient as the scalpel rapidly hit the skin in a slashing fashion. The planned procedure was an exploratory laparotomy that searched for a perforation in the patient's bowels, causing pain, fever and free air on an x-ray.

Within two minutes Fast Eddie was cranking upon a self-retaining retractor that held open the patient's abdomen cavity, exposing the matrix of small and large bowel. Phil was always amazed as to how much bowel footage was so tightly contained within the peritoneal cavity.

"Crap in the hole!" yelled O'Neil upon finding a collection of fecal material and pus. He rapidly began irrigating out the cavity with saline as Phil suctioned out the concoction of lethal fluid. A fierce stench overtook the surgical team.

"I'm getting too old for these late cases," said the face of an elderly anesthesiologist who suddenly appeared from the tower of sheets above the patient's head. Phil noticed that he wore his surgical mask only over his mouth, exposing a nose that was bulbous and littered with intranasal hairs. Sagging skin beneath his eyes suggested a care provider nearing the end of his career.

"For Christ's sake, it's only ten o'clock Norm," said O'Neil with a laugh. "Try to hang in there with us old timer. We will get you home in time for your Manhattan."

"I'm up to three Manhattans a night," drawled the anesthesiologist. "It's the only elixir that helps blunt the horror of a vocation in medicine."

"I can't wait for nationalized health care," said O'Neil, as he pointed out to Phil the perforation in the patient's bowel. "Believe me my life will become a lot more easier. Put me on the government payroll and watch my production plummet."

"America has no idea what they are in for," said the elder anesthesiologist. "No idea."

"I tell my patients it's like UPS versus the postal service, said O'Neil. "Our current medical system is incentive driven like UPS. The harder you work, the more money you make. Capitalism is what made America great fifty years ago. Hand a package to UPS and it will be expertly handled and delivered ASAP. No doubts, no fuss. Done! They want your business back." Fast Eddie was rapidly excising the diseased portion of large bowel that had ruptured. Phil was amazed at the speed of his movement. "Turning our health care system over to the imbeciles in

Washington will create the biggest, most inefficient bureaucracy in the world – doomed to colossal failure."

"Like the Postal Service," said the anesthesiologist. "Losing billions of dollars a quarter and awash with mediocrity. Solely dependent on the skyrocketing national debt."

"Exactly," said Dr. O'Neil as he rapidly began the surgical anastomosis that would connect the two ends of disease free bowel back together. "But there is no stopping the train. The masses think they are in for a free ride, a treat, but in reality they are going to get a bum product, trust me. Take away incentive and you destroy everything."

"I pity these young doctors," said the gas passer as he stuck out a knobby thumb in the direction of Phil. "Sunk in med school debt, yet facing declining reimbursement and salaries." He smirked and shook his head saying, "What a shame."

Phil just shook his head up and down without speaking. He had heard this old song and dance a thousand times over the past several years. It was now commonplace to him.

"Don't think your practice is going to be like the Taj Mahal that you are working at across the street," said O'Neil with a snicker. "What's going on over there is out of this world. Abnormal."

"Somebodies cooking the books over there," said anesthesia in reference to the Tuckett Institute. "Nobody can tell me they are making all that money on replacing five or ten joints a week. I mean it's a one man show."

Phil knew when to keep quiet. He always felt deep in his heart that the opulence of the center was a result of the Tuckett Cup, and its worldwide sales. However the recent flash drive revelation shook his confidence.

"Let's start closing up," said O'Neil with continued rapid movements. Phil looked up at the clock, which was approaching eleven PM. Just then the door behind him opened up and in walked two scrub nurses, about to relieve the day shift of their duties. It was only at this moment did the rapid hands of Eddie O'Neil cease moving as he looked up in bemusement. Phil noticed his blood shot eyes to widen, as the attending surgeon stepped back from the table holding his hand to his heart, in mock fashion of having a heart attack.

"O.M.G.," yelled Fast Eddie. "I don't believe it!" Phil rapidly turned around to see what prompted the actions from the head surgeon. He was equally shocked to see nurse Nikki Bryant walking into the room, absent her trademark clog shoes, tight scrub pants and self assured saunter.

"The prodigal daughter has returned!" shouted O'Neil. "Kill the fattened calf!"

"Good evening gentlemen," said Bryant as she quickly gowned and gloved, thus relieving her day shift coworker.

"Someone pinch me quick," yelled O'Neil, "I must be dreaming."

"Did the Center of Excellence burn down?" asked the anesthesiologist, "Disappear into a mine subsidence?"

"Let's continue on with the case doctors," said Bryant plainly. "Let's get this old gal off the table."

Eddie O'Neil then returned his attention back to the patient, yet continued to barrage the apparently exiled nurse with questions. His pursuit was relentless since this was the first sighting of Bryant back in the hospital proper in two years. Certainly O'Neil was dredging for gossip information regarding her current status with Dr. Ian Tuckett. Throughout the inquisition the proud nurse held her ground, occasionally answering in polite yet vague fashion, which only flamed O'Neil's fire of suspicion.

"Will we be seeing more of you nurse Bryant?" asked O'Neil as he helped place a bandage on the patient's abdomen wound. "Or is this just a cameo appearance among the peons?"

"Time will tell," said nurse Bryant. "Time will tell."

Phil noticed that she appeared tired and somewhat aged, wearing bland hospital scrubs that did not conform to her toned frame. Her height was now below average without the benefit of clog shoes. The sassy sparkle in her eyes was also absent, as was the acidic tongue that existed in her mouth. Surrounding her was the drab of St. Mike's hospital, which only added to the bleakness of her persona. Throughout the remainder of the evening, she spoke no more.

Phil returned home late that evening. Upon entering the apartment he came across Rick Polk who was asleep on the couch, with the television remote control still in his hands. He passed by his cellmate quietly towards his room. It was then that the apartment door opened and in walked Jackie Rhimes, absent his characteristic energy.

"Hey Jack," said a fatigued Phil.

"Yo, Yo," said Jack in unenthusiastic fashion. Phil noticed the absence of his trademark pimp roll gait, which was honed over time on the streets of Philadelphia.

Then without much thought Phil asked, "Where you coming from, Candyland?"

"Candice Adams wasn't ready for Jackie Rhimes," said the resident slowly and quietly as he disappeared into his room for the night, never to be heard of again that evening.

Phil was too tired to try and decipher Jack's body language and comment. He turned towards his room in order to pack for tomorrow's early morning departure to Chicago. The entire orthopedic team was headed to a three-day conference in the Windy City, compliments of the TOI. With the late hour Phil had no time to consider further options regarding the flash drive. A quick suitcase pack was followed by a phone call to Jennifer and a sound sleep.

Early the following morning a TOI limousine picked up Phil and drove both he and Franklin Stortz to the airport just outside the city limits. The airport itself was small and prior to the TOI creation represented an airstrip for recreational aviators. The runway was expanded and updated recently to handle jet service, including the private transport of Ian Tuckett. The limo itself drove directly onto the runway and dispatched the young doctors just a few steps away from the waiting twin engine G660 jet aircraft.

Upon entering the craft Phil was greeted by Emily Reyes who was playing the energetic role of stewardess. Phil's six foot-five inch frame barely fit into the overhead space of the luxury craft. Behind Phil lumbered Franklin Stortz who immediately proceeded to crash his head onto the low ceiling, opening up a bloody abrasion that Emily Reyes tended to promptly. Both physicians sat down in the aircraft, whose engines were running on a low idle. Opposite them sat lobby attendants James and Madison, whose comfortable appearance suggested they traveled aboard the aircraft frequently. Into the cabin then entered a uniformed male, who was apparently one of the craft's pilots.

"Ready?" asked the pilot to Reyes.

"No, not yet," said Reyes looking out the door towards the runway. "One more passenger."

The pilot nodded in consent and returned behind a thick curtain to the cockpit. For the next several minutes the trio discussed plans for the Chicago trip. The junket centered around an orthopedic conference in which Dr. Tuckett was to perform live surgery, via a video feed from a local hospital. The surgery was to promote the benefits of the Tuckett Cup and hopefully increase sales nationwide. Tuckett and Dr. Lee had been talking about the importance of the surgery for weeks, quite aware of the need for a smooth presentation. Both Lee and Tuckett had flown to Chicago two days earlier to meet the patient and prepare the operating room for his technique. Tuckett was adamant that the patient involved should be thin and present with a "run of the mill" arthritic hip, one that from a technical standpoint should not present the surgeon with any difficulty.

Phil then noticed Ms. Reyes to check her watch and anxiously shift in her seat, while peering out the window. She was obviously getting upset about the final passenger's late arrival. Everything ran on time for TOI, no exceptions.

Then without saying a word Reyes bolted out of her seat to the aircraft door. She extended a hand to the final passenger who needed some help getting up the few steps to the cabin. With a thrust of her forearm she then catapulted a smiling and vivaciously dressed Candice Adams into the craft. Her six-inch high stiletto platform black patent peep-toe shoes made the climb aboard the G6 tricky. A quick girl-to-girl hug welcomed the nurse aboard who then pranced over to a seat opposite Phil. Her tight black skirt barely made it physically possible for her to sit down. With a smile and crack of gum she waved to Phil and Franklin as the roar of the jet engines increased. An attendant outside of the craft then closed the door, which was then secured inside by a co-pilot. Phil barely had time to buckle his seat belt before the jet taxied quickly onto the runway, preparing for take off.

As the jet rocketed down the runway Phil looked at Candy Apple with a smile and shake of his head. She wore a tight blouse, barely held together by buttons under extreme duress. Phil noticed her hair to be fashionably styled with a fresh cut look. The surgical nurse then opened up a small cosmetic case with a mirror to apply some luscious red lipstick, with a sparkle tint. The primp job was followed by a smug snap of the cosmetic case and a smile. Nurse Adams then puckered her lips towards Phil and threw him a mercurial kiss. As the jetliner became airborne she snuggled her taut body into the leather seat and looked out over the valley below. The former runner-up professional cheerleader was firmly back atop her pedestal, being more than ready to accept all the obligations and exaltations of the so dearly coveted position.

CHAPTER THIRTEEN

LIVE SURGERY

PERFORMING LIVE SURGERY for the benefit of a national convention is risky business. However Dr. Tuckett enjoyed going about his business in a grand and entrepreneurial way. He knew that the New York City Orthopedic power brokers would be in attendance, watching their former exiled surgeon ply his trade and sell his product. A successful sales pitch was paramount to the continued success of his brainchild.

Much to the chagrin of Tuckett was the volunteer patient on the table who had a worn out hip, yet was a bit overweight for his liking. In orthopedics the saying "thin and win" refers to the ease of an operation being performed on a slight framed patient. Cellulite only added to the necessary dissection and depth of a surgical wound, making the insertion of instruments and hip components more difficult. Unfortunately a thinner patient did not exist, and with a deadline approaching, Tuckett and Lee decided that a mildly obese patient was better than no patient at all.

Surrounding the operative table was Tuckett, Drummer and Stortz. It was made clear to the senator's son that his meat hook hands would stay clear of any sharp instruments, being available for retractor duty only. Phil would handle the operative leg and suction, clearing the view for Tuckett. Both he and Stortz would be on the opposite side of the operative table, with nurse Adams standing next to Tuckett.

Dr. Tuckett wore a microphone and calmly said "good morning" to the audience of approximately two thousand, sitting in a posh conference center just five miles away. Phil was astonished by the amount of video cameras hung throughout the OR, including cameras attached directly to the overhead surgical lights. Surrounding the surgical team was a series of large LCD screens that provided a glimpse of the video feed being seen by the medical gathering. Of course, circulating about the perimeter of the room was Dr. Lee, who exhibited an extra bit of nervous energy that morning. At the head of the table was an anesthesia team that was foreign to all of the surgeons, being part of the host medical center physician staff.

Back at the surgical conference was a moderator who also had a microphone attached, being the only one able to communicate with Tuckett, thus offering an avenue for questions throughout the procedure. Ironically the moderator was a senior surgeon from Tuckett's old NYC hospital, a crotchety old establishment surgeon, who personally didn't care for Tuckett and his self-proclaimed fame.

"Good morning Dr. Tuckett," said the moderator. "Please begin, we are all anxious to see the benefits of the Tuckett Cup."

Tuckett knew the moderator well and internally translated his kind remarks to mean, "I hope you screw up in front of everyone, you pompous ass."

"Thank you Doctor," said Tuckett politely, who then explained that he would be using the standard posterior approach to expose the hip. Then he began his surgical mission of a proprietary nature with a slash of the scalpel. The approach was uneventful as was the dislocation and removal of the hip ball. Then came the placement stage of the Tuckett Cup.

"Dr. Tuckett can you please tell us the benefits of your cup in relationship to the traditional cups being used throughout the country," asked the moderator.

"The posterior matrix design of the cup is an engineering breakthrough that we have developed," said Tuckett as he began reaming out the worn down acetabular walls. "In conjunction with our engineering department we have developed a..."

Phil looked opposite the table while holding his ground. He peered directly at nurse Adams who despite not having scrubbed on a total hip replacement in years smacked the instruments into Tuckett's hands with a level of professionalism that was forceful and strangely seductive. She stood directly in Tuckett's personal airspace yet somehow did not hamper his quick movements. She maintained an unbreakable gaze on both the surgical field and head surgeon. It was apparent to Phil that they had danced this dance many times before.

"We reamed to a size 52 cup," said Tuckett to the crowd with authority. "Now we have to decide upon a line to line fit versus...."

Phil then gazed down upon the hands of fellow Stortz, which were holding retractors that exposed the view of the patient's pelvis. It was then that Phil noticed an obvious rip in the double gloves that Stortz was wearing, exposing a few strands of dark black hair that grew from his knuckle area. Phil quickly pondered his next action, balancing the risk of a possible infection with that of breaking Tuckett's smooth stride. It was then by chance that Candy's eye caught his and with a very subtle nod of his head Phil directed her attention towards the behemoth's hand. She immediately spied the dark hairy protuberance that contrasted the opaque nature of the latex glove. Her eyes screamed yet she dare not speak.

"Let me show you the backside of the cup," said Tuckett to the crowd as he spun the cup on the insertion rod. Tuckett then stepped two feet to his right in order to place the cup in front of the camera. "As you can see the design of the Tuckett Cup allows for bony ingrowth in a breakthrough fashion...."

Immediately sensing an off camera opening, Phil spontaneously snatched the retractor from Franklin Stortz while nurse Adams grabbed his massive hand. She quickly pointed to his ripped glove making the dim witted fellow aware of his national indiscretion, which was fortunately off video field at the moment. Then with a speed previously unseen by Phil, the prima donna of the show slid a new sterile glove atop the fellow's hand, thus covering up his break in sterility. Phil then relinquished the retractor back to Stortz, as the overhead camera light signaled red again. Nurse Adams then focused her sole attention back to Tuckett.

"Now," said Tuckett to the crowd. "Let's see how this cup fits." With a series of smashing hammer blows he whacked the cup's long metal driver, sending the product deep into the patient's pelvis. Then came the moment of truth: the removal of the driver and testing the security of the cup's press fit. A firm fit that required no further manipulation or screw placement would be a colossal grand slam for the product.

The Tuckett Cup fit perfectly snug, bringing a smile to all participants.

"Very nice," said the moderator. "I can appreciate the benefits of the design. Very nice Dr. Tuckett. A wonderful fit."

"Thank you," said Tuckett with a deep feeling of self satisfaction. "Thank you very much."

Tuckett knew that the remainder of the case was an academic exercise, requiring only the insertion of the femoral stem, or thigh component of a hip replacement in place. This required rasping the canal of the thigh bone with a series of increasing sized components, similar to a metallic wedge that is used to split firewood. When done correctly it was nearly impossible to mess up the case from this point forward, especially for an experienced surgeon such as Tuckett. Each rasp was emblazoned with a large number and increased numerically by a size of one millimeter, thus allowing a safe and controlled opening of the canal. Nurse Adam's quickly handed Tuckett a size #6 component, which he expertly hammered down the femoral shaft. Once seated to the hilt, Tuckett quickly removed the rasp and was handed a size #7 component by his proud surgical scrub. Several separate rasp handles were used to expedite the process. In a series of rapid exchanges the duo expertly rasped the femoral canal up to a size #11, with a planned #15 being the final component.

"Dr. Tuckett, may I ask is that Schubert that we are all hearing in the background," asked the moderator. "If I'm not mistaking let me guess, hmmm, *The Trout* I believe."

"Correct you are," said Tuckett with a smile. "Franz keeps us on time every day back at the Institute. Kudos to our moderator, a man of fine music."

However the #12 component didn't smoothly fit the handle that nurse Adams was trying to use. Despite her experienced hands the components would not match and she rapidly reached towards a back sterile table that held a reserve driver. She quickly began to attach the #12 rasp to the backup driver. During this brief moment, Dr. Tuckett continued to peer into the surgical wound while holding out his left arm towards Adams. He knew that his hand was off camera prompting him to impatiently snap his fingers rapidly in anticipation of the size #12 component's arrival.

"Just finishing up the rasping," said Tuckett to the audience as he tried to fill the dead video time which up until that point, never existed.

Nurse Adams would normally speak at this moment but thought best not to, as she struggled now to fit the #12 rasp on the back up component. She suddenly realized that the machine finish of the rasp was faulty, thus not allowing the smooth fit. With her back to the surgical field she struggled with the component, realizing that there was no Plan B to fall back on.

"Quickly," said Tuckett as he peered down the patient's femoral shaft. "We don't want to keep Franz and our esteemed audience waiting." For effect he took the suction out of Phil's hand and cleaned up the surgical field, in an attempt to buy more time.

It was at that moment that the fellow from New England perceived to have the answer, in order to save the day. He reached across the table for the next rasp that Nurse Adams had in line, unaware of a peculiar habit that only nurse Adams adhered to, that being to have the final anticipated component ready, a #15 in this case. He lifted up the #15 rasp and placed it into the demanding hand of Tuckett, who quickly brought it into the field. The head surgeon then lined up the rasp without looking at the number welded to its side. His mind registered loss of time, which he had to make up for in order to seal the deal.

"What's your anticipated final stem size?" asked the moderator.

"A #15," said Tuckett as he delivered the first smashing blow upon the rasp. He thought it peculiar that the rasp did not slide easily into the thigh bone, as he would have anticipated. "We are at a size #12," said the surgeon in error.

"Wait!" yelled nurse Adams upon registering the news and smash of the hammer. She quickly turned back towards the surgical field.

The second blow of Dr. Tuckett's hammer then struck the rasp with a tremendous force, and per the laws of physics, shattered the thigh bone into approximately five pieces. In essence the unknowing surgeon had rapidly gone up in rasp size by a degree of three millimeters, thus placing too much stress of the femur's outer rim, causing the split.

"What!" said Tuckett as his hands froze completely still. No one around the table moved.

"Troubles?" asked the moderator ever so slowly.

Tuckett failed to speak as he took the suction from Phil's hand and inspected the blast zone. It was apparent to the surgeon that a major complication had just occurred, in front of an audience of his peers. He quickly looked at the rasp handle seeing the #15 embossed upon its side.

"This is a #15!" said Tuckett incredulously as he turned towards Adams. "I wanted a #12!"

"I know," said nurse Candice Adams sheepishly. "The #12 wasn't fitting on the driver."

Again, no one spoke, being aware of the cameras and microphones situated throughout the room.

Tuckett turned back towards the field in disbelief. Dr. Lee had to sit down on a chair and held his hands upon his forehead while staring at the ground.

"We are going to need the cables," said Tuckett referring to a reconstruction of the femoral shaft that was now necessary. Tuckett was aware that this would add an approximate hour of time upon the case.

"Did you split the shaft?" asked the moderator smugly, quite aware as to what had just happened.

"Yes," said Dr. Tuckett. "No problems though, we are getting the cables ready already. Should only be a minor delay."

"We have all been there," said the moderator who then allowed a few uncomfortable minutes to pass as Tuckett waited for the circulating team to find the reconstruction cables in the O.R. proper. "These things happen even in the best of hands." The moderator then asked the crowd if they had any questions at that point. There were none.

Three long minutes of unease passed as the entire team sat idle waiting for the unexpected equipment to arrive. During this time Phil noted Tuckett's face turn a fiery red. Nurse Adams just stared at Phil and Stortz, unaware as to how Tuckett got the #15 rasp into his hands. She shook her head in disbelief and her eyes cried out with questions as to what happened.

Then, after allowing the national embarrassment to continue for two more minutes, the moderator spoke. "Dr. Tuckett for the sake of time we should go off live feed now." Tuckett did not respond. "Your time slot is now up and to stay on conference schedule I think it best to take leave of you and your team." Again, Tuckett did not speak as he stared into the wound, with his hands atop the patient's body.

"Thank you Dr. Tuckett for your time and expertise," said the moderator. "We appreciate you informing us of the benefits of the Tuckett Cup. I believe your presentation was most informative and enlightening to all of us." A paltry round of applause then emanated from the audience.

"Thank you," said Tuckett politely. "I'm sorry about the change in plan but..."

"And... we are off air," said the voice of the audio-visual guru that was in the room. "Again, we are off air. The video feed has been cut."

What then followed was an unleashing of vile that rivaled Dr. Richard Knight on one of his worse days. A very brief series of finger pointing immediately centered the entire blame of the debacle squarely upon the somewhat kyphotic shoulders of Dr. Franklin Stortz, who stoically took the beat down in stride. After being lambasted by both Tuckett and Lee the fellow was asked abruptly to leave the room. Without a word he clumsily worked his way around the scurrying scrub nurses who were bringing the necessary equipment into the room to complete the case. His lumbering frame reminded Phil of the "Franklin-stein" moniker that nurse Bryant tagged him with, as he slowly watched the dejected fellow leave the operative theatre.

Dr. Tuckett spoke no more, needing an additional two hours to patch back the shattered femur. Upon completion of the case both he and Dr. Lee vanished, quite aware of the financial fallout that was to occur from the botched live surgery presentation. Most distressing to Tuckett was the bruise that his reputation was about to take in the greater New York City area. The anger in his soul was a painful reminder of his metropolitan exile, so many years ago.

A somber tone sat upon the traveling orthopedic team that Saturday night in Chicago. Dinner reservations were kept at the most expensive restaurants in town, attended by everyone except Tuckett and Lee. Front row tickets were then utilized for the "must see" play in the area, less two empty seats that reminded the team of their saddened leaders. A late night out on the town ended early for everyone as they returned to the posh hotel's penthouse floor. Candice "Candy Apple" Adams then spent a long night in the Presidential Suite, alone and disappointed.

Down the hall rested Phil Drummer trying to sleep next to the snoring hulk of Franklin Stortz. The drone of the big man's nasal passage seemed to shake the mattress that Phil slept upon. As Phil stared at the overhead ceiling a sense of unease and confusion over took him. He tried to rationalize his next step, always asking himself what his father would do in this situation. Just minutes ago he had spoken to Rick Polk who was back at Saint Michael's in cell block five. Polk informed him during the conversation that their apartment was broken into over the weekend. The intruders destroyed the place yet by the description of Polk, failed to take anything of value. With a heavy heart Phil wondered if the flash drive that Anastasia Tuckett gave him still sat safely within his desk drawer. He then stayed awake for hours wondered what ever happened to the beautiful woman who entrusted the cursed device into his care.

CHAPTER FOURTEEN

THE BEAN COUNTER

JOHN OLSON WAS born and raised in Iowa, and attended the same high school as his good friend, Barry Reynolds. COO Reynolds convinced the ultra conservative accountant to join AMG some fifteen years ago during a church weekend retreat. Once on board the AMG team Olson rapidly distinguished himself as a tenacious accountant with an uncanny ability to search the financial books of a hospital and cut costs. Inside his brain resided a keen analytical mind, which never fatigued from the boring repetition of checking and cross matching thousands of invoices and order forms daily. In short John Olson made money for AMG, lots of money. Within the inner circles of Kansas City corporate he was a bona fide all-star that always pushed the numbers into the black. He methodically traveled across the nation on assignment from corporate, visiting assigned hospitals for weeks at a time. During these business trips a dutiful wife stayed back in Kansas City, raising four children. His salary doubled that of COO Reynolds.

"How is the internal audit going John?" asked Reynolds as he leaned back in his chair. Olson was paying a morning visit to the COO in his outdated hospital office. It was the Tuesday after the Tuckett Institute debacle in Chicago.

"Like all audits," said Olson. "Awash with wasteful spending."

"Not at the St. Mike's mother ship," said Reynolds.

"Hospitals are like ships at sea," said Olson. "Being tossed and turned in rolling waters that can make the ride difficult at times. My job is to keep the ship's load as light as possible and plug leaks that occur down below." Olson paused to allow the COO to blow his nose into a cloth handkerchief. "The admirals back in land locked Kansas City are happy when all of their vessels are deemed sea worthy."

"All hands on deck," said Reynolds. "We have a too-sunamey approaching called National Health Care."

"I believe it's pronounced tsunami," said Olson. "The T is silent."

"Whatever," said Reynolds while continuing to wipe his nose. "Any thoughts on what we should do with the Tuckett Institute? I mean I pushed them on the Presidential Wing donation, but corporate wants a minimum of one half million."

"No, but I would love to get a look at their books. Must be some creative processes going on. I wonder if they have ever been audited by Medicare?"

"Tuckett and his band of cronies are starting to get under my skin," retorted Reynolds. "They fly around the country calling themselves a so called "Center of Excellence," where results from total joint replacements are vastly superior than the community hospital standard. Their campaign absolutely destroyed our revenue stream from joint replacements. Yet they completely rely on the hospital to accept their postoperative patients who have a heart attack or deep wound infection. It doesn't seem fair, we struggle and apparently they do not."

"Oh yes, before I forget," said Olson. "Corporate wanted me to get an update on the nurse Adams affair."

"Well you can report back to them that the file is shut on that issue. Per my understanding she was rehired by Tuckett," said Reynolds now with a nervous roll of his thumb and forefinger. "He apparently doubled her already bloated salary and is parading her around the country again, like some sort of a trophy. And I'm sure he is screwing her…"

"Understood, understood" said Olson with a wave of his hand, not comfortable in discussing the lurid details of their relationship any further. The accountant then let a minute go by to calm down the COO's ire.

"Barry, with regards to the Tuckett Institute, why do we purchase all of the implants for hip and knee replacements?" asked Olson.

"What do you mean?" said Reynolds, having no idea what the question meant.

"I noticed that all of the surgical implants for the knees and hips, including the famous Tuckett Cup is first purchased by the hospital, and then the Tuckett Institute buys it from us," said Olson. "Why?"

"Don't know, its always been like that," said Reynolds. "Perhaps you can discuss it with one of the on site accountants."

"Perhaps," said Olson with a shake of his head. "Just seems like a wasted step." Olson continued to stare at the COO, amazed at his lack of concern for detail. His audit to date already uncovered several massive lapses in company protocol that cost AMG millions of dollars over time.

"Something else is peculiar about the ordering of the Tuckett Cup itself," said Olson while tapping his forefinger on hips pursed lips. "I just can't seem to get a handle on it."

"What's that John?" said the COO.

"The cups come through our system with a detailed manufacturer invoice, from a company in California. Each item is marked, matched and then cross-matched with a series of serial numbers. You know standard protocol for surgical implants."

"Yea," said Reynolds while scanning less important papers on his desk.

"But the surgical records coming back to us from the institute on a few rare occasions do not match up regarding the cup serial number."

"So what," said Reynolds. "As long as we get paid for the device. We are getting paid, correct?"

"Sure, sure," said Olson. "That was the whole reason for my detailed analysis of the orders and transaction with the Tuckett Institute. A lot of money is changing hands and we are getting fully compensated for the implants."

"What's the big deal then," said Reynolds. "I have limited understanding of implants but I do know at times an implant may be put in during surgery which doesn't fit, then it's swiped out. I know we both eat the bill for such a misstep, perhaps that can explain the mismatch."

"Well I'm sure it's an oversight," said Olson. "But in today's day and age of audits and accountability, numbers always have to match up." The CPA paused while again tapping his index finger to his lip. "They always have to match up. That is an absolutism in my world, and when numbers do not match, that's when I lose sleep."

"I tell you what John, let me get in touch with a Ms. Emily Reyes over at the Institute," said Reynolds picking up the phone. "She is the only sane person in that asylum across the street. She will be able to direct us in the right direction regarding this matter." While dialing the phone the COO continued to say, "Maybe we can make a big deal over it, now that the Candy Apple affair is officially dead."

Within five minutes the COO fully explained the hospital's deep concern over the serial number mismatch to Ms. Reyes. He embellished the situation to hopefully make both Tuckett and Lee acknowledge his existence and watchful eye. Ms. Reyes stated that she would discuss the situation with Dr. Lee, who keeps all implants fully stocked. Within thirty minutes she called back stating that Dr. Lee was looking into the matter, and would be happy to discuss Mr. Olson's concerns over dinner that night, at his estate. The COO agreed to the invitation without asking for his fellow Iowan's consent, thereby booking a dinner date between the two to "iron out" a matter of "extreme and pressing legal importance" to the hospital system itself.

"The estate, wow!" said Reynolds upon hanging up the phone. "I've only been there once. What a palace! In the middle of nowhere but what a place."

The Dr. Lee estate was situated twenty miles outside of town, in a remote canyon accessible by a series of winding roads that zigzagged through a vast state park. The good doctor purchased the property in a behind the scenes deal that involved the state governor, his brother, a corrupt casino oversight committee, complimentary jet service and a medley of luscious prostitutes. It was a win-win situation for everyone involved, except the governor's brother who developed some unsightly genital lesions from the sordid affair. Beneath the property sat a rich supply of natural gas compliments of the Marcellus Shale Formation. Upon the sacred ground rose a magnificent home, surrounded by nature and a state of the art security system, complete with cameras, sensor devices and on sight security sentries.

John Olson arrived via rental car at exactly five o'clock, just in time for cocktails and hors d'oeuvres. He was nauseous from the windy canyon road, which seemed to traverse over a never-ending series of bridged ravines. While stepping out of the car the accountant was met alone by Dr. Lee. No handshakes were exchanged between the two. While being led into the estate, a lone coyote howled in the distance.

Cocktails were served on a patio deck overlooking a lush meadow, complete with butterflies and white tail deer. Their conversation was that of a non-business nature, occasionally being interrupted by male waiters serving brown trout caught earlier that day in a nearby stream. As the sun disappeared over a steep mountain to the west, the couple retreated to an inside formal dining area, complete with spectacular works of art. At exactly six o'clock a series of waiters delivered cuisine that rivaled the best restaurants of Europe, filling the honored guest with a memorable banquet, capped off by a delectable dessert and series of port wines from Portugal's Douro Valley.

At exactly eight o'clock the accountant was invited into the doctor's great room. It was only then that John Olson began to feel ill at ease, wondering why the incompetent COO that set up the meeting failed to invite himself. The ambience of the room was that of power, heavily laden with oak and leather in a formal British tone. It was at that moment that the business at hand became the main discussion point.

"All total joint implants are first purchased by the hospital," said Dr. Lee in a nasal voice as he sat opposite Olson. "The insurance payment to the hospital for the implant is greater than for a free standing outfit like the Institute." Lee paused to wipe a fleck of dust off his sport coat. "Then we buy it for 80% of the original cost, less 10% for the Tuckett Cup itself. The transaction benefits the hospital and was set up years ago, netting your company about five hundred dollars per implant."

"Very nice," said Olson who sensed there was more to the matter at hand. "We appreciate your generosity and my internal audit will show that the current set up is financially sound for St. Mike's Hospital."

Dr. Lee nodded his head. He waited approximately one more minute before speaking as if to both size up and frighten his guest. During the sixty-second gap there was complete silence in the house, although John Olson did appreciate some movement in an adjacent room.

"So what's the concern?" asked Lee.

"The serial numbers on a few acetabular cups do not match up," said Olson. "Specifically the Tuckett Cup itself." The Midwestern accountant then proceeded to lay out in detail the mismatch between the invoice and the final operative record that documented each implant serial number. He specifically noted that the sticker from the acetabular cup box, which was placed on the operative record by the circulating nurse, didn't match the final cup invoice for the patient. "It has only occurred three times so far this year," said Olson. "Last year it only occurred once."

Dr. Lee just stared back at Olson without blinking or moving.

"I'm sure it represents a misstep by the operating room staff," said Olson who somehow felt obligated to make his host feel better about the concern.

"Do you have any more information on these so called mismatches Mr. Olson?"

"No," said Olson, "Well yes Dr. Lee. I actually have the names of the patients involved this year."

"May I have the names?"

"But of course Dr. Lee," said Olson. "I'm sure that will benefit your inquiry into the situation." The CPA then opened a lap top computer that he brought to the meeting in a leather carry bag. While turning on the computer not a word was spoken by the host who sat motionless in his chair. It was during this time that Mr. Olson appreciated the scent of an alluring perfume, a bit feminine in nature, but quite delightful.

"Let's see, so far this year the patients involved in the mismatch were a Mr. Harold Walters, Mr. Stanford Rupert and oh yes, a most peculiar name, Mr. Anthony Crackstone."

"Any other names?" asked Lee.

"No."

"Very good, I will look into the situation immediately and have an answer for you no later than twenty-four hours from now," said Lee.

"Thank you," said Olson not sure as to where the conversation would head next. The level of unease was high in the room.

"A Medicare audit is what we don't want, do you agree?" asked Lee.

"Fully. AMG has suffered through too many an audit."

"I mean, who would investigate such a miniscule point such as serial numbers from an operative report not matching an invoice?" said Lee. "Certainly not the Medicare hacks that snoop around looking for gross oversights to justify their existence."

"Well, I'm somewhat of a neurotic bore," said Olson with a smile. "That's my job, minutia. Something has to occupy my mind as I sit looking at hospital numbers in hotel rooms across the country."

"Have you handed in your preliminary information to corporate back in Kansas City yet Mr. Olson?"

"No. I've only discussed it so far with Barry Reynolds."

"It would be of great personal and financial interest to the Institute that this slight oversight not become privy to anyone outside of this room," stated Lee. "I'm sure you can understand the possible emotional and fiscal fallout from such a gaff."

"Yes," said the accountant with hesitancy. "But I work for AMG and they sign my check. To AMG I must report. Where it goes from there is out of my hands."

"Would an offer of five hundred thousand dollars for the new hospital wing construction change your mind, Mr. Olson?"

Olson was uncomfortable as to the pronunciation of his name by Lee. He knew his job well, and not to get involved with the backdoor politics of running a for profit hospital.

"I can only report that generous offer back to corporate," said Olson. "I'm sure they will be most thankful."

Lee just stared at his guest and slowly shook his head in the positive. He then arose to excuse himself, stating he would like to discuss the hospital wing donation in detail with Dr. Tuckett by phone. Prior to walking away he cleared his throat before saying, "Mr. Olson my dear friend, all guests at the estate are afforded a complimentary after dinner mint, if they so desire. I hope you enjoy what others have come to appreciate as the "house special." Please, do feel free to take your time. There is no rush." He then walked out of the room.

At that very moment a side door opened and in walked two women smiling at Dr. Lee as he walked coldly past them. The confident click of high heels on the hardwood floor announced a seductive approach from the tightly clad harlots. One was blonde and the other brunette, both were well endowed and good at what they were paid to do.

Each escort then sat down on the couch next to Mr. Olson, one to his right and the other to his left. Their scent was luscious as was their inviting curvaceous figures, complete with skintight dresses and stiletto heels. They smiled and lightly laughed at the CPA while mumbling some inconsequential words prior to commencing a slow, coordinated manual assault on his body. Their quick movements caught the bean counter off guard and strangely complemented the two glasses of port wine that he had just consumed. Up until that point in his life Mr. Olson's experience with marital infidelity was that of a guilt-laden porn video occasionally watched on a lengthy business trip, alone in a hotel room. His senses began to blur as the buxom blonde stood up in front of him and slowly began to sensually disrobe in a fashion that suggested this was her full time occupation. While peering up at the beautiful women he appreciated the brunette to his right lean against him and begin to loosen his tie. The physical contact of her body signaled to him the onset of adultery, which was beginning to feel sinfully good. It was only when the blonde siren took off her corset in dramatic fashion, that fifty years of fire and brimstone Sunday sermons brought him back to his senses.

"Whoa, whoa," mumbled the flustered guest as he stood up. "Ladies, please we have a misunderstanding."

Despite his tepid pleas the two overpriced prostitutes continued to ply their trade, having both been down this fragile yet historically brief moral road of hesitation. They pressed on in a professional manner that the nearby Dr. Lee knew had broken the will of many a guest of his manor. Yet, despite their best sordid effort, complete with sensual and filthy promises, the dullard from Iowa held his ground, and successfully fended off the sneak attack.

"I'm sorry ladies," said Olson while stepping back. "We seem to have had a misunderstanding. You see...."

"Thank you girls," said Dr. Lee while approaching from a side door. "That will be all." Both girls then gathered their garments and left, without saying another word, pleased to have garnered a paycheck without being violated in the vulgar fashion they were accustomed to.

"My apologies Mr. Olson," said Dr. Lee who then signaled to his guest to sit back down on the couch. At that moment a young male dressed as a waiter entered the room and stood approximately ten feet behind Lee in an attentive manner. The attendant was impeccably groomed with a handsome, lean physique. "I have misread you Mr. Olson," said Lee. "Perhaps Anthony can be of assistance to you?" was the next line from the host while extending his hand towards the valet, dressed in a black tuxedo. "Yes?"

"That's it, I'm leaving," barked the AMG accountant. "I'm sorry Dr. Lee but I have absolutely no interest in your shameful business propositions. None whatsoever." He then began to walk past Dr. Lee wondering how to find his way out of the house.

"Please Mr. Olson," said Lee while stepping directly in front of him. "My apologies, but from prior experience businessmen of your stature frequently expect such perks. I apologize. Please sit down."

"No thank you."

"Mr. Olson I have just gotten off the phone with Dr. Tuckett and he too is distraught over the serial number mismatch and concern for a future Medicare audit," said Lee quickly.

"Goodbye Dr. Lee," said Olson now standing face to face with his host, who was blocking his exit. "Please excuse me, I would like to leave."

"We would like to increase our offer to one million dollars regarding the new hospital wing," said Lee with a smile. "Of course, this would be in exchange for your reciprocal oversight of the numbers mismatch which would be corrected by our surgical team in the meantime." Lee just stared coldly at his guest, hoping for a positive answer. "A deal my good friend?"

"That's not for me to decide," said Olson. "I can only pass my audit numbers on along with your generous offer. Corporate will make the final decision based on the information they receive." A brief moment passed as the two stared at each other. "Now please Dr. Lee, let me pass by."

Dr. Lee drew in a long slow breath upon hearing the word "corporate." He knew that his gambit was up, leaving him with no other alternative. "I'm sorry to hear that Mr. Olson, you may leave. I thank you for your time." An attendant then entered the room to politely escort the guest back to his rental car. It was nine o'clock in the evening.

While driving away from the enclave Mr. Olson shook his head in disbelief. He then sent a text out to his wife, saying he was headed back to the hotel, at which time he would call her. Surreal amazement overtook him as he mindlessly followed his vehicles' GPS directions through the desolate state park roads. It was a dark, moonless night.

His route took him around a near ninety-degree mountainous curve before opening up onto a stone bridge constructed by the Civilian Conservation Corps some seventy years ago. The bridge was a quarter mile long and spanned a small stream that flowed 400 feet below. The span was one of seven stone masterpieces in the state park built by then President Roosevelt's New Deal program. As Olson began his traverse across the bridge he immediately noted a distant vehicle in distress, pulled off to the roadside. The driver's side door was open and the silhouette of a female stood in front of the SUV, staring downward at the front wheel. Flashing hazard lights from the stationary vehicle prompted the Good Samaritan from the Midwest to slow down his approach. He stopped his car approximately fifteen feet from the rear of the vehicle. Upon peering forward he immediately recognized the damsel in distress to be the shapely blonde who had just gyrated before him in earnest. She shook her head in a feminine disgust while her body language voiced dismay. Without hesitation the accountant opened the driver side door to exit his vehicle, eager to offer any roadside mechanical advice. Memories of summer days working in a filling station back home came to mind as he stood outside the door and began his approach. After taking five steps forward the working girl looked up with a smile of gratitude and began walking towards Olson. She then quickly slid back into the inner confines of the posh SUV, closed the door and slowly drove forward, vanishing from sight. Per instructions, she did not look back into the rear view mirror.

Bemusement overtook John Olson as he stood in the road, alone in the middle of the dark night. Trepidation began to enter his mind, as did a keen instinct of a presence behind him. A need to get back into his vehicle overcame him. Then, as he began a turn about, a tremendous force exploded across his mid back. The impact of the thug's metal pipe immediately broke three ribs and caused the CPA to crumble down upon his knees. A series of coordinated kicks then pelted his abdomen, causing him to curl up in a protective fetal position. Upon peering upwards he noticed two or perhaps three hooded men aggressively attacking him, raining blows upon his head with their boots. He attempted to arise from the ground but was overwhelmed by the combined force of the assault team. He was knocked prone and felt the skin on his face being forcefully peeled off by the cruel grind of the macadam below. His sensorium temporarily blunted as he felt his body being propelled upwards and towards the left. Horrific grunts from the inner souls of the assailants were heard, as was the painful dislocation of his left shoulder. Attempts to regain control of his body were unsuccessful and a rapid appreciation of lateral momentum arose. It was only then that the accountant briefly recalled that he was on a bridge, apparently above a precipice of unknown height to him. He screamed out in vain as his damaged body was hurled over the side of the guardrail, sending him on a rapid descent to the ravine floor below. He tried to yell out, but could not, appreciating only rushing air and the deepening darkness of his downward decline. His last thought was that of his wife, who was patiently waiting for his promised phone call back home. The initial encounter with the jagged rocks below was horrifically sudden, peeling the aorta off the anterior border of his thoracic spine. Pain was not a factor, as his cranium mercifully shattered into multiple fragments, rendering him dead upon impact. A gravitational role then deposited his corpse face down, in a cool shallow mountain stream.

The enemy above then approached his car to place a suicide note upon the driver's side seat. They left the engine running and driver's door open, allowing a state park ranger to come upon the scene some nine hours later. The note described an addictive life of pornography, alcohol and gambling debts that led to a fateful decision. It made no mention of his family back home, an omission that brought eternal consternation upon his grief stricken wife.

CHAPTER FIFTEEN

KENDRA

KENDRA MASON WAS the product of a tough North Philadelphia neighborhood. Her father faithfully worked in the physical plant of a nearby hospital, and her mother sought part time work in a local garment shop. She was raised in a home below the national poverty level, yet provided everything to a child that was necessary for moral success. Her parents preached and practiced austerity, while inspiring their three daughters to excel, which Kendra did. She accepted a well deserved undergraduate scholarship to Temple's School of Nursing. Her parents encouraged her to pursue a career in nursing which prompted her commitment to the field.

Kendra possessed natural beauty that complemented a five foot five inch athletic frame. She excelled in high school basketball and garnered second team all city honors in the rugged public school league. She never lacked available male suitors. Men did not dominate her life, but her presence blunted the thought process of males around her. Just prior to her departure for St. Michael's she broke up with her high school boyfriend, a decision that pleased her parents, in quiet hopes that their oldest daughter would ultimately marry a medical doctor.

She met her roommate Stephanie Thomas in nursing school and they became close friends during the first two years of didactic lectures. Stephanie was from a small town in New York State's southern tier and was uncomfortable in the large city environs. They complemented each other with regards to their professional aspirations and commitment to a career in nursing. It was fitting that they began their third year of nursing school together at St. Michael's Hospital.

"Almost ready?" yelled Stephanie to her roommate who was applying a final layer of makeup upon her face. Stephanie was glaring at her computer screen, sating her addiction to social networks.

"Yep," said Kendra as she bounced back into the living room of their shared apartment. The deep thumping base of the music next door vibrated through the walls of their apartment, a sign that the Friday night party hosted by Dr. Jackie Rhimes was starting to heat up. "Can you be the designated driver?" asked Kendra in jest. "I may have a drink tonight."

"Is the competition going to be there?" asked Stephanie in reference to Jennifer Ranier.

"Don't know," replied Kendra. "I hope not."

"You're up against one beautiful girl, or should I say woman," said Stephanie, while multi-tasking three ongoing conversations on the internet. "She seems very nice too."

Kendra sat down opposite her roommate with a look of concern on her face. "I know, she seems like a great girl."

"They seem very happy together."

"Yep," was Kendra's reply followed by a pensive pause. "Almost too happy."

"I know," said Kendra "But I have one advantage over her. One great advantage."

"What's that?"

"Proximity," said Kendra with a subtle smile. "At least for the next four months."

"That's all that matters with males," said her roommate. "I'll give it two months before his little man starts doing the thinking. Never fails, they can't help it. Poor pathetic souls."

"I am right across the hall and the beautiful and fetching Jennifer Ranier is three and a half hours away," announced Kendra confidently while standing up to leave. "It's a recipe for success."

"Agree," said Stephanie with a smile. "He doesn't have a chance."

Within minutes the two nursing students joined the festival across the hallway. The party was rocking and it appeared that all the regulars were present except nurse Candice Adams, who was rumored to be in Las Vegas servicing her sugar daddy that weekend.

"Candy Apple wasn't ready for Jackie Rhimes!" blurted Jack to his guests while carrying out two pitchers of ice cold beer.

"Aren't you on call tonight," said Phil who was happy to see Kendra and Stephanie enter the confines. Jackson Rhimes was indeed on call that night and was scheduled to return home tomorrow for a family funeral. Phil graciously offered to take his Saturday call, thus keeping him in the valley for the weekend, an act of kindness not well received by Jenna back home in Philadelphia. "You shouldn't be drinking when on call."

"Listen," said Jackie with bravado. "I'm learning a lot from Doc O'Neil. He said if you can't operate drunk, you shouldn't be operating." His warped line was followed by a hearty cackle and request to turn up the music, which occurred with ear piercing promptness.

Phil just shook his head and watched Kendra work her way into the room. She was young, beautiful and energetic. That night she wore a tight pink skirt and white halter top which complemented the stifling heat outside. A single silver bangle on her wrist complemented a much thinner one on her ankle. Black heeled shoes brought her sultry frame up to the five foot eight inch level. A perfect tan complemented her long legs, which were toned to perfection. While speaking to a group of fellow students she peered across the room and smiled at Phil, who waved back. It was then that Phil felt a nudge from Rick Polk who was sitting on a couch beside him, playing a round of Seinfeld trivia with some fellow students.

"Romeo, snap out of it," said Polk with a smile and chug of beer. Polk was sitting on a couch with a group of male and female nursing students sitting around him in a state of awe. Over the past fifteen minutes they peppered the intern with a series of Seinfeld trivia questions, astonished by his knowledge of the sitcom. As Polk went to speak the questions continued to assail him from multiple directions.

Phil leaned forward with a smile, bringing his ear closer to Polk in an attempt to hear above the music.

"Newman saw Jerry making out during what movie?" shouted a guest.

"Don't insult me, *Schindler's List*," said Polk with a wave of his hand.

"What unreturned library book from 1971 was Jerry being fined for not returning?" asked a student, who was apparently pulling questions off of his smart phone.

"Child's play," said Polk with a pathetic wave of his hand. "The book was *Tropic of Cancer*."

Polk went to speak but the barrage continued. It was apparent the group was not willing to stop until they stumped the self proclaimed Svengali of Seinfeld Trivia.

"What magazine was George reading when his mother caught him "treating his body like an amusement park?" shouted a young female.

"I believe that was from the controversial 51st Seinfeld episode," said Polk with a professorial tone and stroke of his chin. "Let me see, the 11th episode of season four to be exact. A memorable little skit called *The Contest*." The portly intern then paused for effect, as the crowd peered forward in anticipation, hoping to finally stump the great one. "*Glamour* magazine," was the correct response, sending the onlookers into a wild search for more questions.

"What were George's parents names?

"Frank and Estelle."

What holiday did George's dad make up?"

"Festivus."

"What was Kramer afraid of?"

"Clowns."

"What did George's high school gym coach call him?

"Can't stand ya."

"I've got it!" yelled a female sitting opposite Polk. "I found a trivia question guaranteed to stump any Seinfeld fan."

The crowd grew silent as they peered towards the excited young woman with a devilish smirk on her face. She was staring into the screen of her phone and then looked upwards, casting her eyes upon the Svengali.

"The question is actually titled–Guaranteed to Stump any Seinfeld Fan," said the female.

Polk sat up erect and rubbed his two hands together in anticipation. He took a deep breath and said, "Please, young lady from across the room, what exactly is your question?" Confidence exuded from his ample frame.

"What major league baseball player spit on Newman and Kramer after a Mets game at Shea stadium?"

Shouts of "I know this one!" and "What kind of question was that?" abounded from the crowd.

"Please, please," said Polk with a lift of an outstretched hand, restoring silence and order.

"A wonderful question indeed," said Polk, who then stood up. "If I'm not mistaking the question posed evolved from a wonderful two part episode entitled *The Boyfriend*." Polk looked around at the drunken congregation while then saying, "As a side note in the 'Extras' section of the Season 3 DVD, Mr. Seinfeld himself says this is his favorite episode." Polk continued to look at the faces staring back at him. "Think of what I just said, his favorite episode, can you believe it?" No one spoke.

"The correct answer is Roger McDowell," said Polk sharply. "Roger McDowell is the correct answer to the question."

An immediate uproar ensued with shouts of "Keith Hernandez" being heard throughout. The mob began to celebrate the slaying of the trivia king.

"Chief, I even know that one," said Phil to his roommate. "It was Keith Hernandez, remember the Magic Loogie Theory? Please, you're embarrassing me."

"He's right," said the young lady who offered the question. "According to this website he is absolutely right – it was Roger McDowell."

A smug smile came across the face of Polk as outrage erupted amongst the trivia rookies.

"The correct answer is indeed Roger McDowell," said Polk. "Hernandez admitted it in Part 2 of *The Boyfriend* episode. Kramer and Newman were taunting McDowell throughout the game, thus prompting his heinous act."

An immediate round of applause broke out, bringing glory to Dr. Polk who allowed the exaltation to proceed in unabated fashion. Order was restored in his kingdom, allowing him to turn and speak to his friend.

"I see Kendra just walked in," said Polk with a smile. "Kendra in one month," was his prediction while waving his index finger outward. "Down goes Frazier!"

Phil just smiled back, knowing that he was on the precipice of trouble.

"My prediction is one month," said Polk. "No longer than one month." He paused before concluding by saying "Game over!"

"*The Frogger* episode," said Phil with a smile. "Final season."

Polk grossly overestimated the staying power of his roommate. After three more hours of wine, women and song, the defense mechanism of Phil Drummer was battered and beaten. At approximately 2 A.M. eastern standard time, he walked outside to get a breath of fresh air, with Kendra at his side. She had been hovering within his personal airspace for the past two hours. Her essence was captivating, as was everything about her. Phil walked outside like a prisoner condemned to the gallows, being acutely aware of his sealed fate, yet emotionally distraught over his presumed guilt and or innocence. His sensorium was clouded by the historical lethal combination of alcohol and hormones.

The couple meandered a block or two away from Skid Row and leaned upon each other's body throughout. They sat atop an old stonewall which ran around the perimeter of a church recently closed amid public outcry by the local Roman Catholic diocese. For ten minutes they held each other until a nearby train whistle pierced the silence of the warm summer night. An indescribable force of passion then overtook the young couple, in a manner that is wasted on the young. Phil then thought he heard the church bells from the abandoned steeple overhead chime just before his lips met those of Kendra Mason's. Their intimate introduction continued onward for several minutes before a mutual sense of respect created an emotional pause. It was then that they pulled back and looked into each other's eyes. Phil loved the smell of her breath, a wonderful mixture dominated by peppermint schnapps and strawberry bubblegum.

"I have to stop," said Phil. "I just have to."

Kendra continued onward with one more minute of bonus lip service before agreeing. "I know," she said, "It's the right thing to do." She kept her face close to Phil, prompting confusion amid moral fiber.

Alcohol fueled another round of respectful admiration before the young couple decided to abort any further advancement, content that their fateful encounter was just the first step of a budding relationship. They sat upon the wall for another hour, listening to the silence of the night before returning back home to their separate apartments. Phil felt no guilt as he laid himself to rest, comfortable with his perceived loyalty to Jenna, no matter how jaded.

The following morning Phil awoke early to head downtown. His apartment was a mess as unidentified drunken bodies lay about the apartment proper. The only movement seen was the body of Rick Polk rolling over on the couch prior to blurting, "Down goes Frazier, down goes Frazier."

The fresh early morning air helped to ease his sense of guilt, as he walked towards the local police station. There he would meet with officers to discuss his role in the disappearance of Anastasia Tuckett.

The flash drive that Anastasia Tuckett gave to Phil was indeed stolen from his apartment while he was in Chicago. Over the past several days he spoke to his father and the interim chairman of the PGH General Surgery department about the events in question. A unanimous decision was made for Phil to completely disclose all of his information to the local authorities and distance himself from any further involvement in the matter. Phil had requested the meeting several days later, which was delayed per the request of the authorities. Undoubtedly the series of events cast a shadow upon Phil and his presence in the valley.

He was acutely mindful of the fact that someone was privy to his contact with Anastasia just prior to her accidental death. He wished never to have opened the flash drive, now being conscious of apparent violations in the privacy of text messages. His goal that morning was to disclose all information and put the whole ordeal behind him. It was step one of a plan to simplify his life, which was starting to become very cluttered.

Phil first met with two police officers that took his preliminary information. He then waited in a detective's office for the lead investigator assigned to the case, which up until that point was a standard burglary of an apartment. Within five minutes a middle-aged man of fit stature walked into the room with an energetic gait. He was dressed in a sport coat and tie, exuding a professional attitude, which Phil appreciated.

Introductions were made and the detective apologized for being late, having been delayed earlier that morning in the investigation of a suicide. Over the next hour Phil provided all the details of his brief encounters with Anastasia Tuckett prior to her death. His memory banks were able to recall a significant amount of material regarding the text messages of Mr. Edward Banks. The release of information to the public servant was a catharsis to Phil's soul.

"Interesting information," said the sleuth who was penning the data on a notepad as Phil spoke. He continued to stare down at the information while saying, "What was the demeanor of Ms. Tuckett when she handed you the flash drive?"

"A combination of relief and nervous anxiety," said Phil. "She seemed in a hurry to leave."

"What was the one lasting impression from your encounter with her, the encounter regarding the flash drive given to you?"

Phil hesitated knowing that certainly it was the appreciative kiss from the socialite, complemented by her perfume and hint of Chardonnay. He then said, "The feeling that I was a fresh outsider, someone who was not from the valley."

"A valley where everyone knows everyone else's business, correct?"

"Exactly," said Phil.

"Well thank you Dr. Drummer," said the detective. "I'm sure this has been a most disturbing experience for you."

"It has," said Phil. "But I do feel better handing over all the information to you. It's a weight off my soul."

"I understand fully. Please, excuse me Dr. Drummer," said the detective while getting off his chair and walking towards another room. "I would like to give you my card and contact information." He then left for several minutes, exiting into the confines of the police station.

During that time Phil stood up to stretch his six foot five inch frame. He took a few steps to the left and began to scan a series of framed photographs commonplace to all offices. It was then that he noticed a photograph of the detective with Dr. Tuckett and Dr. Lee, standing shoulder to shoulder on a golf course, with their drivers symmetrically placed before them. The surrounding landscape and structure revealed a tropical venue of wealth and plenitude. They all had broad smiles upon their faces. Other photos showed the smiling detective about to get on the G6 aircraft of the Tuckett Institute. He stood atop the short stairwell that entered the plane with one arm holding onto the craft, while his body leaned back for the snapshot. An adjacent photo captured Anastasia Tuckett in a formal gown at the Brookside Country Club, standing amid a group of males in formal tuxedos, including the detective. An eerie sense of Anastasia's presence overtook Phil as he looked into her glassy eyes, warning him of the valley's provincial social network. He peered closely at her young and energetic face. It was then that Phil was alarmed by the sudden return of the sleuth, causing him to quickly pivot back towards his chair, embarrassed for having scanned the photos.

"Sorry to have startled you," said the detective. "As you can see, I knew Mrs. Tuckett quite well. Her death greatly affected me."

"It seems like everyone knew her well," said Phil.

"True, she was a beautiful human being," said the lawman while extending out a business card towards Phil. "Here is my contact information, feel free to contact me anytime." The detective then smiled at Phil and paused. "Seven days a week, anytime, anyhow. The card has all my info including home phone, cell phone, email, etcetera, etcetera." He then paused and said with a firm conviction, "Don't ever hesitate to contact me Doctor Drummer."

"Thank you," said Phil while staring down at the card. He glanced at the detective's peculiar name having heard it upon introduction but unable to commit it to memory. "It was a pleasure meeting you Detective…"

"Crackstone," said the gumshoe with a warm smile. "Tony Crackstone."

CHAPTER SIXTEEN

THE INFECTION

AN INFECTED TOTAL hip replacement is an orthopedic disaster. Mr. Banks initially felt some increased pain in his groin, followed by redness and swelling around the surgical incision. His call of concern to the Tuckett Institute was met with reassurance that such symptoms were not uncommon at his stage of recovery. Dr. Tuckett treated his concern with a good dose of "benign neglect," which is an age-old tenet of Orthopedic Surgery. Unfortunately the bacteria load replicating exponentially inside the confines of Mr. Bank's artificial hip was anything but benign, and could not be neglected. His increasing pain prompted a visit to a prominent Orthopedic surgeon in the New York City area who just happened to be the smug moderator that presided over Dr. Tuckett's national embarrassment in Chicago. The local surgeon jumped on the opportunity to embarrass his exiled colleague further by immediately proceeding with an aspiration of Mr. Bank's hip joint. This procedure involves passing a fine needle into the surgically replaced joint and removing joint fluid, which is then sent to the microbiology lab for evaluation. Within forty-eight hours of the joint tap, the fluid cultures were growing out the dreaded Methicillin Resistant Staphylococcus Aureus, or MRSA. MRSA is a particularly virulent bacteria that will not expire when exposed to common antibiotics, due to a mutated resistance over time. It represented an infection that would be extremely difficult to eradicate. Mr. Banks was quickly informed that he now had a real tempest on his hands, one that would require two to three additional operations and the prolonged use of intravenous antibiotics. The local surgeon recommended immediate admission to his New York City based hospital in order to care for the deep-seated infection, and prolong the pummeling of Dr. Tuckett's reputation. Up until that point Dr. Tuckett was unaware of the local workup and professional recommendation by his despised former colleague.

Mr. Bank's then graciously returned a call to his treating surgeon and explained to him the situation, which sent a chill down Tuckett's spine. Tuckett immediately informed the banker that the private jet would be in route to bring him back to the Institute and begin the necessary treatment, which would involve removing all of the infected surgical implants, including the Tuckett Cup. The original operation would have to be undone, followed by a secondary "wash out" procedure two days later, followed by a final re-implantation of all devices approximately six weeks later. Tuckett demanded his return to the valley, claiming only he knew what implants were inside, and this knowledge would guarantee a successful outcome. Despite Tuckett having no medical basis for this bold prediction, Mr. Banks thought the reasoning sane, and prepared to board the Tuckett jet. It was mid-afternoon on a Saturday when the jet landed back in central Pennsylvania, followed by an ambulance racing the ailing patient back to St. Michael's Hospital. On such short notice it was predetermined that the emergency procedure be performed in the main operating room at St. Michael's, where afterwards the patient would be admitted directly to the hospital. Having Tuckett and his staff appear, yet alone operate within the confines of the hospital was a rare event. It represented a collision between the haves and have-nots, which in this case involved two fiery scrub nurses called in to assist.

The scene took place in Operating Room One. The on call surgical team consisted of exiled nurse Nikki Bryant and semi-retired circulating nurse Kline, who frankly didn't care to be working that Saturday. Nurse Bryant prayed that Tuckett wouldn't call in his personal scrub nurse whom she loathed, but he did, and nurse Candice Adams appeared, full of attitude and sass. Phil and Fellow Stortz played the role of innocent bystanders. It was Phil's last week of rotation on Orthopedics.

By chance the operating team of Fast Eddie O'Neil and Jackie Rhimes were in the midst of a laparoscopic appendectomy in Operating Room Two when they noticed a flurry of adjacent activity. The surgical rooms were partly separated by a glass partition, allowing the occupants of each room to view that of the other.

"What the hell is going on over there?" yelled O'Neil over the blaring disco music. Up until that point he was allowing Dr. Rhimes to struggle through the procedure himself. "Looks like one big cluster...."

"Septic hip," said the circulating nurse. "V.I.P. from the Institute."

"The Institute, what the hell? Was there a power outage over in the Taj Mahal?" blurted O'Neil as he stepped further away from the table to peer through the window into Room One. "Wow, even the pharaoh himself is present with his reclusive little henchman."

Dr. Tuckett was not a happy man when he stormed into the operating room. The anesthesiologist was passing a breathing tube down the patient's windpipe when he let out a tirade of vile accusations that blamed everyone else for the infection except himself, the true sign of an expert in the field. "The nurses must have been picking their noses up on the floor when they changed his post op dressing," yelled Tuckett who began to rapidly position the patient on his side for the procedure. "Maybe this was the case that our esteemed fellow's finger poked out of his glove, yes? See Dr. Stortz what happens when you break sterile conditions in a case? It's my albatross now. MRSA yet!"

Phil kept silent and noticed Dr. Lee to exhibit a level of nervousness above and beyond his baseline. Looking to the left he then noticed the oversized derriere of the plump circulating nurse inadvertently touch the edge of Nurse Bryant's sterile instrument table. The nurse wore scrubs that were about to explode from their expansive grip on her backside. She didn't even notice her rump abut the sterile field as she bent in the opposite direction to pick up an item on the floor.

"You hit the table!" screamed Dr. Lee at the nurse. "For God's sake you just hit the sterile table."

"No she didn't," said nurse Bryant sharply. Since they were in Saint Michael's O.R. the sterile table was her sole responsibility and nurse Bryant protected her turf with a fierce retort.

"I did not," said nurse Kline.

"Do you think I am blind?" said Lee incredulously.

"Maybe," said Kline.

"You are going to cause an infection," blurted Dr. Lee.

"It's already infected," said the circulating nurse. "Too late to worry about that."

"That will be enough nurse," barked Tuckett. "Another word and I'll ask you to leave."

"Go ahead," said the defiant nurse quietly. "Make my day."

"Get the hell out of here!" screamed Tuckett at the top of his voice. "Get out right now!" The angered surgeon took a deviant step towards the portly nurse who just shook her head at him.

"COO Reynolds will be hearing about this!" yelled Lee.

"O.M.G.," said the nurse sarcastically as she turned to leave the room. "Good luck finding a replacement, there is no back up call team today."

Across the hall Fast Eddie O'Neil continued to crane his neck towards the room, completely oblivious to Jackie Rhimes and the appendix at hand. "Lot of screaming going on across the hall," said O'Neil as the door to his room suddenly opened up. He looked to see the exiled nurse stick her head inside the door-jamb with a smile.

"Check out the side show next door," said nurse Kline. "Some raging female hormones are about to ignite."

"Catfight!" yelled O'Neil with a sick feeling in his stomach only appreciated by those with a Y chromosome. "Catfight!"

"Ah, Doc O'Neil I have no idea where I am at," said Jackie staring at the screen in front of him. "Please, a little help."

Fast Eddie turned back towards the table and peered at the screen saying, "For God's sake son, that's the gall bladder! You're way off." He then rapidly returned to the other side of the table to assist the resident. "Let's get this over quick to kick start the show." He then took over the case with a speed that even astonished the younger resident at his side.

"We need a circulating nurse," said nurse Bryant to Tuckett who was now stepping up to the table. At his intimate side was Candy Apple Adams who didn't even acknowledge the presence of the exiled diva. She tucked her body close into that of the operative surgeon, fully aware that one of the two nurses would have to break scrub and circulate in the room, a step down for whomever was chosen. "I can't do it, I'm the primary scrub nurse."

"No you're not," barked Adams. "This is an orthopedic case and I am the orthopedic scrub nurse."

"Maybe you are across the street, but not in my house," said Bryant firmly.

"Nurse Bryant I suggest you break scrub," said Dr. Lee in a nervous, nasal tone. He was still trying to calm down from his previous exchange with the banished hospital employee.

"I don't take orders from you," said Bryant defiantly. Nurse Bryant knew she had the upper hand in the argument. She felt this was her one and only opportunity to voice her opinions to the Tuckett Institute cadre without risk of retribution. "Your not even a medical doctor, just some sort of an equipment rep," said Bryant. "Don't tell me what to do."

"I'll report you to the hospital board of…"

"I'll break scrub," said Candy Apple. "Let's do what's best for the patient on the table." She then stepped back from Tuckett's personal space and tore her gown off with panache. She then looked smugly at nurse Bryant and gyrated her body away from the table, taking the high road, fully aware of the compassionate light shining upon her.

"Thank you nurse Adams," said Dr. Tuckett. He then extended his hand without looking at nurse Bryant saying, "Knife."

Fast Eddie finished the case in record time across the hall and instructed Rhimes to close the small puncture wounds on the abdomen. He then stepped rapidly to the other side of the table and yelled "Let's give the boys from across the street a warm, St. Michael's welcome. Hit it nurse Jones!"

A young nurse with a smile behind her mask then pressed the play button on the stereo system funded by O'Neil to bring state of the art acoustics into Room Two. The nurses along with the anesthesiologist quickly lined up next to Fast Eddie in a formation that looked directly through the glass into Room One. The blast of the music even shook Rhimes, who was accustomed to such loudness.

The blare of the first four notes brought a smile onto the face of Jackie Rhimes as he looked at the behinds of the dance troupe before him, who starting strutting to familiar disco lyrics.

The shake of the walls and glass caused all heads next door to quickly look up. As they peered through the glass into Room Two their eyes focused upon the cabaret line now in full swing, whirling to the music in hedonistic fashion.

Tuckett shook his head in disbelief and returned his gaze upon the wound while trying to concentrate on the task at hand. Dr. Lee turned ashen white and appeared ready to implode. A smile and rhythmic bob of the head came from nurse Bryant and the anesthesiologist, peering above the head sheets.

"No wonder we don't do cases over here," said Dr. Lee with a repulsive tone. "That wouldn't happen at the Institute."

"Inappropriate," said nurse Adams with a shake of her head. "So unprofessional."

"But Candy Apple, this is your song," said the gas passer in a disappointed tone. "A month ago you would have been shaking your money maker to the beat. What have they done to you, my precious child?"

Nurse Adams took the medicine in stride knowing full well that the anesthesiologist was right. Her DNA screamed for her to dance, but she would not.

Throughout the ordeal Phil and Franklin spoke not a word.

"Rhimes, what are you doing?" screamed a now sweating Eddie O'Neil. "Get the hell over here! Bust a move."

Upon entering the hip capsule of Mr. Banks a tremendous release of pus was encountered, suggestive of MRSA. Deep cultures were obtained and Tuckett cursed the gods above, knowing quite well how long it would take to eradicate the infection. With anger he dislocated the hip and rapidly removed the femoral stem with forceful blows from a slap hammer. It was then that he centered his attention upon the last remaining piece of hardware to be removed – the Tuckett Cup.

As Phil listened to the final stanza of the song he looked back across the glass in Room Two, appreciating the absolute joy upon the faces of the dance team.

He then looked up at Candice Adams who, although attentive to the surgery, had a sideways glance casted towards Room Two. He was sure that she was peering at Jackson Rhimes, hopefully wondering if she made the right move, which Phil knew hurt Jackie.

"Suck in the wound Stortz," said a dejected Tuckett, "I can't see the liner."

Within five minutes the lead surgeon had dislodged the Tuckett Cup from its previously called "final resting place." Tuckett quickly inspected the cup and handed it off to nurse Bryant who placed it on her sterile table, adjacent to the entire hardware construct. Tuckett then began to irrigate out the wound with a pressure saline mechanism, planning to run a total of nine liters through the zone of infection.

"I'll take the cup," said Dr. Lee as he rigidly stepped next to nurse Bryant's table.

"No you won't," said Bryant. "Hospital protocol. Any implant removed must go to pathology first."

"Nurse, please," said Lee politely and with authority. "We have a program that fully inspects any removed Tuckett Cup, part of our overall Quality Assurance process."

"I can only assure you one thing sir. That this cup is going straight to pathology, in the hospital. If not it's my ass on the line."

"I can assure you that upon completion of our inspection, the cup will be delivered promptly to the hospital pathologist," said Lee.

"Sorry," said Bryant who then relocated all of the removed total hip components to the center of her table, thereby making them inaccessible. It was quite clear that she was not going to release the cup to Dr. Lee.

Just then the door to the room opened and in walked Fast Eddie with Jackson Rhimes in tow.

"It's our lucky day, the great one has come down from the mountain to visit the village people," said Fast Eddie. "What happened, a mine subsidence beneath the Taj Mahal?"

"Nice dance," said Tuckett who continued to run fluid through the wound.

"Thank you but that was the B-team squad," said O'Neil. "You hijacked our number one dancer." He pointed a thumb at Candy Apple with the line. "We want her back." He then looked at Candice saying, "Candy please, come back to your home."

Tuckett laughed in an uncomfortable way, waiting for someone else to speak. Suddenly nurse Bryant let out a yell.

"Hey, that's a sterile field!" was her cry that spun everyone's head towards her.

Immediately prior to the scrub nurse's outburst, Phil witnessed a rapid and coordinated effort by both nurse Adams and Dr. Lee that prompted the scream. Nurse Adams had just put on a pair of sterile gloves and reached onto nurse Bryant's table in order to grab the Tuckett Cup. She then rapidly brought the cup away from the table and put it in a clear plastic bag that Dr. Lee held in open fashion. Upon receiving the goods, Dr. Lee zip locked the bag, pirouetted, and departed.

"What are you doing Adams?" yelled Nikki Bryant. "I'm writing an incident report! You're my witness," said the angered nurse while looking at Fast Eddie. "You're all my witnesses!"

"Just following orders," said Adams with verve. "Just following orders."

"Everyone just please calm down," said Tuckett, trying to regain order within his room. "What's the big deal?"

"The big deal is that a surgical implant that was removed is now missing," said Bryant. "Do you have any idea what happens to me when that happens?"

"I will take full responsibility for the cup," said Tuckett. "Dr. Lee is fanatical about his product. I can assure you it will probably be in the pathology department within an hour or two. Trust me on this one."

No one spoke. Phil sensed that nurse Bryant was about to attack nurse Adams. Fast Eddie had a crazed look in his eyes, hoping that a brawl would break out. Tuckett just continued his surgical closure, seemingly immune to the chaos around him. Phil then smelled the expelled gas from the lower bowels of Franklin Stortz, who shifted nervously besides him. He shook his head in disbelief as to how he was thrown amid such a cast of characters, thankful he had only one more week of Orthopedics remaining.

The last week of Phil Drummer's orthopedic rotation proved oddly uneventful. Once the team returned across the street to the Institute they became insulated from the gossip of the hospital proper. However an uneasy sensation continued to haunt Phil, as he was constantly aware that someone knew of his involvement with Anastasia Tuckett, and perhaps may have been privy to information of a deeper concern. The young doctor had to continually reassure himself that once off Orthopedic rotation, life would revert back to normal, absent the Kendra factor.

Unfortunately the last patient of the day shattered his false sense of serenity that Friday afternoon. Upon entering the V.I.P. room he was surprised to see detective Tony Crackstone sitting upon the examination table. Mr. Crackstone was in for his one year anniversary checkup. Up until that point his total hip replacement performed by Dr. Tuckett had been doing just fine.

CHAPTER SEVENTEEN

WHAT HAPPENS AT SEA

THE SENATOR FROM New England sat relaxed in the posh great room of Dr. Lee's estate that Saturday night, pleased with the complimentary jet service from Dr. Lee that he had grown accustomed to over time. The meal as usual was magnificent, as was the port wine shared by the duo. Firmly entrenched in his third term, a cocky confidence exuded from his persona. The toxic mixture of power, arrogance and narcissism anchored the ego of the seasoned legislator. His anticipation grew with each passing moment, as he settled in for private discussions with the wealthy benefactor of his past two campaigns.

"It's an honor to have your son spend an academic year with us at the Tuckett Institute," said Dr. Lee. "He is a truly talented young man."

"Why thank you Dr. Lee, I greatly appreciate your willingness to teach him the finer points of the surgical trade."

"It's our pleasure," said Lee. "Dr. Tuckett is quite impressed with his surgical skills, which is quite a compliment in itself."

Both men then inhaled a deep sense of pride and accomplishment in regards to the senator's son, absent any sense of reality. With his deep inspiration the New England spokesperson appreciated a familiar perfume nearby, which sent an immediate tingle down his spine.

"Thanks for that tip on the McCoy merger," continued the senator with a grin. "Tripled my money in a matter of two days."

"My pleasure," responded Dr. Lee with a smile. "All of us here appreciate your effort to get FDA approval for the Tuckett Cup. Without your help, our product would never had made it to market."

"No problem," said the senator, drawing a deep puff on his Cuban sourced cigar. "You've never been wrong on the market, how is that possible?"

"The stock market has been a hobby of mine for decades," responded Lee. "If you understand history, then you understand the market."

"I see, but you are always so well ahead of the curve."

"I've got my system," said Lee. "With today's computer technology and a little effort, trends are easily seen. Then it just takes guts to drop a load of money down when the time is right."

"The first million is always the hardest," joked the elected official with puffs of smoke now encircling his head.

"Any progress with the Tuckett investigation out West?" asked Lee. "As you know the whole event has brought a considerable amount of remorse and angst upon us."

"I can understand your feelings, especially that of Dr. Tuckett. Losing a loved one is never easy."

"Did you have an opportunity to speak to the local district attorney?"

"Better yet," said the senator, "I spoke to the Attorney General of California who is an old friend of mine. I supported his election and he owes me a few favors."

"And?" asked Lee, realizing this was the final talking point on his agenda for the evening.

"There were a few loose ends hanging out there regarding the investigation, could have gone on for another year or two," said the senator.

"Emotionally that would be tough for Ian," said Dr. Lee. "He needs closure. I'm sure that you understand that."

"Exactly," said the senator with an anticipatory tone, realizing that his next comment would secure the house special that he had become accustomed to at the Lee estate. "I impressed upon him such a need for closure, and I am happy to report that as of three o'clock today, the case was officially closed."

"Wonderful senator, wonderful," replied Lee with a clasp of his hands and slight bow to the senator. "Bravo, bravo."

"Cause of death is Accidental Drowning – Missing at Sea," said the senator. "It's official."

"Amen, may she rest in peace," said Dr. Lee.

"What happens at sea, stays at sea," said the senator with a nod of his head. "That was our motto back in the service, it's a great maxim for life in general." He then paused to look at his host, content with his role in bringing closure to the Anastasia Tuckett affair. A smile came upon his pretentious face. He then reiterated slowly, "What happens at sea, stays at sea Dr. Lee, don't you agree?"

"Absolutely," responded Dr. Lee. "As usual it has been a pleasure having you over for dinner Senator. You have brought great solace to Dr. Tuckett and the Institute, and for that we shall forever be grateful." Dr. Lee then arose to leave the room while rubbing his still clasped hands together. "The limo will take you to the airport tomorrow morning at nine o'clock Senator – please do enjoy the rest of the evening."

"Why thank doctor," said the Senator while popping two Viagra tablets into his mouth. "I bid you peace."

Then on silent cue, the trashy blonde and brunette harlots employed by Dr. Lee entered the room in grandiose fashion. One wore a chambermaid's outfit and the other that of a police-woman. Their sensual entrance was the expectant crème brulee that had whetted the senator's appetite over the past two hours. An enticing gust of perfume overwhelmed the senator in intoxicating fashion just prior to the foreplay that rapidly ensued.

"Ooh, la, la!" exclaimed the New England senator upon seeing his two favorite escorts prance in front of him. "Please ladies, there must be a mistake, I am a happily married man."

"You're under house arrest for adultery," was the last line that Dr. Lee heard shouted to his guest as he walked slowly down a long hallway towards a private study. Although Lee deeply disliked the senator, he respected the influence and power that his office possessed.

Lee then entered the private confines of his study. The room was austere, with a hint of an oriental theme. A single large computer screen sat atop his desk, shining bright in the dark ambience. The doctor sat upon the leather chair directly in front of the screen and slightly leaned back. He picked up a phone next to the computer and hit the top speed dial number, then awaited the voice on the other end of the line. While waiting he began to scroll down the computer screen in front of him. A never-ending series of pages rapidly rolled before his watchful eyes.

"Hello?"

"Mission accomplished," said Lee.

"Great. Even the investigation out west?"

"As of 3 PM today the case was officially closed," said Lee. "Official cause of death is Accidental Drowning."

"Wonderful, absolutely wonderful. Where is he now? With the whores?"

"Yes," said Dr. Lee. "They both tell me he is a real pervert, so it won't be difficult to keep him on the payroll.

"Documenting it?"

"Of course," replied Lee. "An orgy video with a senator in the lead role may go a long way in the future."

Dr. Lee continued to scan down the computer screen as the conversation continued.

"Any further questions on the cup?"

"Thankfully no," said Lee. "The final pathology report should come out soon. I don't anticipate any problems, since we got to it first."

"Close call, how can we prevent that from happening again?"

"You can't," said Lee. "Just make sure that any infections or hip revisions come back to the Institute, at all costs."

"Understood."

Dr. Lee then focused his attention of the screen in front of him while saying, "We still have a problem with the resident. Seems to be still communicating with the authorities about a hand written note from the deceased that wasn't picked up in the apartment sweep."

"Go on," said the concerned voice.

"Sounds like a thank you note for keeping the flash drive with a silly heart drawn on it, must have fallen out of the envelope."

"Shouldn't be a problem."

"Agree," said Dr. Lee. "Hopefully the resident continues to step away from the situation, but we have to be careful here."

"As usual I trust your decision process in this matter. You have never steered me wrong."

"Things are settling down so let's just stick with the plan now," said Lee.

"Agree," said the voice on the other end, upon which the conversation was terminated.

At that moment a scream of exaltation echoed down the hallway, prompting the doctor to view a video screen besides him. He remained unemotional while watching the depraved senator ignore basic tenets of decency in his quest for personal gratification. A quick check of the system assured the doctor that the video recorder was functioning well.

Turning away from the screen he again inspected information that was streaming in via live feed to his computer hub. The innocent and energetic face of Phil Drummer entered his mind, as did the fact that his orthopedic rotation ended that week. Deep in his heart he hoped the naïve resident would stay clear of the recent collateral damage. However his paranoid mind always needed a Plan B, ready for immediate implementation. With a sigh he reached forward to the keyboard and logged onto his search engine, typing in the words Jennifer Ranier, Physician's Assistant, Philadelphia General Hospital. What he discovered that evening was of great interest, as his cold, cunning mind began to construct the foundation of Plan B.

At that very moment one hundred and fifty miles away sat the cramped body of Phil Drummer in the front seat of a car bearing down on Philadelphia. At the wheel was Rick Polk, trying to figure out where he was going to stay in the city that weekend.

"I'm taking over the Polk Lounge again," yelled Rick. "A coup d'etat!"

"Just stay with Jen and me," said Phil as he repositioned his body in an uncomfortable fashion. "What's with this car, it's been throwing off heat in my face despite the air-conditioning being on. I feel like I'm in a nuclear reactor."

"No way am I staying with you," said Polk. "Once you tell Jen about your little run in with K-E-N-D-R-A she is going to melt down like a nuclear reactor gone bad."

"I've got to come clean for the betterment of the relationship," said Phil. "It was an innocent contact between us that won't happen again."

"The China Syndrome or something like that. I'm not getting near the blast zone."

"Jen is a mature adult, and it's better to get it all above deck now as opposed to later," said Phil.

"Listen to me," said Rick as he steered his vehicle onto the Schuylkill Expressway. "Don't you remember what I told you on day one of this rotation, when we bolted out of the Greycliff like sailors in front of Jen?"

"No"

"I said what happens at sea, stays at sea," said Polk in exact fashion.

"I don't remember you saying that."

"Well maybe I didn't, but I'm saying it now," said the driver. "Don't be an idiot Phil. You've got a good thing going with Jen, don't blow it."

"I'll go with my heart if the moment moves me," said Phil.

"You've also got a good thing going with Kendra," said Polk. "She is amazingly beautiful and gaga over you. Don't blow that either."

Phil just looked at his best friend, then laughed out loud knowing that he was right. His heart was torn in the direction of two absolutely beautiful women, both with qualities that attracted him. He took a deep breath and visualized Jennifer anxiously awaiting his arrival. Maybe Rick was right he thought, at least for the weekend it may be best for him to enjoy the moment at hand. He and Jennifer had been through so much, and Kendra was just a passerby in his training schedule. In four months he would be back in West Philadelphia and then all would be normal. His mind continued to wrestle silently for several minutes before Polk pulled up in front of the Greycliff Apartments.

"Get out," said an exhausted Polk while rubbing his eyes.

"Thanks," said Phil while grabbing his pack from the back seat. "Thanks for your sage advice."

Polk just stared back at him and said, "Don't blow it chief. Trust me on this one."

As Phil approached his apartment on the seventh floor of the Greycliff it felt good to be home. As he reached the key forward to unlock the door, he heard laughter in the apartment that continued as he opened the door.

"Phil is that you?" screamed Jennifer as she turned the corner from the galley kitchen and jumped into his arms. She looked and felt great.

"Hey Phil," said Troy Huckabee, as he emerged from the kitchen area. He gave a weird wave with his left hand as if he was peering into a video camera.

Jen then kissed Phil and stepped back with a broad smile on her face. "Skeeter came over for dinner tonight just to keep me company."

"Thanks Skeeter," said Phil as he looked at the intern grinning behind Jennifer. "Much appreciated."

"No problem," said Skeeter. "Jennifer is just too beautiful, I can't stay away from her."

"Where's Rick?" asked Jen as she straightened out her hair and pulled her shirt taut.

"Going to stay at the hospital tonight," said Phil. "Back in the Polk Lounge."

"I heard about him," said Skeeter Huckabee with a southern drawl that slightly annoyed Phil at that very moment. "He is a legend."

"How's internship?" asked Phil as he walked into the apartment noticing Skeeter wore a pair of surgical scrubs that were too short, exposing a pair of blazing white socks at ankle level.

For the next few minutes Troy "Skeeter" Huckabee described his first two months of internship. He stated there was no definitive word on the search committee's decision regarding the department of surgery chair, although he mentioned a surgeon from Boston with Chicklet teeth who was in the running and had recently visited the Philadelphia General. Skeeter then reported that Dr. Knight was starting to see some patients in the office on a limited basis, but as of yet had not returned to the operating room. Lastly he noted that the cardiothoracic program had reopened, with a slow but steady increase in the volume of coronary bypass procedures.

"I'm gonna leave you two love birds alone now," said Skeeter as he headed towards the door. "Thanks for dinner Jen."

"Nice kid," said Jennifer as she embraced Phil to start what was to become a lengthy welcome home party. "Good company for me."

"Yea, real nice," said Phil as he held Jennifer in his arms suddenly realizing that the now legendary Richard Polk was indeed right.

What happens at sea–stays at sea.

CHAPTER EIGHTEEN
PHIL'S MORAL SLATE

TONY CRACKSTONE WAS good at what he did having been raised by a father who was a local police chief. He was a product of the valley and knew just about every family and their history, both good and bad. Although somewhat cavalier in presentation, his ability to process and interpret information in relation to a crime was quite keen. While growing up he never missed an episode of *Columbo* on television, constantly amazed with the fictitious sleuth and his ability to stumble upon information, via a never ending grind forward, no matter how mundane the details. While sitting across from the COO of Saint Michael's, he was underwhelmed by the figurehead in front of him. Barry Reynolds appeared disheveled and anxious to end the just commenced meeting. Detective Crackstone arranged the interview as part of the ongoing investigation regarding the death of John Olson. COO Reynolds had just provided him with the background of their relationship, forged while living back in Iowa together.

"Sounds like a clean living man," said Crackstone. "No skeletons in the closet."

"None," said Reynolds. "That's why the whole situation is so shocking to me." The COO nervously bobbed his left foot up and down on the floor, a point noted by the detective. "Gambling debts, pornography, alcohol, that's just not John."

"Why didn't you go with him to the mansion?" asked the detective.

"Wasn't invited," said Reynolds bluntly. "Only a select few get invited to the mansion." He paused as if calculating his next comment. "I've only been there once."

"But you helped arrange the meeting, isn't that true?"

"Correct. I contacted Ms. Reyes at the Institute to discuss a matter that had come to our attention. We were actually just trying to put pressure on the Institute to donate money to our Presidential Wing project, which has been a thorny subject between corporate and the Institute."

"What was the matter of attention?"

"I'm having troubles recalling the exact details," said Reynolds who now again began bobbing his right foot up and down. "I'm no accountant, had to do something with the Tuckett Cup."

"Go on."

"Apparently the hospital buys the cup first, then the Tuckett Institute reimburses us for the charges. After that he lost me on the details, but I do remember the handling of the cup was a win-win situation for everyone involved."

"Anything else regarding details of the cup's transactions?"

"Nah," that's all I can remember," said the corporate lackey, now wondering where he would be getting lunch that day. "Why all the questions detective? I mean a suicide is a suicide. Some questions will never be answered surrounding such an occurrence."

Crackstone just stared in disbelief at the COO, not sure if he was holding back on critical information, or just an absolute dolt.

"What about his personal papers or computer?" asked the COO. "Perhaps that will help you with the details of his concern regarding the Tuckett Cup."

"Good point," said Crackstone, already aware of the laptop computer found in Olson's car. The computer unfortunately contained a virus that turned all information within the local disc into incomprehensible characters. Crackstone had sent the laptop to FBI headquarters in Philadelphia, where their top

Information Technology team was assessing the matter. "I'll have to look into that."

"Hey, maybe I should have been a detective?" said Reynolds with a chuckle.

"Mr. Reynolds, I have one more question to ask before I leave."

"Fire away."

"Do you enjoy living in the valley?"

The question caught Barry Reynolds off guard. He cleared his throat and squirmed slightly in his chair. Crackstone looked at the bookshelf behind the COO, with pictures of his wife and children.

"Sure," mumbled the COO. "I love the valley, been here a long time."

"How about your wife? Does she like the area?"

"Well," stuttered Reynolds with a clearing of his throat. "Women, you know, they have a somewhat different outlook than men." A brief pause ensued before he continued saying, "But of course she likes the valley too, wants to be here for many more years."

"Thank you Mr. Reynolds for your time," said Crackstone as he arose to shake hands. "I'll keep you posted of any further developments in the investigation."

"My door is always open," said Reynolds with a heavy sigh. "John was a dear friend of mine."

"Oh Mr. Reynolds," said Crackstone as he turned back towards the COO in the doorway. "Will you be attending the Senator's fund raising gala at the Brookside? I hear he is considering a run for the presidency."

"The senator from New England?"

"Yes," said Crackstone. "If I'm not mistaken his son is spending a year of training with Tuckett. The Institute is apparently a big financial backer of his political career. I just heard the news, the event will be in a month or two."

"Wow," said Reynolds. "No, I haven't been invited yet, but I'm sure his campaign will be asking for our money."

"Interesting how money makes strange bedfellows, isn't that the truth, Mr. Reynolds?"

"Yes, yes it is Detective Crackstone," said the COO realizing that the gumshoe was continuing his investigation while walking out the door. "Money is the root of all evil."

"Funny," said Crackstone. "In our line of business the saying goes the *lack* of money is the root of all evil." Crackstone then smiled at the COO before saying, "Have a good afternoon Mr. Reynolds. Let's keep in touch."

A queer feeling overtook the COO as he sat down behind his desk. The combination of hunger and nervousness caused his stomach to gurgle aloud. Without hesitation he lifted the phone on his desk to call the chief financial officer of the hospital, prompting a meeting between the two later that day. He requested that hospital legal counsel be present at the meeting.

At the same moment across the street another meeting started, as the day marked a rotation switch for all the junior residents. Jackson Rhimes strolled into the Tuckett Institute with a nasty chip on his shoulder. He never loved Candice Adams but enjoyed her uninhibited companionship immensely. Her rapid disposal of him still stung as he walked into the building whose namesake was responsible for the rift. Rhimes was a bit of maverick, a free spirit who wasn't afraid to make his presence known. Despite being dismissed from his prior residency program for behavior unbecoming a physician, an ardent zest for life burned in his soul. Jackson Rhimes wasn't afraid to challenge the establishment, quite confident in his physical prowess and intelligence.

"Welcome to the Tuckett Institute," said Ian Tuckett as he strolled into the operating room that morning. "Dr. Rhimes I presume?"

"Yes sir," said Jack. "Just call me Jackie."

"A prior Temple resident, correct?" asked Tuckett.

"Temple wasn't ready for Jackie Rhimes," said Jackson with a pimp roll of his arm.

"Yes, I see," said Tuckett. "Well please take your time scrubbing Dr. Rhimes, we are currently dealing with an infection upstairs that makes all of careful to avoid such a repeat complication."

Jackie was then steered out of the OR towards the scrub sink area while Dr. Tuckett and Dr. Lee studied some preoperative x-rays on the view box. Upon entering the scrub area he came face to face with nurse Adams, who despite having on a surgical mask was nervously chewing some gum, in anticipation of their inevitable meeting.

"I'm sorry," said Adams immediately without hesitation. "I'm just so very sorry."

"You should be," said Rhimes. "We spend the day together and then you board a jet to Chicago the next morning with Tuckett?"

"It's just so complicated," said Candice. "You have to understand that Ian and I have a history together, a history that predated your arrival. Why haven't you answered any of my phone calls?"

"No reason to," said Rhimes. "The guy is out of my league, but I would appreciate a little warning next time," said Rhimes. "At least get your underwear out of my apartment, it's starting to stink it up."

"It all happened so suddenly," said Candice. "I mean it was like a text message that evening, just prior to departure. I didn't even have time to think it through." The nurse rapidly continued to run the scrub brush up and down her forearms while peering into the O.R. at the head surgeon. "It's just that Ian is still emotionally recovering from...."

At that moment the massive frame of Franklin Stortz turned the corner, bringing the uncomfortable conversation to an end. After introductions, the team worked their way into the surgical theatre of Dr. Tuckett, all aware of the delicate situation existing between the head surgeon, his concubine nurse and Rhimes. A nervous Dr. Lee peered at the squad in wonderment, hopeful that emotions would remain in check throughout the next two months. He wondered if the young Franklin Stortz had any inkling of his father's perverse genetic makeup. The case commenced with Schubert's *Trout Quintet*.

"Oh no," said Rhimes spontaneously as the classical music entered his gangster rap infested mind. "Is this opera?"

"No," said Tuckett as he stared down at the open wound, "It is classical. Franz Schubert to be exact."

"Fast Eddie was into the 70's music," said Rhimes. "In some sort of a disco time warp. His room was always rocking, loved it."

Dr. Tuckett paused and then cleared his throat before saying, "That's a risk we all take, having to listen to disco music that is."

"What type of music do you like chief?" said Rhimes as he looked upwards at fellow Stortz. "Heavy metal?"

"Ah, don't really have a specific genre," replied Stortz, caught off guard by the attention directed at him. "Easy listening, soft rock maybe."

"You know you look like an old Indian chief," said Rhimes. "Did anyone ever tell you that? Mind if I call you the Chief?"

"Ah…" mumbled Stortz as he fumbled for a retractor to hold onto.

"Do you play basketball?" asked Rhimes. " We had a killer team back in my old residency in Philly. Playground league in North Philly, that's where the real talent is. I was the power forward, the enforcer of the league."

At that moment Dr. Tuckett stepped back from the table and paused, looking across the table at Rhimes. Nurse Adams just slowly shook her head as she stared at Jackie with pathetic eyes, knowing full well what was about to unfold. Dr. Lee stood rigidly erect behind Tuckett without moving a muscle. The circulating nurse paused the music and silence gripped the room. The anesthesiologist arose from below the patient's head sheet, sensing something amiss.

"Dr. Rhimes, I am performing reconstructive hip surgery on Mr. Patel here who has traveled all the way from Boston for the surgery," said Tuckett calmly. "Every step that he takes for the rest of his life will be affected by what we do this morning. He is expecting our A-game, and nothing less. I hope you understand that."

"Of course I do," said Rhimes.

"Here at the Tuckett Institute we pride ourselves on excellence and a very high standard of professionalism. Do you understand?"

"Yes."

"I respectfully request that you abide by our standards and conduct yourself in a professional manner while in my operating room. Do you understand?" asked Tuckett.

"Of course I do," said Rhimes. "I was just trying….."

"Dr. Rhimes, please be quiet," said Tuckett firmly. "I don't want to hear another comment from you this morning. Not one more word." Silence ensued for thirty seconds before the circulating nurse restarted Schubert, allowing Dr. Tuckett to get back on schedule. Within fifteen peaceful minutes he expertly sent another Tuckett Cup to its final resting place. All was well until the lead surgeon focused his attention on the femoral shaft.

"Oh my God!" blurted Rhimes with a step back from the table. "Holy crap!"

"What?" said Tuckett with a surgeon's alarm in his voice, "What?"

"Oh my God, who ripped one?" yelled Rhimes with a wave of his bloody hand, "Wow, Stortz was that you?"

"What are you talking about?" said Tuckett.

"Chief you're killing me," said Rhimes as he peered upwards at the Senator's son, "You need to see a doctor man."

"Dr. Rhimes….." said Tuckett in amazement.

"My eyes are watering," said Rhimes. "I can't see!"

As the dense stench from fellow Stortz's large intestine filtered its way into the airspace of Tuckett and nurse Adams, it was only their highest level of professionalism that maintained a stoic composure. A subtle wince on the face of nurse Adams was the only indication that their olfactory glands were in working order.

"Dr. Rhimes please leave the room at once," said Tuckett sternly. "At once!"

"Me?" said Rhimes as he stepped away from the table. "You got the wrong guy. He should be fined for that one." Rhimes shook his head while walking away saying, "You need a hazmat team in here."

"Out!" yelled Tuckett whose face was now turning bright red. "Head immediately to your residency director's office and stay there! Do you understand?"

"A gnarly one from the Chief," said Rhimes as he left the surgical room for the day, confident in the curious position he held within the Institute – the ex-beau of the current filly in Doc Tuckett's stable. The chiseled resident then graciously accepted a latte and apple tart from an attendant in the lobby prior to heading back to cell number five. During his pastry break he thought that perhaps the Tuckett Institute wasn't ready for Jackie Rhimes.

An hour later Phil awoke to the door slamming behind Jackie, as he entered cell number five. At first Phil was confused as to his whereabouts, thinking he was back in Philadelphia at the Greycliff. He discerned a perfume that reminded him of Jenna. He looked to his right, immediately noticing that Jenna's picture frame was not present on his night table. The clock read two o'clock in the afternoon. He recalibrated his sensorium by recalling that his attending for the next two months, Dr. Martha Brace, didn't work two days a week, due to stress and an alcoholic husband. Therefore he had two full days off in the middle of the week providing him with too much time on his hands. That morning he did some medical reading, worked out with some weights and went for a run, with Kendra. The autumn sun was hot and the humidity high for September, causing the duo to sweat profusely. They pushed their running limits to the maximum by adding speed and distance to their routine, which triggered an opiate like endorphin rush throughout their bodies. Phil drew a deep breath as his short-term memory recalled how sultry Kendra looked after the run, so sensual, tanned and so very near by. It was then that his moral conscious blurted out a frantic alert with shouts of fidelity, trust and respect, only to be shattered by the hot pink underwear and sports bra lying on the floor, next to Kendra's socks and sneakers. A subtle purr of satisfaction emanated from behind him as Kendra Mason snuggled her warm, taut body back close to his. It was then, that

Phil Drummer realized he had failed miserably. Despite all his best intentions and true love for Jennifer, he had committed the oldest sin known to man–infidelity. His moral slate was no longer clean. He looked one last time up at the night table hoping that he was dreaming, but the picture of he and Jenna was gone, tucked away deeply into a nearby desk drawer. As the rap music of Jackie Rhimes took hold of the apartment complex the two bedfellows then turned to face each other, immediately aware as to how perfect they felt in each other's arms.

CHAPTER NINETEEN

BIG NEWS

THINGS WERE NOT going as planned between Ian and Candice. At first their liaison was new and exciting, yet it rapidly deteriorated into the sham project contrived in response to a threat from the AMG group. Ian Tuckett missed Nicky Bryant, whose company he craved despite her drunken lapse in San Diego. Tuckett occasionally found Candy Apple's actions contrite and scripted, with an utter lack of emotion and spontaneity. It became quickly apparent to both parties that their time together may be brief, yet Candice did her best to maintain her coveted prima donna status. During the workday she remained a trusted assistant in the operating room, providing a top rate professional service. During the weekends she also provided a top rate service, pampering Tuckett with a femininity that normally would satiate any male's appetite. Unfortunately these were not normal times for Candice, as she was dealing with a man who seemed off his game, in part to the recent death of his estranged spouse. Despite the conditions nurse Adams pushed forward, well aware she was just one text message away from banishment back to a life of mediocrity. It was this fear that stirred in her heart as she sat next to Tuckett that Friday night, having just spent an evening together in New York City.

"Great day in the city," said Tuckett. "Did you enjoy it?"

"Absolutely," said Candice. "That restaurant was amazing. How did you get reservations on such short notice?"

Tuckett just smiled as he got up and headed to the hotel room's refrigerator for an overpriced beer. He popped the cap and headed to the window, which offered a commanding view over Times Square. The light from below shone upon the surgeon as he gazed pensively out towards Broadway.

"God I miss the city," said Tuckett.

"I know," said Adams. "But we are both from the valley, and in the valley we reside."

"If only I had stayed," said Tuckett. "I lie awake at night always wondering what could have been back here. If only...."

"It wasn't meant to be."

"If it wasn't for her father and that ridiculous ponzi scheme that he got involved in," said Tuckett with a slug of beer. "Once the money goes, then all hell breaks loose." He paused shaking his head slowly. "Nothing good happens after that."

"Do you miss her?"

"Of course I do," said Tuckett. "She was the mother of my two kids, and a great mother at that." He paused while continuing to peer down at the streets below. "I just still have trouble accepting the fact that she is gone. Something deep inside me won't let go. I still expect her to show up at my door."

"She is gone Ian," said Candice as she sat up on the side of the bed. "Lost at sea, it's official per Dr. Lee. He certainly has been a help in this whole matter."

"Lost at sea, so they say," said Tuckett. "So they say."

Idle conversation then continued between the two prompting Tuckett to open another cold beverage. "Do you miss him?" he then asked.

"Who?"

"The resident, you know Rhimes," said Tuckett.

"Oh no," said Candice quietly and somewhat unconvincingly. "He was just a handsome, carefree person who filled a void." Candice paused, trying to sound more believable by stating, "You were always..."

"He is kind of cocky, don't you think?" asked Tuckett.

"Yes, but...."

"Good God, when I was a second year resident I dare not say a word in the O.R., it just wasn't allowed."

"He has toned it down," said Candice. "The residency director must have come down hard on him. He has been quiet as a mouse."

"I agree," said Tuckett. "But a kid like that will only toe the company line for a short period of time before he pops off again. Let's see if he makes it seven more weeks."

"It's a tough situation for all of us," said Candice. "Let's be honest with ourselves Ian. I mean the young man has feelings too."

The orthopedic surgeon spoke no more as he slowly finished his drink, continuing to stare out the window. The couple then went to bed with Ian wondering about Anastasia, and Candice dreaming of Jackie.

The following Saturday morning found them heading west towards Pennsylvania, inside Tuckett's new Porsche. It was the latest model, capable of speeds beyond safe. The hum of the engine felt good to Candice as she stared out towards the mountainside. They were passing through the Delaware Water Gap, halfway home.

"How does the new vehicle ride?" asked Tuckett, proud of his new toy.

"It's certainly doing something for me," said Candy Apple. "How can you tell which car in the parking lot belongs to an Orthopedic Surgeon?"

"Don't know."

"It's the Porsche with the comic books in the back," said the nurse with a smile.

Tuckett burst out laughing, fully aware of the perception that Orthopedic Surgeons were perceived as having more brawn than brains.

"How many nurses does it take to screw in a light bulb?" asked Tuckett.

"Tell me."

"None, they have the nursing assistant do it," said Tuckett with a laugh.

"Very nice," said Candice. "How do you save a doctor from drowning?" She paused, but there was no response from the driver. "You take your foot off his head."

Laughter again filled the vehicle as it sped home, to a place where both occupants were important. Sophomoric hijinks continued as Candice realized the enigma that rode beside her. Ian Tuckett was a skilled surgeon, world renowned, who practiced his trade to the tune of classical music. Yet outside the medical realm he was an average Joe, at times acting like a teenage skirt chaser. Somehow, in an odd way, it worked perfectly. In short time the Porsche was roaring down the mountainside into the Valley. Candice was dropped off at her apartment, and Ian raced home.

Ian Tuckett's apartment was modest and befitting a man who lacked any semblance of interior design. Despite his wealth and intelligence, the apartment was similar to that of a graduate student on a university campus, comfortable yet lacking any hint of excess. Tuckett lived there since the split with Anastasia, allowing the confines to serve his basic needs for food and shelter. Upon entering the apartment he was slightly startled by Dr. Lee, sitting rigid in a chair, which he had just polished clean. It was not uncommon for Dr. Lee to appear unannounced at all hours of the day to discuss yet another matter of "extreme importance." Tuckett knew well that Lee's world was one of strict order and immediacy, two traits that rarely affected his own actions.

"We have problems," said Lee in his characteristic nasal tone. His body didn't move a muscle. Tuckett thought he must have been sitting on the chair for hours in wait.

"The world is full of problems Aran, we have solved a lot of them, haven't we?"

"Crackstone is pushing the envelope on the suicide investigation."

"Tony is just doing his job, don't forget there was a corpse found at the bottom of the ravine."

"I've provided him with two sworn statements already, as has my staff," said Lee. "I also provided him with all of the security video surrounding my home, which basically takes him two miles away from the front gate."

"Then it shouldn't be a problem," said Tuckett. "Trust me, Tony is a trusted friend of mine, if he had any major concerns he would come directly to my front door, and I haven't seen him since his last office visit."

"He has been keeping in touch with your former resident, Dr. Drummer, which is another concern of mine," said Lee, now getting up and pacing the room. "You are aware that Anastasia visited Drummer just prior to her departure from the valley."

"Yes, I remember you telling me that," said Tuckett as he slumped his body upon a couch. He then kicked his shoes off and rested his feet upon a pillow. A sharp ache in his back reminded him of nurse Adams. "Probably a hospital medical staff concern of some nature with the resident."

"Ian, your wife has vanished, an AMG employee has committed suicide and a detective, who we both know very well, continues to ask questions."

"Let him ask," said Tuckett. "Tony and I went to high school together, our fathers were best friends, for goodness sake we both dated the same cheerleader in high school. Stop worrying."

"Why did you log into your computer the night before Anastasia left the valley?"

"What are you talking about?" asked Tuckett.

"Remember when you came back from San Diego, I asked why you logged into your computer in the middle of the night?"

"No," said Tuckett who then reached for the TV's remote controller.

"Ian did Anastasia spend the night here? The night prior to her departure for the west coast?"

"Sure, she may have. I can't remember," said Tuckett. "But you know that we occasionally got back together. She was an emotionally needy woman." He turned on the television saying, "What's the big deal?"

"I'm very concerned she disclosed confidential material regarding the Tuckett Institute to Dr. Drummer," said Lee. "Just prior to her departure. And that is another major problem of mine."

"Aran I'm exhausted," said Tuckett. "You are the detail man of the operation, just take care of the details like you always do. I replace the hips and pamper the VIPs, and you take care of the rest."

"I'm not sure it's so simple," said Lee. "We are dealing with a resident from a medical institution, we have to proceed carefully here."

Dr. Tuckett then concentrated on the sports show blaring from the television, with the blonde anchor smiling at him. Lee continued to pace the room in a slow fashion. They were acting out a scene that had been acted out a hundred times before, with Lee playing the heavy and Tuckett playing the fool.

"I arranged an impromptu meeting with Dr. Drummer last night, as he exited the hospital," said Dr. Lee. He waited for a reply, but there was none. "To be blunt I told him that Anastasia had some emotional problems, magnified by alcoholism."

"Nice."

"I asked that he be careful regarding any conversations that he may have had with her, since she was not in her right mind."

"You have a way with words."

"He seemed reasonable, stating she did speak to him and the conversation was benign with regards to content," said Lee. "I stressed the need for tact and caution, especially in light of her death. He stated that he notified the authorities of his conversation, and his role in the whole matter was over."

"Case closed," said Tuckett. "See, you always worry about nothing."

"Ten minutes after my conversation he sent a text message to Detective Crackstone," said Lee sharply. "Case not closed."

"What's the big deal?" said Tuckett, now annoyed. "And how do you know he sent a text?"

"I have my friends," said Lee. "Drummer cannot be trusted."

"What about his partner, Dr. Rhimes?" asked Tuckett. "That's more of a concern to me. We have seven more weeks with him, what's your opinion on that keg of dynamite?"

There was no answer as Dr. Lee stewed on the Phil Drummer issue. His goon squad secured the flash drive from Drummer's apartment, but he was unsure as to whether or not Drummer had viewed the information regarding Mr. Banks. He had no way to know if Drummer passed on the information to the authorities. As he stared at Tuckett, he knew his associate's insatiable libido was the reason for the current predicament, which was now threatening the grand plan, which was so near to completion.

"The senator informed me he will be making a run for the presidency in three years," said Lee. "He is expecting our full financial backing."

"Great, book the Lincoln bedroom for me and Candy."

"We are going to have to prime the pump for the funds," said Lee.

"Can you imagine if he wins?" said Tuckett. "I'll be the surgeon general and you will be the goddamn ambassador to whatever country you choose."

"He is going to want a ton of cash," said Lee. "We need to do our part."

"Agreed," said Tuckett as he stared at the sports anchor, wondering if she was from the New York metropolitan area. "You're the brains behind the cash flow, I fully trust your ability to generate cash funds. You have my complete backing, get the senator his cash."

"Switzerland," said Dr. Lee. "That's would be my top choice for an ambassador position."

"Why?"

"It's an orderly country, with a banking system that we both love."

"Brazil," said Tuckett. "Rio to be exact. That's where the most beautiful women in the world live."

Both men paused as the sportscaster babbled on about a professional basketball player's legacy being besmirched by the recent tweet of another player, long retired.

"Ian, part of the senator's campaign platform will be an attempt to move National Health Care a bit to the right," said Lee.

"I think I know this broadcaster," said Tuckett. "Her kids may have gone to Montessori school with mine. She still looks great."

"I have some big news for you," said Lee proudly.

"I wonder is she is still married, her husband was a jerk."

"Ian, the senator wants to make his national announcement regarding his candidacy for the president here in the valley, at the Tuckett Institute itself," said Lee.

"What!" screamed Tuckett as he elevated off the couch. "Are you kidding me? Don't be messing with me Aran."

"His staff called me this morning. It's official, I agreed to it," said Lee with an excitement that almost levitated his petite body. "I assumed you would agree to such a joint venture."

"Yes, yes, yes!" said Tuckett. "Oh my God, imagine the press that we will get! When, when will it occur?"

"Three weeks from this Friday," said Lee. "He wants the nation talking about it all weekend."

"In your face New York," said Tuckett with a high five to his longtime friend. "In your face!"

"I did agree to two conditions regarding the announcement," said Lee in a somewhat pensive tone.

"Yes?"

"One. We back him with an initial donation of two million dollars for the chosen venue."

"Ouch," said Tuckett with only a moment of hesitation that followed. "But it will pay itself back tenfold, so go ahead."

"Two. We perform a hip replacement on his good friend Harry Street, who has been shopping around for a surgeon."

"Don't know him, but add him on the schedule," said Tuckett. "Easy request to carry out."

"Ian, Harold P. Street is the current co-chairman of the United States Federal Reserve, he is one of the most powerful men in the nation."

"Great," said Tuckett, "Another feather in the Institute's hat."

"He wants the surgery done the Friday morning of his announcement, so he could be in town to see his friend through it."

"No problem," said Tuckett. "Just clear the entire day for him, one surgery and then onto the gala announcement that evening. Get Ms. Reyes to coordinate it, she will make it a world-class event. I can't believe it."

"So you agree?" asked Lee. "To the donation and surgery."

"Absolutely! Do we have two million to spare?"

"Not exactly, but I believe we will shortly," responded Lee with a smile.

Ian Tuckett slept well that evening, knowing the Tuckett Orthopedic Institute, his namesake Center of Excellence, would be the focus of national attention in several weeks. In the process, the New York establishment would realize what an all-star they exiled. An all-star that was molding national health care as it pertained to orthopedics. If only Anastasia were here he thought, while drifting asleep. Certainly she would have enjoyed this crowning achievement.

Sleep however did not come easy to Dr. Lee. Nervous energy surged through his body. Too many pots were on the stove and they were all coming to a boil. Tony Crackstone was pushing forward with his investigation. AMG's chief financial officer was pressing for a meeting regarding the Tuckett Cup and its purchasing process. A United States Senator with a perverse id was announcing his candidacy for the Presidency of the United States at the Institute. Last but not least, the Co-Chairman of the Federal Reserve was soon to drop out of the sky, into his lap, like manna from heaven. Certainly he thought, this would be the last time, the very last time. His calculating mind then began to slowly churn through every detail of the upcoming event.

The following morning Tony Crackstone slowly lumbered into FBI headquarters in downtown Philadelphia. A traffic jam on the Schuylkill Expressway kept him corkscrewed in his import sedan for much too long a time. He met with two FBI officials with expertise in computer analysis, who informed him that a real pro had erased all the data from John Olson's laptop computer. Crackstone was now convinced that foul play was involved in the death of the Midwesterner. He was then notified that the scrapes of skin found on the road fifteen feet from the guardrail matched the DNA from Olson.

"You have a murder on your hands," said senior agent Flood from Philadelphia. "We are standing by to assist."

"Thanks," said Crackstone with a sad nod of his head, realizing that his friendship with Dr. Lee and Tuckett was about to be tested. "I'll keep it local for now, but I appreciate the offer."

Handshakes were exchanged, and Crackstone headed towards the exit.

"Oh Tony, one more thing," said the senior agent. "I almost forgot."

Crackstone turned towards the elderly officer while still trying to digest the information at hand. "Yes?"

"Security informed me that you set off a third level alarm when entering the building, which apparently is an uncommon event."

"Third level?" asked Crackstone. "Help me out."

"It's a scanner beyond the obligatory metal detectors in the entrance of the compound, apparently more sensitive then the older units. Beyond that don't ask me anymore about it, technology has long passed me by."

"Must be my hip replacement," said Crackstone. "It set off the first scanner. Usually does at an airport also. Made out of titanium."

"I'm sure it was," said the FBI agent, "Security is however asking that you exit out through the scanning room, just to be sure."

"No problem," said Crackstone with a smile, "Just call me the bionic man."

Anthony Crackstone exited through the entrance scan room, confident that his metal implant was the source of the alarm. During his long trek home the detective's mind was occupied with the facts surrounding the murder of John Olson. His thought process kept coming back to two points: COO Barry Reynolds and his role in setting up Olson's dinner at the estate; Mr. Banks and the information that Phil Drummer recalled regarding the McCoy Deal. Some pieces of a peculiar puzzle were starting to appear, yet none interlocked. Fortunately the three-hour ride home offered plenty of opportunity for the detective to try and connect the dots. During this time, Crackstone was completely unaware of the flurry of activity amid the security gurus back in Philadelphia, who were bemused by the data collected from his very body.

CHAPTER TWENTY

HURRICANE JENNA

THE EMAIL SAT in Jennifer's junk mail for three days, compliments of a spam program she purchased through her internet provider. It was only when she was searching for an erroneously deleted email, did she stumble upon the message entitled "Jennifer–Check Out What Dr. Drummer is Doing." The catchy title caused her to click open the message, which immediately brought up images of Phil and Kendra together. The majority of photos involved Phil and Kendra running throughout the valley, and occasionally walking along the hospital grounds. One photo was a night time shot of them walking out of Cell Block B arm in arm, with Kendra wearing a tight pink skirt, white halter top and black high heel shoes. It wasn't the togetherness that bothered Jennifer, rather the happiness in their faces that stirred a combination of hurt and anger inside her. From the moment she met Kendra, she knew her proximity to Phil would be a problem, along with her athletic beauty. Jennifer's mind raced as she scanned to the bottom of the email, which read–"Have the good doctor mind his business, or more photos will come – a concerned neighbor." Within the hour she was in a car barreling northwest to the valley. Her arrival time would be nearly one o'clock in the morning. No warning was given to Phil with regards to the tempest and her rapid approach.

That evening Phil was already in trouble while operating with Dr. Martha Brace, his esteemed attending surgeon. The case started out as a simple exploratory laparotomy of the abdomen in a healthy sixty nine year old, yet quickly evolved into a blood bath that involved the splenic artery. As the clock struck midnight Phil was holding pressure upon the artery, whose bleeding was unable to be controlled by Brace. At the head of the table was anesthesiologist Norm Carter, already two hours late for his first Manhattan of the night.

"I think we should hang some blood," said Norm in a slow drone, with his trademark surgical mask not covering his nose. "Her pressure is kind of low."

"I should have been anything but a doctor," said Brace. "When is Eddie getting here?"

"We called him twenty minutes ago," said surgical nurse Nikki Bryant. "Maybe we should type and cross some blood?"

"Go ahead," said Brace in a slow trance like tone, "Probably wouldn't hurt."

Phil stared at the attending that had majestically underwhelmed him during the past month. Dr. Brace was his first experience with an incompetent community surgeon, who somehow still managed to attract patients as a treating physician. This was by far the biggest case she had recently attempted, with the patient being an old high school teacher who trusted her completely. Brace was in a dysfunctional state, staring down into an abdomen full of fecal matter and blood, waiting for her colleague to arrive.

"Hang two units of blood," said Phil. "Stat."

"I agree," said Doc Carter. "Her systolic is really low, about sixty."

Just then the door burst open followed by a tremendous sigh of collective relief. Fast Eddie O'Neil arrived with Rick Polk, whom he picked up on the ride into the hospital.

"Martha, what the hell is going on?" yelled O'Neil as he quickly stepped up to peer into the wound. "You shouldn't be doing these cases so late!"

"Exploratory lap, some free air on x-ray," said Brace. "An emergency, she is my old home room teacher. The family requested me."

"Norm, what's the pressure?" asked O'Neil as he peered up at the monitors.

"Sixty over thirty," said the old anesthesiologist.

"Holy crap!" shouted O'Neil, "She is going to code soon."

"I thought the perforation was along the descending colon," said Brace, "I started a careful dissection towards…"

"Norm for god's sake open up all the fluids wide and give her some pressors," screamed O'Neil. "Call the lab, two units of packed red blood cells, STAT!" O'Neil then spun towards the scrub sink area and yelled at the circulating nurse, "Susan, hook up another suction canister and open my vascular set."

O'Neil ran out the door with Polk following and within twenty seconds they both returned with water dripping from their hands. Nurse Bryant rapidly gowned and gloved the duo and within two minutes Dr. Brace's role was mitigated to that of spectator.

"Let go of your pressure," said Fast Eddie to Phil, upon which a surge of blood roared up towards the team. "Get the suctions down in there boys," said O'Neil to Phil and Polk who responded immediately. "Large hemostat times two," yelled the surgeon over the loud, sickening sucking sound emanating from the bloody field. Then with a level of skill and agility befitting his name, Dr. Edward O'Neil expertly identified the bleeding artery and cross-clamped it, much to the relief of the surgical team. The frightening pulsations of bright red blood ceased immediately, as did the noise from the suction system.

"Got it," said O'Neil. "Got it."

"Amen," said Norm.

"What was it?" asked Brace.

"The splenic artery Martha, what the hell were you doing near the splenic artery?"

"Maybe that was the source of her pain, a spontaneous bleed," mumbled Dr. Brace.

"No, it wasn't," said O'Neil who now was rapidly inspecting the patient's bowels. "Here is the source, a ruptured diverticular abscess." O'Neil just lifted his head and stared at his colleague. "Please Martha, call me in at the beginning of the case, it's better for everyone involved. Please we have had this discussion before."

"I just thought…"

"Let's do the splenectomy first, followed by a temporary colostomy," said O'Neil to nurse Bryant. He then looked up at the circulating nurse while saying, "Get an ICU bed set up, have the hospitalist running the show tonight call into the room ASAP. Norm, what's the pressure?"

"Ninety over sixty and rising."

"Great, keep the fluids wide open and hang the blood the moment it arrives." The patient stabilized and within an hour, the case was completed.

After the case the male surgical team spent a few moments together in the O.R. lockers. Like most old time physicians, Norm Carter always showered before leaving the hospital facility, a safety measure that predated modern antibiotics. As he stood facing his locker he took a white towel off from around his waist while speaking, allowing the sag of his torso to visibly shock the audience.

"Norm, for God's sake cover up your Johnson," said O'Neil. "There are children around."

"I got an invite to some Senator's announcement at the Institute," said Carter as he applied some crusty white deodorant to his hairy armpit area. "Open bar I hope."

"Rumor has it he's going to announce a run for the presidency," said O'Neil. "Only hearsay, but I've got it from a reliable source."

"His son is the fellow spending a year with Dr. Tuckett," said Phil in a fatigued tone.

"The Tuckett Institute never ceases to amaze me," added Carter as he turned directly towards the group, allowing a direct visual of his seventy- year old frame. He stuck an index finger down his right ear canal and jiggled it violently, attempting to clear some water from his eardrum. "Say what you want about them but they just continue to plow forward, leaving everyone else behind. Amazing."

"Norm, cover up," said O'Neil as he turned away from the veteran anesthesiologist. "You're going to give me nightmares."

"How do they do it?" asked Norm with a shake of his head. He then slowly stepped into some faded white underwear, one bony leg after another, much to the relief of his counterparts.

"Not legally," said Eddie. "I don't care how hard they work or how many cups they sell. There have to be powerful entities and forces lurking in the background of that center."

Phil again kept quiet but Polk did not.

"Jackie Rhimes is going to get to the bottom of it. He told me so," said Polk. "Said something about him being the truth serum."

"That kid has got some bluster," said O'Neil. "Good set of hands too."

Phil cringed knowing full well that Jack's attitude would not fly in the Tuckett Institute. He was surprised things were going well up until that point.

"Do you think he will want a donation?" asked Norm. "You know, the Senator."

O'Neil burst into laughter, "Norm, you're a Republican, don't be silly, save your quarters." He then slapped the anesthesiologist on the back and headed to the exit. "Need a ride boys?"

The residents declined, preferring a walk home with some fresh air. Within minutes they exited the hospital onto the street. It was two o'clock in the morning and they took their usual route through the sleepy neighborhood surrounding the hospital. All was quiet.

"What's up Phil?" asked Polk about one block away from the hospital. "You're not yourself."

Phil shook his head in agreement while inhaling some cool autumn air. "Too much going on," said Phil, realizing that he could not fill Polk in on all the details surrounding Anastasia. "How did things get so complicated so fast?"

"Kendra versus Jenna?" asked Polk.

"Exactly, Kendra versus Jenna."

"Sounds like a pay for view event on closed circuit TV."

"What am I going to do Rick?"

"Go with your heart," said Polk while looking straight ahead. "If you go with your heart, no matter what the outcome, you will have peace of mind." One minute passed until Polk spoke again asking, "What does your heart say?"

"I think Jenna," said Phil. "But at times when Kendra is around me I just can't think straight."

Just then the duo heard a metallic crash behind a fence just ahead of them and slightly to the right. A beam of light then flashed quickly between two garages. The sound suggested to both physicians that a person had fallen over an object nearby. Phil then peered backwards and noticed a slow approaching vehicle, with its lights off. A dog began barking inside an adjacent home.

An inbred Philadelphia instinct prompted both men to break out into a sprint, initially forward and then across the street. Phil sensed a body rapidly moving towards them from the direction of the metallic rumble. The car behind them accelerated loudly in a forward attempt to close the gap. Polk lagged behind Phil, and stumbled over a tree root as the duo made it to the other side of the street, causing him to fall upon the ground. Phil turned to help his colleague and immediately saw a sturdy male, dressed in black darting between two parked cars directly towards him. The street lamp above gave Phil a brief look at the assailant's face, which then disappeared from sight as he tripped over the fallen frame of Polk. A thud signified the aggressor's head hitting the base of the metallic lamppost, temporarily disabling his plan. Polk was able to upright his body and the duo continued their sprint forward towards the side street's intersection with Main Street. Upon approaching the intersection the vehicle from behind pulled even with the pair, causing them to dash to the left across a darkened yard, behind a house on the intersection corner. They briefly paused, short of breath, in the darkness of the night. The automobile then accelerated with a screech, turning right on Main Street and disappearing from sight. Without haste the junior residents found their way down a driveway onto the main thoroughfare, and sprinted to the left towards Cell Block B.

"What the hell?" yelled Polk slamming the apartment door behind him, blood oozed from an abrasion across his left forearm.

Phil was unable to speak, winded and bent forward, with his hands on top his knees. A quick look forward spotted Jackie sitting on the couch with a computer on his lap.

"What happened?" asked Jackie.

"We were mugged," yelled Polk. "Mugged in Hicksville, USA."

"What are you talking about?" said an approaching Jackie. "Mugged?"

Phil proceeded to recount the event to the astonished Jackie Rhimes. During the discussion Rick Polk took his own pulse and stumbled over to the couch, where he collapsed. Phil and Jackie sat upon adjacent chairs as the description continued.

"Sounds like a coordinated attack," said Jackie.

"What's come of this world?" asked Polk. "Neither one of us has a dime on our body."

Phil didn't speak as a sense of doom overtook his thought process. He knew the attack was a result of his involvement with Anastasia. Suddenly the door to his bedroom slammed, causing both he and Polk to leap upwards in alarm.

"Oh I forgot," said Jack. "Your filly is here, in your room."

"What? When did she get here?" asked Phil.

"Scared the hell out of me," said Polk.

"About an hour ago," said Jack, now turning his attention back to the computer. "Said she needed to talk to you like ASAP, something urgent."

Phil stood up and began walking towards his room, wondering what Kendra could possible want at this hour. His jumbled mind did not allow him to make any further sense as to why she was there.

"K-E-N-D-R-A," spelled Polk, "The poor soul."

Rhimes looked up with a smirk directly at Rick, and then paused for effect before saying, " Wrong my dear friend. J-E-N-N-A."

Rick Polk's eyes suddenly grew large as he then hunkered down with his roommate, in anticipation of the storm front's initial blow.

Phil turned the corner into his room and was shocked to see Jennifer sitting in a chair, her arms folded across her chest. She stared directly at Phil, yet did not say a word. He then noticed the absence of their photograph together on his nightstand, a sobering reminder of the afternoon spent with Kendra. Fatigue was upon Jennifer's beautiful face, coupled with a tear in her left eye. She wore a pair of old jeans and a tee shirt that suggested a hasty departure from Philadelphia. The entire apartment was now eerily quiet as the young physician fumbled for words.

"Jenna, what are you doing here?" asked Phil as he approached his girlfriend. "Did something happen?"

Then, without warning, Phil was rendered useless by the dreaded line that all males experience at least once in their life. Four simple words, that when strung together immediately cripple a man's Y-chromosome. A lethal dictum for which there is no known antidote. An adage that despite feminine overuse is somehow never cliché.

"We need to talk," said Jenna in a tone that no known adjective could describe.

Psychological paralysis was immediate.

What followed was a two-hour beat down hurled upon Phil by the woman he loved. A woman who conducted a fiery inquisition that expertly weaved a myriad of emotional issues into a common theme – the theme of trust. Phil offered hapless responses to moral questions centered upon commitment and devotion. The precipitous onslaught brought about his full and unadulterated confession of perfidy at exactly the two-hour mark of the interrogation. Full disclosure then generated a putrid combination of tears, anger and profanity, followed by the sentencing phase of his arraignment. As the sun rose above the horizon a miracle occurred, in so much that the death sentence was avoided. However, the defendant was harshly sentenced to immediate physical and social excommunication from the plaintiff, via a restraining order laden with guilt. Judge Jennifer then stormed away from the apartment complex to return to Philadelphia. On her way out she threw the nightstand picture of herself and Phil into a nearby garbage can.

CHAPTER TWENTY ONE

THE LAND LINE

EXCITEMENT WAS BUILDING at the Tuckett Institute for the big announcement and no one exhibited that more than Emily Reyes. Drs. Tuckett and Lee placed her in charge of preparations for the national event, now one week away. The speech was scheduled to take place in the elegant lobby of the Tuckett Institute, modeled after the Roman Pantheon and designed by the gods of the Tuckett Institute themselves. The large inner lobby rotunda had seating capacity for five hundred people, and frequently served as a lecture hall for Dr. Tuckett when he hosted medical conferences. The senator's staff scheduled a thirty-minute speech to begin at exactly 4 P.M., followed by a gala dinner reception at the Brookside Country Club. Ms. Reyes was instructed to spare no expense for both events. That Friday morning she was working with Mrs. Dorothy Reynolds, who volunteered her services for the event, together with the marketing gurus from AMG in Kansas City. A generous monetary donation to the Tuckett Institute allowed the AMG banner to be hung just behind the right shoulder of the Senator, adjacent to the majestic TOI symbol, which commanded the center slot.

"He is so handsome," said Mrs. Reynolds as she stared up at a large photograph of the senator that hung from one of the balcony rails.

"I agree," said Emily. "I've met him twice and he has natural charm and charisma. The soccer moms will put him in the White House."

"A real family man from I understand," said Mrs. Reynolds. "His wife is beautiful and they have three handsome boys."

The two women continued to carefully place a red, white and blue banner around the brim of the stage that would hoist the Senator to fame. Behind them toiled a lighting and AV team concentrating on the brightness and acoustics of the chamber. James and Madison, the omnipresent lobby attendants, escorted a squad of florists around the stage while requesting massive bouquets of fresh cut flowers.

Seating on stage was set to accommodate fifty VIP guests. Rumors swirled as to the expected dignitaries planning to attend the event and included several Hollywood personalities. Senator Stortz's platform was anchored by many themes, one being a cautious pullback of government involvement in national healthcare. As a Democrat the Senator was quite aware of his need to march to the national healthcare drumbeat. Massive voting blocks mandated his dance to the left in this regards. Yet his consultants assured him of the fiscal catastrophe associated with a bureaucratic health care system, prompting him to allow some wiggle room in the network. This in turn opened the door to massive amounts of cash from insurance companies and health care system lobbyists. The fine line that the Senator walked was a win-win situation, and what better place to garner more cash from hospitals and physician networks than the Tuckett Institute, the East Coast paragon of cutting edge medical care.

"You do know his son is spending a year here at the Institute," said Ms. Reyes.

"No I did not," said Mrs. Reynolds. "My husband doesn't talk much business when he is home. Is he as handsome as his father?"

"Yes he is, a tall and very polite young man. Good surgeon from what I hear."

"Like father, like son," said Mrs. Reynolds who was thoroughly enjoying her time that day with Ms. Reyes. "I am looking forward to meeting the Senator and his family at the Brookside dinner. For once I won't mind going to a hospital function."

"Dorothy, does your husband enjoy his work?" asked Reyes. "He always seems so happy." Emily appreciated the fact the Dorothy Reynolds was at least ten years younger than her spouse, being more attractive than one would expect in comparison to her drab husband.

"Yes and no," said Mrs. Reynolds. "It doesn't take much to make him happy, but the constant pressure from Kansas City can take a toll on anyone. Even me."

"Do you like it here in the valley?"

"No," was the rapid response. "I mean we love the people here but we are Midwesterners, who belong back in the Midwest. Hopefully after our last son heads to college we can return home," said Reynolds. "Are you from the valley?"

"No," said Emily Reyes with a smile. "No I am not."

"Where do you call home?"

"That's difficult to answer since my father was a European businessman who lived in seventeen countries throughout his career." Reyes then paused as if to further measure her answer. "I've traveled all over the world during that time."

"Where were you born?"

"Again, difficult to say. My mother was traveling between Switzerland and Italy when she went into labor. My dad always said I was born in a hospital right on the border, kind of family folklore."

"Are your parents still alive?"

"My mom is," said Emily. "Dad passed away five years ago. She spends winters in Florida and summers in Europe."

"How did you end up here?" asked Reynolds.

"Well it all happened when my dad was on business in....."

"Ladies, ladies we need your help," cried out James as he helped position an urn full of planted roses on the corner of the stage. "Do you think red or white roses accent the Senator's attire? Remember he will be wearing a fuchsia tie that is almost baby pink, along with a deep navy suit. I say white but Madison thinks red."

The beautification committee then spent ten minutes debating the question, with white roses decided upon.

Several floors above the lobby and floral preparations, Franklin Stortz was being escorted out of the operating room. He had just cut his left hand with a scalpel; a self-inflicted wound that instantly made Stortz a blood relative of the unsuspecting patient on the table. Even the watchful eye of Dr. Tuckett couldn't prevent the ineptness of the fellow from generating an intraoperative event. Stortz was being ushered to the emergency room over at St. Mike's to be seen by a plastic surgeon. There was a concern that he may have lacerated a sensory nerve on his index finger.

"He is a one man wrecking crew," said Tuckett in disgust. "There is no way he is going to scrub in next week for the VIP case. No way!"

"He is under our charge for the next nine months," said Dr. Lee. "Just be happy he didn't cut one of your fingers off."

"It's exhausting to just be around him," said scrub nurse Adams.

"Cut the chief a break," chimed in Jackie Rhimes, who always championed the underdog. "He is trying his best. He is here to learn."

Before anyone could respond to Rhimes' comment the operating door opened and in walked the head of anesthesia, Jerome Floret. Dr. Floret was hand picked by Tuckett years ago to anchor his anesthesia team and was the best in the business. Tuckett implicitly trusted his expertise, aware that the well-being of his patients rested in his knowledge base.

"Gentlemen," said Dr. Floret, "I've just reviewed all the pre-operative labs on Mr. Harold Street."

"And…" said Tuckett as he was starting to finish up the total hip replacement before him.

"He is a high risk surgical candidate. In my professional opinion his case needs to be done in the hospital proper, followed by a night on a monitored floor."

"Absolutely not!" said Dr. Lee. "Not after our last visit to that mad house across the street."

"Jerry, Jerry please," added Tuckett. "I'm just so comfortable doing the case here. "

"No." said the anesthesiologist sharply. "He needs a monitored bed postop, maybe the ICU to be safe, especially with his national profile. We don't want a medical disaster on our hands."

"No," said Lee with a slight stomp of his polished shoes upon the ground. "Not an option. The case will be done here, at the Institute where Mr. Street wants it done."

"Listen Aran," said Floret. "Mr. Street is a cardiac train wreck with three arterial stents and an ejection fraction of forty five percent. We can do him here and then wheel him across the street in a hospital bed if you like, but that might look bad for the camera crews."

"No chance at all Jerry?" asked Tuckett. "Not even if we create our own little ICU here?"

"No chance, at least not with my name on the chart."

Silence gripped the room as Dr. Lee stared at Tuckett, waiting for a firm response to reverse the medical recommendation.

"O.K." said Tuckett. "Under one condition."

"What?" asked Floret.

"I want Norm Carter to do the case. You're fired."

Dr. Floret broke out into laughter saying, "Don't worry my good friend, I will be at the head of the table. After all we have been through, this is our Super Bowl together."

"It's a deal," said Tuckett, laughing with a quick glance at nurse Adams, unaware that Dr. Lee stormed out of the room behind him, never to be seen for the rest of the case. "Jerry, please call COO Reynolds to arrange a VIP room with all the trimmings, tell him the Senator requested we use the great Saint Michael's hospital."

"Will do," said the anesthesiologist as he left the room.

"Aran, Aran? Where did Aran go?" asked Tuckett while looking behind himself. He then just shook his head and returned to the task at hand while saying, "What's best for the patient. Remember, always do what is best for the patient."

Tuckett completed the surgical procedure over the next thirty minutes, his speed accelerated by an afternoon tee time at Brookside's North Course. During this time he failed to perceive the coy eye contact between his scrub nurse and the chiseled resident opposite the table.

Later that night a fatigued Tony Crackstone drove back into the innards of Pennsylvania, after a full day in New York City. He hated New York with a passion, however Mr. Banks' schedule demanded his personal appearance in the city. Crackstone's interview occurred with Mr. Banks' corporate and personal attorneys present, and lasted three hours. An in depth discussion occurred regarding the McCoy detail and the absolute secrecy of the transaction itself. Only Banks and two trusted colleagues knew of the deal, which involved a cash and stock buy out of a upstart company that promised to hold the cure for adolescent acne. Immediately after the deal their firm received a notice from the Security and Exchange Commission regarding a large stock purchase of the start up, just days before public notice of the arrangement. Mr. Banks was actually relieved to hear that some breach of his text messages had occurred, thus providing him with an explanation for the perceived insider trade. What concerned Banks and his legal team, was how his text messages were compromised and the timing of the theft, occurring between his hip replacement surgery and subsequent postoperative visit to the VIP room. Lastly a detailed conversation occurred regarding Mr. Banks' infected hip replacement and need for the complete removal of all metal components from his body. Upon completion of the meeting, all parties had more questions than answers, with promises to keep in close contact regarding the investigation. Banks was not made privy to matters regarding Anastasia Tuckett and John Olson.

Crackstone's mind was racing as he traveled the highway leading into the valley. On his hands were a murder, a missing person and theft of personal data that apparently led to a lucrative stock purchase. At the center of the matter was his close and trusted friend, one who replaced his own arthritic hip a year ago. Fatigue muddled his thought process as he pulled into the driveway. "Ian, what the hell is going on?" thought the detective as he entered the dark confines of his home.

Upon turning on the kitchen light he tossed his keys atop the table and flipped through some mail. While walking in search of the television remote he noticed the message light blinking on his answering machine, a relic that adults of his generation still maintained. The first message was from a telemarketer. The second was from Detective Flood, the FBI agent whom he had met with to discuss the Olson affair in Philadelphia. Flood's message was short and to the point, asking him to immediately return his call with the specific instructions to use a land line as opposed to his cell phone. Detective Crackstone immediately responded to the strange request, it was eleven thirty in the evening.

"Thanks for calling," said David Flood on the other end of the line. "Are you on a land line?"

"Yea I am," said Crackstone. "What's up?"

"Tony do you remember setting off the alarms during your last visit here in Philadelphia."

"Yea," said Crackstone as he walked over to a patio door and looked outside. "My hip replacement, remember."

"Of course I remember," said Flood. "That's what you and I thought, but people smarter than us have other ideas."

"Like what?" asked Crackstone. "Am I radioactive or something?"

"The local boys were confused so they sent your scan data down to Washington DC. To my understanding the info made it to a CIA lab and today some scientist from their department called back."

"Yea, and what's the concern," said Crackstone, now sitting down on a kitchen chair. A pitiful ache started to arise in his stomach. "What do you mean by some scientist?"

"Tony I'm going to be blunt," said Flood, "You have some sort of a radiofrequency device on body. Exactly where on your body I do not know."

"What!" said Crackstone as he stood upright.

"A device of some nature, a transmitter perhaps, something that is either receiving or sending data, or both. "

"What the hell are you talking about?" yelled Crackstone. "And what's it doing on my body?

"The boys in D.C think it is some sort of gizmo about the size of a grain of rice, that can gather information. I would call it some sort of technology chip."

"What type of information is being gathered?"

"A myriad of things, according to the pros," said Flood. "Like your whereabouts, what items you buy and use. When stored over time and interfaced with data from other chips it can basically track your every move."

"Are you kidding me?"

"That's what the boys in the lab say," said Flood. "Apparently this is nothing secret, the technology has been around for a while. It's just that the covert use of transmitter chips is now becoming a hot topic. Seems like the mainstream press has latched onto it being used by retail stores. They apparently have been putting them on merchandise bought by John Q. Public."

"Are you sure this radiofrequency device, or chip is on me, and not my clothes or shoes?"

"The D.C. gurus are not absolutely sure. It's either on you–or in you Tony. They want to run a few more tests to be definitive. Apparently a transmitter inside someone is not that uncommon in their line of work."

"Dave, you're freaking me out. I don't even know what a transmitter or radiofrequency chip is and you're calling it commonplace."

"Listen Tony take it easy. Get back down here as soon as you can for further testing," said Flood. "Once that is over we can be definite as to what type of chip it is and more importantly where is it."

"And how did it get there!" yelled Crackstone. "Dave, do you realize what you are telling me?" The detective thought of the three surgeries he had in his life including a hernia repair, hip replacement and appendix removal.

"Yes I do, remain calm. Do not, I repeat, do not do anything drastic or out of the ordinary," said Flood followed by a pause. "The experts did ask not to use your cell phone or send text messages that contain material of a private nature. Don't stop using your phone, but do take care as to the content of your communications."

"Why?"

"Apparently some of the newer technology chips can collect data from your personal airspace, such as phone conversations and text messages."

"Dave, someone is spying on me? Correct?"

"It appears so Tony, the question is who, and why?"

Crackstone wondered how long the reported chip was present. He immediately thought of thousands of text messages sent over the years to clients and confidents in regards to a multitude of private matters. His mind was unable to process the landslide of complications that would occur if such information would be made available for public consumption. His mentation froze while he stared at the cellphone sitting on the kitchen table. An eerie sense of violation overcame him.

"Tony are you still there?"

"Sorry. Yes, yes I am."

"Listen Tony, it appears things are getting a bit complex up there in the valley. How about I send up a few agents to help with the case, just for a week or two?"

"No, thank you David. Let me digest this info overnight and I will call you in the morning. Things are starting to crystalize and my staff is holding up well."

"Are you sure?"

"I'm sure Dave, besides this is my valley, and these are my people. I know how they think. I know each and every one of them, and their families. I'll be O.K."

"Roger, good night Tony. Call me immediately, on a land line, with any problems."

Sleep evaded Detective Crackstone that night as paranoia overtook his thought process. Someone was collecting data from his mortal being. The thought of his text messages being intercepted sent a chill down his spine. Most troublesome of all was the recall of multiple texts sent to Anastasia Tuckett just prior to her disappearance, in an attempt to shield her from perceived harm.

CHAPTER TWENTY TWO

PHIL AND JENNA

PHILLIP DRUMMER WAS at an all time personal low in his life. Problem number one was Jennifer and the expulsion from her world. Multiple phone calls to her cellphone went unanswered, as did a landslide of well-crafted emails and text messages expressing remorse. A return email from Skeeter Huckabee stated she moved out of the Greycliff apartment complex. The intern recalled her talking about some social worker friends who were going to help her get through some "hard times." Skeeter then tactfully notified Phil that a goldfish she gave him upon leaving expired under his watchful eye.

Second on the list was the middle of the night assault that Phil and Rick barely avoided. Phil was convinced that the incident dovetailed into Anastasia and the flash drive event. The morning after the near mugging Phil contacted Tony Crackstone in yet another attempt to step clear of the entire situation. The young assailant's face resonated in his mind, as did the fervor of his forward progress towards Phil that night.

Third was the horrible rotation that Phil was currently experiencing under the misdirection of Dr. Brace. Learning was not an option as Phil was constantly underwhelmed by her lack of guidance and expertise. The plodding surgeon exuded mediocrity that permeated everyone around her, along with a constant whine about the difficulties of the medical profession. More damaging was her part time presence at the hospital, which translated into too much free time for Phil, and directly led to the final problem of Kendra Mason.

Phil felt a deep physical and emotional attraction to Kendra, which triggered one additional soiree with the Philadelphia product, prior to his single count confession to Jennifer. The allure between them was undeniable, as was the inevitable forward progress of their relationship. Kendra felt like Jenna did a year ago, irresistible and energetic. Phil knew he was now in love with two women, both beautiful and both captivating. The problem was that he had to choose one, and only one. Kendra was the easy choice with her age and positive vibe. Jenna was the more complex option, one that would bare the element of trust over time. He looked to his right, fully expecting to see the picture of himself and Jenna on the nightstand, yet it remained barren.

While pondering his suddenly complex life the young physician knew that a phone call to his dad would allow him to somehow persevere the storm. Phil's father was his anchor in life, and always someone with sage advice. It was during the end of their conversation that he brought up the conundrum in a seemingly well-disguised manner.

"Dad, did you ever have to make a big decision in your life? A decision that involved a choice between two things you cared deeply about, realizing that the option not chosen would be lost forever?"

"Women problems Phil?"

"No, no Dad. I'm just asking a hypothetical question."

"Listen son, take my advice for what it is worth. Rule number one is to always go with your heart. I've told you that a hundred times before."

"I've got that one down dad. You're right, never fails."

"Rule number two is to take your time. There are few true emergencies in life, trust me. Just take your time and let it play out."

"What if I don't have time dad?"

"Phil, you have time on your side. When you're my age everything is crystal clear in retrospect. Just take your time. Practice patience. It's an art your generation has abandoned. Time is on your side and if your decision hypothetically involves a broken heart – remember that time is the greatest healer of all."

Phil's mind was immediately placed at ease. "Thanks dad, you're always a great help."

"No problem son. Glad I can help. Good talking to you as usual."

After the phone call Rick Polk entered Phil's room asking him to go out for a drink at a local bar. Stephanie and Kendra were tagging along, as was Jackie who appeared to be slowly coming out of his depression. Polk excitedly declared the evening a "Festivus" celebration, but Phil declined, opting to stay in and collect his thoughts. He then checked his phone and computer for any response from Jenna, which did not exist. Phil then attempted to practice the lost art of patience, while praying for the mental fortitude to carry out his father's advice.

That evening Jennifer was sulking in the apartment of Stacey Ricketts, her best friend from the hospital's Social Work department. Jennifer moved into Stacey's spare bedroom the night after Phil's admission of disloyalty, where she planned to remain for the indefinite future. She was stung bitterly by the confession of Phil, having not felt the bite of emotional betrayal since her collegiate days. Simply put, she could not accept the fact that Phil Drummer, her Phil Drummer jilted her. Her center of gravity was dislodged and she was emotionally adrift at sea.

"He's scum," said Stacey. "Like all men, they only have one thing on their mind." Stacey was eating out of an ice cream container while watching the season finale of a reality television series.

"I knew she was trouble the moment I laid eyes on her," said Jennifer. "She looked just so, so…. young. Even her name sounds sensual – Kendra."

"You're still the hottest girl in the city," said Stacey in defense of her girlfriend. "Forget about him. There are plenty of other creeps in the ocean."

"It's not that easy," said Jenna. "Not this time around. Maybe it's that biological clock I'm always reading about. Maybe it's some sort of nesting instinct. What's happening to me Stacey, am I getting old?"

"Listen girl, you and me this weekend, let's cut loose like the old days. We'll get all dolled up, drunk and carefree, that always generates a crowd around us, well at least around you."

"Maybe," said Jenna sadly. "Maybe."

"Oh my god!" screamed Stacey at the television set as it blared. "OMG! I can't believe Gary and Brittany won! It's rigged. Brian and Tanya were the bomb, they were my pick." Stacey immediately picked up her cell phone and started to rattle off a rapid series of text messages to her reality junkie friends. "No way, it's fixed!"

As Stacey hollered at the television set, Jennifer just stared blankly down at her cell phone. She wanted so badly to respond to one of Phil's text messages but she could not, certainly not after what he had done. Panic was in her mind, knowing that Phil was living just across the hall from Kendra, having already tasted the forbidden fruit. She moaned a deep and depressive sigh while getting up to head to her room.

"Good night Stacy, and thanks for listening."

"No problem," said Stacey as she stared at the television watching the highlights from her show's last season with a tear in her eye. "Poor Brian, he was so cute."

Jennifer collapsed on her bed and cried, as the pitiful pang of a breakup stirred inside her stomach. While listening to the sounds of the city outside her window she sadly turned to the right, towards her nightstand. There sat the photo of Phil and her on their first date, so happy in each other's presence. She reached over to grab the snapshot and brought it towards the front of her face, and continued sobbing softly. She cried herself to sleep that night alone on top of the sheets, with her clothes on. During the early morning hours a horrid dream occupied her mind, one that relived the Schuylkill Expressway crash involving Dr. Knight. As the out of control Porsche impacted the concrete median she awoke with a scream and reached to the left for the comfort of Phil, who was not there. She never felt more completely alone in her life, suddenly fearful of growing old without a soul mate. She stared at the ceiling until her alarm clock went off two hours later, wondering how she would make it through another day.

Jennifer boarded the Broad Street subway line earlier than usual that morning, from Allegheny station. Despite the early hour the subway was jammed with passengers bound for center city. During the trip Jenna reached into her leather satchel, which contained her lunch and various work papers. From the front of the satchel she pulled out a crinkled and heavily stapled six by nine inch manila envelope to inspect. She picked up the envelope yesterday afternoon on her way home, from the Philadelphia General Hospital mailroom. The postmaster informed her that the envelope was astray within the postal service secondary to a poorly written address. Apparently it took some time to make it to the PGH where it then sat for another week or two. Jennifer raised the envelope to inspect it, curious of its content.

The envelope was simply addressed to Jennifer and misspelled her last name as Raner. There was no street address below her name, but rather the words PGH, Philadelphia, PA. There was no zip code. The name and address were printed in a fashion that suggested haste, with a colored crayon similar to a child's prop at a restaurant. The return address in the upper left hand corner simply said "A. Tuckett." A single clasp held the contents closed along with a series of staples haphazardly aligned across the top flap. Crinkles throughout the manila hemp fibers suggested a rough ride through the postal system. There was no stamp on the package, but an emblazed "Postal Due" mark adorned the upper portion of the envelope. The upper right corner however did clarify the post office of origin, that being San Diego, Calfornia.

Jennifer turned the parcel over once again trying to make sense of a hand written warning, which was penned across the top flap sealing the packet. "Don't trust Crackstone" were the words written after the envelope was sealed, certainly as an afterthought. What it meant she had no idea. The urge to open the package addressed to her was strong, almost irrepressible. She had heard the name Crackstone from conversations with Phil, realizing that he was a lawman involved in the Anastasia Tuckett disappearance. It was obvious that the contents of the envelope represented evidence from a missing person, whom she had met once under surreal circumstances just three months ago. A combination of sorrow and anger prevented her from disclosing the matter to Phil. Respect for Anastasia and the legal process curbed her feline curiosity to open the envelope. Suddenly the illegible voice announcing the next subway stop crackled in staccato fashion overhead. Only native Philadelphians could decipher the lingo, alerting them that Suburban Station was approaching. Jennifer quickly stuffed the manila envelope back into her satchel and stood up, joining the packed mass of commuters planning to exit. As the subway doors opened she was bounced in pinball like fashion against the bodies of other travelers, and suddenly expelled outside the car onto the platform of Suburban Station. The strong smell of coffee and urine permeated the underground passage. Mindlessly she followed the throngs exiting the catacombs of the rail system, rapidly appearing above ground on JFK Boulevard. Skyscrapers from above hid any early morning sunlight, adding to the chill of the cool autumn morning.

Jennifer walked two blocks north into a Philadelphia Police Precinct where she was introduced to Special Agent Flood. Her phone call to the police the evening prior led to her contact with the agent. Jennifer handed over the package to the lawman while explaining how it came into her possession. Agent Flood thanked her for her prompt action in the matter. He then asked Jennifer if she ever had contact with Detective Crackstone. Her answer was no. Their meeting was brief but exact, allowing Jennifer to ambulate back to Suburban Station, where she boarded the Market-Frankford El train to West Philadelphia.

CHAPTER TWENTY THREE
An Evening in the Valley

It was a beautiful October evening in the valley, one that followed a most delightful autumn day. The lowlands were surrounded by mountains whose trees were painted with an array of harvest colors at their peak. The warm sun was setting over the western horizon as a flock of geese heading south adorned the sky, honking with joy. Local farmers were sheltering their tractors after reaping a bumper corn crop, destined for silos across the land. Organizers were finishing downtown preparations in anticipation of the annual weekend Harvest Festival, with forecasters promising bright blue skies. All was well in the valley, or so it seemed.

Over the past forty-eight hours an uninvited national attention had rudely disrupted the idyllic valley landscape. Upon hearing word of the Senator's speech, with presidential implications, a press corps from the nation's four corners descended upon the region like buzzards to road kill. Rural lanes suddenly became jammed with semis hauling satellite dishes. Hotels rapidly filled up denying weekend tourists their annual visit. Locals were uncharacteristically placed into the national spotlight with microphones thrust in front of their face, searching for opinion.

A few old timers recalled the last time such a event overtook the valley, back when Calvin Coolidge spent a hot presidential night downtown in route to his summer white house in the Black Hills of Dakota. The reticent President reportedly spoke to a crowd of three thousand locals after his breakfast, which lasted a total of two minutes and was heard by only those in the first twenty rows. The local newspaper photographer was unfortunately sleeping off an alcohol daze that morning and failed to make it in time for the speech, thus rendering the event to the aging memory of a few oral historians. Regardless, the thought of having a future president give a speech in the valley, their valley, was historic news to the local populace.

The invading press had multiple questions, but their most common inquiry regarded the Tuckett Orthopedic Institute, and why it was the setting of the Senator's speech. The outsiders soon discovered that there was no obvious answer, besides the fact that the Senator was attempting to move the National Health Care agenda a bit to the right. Frequent explanations however contained the "Center of Excellence" angle, which became a catch phrase for the weekend festivities.

"A Center of Excellence is a nationally recognized joint replacement center," said Tuckett to the television network camera facing him. "When a team of professionals performs the same operation over and over, the results are superior, both for the patient and for the health care dollar spent."

It was Tuckett's third and final interview for the day, and he was impressed with the stunning middle-aged woman conducting the dialogue. She was from the New York metropolitan area, which prompted Tuckett to add a little pizazz to his answers knowing quite well that the New York Orthopedic establishment was tuning in.

"Dr. Tuckett, as we wrap up the interview, do you have any advice for the many baby boomers listening in who are on the precipice of a joint replacement procedure?"

"Of course. Find a surgeon who you are comfortable with, and ask that surgeon to administer community accepted standards of care throughout your perioperative period," said Tuckett. "Do not over analyze the procedure and for goodness sakes, stay off the internet. Trust your doctor. We are all professionals."

"And try to get to a Center of Excellence?" asked the moderator.

"Trust your surgeon," said Tuckett emphatically. "And if he or she happens to be at a true Center of Excellence, then all the better."

"Thank you Dr. Tuckett. Thank you for your time and expertise."

Ian Tuckett was pleased with the interview. He retired to his apartment that evening content that his crown jewel would shine in the national spotlight the following day. Mr. Street's pending surgery didn't even register in his mind as he lay awake that night, thinking of Anastasia. If only she could be there tomorrow, to see the glory bestowed on the Tuckett Institute, their Institute, built upon years of hard work and commitment. If only she could be there.

Across town nurse Candice Adams sat on her balcony smoking a cigarette, also not worrying about tomorrow's surgery on Mr. Street. Her thoughts centered about the potential demise of her prima donna status at the Institute. She was in love with someone else, yet couldn't declare this openly, since it would announce her resignation from the coveted roost in Tuckett's hierarchy. Then, the despised Nikki Bryant would soar back into the nest, and she could never permit that. As the evening breeze slowly vented the nicotine laden carcinogenic potpourri from her lungs, she pondered a respectable way out of her current conundrum.

Meanwhile, unrest was the order of the evening at the home of Barry Reynolds. The COO of St. Mike's had absolutely no recollection of Mr. Street's pending surgery the following morning in his hospital, for he and his wife had just finished a hostile verbal exchange uncommon to the Midwestern genre. Dorothy Reynolds drew a line in the sand that evening, demanding to move back home within one calendar year, with or without her overworked husband. She verbally castrated her spouse with cries of anger that violated norms of decency, banishing him to the basement to smoke a cheap cigar and wonder what had gone wrong in his life to deserve such a lot.

Fast Eddie O'Neil was in St. Mike's hospital operating room that evening, helping out Martha Brace, who thankfully called him before she started a bowel case. The seventies music blared over the speakers as Dr. O'Neil expertly performed an anasto-mosis of the lower intestine, with a speed that seemingly defied the laws of physics. O'Neil was in his comfort zone, fully aware that for some surgeons, no better place existed on earth. He wasn't even cognizant of the room set up in the adjacent surgical suite, awaiting the VIP hip surgery the following morning. Neither surgeon missed anesthesiologist Norm Carter, who was relaxing at home working on his second Manhattan.

The Senator and his son were spending the night at the Lee estate. They had just enjoyed a seven-course meal, compliments of their host and a series of all-star chefs hired for the evening. Joining them was Mrs. Stortz, who fussed over the dress she had chosen for the big event. The Senator ran through his speech once more in front of the duo. Every detail of their next thirty-six hours had been mapped out to the minute, including Mrs. Stortz's rapid departure from the valley after the Brookside banquet, which would allow the Senator to tend to "mundane campaign matters with his strategists."

Nikki Bryant worked out like a woman possessed in her basement that evening, toning her body to fit the sleek black dress she picked out for the event. With sweat dripping down her face she looked into a mirror while drinking some water from a plastic bottle, noticing how tight her buttocks looked. She noticed a chip of red paint off her left index finger nail, prompting her to reapply a finish to the recently manicured digit. When the nail polish dried she pumped up the overhead music and returned to her workout, confident that her figure would someday be reinstated atop the Tuckett pedestal.

Tony Crackstone sat in his office that evening just trying to make sense of what was going on. On his plate were a missing person who he knew quite well, and an apparent murder. Complicating the issue was the theft of classified Wall Street trading info that garnered someone a large sum of cash. Most disturbing to him was a possible technology chip lodged somewhere in his body, recording data for an unknown entity. The thought of a United States Senator being nearby generated added concern. The somber detective then peered down at a pathology report lying in front of him regarding the infected hip components removed from Mr. Banks. The report's conclusion noted quite plainly, "Unremarkable Orthopedic Hardware." Somehow, everything had to connect thought Crackstone, but why?

Cell Block B found Rick Polk and Jackie Rhimes playing a video game inside Jack's bedroom. Rap music blared as the duo deposited their body and soul into a fantasy world that involved military platoons, attack helicopters and enough ammo to re-enact the Battle of the Bulge. Polk and Rhimes were part of an elite brigade attempting to capture a flag on a remote hillside. They were testing their skills against twelve other teams spread out across the world. Polk's screen moniker was Baba Yaga and Rhimes' was The Holy Redeemer. Chaotic bliss had occupied their minds for countless hours throughout the quest, with no end in sight. Both combatants had not a single care in the world.

Across the hall Stephanie Thomas was pleased with a selfie she just posted on the internet. The photo had immediately garnered over one hundred "likes" and the nursing student was on a campaign to double that number. She feverishly pumped out a landslide of text messages, beseeching her followers to "like" the photo. She was momentarily distracted by the hum of her desktop computer, signifying a possible communal emergency, thus imploring her to please remain on social media for the next several hours. While smiling and holding her cell phone to within three inches of her face she completely ignored her roommate Kendra, who sat gently crying on her bed.

Across the hall Phil Drummer sat distraught upon his bed. Despite his best efforts, absolute radio silence enveloped Philadelphia. A sense of doom was crushing his thought process, as he tried to practice the lost art of patience. As rap music and shrill battle cries emanated from nearby, he said a prayer to his mom, asking her for guidance. Certainly her guiding spirit would lead him out of the valley of confusion, and give clarity to his plight. He spent the night pondering his options, aware of the barren night table at his bedside.

Later that evening Dr. Lee sat alone, on the top research floor of the Tuckett Institute. He had just finished soldering a spy chip onto the back of a Tuckett Cup. The black metallic chip was only eight millimeters long, and fit quite well into the coarse honeycomb matrix of the cup. Earlier in the day he had calibrated the spy chip to a scanner, which would allow the collection of data whenever the chip was nearby. A smile came upon Lee's face as he held the cup up to the light and spun it gently around, noticing how well the chip was hidden. It always fascinated Lee that the chip could not be seen or damaged by routine x-rays, being completely obscured by the metal cup. So simple yet so lucrative was his brainchild.

The spy chip was a state of the art model, compliments of some nefarious technophiles that spoke and shared the common language of greed. A technological marvel, the chip collected data from any cell phone within a six foot radius of itself, capable of capturing both text and video from the nearby cell. Once gathered, the info would remain within the chip, until recovered by a scanner that was exactly synched to its frequency.

Dr. Lee had implanted a total of nine chips so far into a carefully selected cohort of unknowing patients, including Tony Crackstone. This allowed him unparalleled access to privileged information from law enforcement officers, bankers, brokers and financial gurus who knew what lay ahead of the curve. The collective knowledge that Dr. Lee illegally obtained garnered him riches beyond a mortal man's belief, and ultimately permitted the doctor to befriend a Senator with a perverse genome.

All was well with his twisted plan until Anastasia unexpectedly got involved. Dr. Lee was aware of her drunken visits to the flat of Ian Tuckett, whose boyish libido could not resist her overtures. New however was a crazed jealousy that Anastasia developed for the reigning "diva of the month" in Tuckett's stable. Lee postulated that Anastasia downloaded random information from the Institute's computer system in an amateurish attempt to confuse her ex-husband. It was this apparent combination of dumb luck, alcoholism, hormones, and limited computer knowledge that led to information concerning Mr. Banks ending up on a flash drive, which fortunately was recovered by Lee's henchmen. Why Anastasia gave the chip to Phil Drummer, and whether any information viewed on the flash drive was shared with the authorities, were both unknowns. Certainly Drummer had contact with Crackstone, which in Lee's mind was expected, since he met with Anastasia just prior to her departing the valley. His plan to put a scare into Drummer surely worked to perfection, including the dive that his thug took prior to any actual physical engagement. His threatening email to Jennifer Ranier reinforced the message.

Regardless, Mr. Street would be the last victim of Lee's illegal activity, since access to the text messages of the Federal Reserve would generate enough cash to even satiate the delusional ideals of the plan's architect himself.

A size fifty-four Tuckett Cup was chosen for Mr. Street's case based upon radiographic measurements that Lee and Tuckett performed earlier in the day. The size chosen was usually quite accurate, and once Lee was satisfied with the stability of the chip, he would then re-sterilize the entire implant and package it up as if new. It was this cup that he would personally open up during the case, permitting nurse Adams to place it on the wand, allowing Dr. Ian Tuckett to bury it deep into the pelvis of Mr. Street, where it would remain in the proverbial "final resting place."

The purr of Dr. Lee's cell phone at his side did not alarm him, as he was expecting the call per standard operational protocol.

"All set," said Lee. "Are you ready?"

"Yes," was the confident answer, "No problems from my end, how about you?"

"All systems are go," said Lee followed by a pause. "The stakes are a bit higher tomorrow, do you foresee any possible problems?"

"No, I've looked at every angle, all clear."

"I agree, but remember the abort plan. Did you commit it to memory?" asked Lee. "Just in case."

"Yes, nothing on paper or computer, just in my mind."

"Everything? The flights, bank numbers, alibis and rendezvous timetable."

"Yes, of course. We've been through this a thousand times."

"Even our final resting place together?" asked Lee in a softer tone.

"Of course," said the voice. "It's where we first met, so long ago. You doubt me?"

"Of course not," said Lee, "But you know me, every plan has an even better back up plan."

"That's what makes you special," said the voice.

"Special?"

"That's right, so very special," said the voice with passion. "I love you."

"I love you too," said Dr. Lee with uncharacteristic emotion that belied his stoic ancestral heritage. "I love you too." The call was then terminated.

Across the avenue rested Mr. Harry Street, alone in his hospital room. He had just turned off the light in order to get some sleep, calm and confident in his Center of Excellence whereabouts.

CHAPTER TWENTY FOUR
THE BIG DAY

"LOOKS LIKE A fifty-six," said Dr. Tuckett as he pulled the reamer out of Mr. Street's exposed acetabulum. Up until that point the surgical case had been uneventful, as the third movement of *The Trout Quintet* began. "Fifty-six Aran."

"The x-rays template a fifty-four," said Dr. Lee as he stood behind Tuckett. "I have a fifty-four in my hand, ready to go."

Dr. Tuckett then reassessed the situation before him, while again testing a fifty-four cup followed by a fifty-six. He stared into the depths of Mr. Street's pelvis before stating confidently, "Nah, a fifty-four is too loose. Let's go with a fifty-six. Final answer."

Silence ensued behind the surgeon as nurse Adams stared impatiently at Dr. Lee, awaiting the Tuckett Cup.

"He said a fifty-six," chimed in circulating nurse Kline loudly, as she stood with her hands on her hips next to Dr. Lee.

Nurse Nikki Bryant had called in sick that day in an attempt to concentrate all her energy towards a stunning physical presentation at the Brookside gala that evening. She therefore scheduled a hair appointment that morning, which per the laws of femininity could never be cancelled. On short notice nurse Kline was called upon to circulate in the operating room, which she agreed to–if paid time and a half. The fiery semi-retired plump nurse that was thrown out of the room during the Mr. Banks infection case despised the Tuckett Institute and everything about it. She bitterly recalled being told by Dr. Lee that her rump brushed up against the sterile table that day, being quite sensitive to any derogatory remarks in reference to her oversized derriere. That morning she wore her trademark tight scrubs which appeared to be under extreme duress at the seams.

"Hello, Dr. Lee is anybody home?" barked nurse Kline.

"Aran a fifty-six please," said Tuckett.

"I respectfully ask you to reconsider," said Lee calmly. "We are usually right on with regards to the pre-op template. I strongly recommend a size fifty-four cup."

"Too loose," said Tuckett with a snap of his hand suggesting that the cup make it to the surgical field promptly. "Let's go."

"A fifty-four usually fits a man of Mr. Street's stature," said Lee. "I again would, with all due respect......"

"Fifty-six looks perfect," said Jackie Rhimes who was opposite the table of Tuckett, holding retractors to protect the acetabulum. Beside him was Phil, who had been called in to assist. The two junior residents stared at Dr. Lee in anticipation of some movement. Standing in the corner of the room was fellow Stortz, having been instructed to keep quiet and offer no assistance whatsoever.

"Fifty-six!" yelled circulating nurse Kline with a voice that would test the steel of any mortal man over time. "For heaven's sake, F-I-F-T-Y-S...."

"I'll get one off my cart," interrupted Lee as he pirouetted towards a door that led to the equipment room. He then rapidly vanished from sight as the entire surgical team awaited his return, with the fifty-six cup.

"Must have overslept today," said nurse Candy Adams. "Moving a bit slow."

"Nah," said Tuckett. "His mind is preoccupied with the Senator's speech today. He has been fussing over that for the last few days."

As Dr. Lee stepped outside the room he stood directly facing a large metallic cart that contained a myriad of cup sizes from forty millimeters to eighty, rising in increments of two. He had been down this road before and quickly reached for a fifty-six cup, which was wrapped in a box with a tight plastic seal around it. The maneuver about to be performed would create another serial number mismatch, similar to those that triggered the corporate bean counter's interest, but the bean counter was now dead. The plastic wrap sealing each box was then swiftly removed. He pranced back into the room holding both the fifty-four and fifty-six cups. With his right hand he held the box containing the fifty-six cup up to both Dr. Tuckett and nurse Adams for their review. He kept his left hand with the fifty-four cup down at his side. The requested fifty-six cup did not contain a spy chip–only the fifty-four cup did.

"A fifty-six cup per your request," said Lee. "Under protest I must add."

Per protocol both Dr. Tuckett and Candice Adams stared at the package while reading the print, assuring the size of the implant.

"Agree," said Tuckett. "Fifty-six. Open it up."

Dr. Lee then stepped back from the surgical field towards a table behind him, under the wary eye of circulating nurse Kline. He laid both cups upon the table and like a street huckster playing the shell game, rotated them in rapid succession, while peeling off the sticker for the fifty-six. He handed the sticker with the serial number to nurse Kline who then turned away to place it in the patient's chart. Dr. Lee then opened the box of the fifty-four cup and returned to nurse Adam's table, where she carefully hoisted the sterile implant out of the box. Within seconds the slightly undersized fifty-four cup, with an attached spy chip, was ready to be implanted.

Tuckett grabbed the cup atop the driving rod and immediately lowered it into the patient's pelvis. Then with a large steel mallet he began smashing the cup into place with fierce blows, prompting blood to fly back towards him. After the fifth blow he toggled the driving rod to confirm a firm fit, but there was a slight wobble to the component. Being an orthopedic surgeon, he then began to hit the implant even harder with the mallet, confident that his brute force would rectify the situation. It did not.

"Hmmm," said Tuckett. "Still a little loose. Maybe we should have gone up to a fifty-eight."

"That would be shocking to me," said Dr. Lee. "In all my years of experience I've never seen a cup put in four millimeters larger than our template. Never."

"It's loose," said Jackie. "I can see it from here."

"I agree," said Phil.

"Then put in a couple screws to secure it," said Lee. "Let's keep moving, the Senator is waiting."

The Senator was indeed waiting in the recovery room that morning. Waiting for his childhood friend to emerge from the surgical greatness that he himself had recommended.

"The cup is definitely a fifty-six?" asked Tuckett as he innocently spoke aloud, while fingering the cup's rim fit. "Still seems loose."

"Show me the implant box again," said nurse Adams to Dr. Lee. "Just to be sure it was a fifty-six."

"How dare you question me!" yelled Lee at the scrub nurse. "How dare! I've been doing this job for over twenty-five years and you question my professionalism."

"Let's not out think ourselves," said Tuckett while ignoring the hissy fit of his long time colleague. "It's loose, so just give me a fifty-eight."

"Ian, just put in a few screws and move on," said Dr. Lee. "A fifty-eight could possibly fracture the acetabulum. Remember, do no harm."

Phil sensed something amiss at that point in time, for Dr. Lee never called his comrade by his first name in public. He watched Tuckett just stare into the wound while measuring his answer. Besides him was nurse Adams, who was starting to roll her eyes and rapidly rearrange the instruments atop her table, signifying impatience. Nurse Adams also had a hair and wax appointment in two hours, barring any unforeseen act of God. He noticed the left eyebrow of Dr. Lee beginning to twitch, as sweat stained the front of his surgical cap.

Suddenly to the left of Dr. Lee the bodily mass of nurse Kline began to lurch towards the rear table, which held the empty box of the Tuckett Cup. Phil was impressed by the speed of Kline's first step, prompting her backside to gracefully swing right to left per the laws of classic physics. It was obvious to Phil that she was on a direct route to check the discarded implant box, to assure that a size fifty-six cup was opened.

Dr. Lee nervously sensed mass and momentum behind his frame. He briskly turned ninety-degrees to his left which placed his slight body directly in front of the charging circulating nurse, who was unable to reverse the forward thrust of her genetic constitution, causing a collision between the two. The propulsion of energy caused Dr. Lee to be thrown backwards and down upon the floor, with a slight high-pitched scream.

"You fool!" shouted Lee as he regained his upright position in a hurry. "You absolute fool!"

It was then that Franklin Stortz decided to assist, taking a few steps forward to grab the empty box. He elevated his arm slightly parallel to the floor, setting the box at eye level with Candy Adams, who squinted to read the print.

"It was a fifty-four!" shouted nurse Adams as she looked directly at the opened box. "You were wrong Dr. Lee. Imagine that?"

The statement compelled Dr. Lee to spin around and face the accusation, causing him to deposit his face directly into the putrid armpit of Stortz. His physique comically dwarfed that of Dr. Lee, who immediately recoiled from the stench of his armpit. In trademark fashion, perspiration soaked the axilla of the fellow's scrub top.

"It was a fifty-four," said Tuckett who was now looking at the box. "That explains it."

"You imbecile, don't ever touch my equipment, do you understand?" shouted Lee looking up at the Senator's son.

"I was just trying to move things along," said Franklin. "She asked to see the box."

"You idiot!" shouted Lee. "I don't care who…."

"Aran, Aran, take it easy," said Dr. Tuckett. "We all make mistakes, just give me a fifty-six and let's move on." Tuckett then began to backslap the fifty-four cup out of Mr. Street's pelvis and handed the cup and driver back to nurse Adams. The scrub nurse then rapidly rotated the cup off the driver and placed it on her table, in anticipation of the true fifty-six cup.

Dr. Lee quickly returned to his back table again under the watchful eye of nurse Kline. Now in damage control mode, he opened the fifty-six cup and delivered it to nurse Adams promptly. Within five minutes the Tuckett Cup was snuggly delivered to its final resting place allowing Tuckett to direct his attention to the femoral shaft.

"Strong work chief," said Jackie to Franklin Stortz as he rotated the thighbone towards Tuckett. "Strong work from the chief."

No one spoke as Dr. Tuckett began the second half of the procedure, which would replace the ball of the hip joint. It was during this time that Phil noticed Dr. Lee approaching the table of nurse Adams.

"I'll need the fifty-four cup," he said tersely, while pointing to the bloody implant sitting on her sterile field. "Nurse Adams, the cup please."

"Not this time," jumped in nurse Kline. "The hospital's pathology department gets the cup."

"Nurse Kline, we have been through this before, the makers of the Tuckett Cup have a quality control team that inspects every implant that is removed from a body. After our complete inspection I guarantee that the cup will promptly return to the hospital, just like before."

"Do you know how much trouble I got in after the last debacle with your famous cup?" protested Kline, now approaching the scrub table. "I almost got fired, as did Nurse Bryant. I get the cup. Besides there is too much paperwork the other way."

Nurse Kline rapidly put on a pair of surgical gloves and extended her hand for the cup, as did Dr. Lee.

"The cup please," said Dr. Lee to Candice. "Give me the cup."

"Let her have the cup," said Tuckett as he was driving the femoral component down the thighbone of Mr. Street. "We will eventually get the cup back. Trust me."

"Ian, I fully disagree with you on this matter," blurted Dr. Lee. Having some hack pathologist enter a derogatory comment into the record regarding the cup can be damaging to sales. I will not allow it. I must have the cup." He then reached forward to the sterile table to grab the implant.

"What are you doing?" shouted nurse Adams. "That's a sterile field! What's wrong with you today?"

"That's it!" screamed Tuckett as he stepped back from the table. "Give the goddamn cup to the hospital." He pointed at nurse Kline saying, "Take it, now!" He paused to settle his anger. "I'm trying to replace someone's hip, does anyone understand that?"

Dr. Lee's face turned deep red behind his surgical mask, yet he did not speak.

"Everybody just calm down," continued Tuckett while returning his attention back to the surgical wound. "Aran, no problem, trust me. I'll work out the details with Barry. We will get the cup back, no questions asked."

Dr. Lee did not speak for the remainder of the case, which was successfully completed in thirty minutes. Tuckett then headed out to talk with the family and Senator. Mr. Street tolerated the procedure well, and was escorted in stable condition to the recovery room. The remainder of the surgical team retreated to their respective locker rooms adjacent to the O.R.

"Chief, high five," said Jackie while extending his left hand upwards towards Stortz. Jackie had his shirt off and his chiseled pectoralis muscles jumped up and down with the maneuver.

"Thanks," said Stortz with a reciprocal gesture and slap of the hand. "Just trying to help."

"Man, did you see Dr. Lee get tossed down like a rag doll?" said Phil who was to the left of Jackie, taking off his surgical scrubs. "He had no chance. He went down like a bowling pin."

"What a candy ass," said Rhimes. "He pouted the whole second half of the case. I wouldn't be surprised if...."

At that very moment the locker room door swung open and in charged Dr. Lee, directly towards Franklin Stortz. A scowl was across his face that remained red with anger. It was apparent to Phil that he was on a collision course with the fellow, who stood dumbfounded.

"Don't ever touch any equipment of mine in the future!" screamed Lee as he nearly levitated upwards towards Stortz with a pointed finger. "Ever! Do you understand, you mindless dolt?"

"Uh, yes, I'm sorry sir, I mean doctor," mumbled Stortz.

"You're a menace to us all Stortz!" shouted Lee, with some saliva projecting from his mouth. "The only reason you are here is because of your father, do you understand?

"Ahh...,"

"I'll have you thrown out of this fellowship," shouted Lee, as he pounded his index finger on the chest of the fellow. "How do you think that would look on your resume?"

Phil was disturbed by the scene and stepped forward to ease the assault, however Jackie beat him to the punch.

"Lay off the Chief," said Jackie sharply. "He didn't do anything wrong. You're the one who screwed up."

"What did you say?" said Lee as he then faced Rhimes. "I screwed up? I screwed up? I've been doing this for over twenty years mister. What if I squash you like a bug, and send you back to Philadelphia looking for a third residency program."

"You don't scare me," said Rhimes. "The chief was in the right."

"That's it! Your rotation at the Institute is over!" shouted Lee. "Over! Don't bother coming back. I'll be talking to your program director immediately."

Phil noticed that only about two feet separated the two. A large vein in Dr. Lee's neck dilated, as did arteries in Jackie's biceps.

"Big deal," shouted Rhimes. "The Tuckett Institute isn't ready for Jackie Rhimes anyway. Center of Excellence my ass, the boys at Temple do a better job with hip replacements."

"Do you know what your problem is Rhimes?" said Lee, as he closed the gap even further, with his index finger pointed at the junior resident. "Respect. You have no respect for authority." While enunciating the word "authority" he tapped his finger lightly upon the exposed skin of Jackie's chest, an action that in Jackie's mind, prompted retaliation.

"Don't touch me boss," said Rhimes. "Do not, I repeat, touch me again."

For one second no one spoke or moved.

"Respect," said Lee in a slow violent manner. He again impressed his index finger upon the exposed chest of the junior resident with a slow steady pressure, while spelling out the word, "R-E-S-P...."

Phil tried to step in, realizing Lee had crossed the red line of Jackie, which in North Philadelphia meant physical combat would rapidly ensue. He reached forward, but was too late.

The punch delivered was a short, crisp right hand jab that landed directly upon the jaw of the elder Lee, sending him backwards with a crash into a row of lockers. A fierce left uppercut met the slumping descent of the doctor with a thud that again propelled him backwards.

"Jack!" shouted Phil quickly in an attempt to stop the assault switch that had been flipped within his friend's head. "Jack, stop!"

Rhimes then grabbed the near unconscious doctor by his scrubs with two hands about his upper torso, and hurled the victim onto the tiled floor of a shower room, awash in fungal molds. The limp body of Dr. Lee rotated in prone fashion one and a half times before it crashed into the sidewall of the washroom, where it lay frightfully still.

Rhimes stepped forward to continue the rampage but was stopped by the combined grips of Stortz and Phil. At that moment, the door to the locker room opened, followed by the voice of Dr. Tuckett.

"Senator, again, it could not have gone better. Let me just change my shoes and we will head over to the recovery room to see Harold."

As Phil maintained his grip on the shirtless Rhimes, he looked to the left and was met by the incredulous stares of Dr. Tuckett and the senator, who trailed behind him. The senator was flanked by a massive bodyguard, with a look of concern on his face.

"Gentleman, what's happening?" asked Tuckett, not yet aware of his colleague's limp torso, now just starting to show signs of life in the stall beside him.

"Franklin, what's up?" asked the Senator with a cocked eyebrow. "Who are your friends?"

"Ohhh," moaned Dr. Lee from the floor, "Ohhh, help."

Tuckett bolted around the corner to find his long time friend beaten and prostrate upon the shower floor. He rushed to his side and turned his body supine, immediately noticing a trickle of blood from his right nostril. His left lower lip was split open and swollen, and a left incisor tooth was cracked.

"Aran, what happened?" asked Tuckett.

"He tripped," said Rhimes, knowing this excuse readily satisfied the police officers that showed up after a brawl in his boyhood neighborhood.

"He assaulted me," said Lee with a shake of his head. "Him, Rhimes," said Lee as Tuckett helped him sit up upon the floor. "Oh my God, my face."

"Is that true son?" asked the Senator in a fatherly fashion. "Did this young man assault Dr. Lee, my very close friend?" The bodyguard slowly moved forward between the Senator and junior residents.

"Dad, it all happened so fast," said Franklin, "I'm not sure exactly what happened."

"He punched me in the face, without warning. A coward," said Lee while being helped up to his feet by Tuckett. "Call the police Ian, I want him arrested."

"Whoa, whoa, gentlemen," said the Senator while holding his hands upwards. "No police action is necessary. Certainly not today."

"I want him arrested immediately for assault and battery," mumbled Lee, feeling the cracked tooth in his mouth. "Your son may have been involved too Senator, I'm not exactly sure how many people hit me."

"Gentlemen. Easy, easy," commanded the Senator. "Ian, take charge here. Let's get some medical attention for the good doctor and talk this over tonight, among each other. We have a press corps just outside waiting to sink their teeth into any storyline that can go viral in a matter of minutes. This is an internal matter. Do we all understand?"

"No," said Dr. Lee emphatically. "Absolutely not. I want an arrest immediately."

"Aran, please," said Tuckett. "I agree with the Senator, especially today. In six hours the Institute will be in the national spotlight. Let's get you over to the Institute, tend to your wounds and just get through the day, then disciplinary actions can be taken care of internally."

"Ian look at me," said Lee as he blotted his nose dry. "I'm missing some teeth and there is a chance my jaw may be broken. I've been physically assaulted."

"All right, listen up everyone, and listen good," said the Senator sharply in an authoritative tone. He stepped in front of the guard, who then peered over his shoulder with a menacing scowl. "Today is the biggest day of my professional life, and I'm not going to have it sullied by a little misunderstanding that in the scheme of things means nothing. Do we all understand?"

No one spoke, but Jackie did shake his head up and down in the affirmative. The Senator then stepped forward to occupy the center of the crowd. Phil noticed his fingernails to be manicured below a shirt sleeve that utilized old fashioned cufflinks.

"Now, I believe this young man in so much that Dr. Lee did trip here, today in the locker room." The senator paused and looked at each member of the group one by one. "It was an unfortunate event, but it undeniably did occur, causing some facial damage to Dr. Lee. Understand?" The Senator again made eye contact with all members of the cabal. "It happened, no denying if asked, but it was an accidental trip. Nothing else."

"I saw it," said Jackie. "Some water on the floor."

"I'm not going to be part of this," said Lee. "I've been...."

"Dr. Lee I've heard enough!" shouted the Senator in a tone that even caught Lee off guard. "I am going to now turn around and with my son, visit my childhood friend in the recovery room. I've chosen the Tuckett Institute over a long list of venues begging me to host this speech. If this day is tainted in any fashion, so help me God, the parties involved will forever regret it."

Phil froze, as did everyone in the room.

"We fully understand," said Tuckett as he continued to help keep his partner erect. "An accidental fall it was. And Senator, believe me, we all so deeply appreciate what you've done for the Institute. There will be no further problems in this regard."

"Thank you Ian," said the Senator calmly while spinning around towards the exit and placing his hand over Franklin's shoulder. "Come on son, show me where the recovery room is, I'm so proud of you."

Phil and Jackie promptly left the scene, allowing Dr. Tuckett time to clean up his associate's face. The duo then left the hospital via a maintenance side exit, allowing the national spotlight to shine upon the Senator, now speaking just outside the hospital adjacent to a beaming COO Reynolds. The Senator thanked the hospital for providing state of the art facilities for his close friend's hip replacement surgery. The impromptu speech would be used for future hospital marketing propaganda.

Ian Tuckett helped ease his colleague's mangled body into the front seat of his Porsche, parked in the hospital garage. A subtle crunch about his right shoulder suggested a broken collarbone.

"Aran, I think your clavicle is broken," said Tuckett with concern.

"Don't worry about that," said Lee. "Just worry about who has our cup."

CHAPTER TWENTY FIVE

THE SPEECH

THE SCENE OUTSIDE the Tuckett Institute was chaotic, replete with an eclectic blend of strangers and locals. All roadways within a mile of the Institute were jammed with pedestrians and vehicles closing in on the venue. Most noticeable was the press corps, whose trucks clogged the streets directly adjacent the hospital, emanating a noisy hum while providing a live newscast to the world. Several of the larger networks set up scaffold towers outside the Institute's main door, allowing their cameras to fixate upon the Center of Excellence.

The speech was scheduled for 4 P.M. that Friday afternoon followed by cocktails and a lavish banquet at the Brookside Country Club. The weather was slightly overcast, with a chill and chance of thunderstorms later in the evening.

Those fortunate enough to secure a ticket for the event were asked to be seated one hour prior to the main speaker, allowing enough time for some lesser dignitaries to pontificate. It was almost 3 P.M. and the inner sanctum of the Institute was jammed with sharply attired clientele, anticipating a wonderful afternoon and evening.

Phil, Rick and Jackie were present, compliments of their residency program director. Absent were any nursing students, who were invited later to the Brookside gala.

"Wow, looks like Abe Lincoln is about to walk in," said Polk as he scanned the crowd. The three were seated in the left rear of the rotunda, just beneath a balcony above them. Red, white and blue banners were draped over every rail in the hall, with flags hanging above. A band to their right was playing a host of patriotic songs, with the current being Sousa's *Washington Post March*.

"I love *The Stars and Stripes Forever*," said Polk while tapping his foot to the tune.

"You idiot, that's not *The Stars and Stripes Forever*," said Rhimes.

"Sure it is," replied Polk while whistling the tune, "I was a band member in high school."

"Don't be stupid," said Rhimes.

"What instrument did you play?" asked Phil as he eyeballed Nikki Bryant strolling in just a tad late. She wore a tight red dress surrounded by black accents that caught the attention of every male in the joint, in a red, white and blue way. She took a seat twenty rows back from the main stage.

"Tuba," said Polk, now starting to gyrate his body to the march.

"It's definitely not *The Stars and Stripes Forever*," said Rhimes emphatically. "That's the one they play at fireworks."

"No it's not," barked Polk. "That's *The 1812 Overture*. I'm sure of that."

"Well it's not *The 1812 Overture*," said Rhimes. "That has cannons firing in it. I don't hear any cannons, do you?"

"I didn't say it was the *1812*," said Polk, now annoyed. "It's definitely *The Stars and Stripes*."

Just then a rumble of excitement rolled through the crowd, causing Phil and his fellow residents to look back towards the main aisle, where all eyes fixated upon the entrance of the voluptuous Candice "Candy Apple" Adams. Her entrance was self-timed to occur just after that of Bryant.

Candy wore a dress that screamed harlot, and looked great on her. Her body swayed back and forth in short step fashion as it teetered on heels that added three inches to her height. Her hair was perfect as was her toned, dark brown body, compliments of the town's only tanning salon.

Phil felt a tap on his shoulder and looked back to see Fast Eddie sitting next to old Doc Carter. Fast Eddie had a twenty dollar bill in his hand, extending it forward for Phil to take.

"Here, pass it down to the band and have them play *The Stripper*," said Eddie, as he glanced back towards nurse Adams. "Quick!"

Phil laughed at the gesture but then noticed Polk take the twenty dollar bill and put it in his pocket while saying, "Will do boss."

Their attention swung back to the final few steps of nurse Adams, which brought her to the front row, just opposite the main stage. As she approached her seat both Emily Reyes and Mrs. Reynolds stood up to greet her, with a rapid exchange of female air kisses. Phil noticed that the majority of dignitaries on the stage gazed upon the local wonder, in appreciation of her debut. Then just prior to sitting down, Candice looked back towards the adoring audience and inhaled deeply. She then snuggled her body every so tightly into the seat that befit her status among the flock.

The first speaker was the mayor of the town, who spent ten minutes praising his local administration. During this time Phil noticed Detective Tony Crackstone make his way into the hall, taking a seat three rows ahead, which had been reserved by a fellow officer. Crackstone calmly scanned the crowd and gave a slight smile and nod of the head to Phil as their eyes met.

"Check out Reynolds," said Polk to Phil. "I'm convinced he gets his clothing at the hospital consignment shop."

Phil eyed COO Reynolds on stage. A broad smile beamed from his face as he attentively listened to the mayor. Phil only recognized a few of the honored guest upon the stage, wondering where the rumored Hollywood stars were. Four seats were empty directly next to the podium, which Phil assumed were being reserved for the Senator, his wife and Drs. Tuckett and Lee, who up until this point were all absent. The mayor then cracked a lame joke that caused COO Reynolds to burst into laughter, slapping his thigh.

As the mayor's speech ended the band promptly began playing Sousa's *Liberty Bell March*. Handshakes and man hugs were exchanged between the mayor and stage VIPs.

"This is *The Washington Post March*," said Polk confidently to Jackie. He was flicking his wrists up and down as if orchestrating the band. "We played it at high school assembly. One of my favorites."

"No it isn't," said Rhimes, "This isn't even Sousa."

"How dare you besmirch the March King's name," said Polk, while continuing to arrange the number. "How dare you."

"It's *The Liberty Bell March*," said Doc Carter from the row behind.

Just then the Governor from the great state of Pennsylvania was introduced to the crowd, provoking a tepid applause. Pennsylvania's governor was historically a Democrat, thanks to the urban masses of Philadelphia and Pittsburgh. The rest of the Keystone State was pure Republican, especially rural Pennsylvania, where the gathering sat. The governor was not popular in the middle of the state, thanks to turning a blind eye to the lucrative gas drilling industry, which was raping the state's rich gas reserves of the Marcellus Shale via controversial methods, untaxed. The governor knew he was on thin ice, yet managed to consume thirty minutes of airtime while at the podium.

During this time Phil witnessed a show of disrespect based upon generational lines. Those over the age of forty in the crowd just crossed their arms and stared forward, not applauding or chuckling at the Governor's one-liners. While those of Phil's age discreetly pulled out their cell phones and starting texting and surfing the internet, oblivious to any words mumbled by the speaker. Phil tried to pay attention to the Governor's words, but his gaze wandered upon Nurse Nikki Bryant, who sat attentive in her chair. He recalled their first meeting together, in the O.R., where she was filled with swagger. Now, just four months later, she was an outcast. Phil then scanned the room and realized the impact of Drs. Tuckett and Lee upon the congregation. He realized how inappropriate the punches thrown by Jackie were, against the Institute's co-founder. He craned his neck about the foyer searching for Dr. Lee, yet could not locate his slight frame.

Just then the Governor's speech ended and the band burst into a roaring rendition of Sousa's *The Thunderer March* in anticipation of the Senator's arrival on stage.

"Don't even say it!" yelled Rhimes over the blare of the trumpets. "Don't even say it!"

"*The Liberty Bell March*," shouted Polk, "No doubt."

Excitement erupted in the auditorium as some balloons and confetti drifted down from the ceiling. A series of flag bearers then began a procession from the rear of the hall towards the stage center. Majorettes, baton twirlers and cheerleaders from Valley High School followed with enthusiastic cheers of joy. The entire gathering rose to their feet as did all the stage occupants in anticipation of the great one's arrival. A burst of hoorays emanated from just outside the hall's great door. Then, as a ray of late afternoon sunshine outlined his frame, the great Senator from New England appeared.

Cheers erupted as the man of the hour waltzed into the room, waving majestically at the crowd. His gait was polished and smooth as was his smile, honed by years of political excess. Phil's height allowed him to see the initial entrance, at which time he noticed two tall, stunning women jumping up and down as the Senator passed by, intoxicated by his presence. One of the girls was dressed like Uncle Sam and waved a flag, while the other appeared to be actually clad in a flag, flapping in the breeze. The Senator slightly nodded his head to the duo while continuing to wave to the adoring crowd. Several rows ahead of him stood TOI attendants James and Madison who clapped wildly in appreciation of the politician's presence. Next the Senator passed by Nikki Bryant who accepted a seemingly random handshake from the legislator with a smile. Finally the procession passed by the first row where the Senator hugged Candice, Emily Reyes and Mrs. Reynolds. The Senator then took a few steps up onto the stage and passed in front of the dignitaries who were applauding fiercely as the march continued. It was then Phil noticed Ian Tuckett and the Senator's wife appear from the side of the stage and trail the leader towards their respective seats. Phil again looked for Dr. Lee, but he was not present as the Governor stepped to the microphone and introduced the

Senator. Pandemonium ensued for several minutes as the band continued to blare out *The Thunderer March*, prompting everyone to begin clapping in unison. The Senator's wife then joined the candidate at his side while holding one arm around his waist, waving together at the crowd. The couple smiled at each other in a scripted maneuver, after which Mrs. Stortz returned to her seat. It was only after the Senator raised his hands in an attempt to calm the masses that the boisterous crowd quieted. He then stepped to the microphone and stared at the cameras fixated upon his chiseled face, and smiled. The front of his podium read "Stortz-Our Future."

"Thank you, thank you," said the Senator to the crowd, now starting to sit down. "Thank you for joining me today on this, our historic first step in a march towards destiny." The crowd erupted again with a standing ovation.

At that moment Phil spotted Dr. Lee, slipping onto the side of the stage in labored fashion. His gait was arduous and his upper body movements slow, especially his right arm, which appeared to be secured to his side. He stood in front of a vacant chair at the end of the second row, to the left of the main speaker. He did not appear capable of applauding with the masses.

"I would like to acknowledge and thank all of the honored guests behind me, including the great Governor of your state, whose work throughout the commonwealth has been exceptional." Reserved applause followed. "I would also like to thank your mayor, whose hospitality has been most exceptional this past week." The Senator smiled and applauded, while looking at the mayor. "Next, I would like to thank my host for this event, The Tuckett Orthopedic Institute and Dr. Ian Tuckett, whose model of medical care and delivery has been exemplary to the nation as a whole." The partisan crowd erupted again in unison as the local surgeon stood with a boyish wave to the crowd. He bowed his head respectfully at the Senator while saying "Thank you."

"Lastly and most importantly I would like to thank my wife, Susan, for being my guiding light in a sea of turmoil." His wife then stood up to a thunderous applause and smiled. "Isn't she beautiful?" said the Senator over the roar. "Wouldn't she look great in the White House?" The Washington reference generated more applause as the Senator stepped back to hug his wife before returning to the pulpit.

The political speech continued, touching upon the nation's forefathers and their dream of democracy. The spirits of Washington, Lincoln and Roosevelt were invoked to bless the congregation and guide their actions over the next several years. Words of war, despair and division were countered by promises of peace, hope and unity. The speaker promised a journey together that would gather laborers, businessmen, farmers and teachers in a quest for a more hopeful America. A short autobiographic dissertation then followed, which outlined the Senator's path in life. Absent was any mention of the incredibly wealthy family he was born into, which fueled his political rise. By the time the oracle uttered words of morality, decency and honor, the crowd was in a fever pitch.

Then he began to recite the words that brought the country's interest to the valley. It was also then that the cell phone in Dr. Lee's right hand pant's pocket vibrated ever so calmly, oblivious to the magnitude of surrounding events.

"That is why, in the setting of this Center of Excellence," said the Senator firmly. "Where it has been shown that those who stand together with common hopes and dreams succeed above and beyond standard expectations."

Lee shifted his body forward as the vibration tone triggered a queer memory. He grimaced and fumbled his injured right upper extremity in an attempt to somehow reach his hand into his pocket. Fear and pain gripped his upper right arm as crepitus was appreciated in his right clavicle, yet he was able to reach the cell.

"I stand before you today..."

While arching his back and somehow remaining seated, the doctor was able to deliver the cell phone to his lap, deaf to the drama around him.

"...To announce my candidacy for President of the United States of America!"

Shouts of elation immediately burst from the crowd, which jumped to their feet, applauding in waves of unbridled enthusiasm with chants of "Stortz! Stortz! Stortz!" Flags waved and arms flailed as the much anticipated words sent the crowd into a frenzy.

Dr. Lee remained seated and squinted down upon the face of his cell phone, ignoring his body being bumped by people celebrating around him. The stage was rocking yet his gaze coldly focused upon the text message that appeared. The message was sent primarily to Dr. Tuckett, with a copy to Dr. Lee and Tony Crackstone.

"Thank you, thank you," shouted the Senator above the screams of the crowd. "Together we can make a difference that shall right the path of this great country of ours!"

Dr. Lee's lame hand then tapped his cell screen, which delivered the message. He was the only person still seated in the building. His heart skipped a beat when he read the text:

"I'm here, just outside. Lots to talk about."

The sender was Anastasia Tuckett.

Suddenly the band and crowd broke into a glorious rendition of Gustav Holst's *I Vow to Thee My Country.*" A pipe organ brought in for the occasion echoed the opening notes in majestic fashion off the roof of the rotunda.

I vow to thee my country, all earthly things above,
Entire and whole and perfect, the service of my love;

Lee looked to his left between the bodies before him and viewed the Senator standing royally before the gathering with his wife at his side, singing together. Balloons and confetti again floated down from the ceiling above, bouncing off their bodies. He then reread the text to assure its accuracy regarding the date and time. In utter disbelief he looked up upon the surreal scene unfolding before his eyes, his scene, the one completely orchestrated by his ideas, money and effort.

As Phil held the program card before him he was in a state of euphoria. Emotions churned in his gut, being sparked by the passion around him. Looking to his left he witnessed Rick and Jackie singing loudly, with tears in their eyes.

The love that asks no question, the love that stands the test,
That lays upon the altar the dearest and the best;

Dr. Lee painfully rose to his feet as a large screen display above the crowd flashed images of the Senator walking among children of all colors in a field of wildflowers, a flag waving in the background of the video. He glanced into the crowd to witness the masses staring down at their song cards before them, swaying to the beauty of the tune. It was Emily Reyes who he initially noticed, staring directly at him, with a look of concern. Candice Adams then looked towards the left of the stage while still mouthing the words of the song, with a smile. His gaze scanned backwards into the auditorium, being stopped dead by the cold look of Nikki Bryant, fixated upon him with sealed lips.

Phil too was on the verge of tears as the song, which he had previously never heard, laid waste to his emotions. His dad was right. Patience was the key, because his choice between Kendra and Jenna was now obvious, clarified by the intoxicating charm of the hymn.

The love that never falters, the love that pays the price,
The love that makes undaunted the final sacrifice.

Peering to the center of the stage Dr. Lee noticed Ian Tuckett staring upwards at the rotunda, fighting back tears. Earlier that day Tuckett notified him he would not be carrying a cell phone that evening, due to his position on the national stage. Lee then noticed Tony Crackstone rapidly speaking to the officer besides him, and then turning towards the rear exit. He had an astonished look upon his face, and a pace that suggested urgency. Within seconds he vanished from the scene.

And soul by soul and silently her shining bounds increase,
And her ways are ways of gentleness,
And all her paths are peace.

With a wave from the Senator the ceremony ended, and a noble procession began outwards into the throng of gatherers.

CHAPTER TWENTY SIX
THE FACEOFF

Dr. Lee retreated from the procession that brought the Senator into a mob scene just outside the Institute. He was in absolute damage control mode, aware that a cup with his spy chip was in the hands of a pathologist, and Anastasia Tuckett was apparently somehow alive. Despite the pain, his gait was quick, and he headed out a side lobby entrance towards a stairwell. While ascending the steps he sent a simple five-letter text – ABORT.

He entered the upper level of the Tuckett Institute Research center alone, wondering how things had gone so awry over the past few hours. Glancing out the window he viewed the Senator amid a crowd of adorers shaking hands, heading towards a shuttle that would transport him and the dignitaries to the Brookside Country Club. He unlocked his office and took three remaining spy chips from a manila envelope, secured within a safe. A quick visit to the bathroom sent the remaining chips down the city's sewer system in a single expensive flush. He then turned his attention towards the computer system, which was linked to his network at home, and backed up by a hard drive in Europe.

Over the next hour the scientist purged his system completely of the vast data retrieved from the spy chip network. Rage boiled within his soul as he watched endless text messages churned into scraps of useless cyberspace debris. The fury was directed at Anastasia, whose drunken jealousy uncorked the whole debacle.

But why she waited so long to resurface was unfathomable. Perhaps to ruin his and Ian's shining moment? It was unthinkable that she was alive, given the amount of money he paid an apparent incompetent group of thug hustlers in Southern California to dispatch of her. A furor also arose towards the Senator, whose career was being catapulted forward by someone whose legacy was being destroyed. Certainly such an injustice could not proceed.

The computer signaled completion of its task with a confirmation message, allowing Dr. Lee to arise. He carefully scanned the room for any other possible links that would uncover evidence of his covert operation. There were none, and there was silence in the Tuckett Institute. Satisfied, he stormed out of the room as an eerie shadow formed through the window, compliments of the sunset behind a nearby mountain ridge.

The frenetic pace of the doctor's feet echoed through the stairwell heading downward. An infinite series of possibilities churned through his mind, yet it was an innate paranoia that caused him to pause, just outside the second floor fire door. Absolute silence ensued for ten seconds, only to be disrupted by the ever so faint sound of nearby movement. Slowly the doctor opened the fire door leading to the clinical floor of the Institute, allowing him to glance inside.

The hallway contained a total of eight rooms, with four per side. The subtle rumble of motion was better appreciated, prompting him to progress inwards towards the examination rooms. It became apparent to the forward moving Lee that the noise came from the last room on the right, better known as the V.I.P. Room. While approaching he withdrew a K5 pistol from a torso belt, using his non-dominant left hand. The movement within the room suggested a cleaning team, which Lee knew would not be present on that day. His heart pounded rapidly as he came within three feet of the door, while stopping to listen. He sensed the slow ripping sound of someone tearing the padding off the top of the exam table within the room. He then slowly turned the corner to see the backside of Detective Crackstone, holding a knife in his hand, while slicing through the exam table's cover. The remainder of the room was a mess, as if a burglar had ransacked it in search of treasures.

Tony Crackstone immediately sensed his presence and turned about the see the swollen face of Dr. Lee, standing with a firearm in his left hand and holding his right arm close to his body. He noticed his left jaw to be massively edematous causing a near closure of his eye.

"Where is it?" asked Crackstone. "The receiver. Where is it?"

"I don't know what you are talking about Detective, but why are you vandalizing our office?"

"You sick bastard," said Crackstone, "How dare you implant some foreign body inside me."

"Put down the knife Tony, before someone gets hurt."

"It looks like that already happened," said Crackstone, while continuing to hold the blade in his hand. "Where is it, the receiver or recorder or whatever you call it. This has to be the room that gathers info, it's the common denominator for all us rats in your twisted experiment."

"Tony, you're not well, put down the knife. We can discuss this rationally if you would just put down the weapon."

"I spoke to Mr. Banks who told me all about the McCoy deal doctor," said Crackstone, while tossing the shank onto the exam table. "The boys at Securities and Exchange are on your electronic trail as we speak, it's just a matter of time."

The two just stared at each other, similar to an old western gunfight, except only one of the two combatants was armed.

"What happened to you?" asked Crackstone.

"Did you speak to her?" asked Lee. "Anastasia."

"Yes, and she is here, alive and well," said Crackstone with a smile. "It all makes sense now, knowing you were monitoring my text messages."

"Oh really?" asked Lee "The words of a wino make sense, how interesting."

"It seemed like who ever was chasing her out west knew exactly what her next step was," said Crackstone. "How convenient, since I was the one trying to steer her out of harm's way."

"Why now? Why on this date did she bother to reappear?" asked Lee. "Can you imagine all the turmoil she put her family and children through? Lee just shook his head in disgust. "It was Ian wasn't it, she couldn't take his pandering. After all the years of turmoil, she still loved him. How sweet."

"Who else knew what you were doing?" asked the sleuth. "Did Ian know?"

Crackstone noted a pensive pause from the gunman, allowing him a moment to assess his physical status. His right arm appeared lame and playing the odds, he was probably right handed. His left eye was swollen shut, which would certainly affect his left visual field. The pinpoint diameter of his right eye pupil suggested the recent use of a narcotic analgesic. A standard issue South Korean 9 millimeter semi-automatic pistol was in his left hand, slightly trembling. The ambidextrous safety mechanism of the pistol was off and the hammer was not cocked. Any assault towards Lee would have to come via his left side in order to succeed. Crackstone was unarmed but still dangerous.

"It's beneath the table top," said Lee with a smile. "Under the wooden table itself."

"What is?"

"The spy chip's receiver Tony, it's under the table, nearest a patient's hip replacement when they are seated on the table, listening to the great Dr. Tuckett tell them what they came to the valley to hear, that their surgery was a smashing success."

"Does Ian know?"

"Anastasia stole data from the Institute," said Lee. "It was her thievery that brought us together, here, in this room."

Crackstone sensed finality to the standoff yet asked one more time, "Does Ian know?"

"That doesn't matter since you are going to die," said Lee with a trembling left hand. Crackstone noted a wince of pain on his face and sweat dripping down his brow. It was now or never.

He bolted to his right and appreciated the thunderous roar of the pistol's discharge, yet no impact. A sharp pivot to his left then landed his body upon that of Lee's, causing the two to tumble sideways, into the wall. A moan emanated from the shooter as the sharp edges of his broken right collar bone pierced through his skin, rendering his right upper extremity useless. Once down the detective easily wrestled the K5 from the injured doctor and pinned his prone face onto the ground. Blood pulsated from his right supraclavicular area, soaking his shirt.

"You're under arrest Doctor Lee," said the detective while panting. "Under arrest for attempted murder." Crackstone paused to catch his breath while continuing to apply a downward force on the doctor. "Now let me ask again, was Ian involved? I need to know."

The doctor moaned but there was no response.

Crackstone then applied more pressure upon the right rear shoulder girdle of his suspect, causing him to scream out in pain. "Tell me now, did he know what was going on!"

The wounded doctor began speaking violently in Korean, signifying either complete disorientation or disregard, prompting the detective to stand him up with his left arm behind him. Together they exited the V.I.P. room and turned towards the stairwell exit. The battered frame of Dr. Lee pushed forward under the guidance of the arresting officer, his feet shuffling heavily on the floor. Crackstone held the pistol in his right hand.

As the duo approached the stairwell another tremendous discharge from a firearm occurred just behind them, sending each man in opposite directions. Dr. Lee was thrown to the left and landed forcefully on the ground, screaming upon impact. Tony Crackstone lurched forward while appreciating a hot burning sensation at the base of his skull. He was able to turn about to visualize the assailant. The detective was unaware that the single bullet actually missed both men, yet ricocheted multiple fragments off a steel beam to his right, sending a solitary fragment into the base of his brain. Instinct caused him to steady himself and raise his right hand in self-defense, prompting another round from the shooter.

The second bullet was spot on, hitting the detective in the midsection. The force of the impact sent him flailing backwards through the fire door and deposited his bleeding body supine on the stairwell landing, upon which he was left to die. As the door slammed shut above him, he thought only of Anastasia Tuckett and her whereabouts.

CHAPTER TWENTY SEVEN

A DIRTY DEAL

THE ATMOSPHERE INSIDE the Brookside Country Club was electric. A mixture of handshakes, smiles and kudos were primed by the essential elements of any country club, money and alcohol. A one-hour "Meet the Senator" cocktail hour was followed by a few short speeches from lesser dignitaries, followed by a dinner. Currently in full swing was another booze recess allowing everyone the opportunity to digest, prior to the keynote speech. The speech would be the Senator's last, after which time he planned a private military induction ceremony with Uncle Sam and her flag bearing patriotic partner.

"I'm officially drunk," said Norm Carter while working on his fifth Manhattan. "And that's said within a reasonable degree of medical certainty."

"I don't know," responded Fast Eddie who was sipping some vodka next to the aging anesthesiologist, "I can't explain it, but I just don't trust the man. I wanted to wash my hands after shaking his."

"Whose hand?" asked Norm with a slight list to his right.

"Senator Stortz," said O'Neil. "Our honored guest. Wake up Norm."

"I'm just glad the drinks are on the house," was the anesthesiologist's response. "Can you imagine how much this shindig costs?"

"Who do you think is going to win?" asked Doctor Martha Brace, holding a coconut based aperitif. "It's going to be a tough contest."

"The primary?" asked Eddie.

"No, the fight between Candy Apple and nurse Bryant!"

"Meow," said Fast Eddie as the group then turned their attention towards Ian Tuckett and the two gorgeous females standing to his right and left.

"I want to be like him when I grow up," said Jackie Rhimes with envy. "A nice piece of arm candy on each side."

"I put my money on Nikki," said Phil, also quite ginned up at that moment, compliments of the Brookside. "She is one lean, mean work out machine." He then looked around to see Kendra, but she was nowhere in sight.

"Nah," said Eddie, "I'd bet on Candice, she is a street brawler, like a hungry alley cat roaming the streets."

"Catfight?" said Polk whose ears perked up. He had been consuming shrimp hors d'oeuvres at a blistering pace from a smiling waitress standing beside him with a tray. "Catfight?" He tried to reference a famous Seinfeld episode centered upon a catfight but his sensorium was too far blunted to access his memory banks.

"I pick Nikki too," said Martha.

"Norm, who you got in a catfight?" asked Eddie. "Between Nikki and Candy."

"Candy Apple," said Norm followed by a nervous gulp of his drink. "No doubt, she curses like a sailor, a real toilet mouth."

Just then the slight body of Dr. Lee walked by the troop, paying no attention to their existence. Absent since the end of the Senator's speech within the Institute's great hall, his right arm was snugly tucked into a sling that wrapped around his neck and torso. A thickness beneath his suit coat suggested a bandage over his right clavicle area. The doctor was headed directly towards Ian Tuckett and the crowd about him parted, like a cold front cutting through a hot summer day. An inebriated Candice Adams saw him first, shocked by the post-traumatic appearance of his face.

"Oh my God, Dr. Lee what happened?" slurred Candice. "Are you alright?"

"Ian, a moment of your time," said Dr. Lee, ignoring Candice while staring directly at Tuckett.

"Dr. Lee, my goodness, there is some blood coming from your nose," said nurse Bryant.

"Ian, we need to speak privately," said Lee while dabbing his nose with a perfectly pressed handkerchief. "This cannot wait."

Ian Tuckett was also alarmed by the intensity of the swelling about his partner's face. Ecchymosis engulfed his left mandible, suggesting a broken jaw. His left eye was now completely swollen shut.

"Aran, you look horrible," said Tuckett. "We need to get you over to the hospital immediately."

"Ian there has been a break in at the Institute," said Lee. "Some damage has been done and I believe the computer system has been breached."

"You need medical help," said Tuckett with a hand gesture to the nurses for assistance. "Let's get you out of here."

Tuckett reached forward to steady his colleague, as did the two nurses at his side. It was then that Dr. Lee spotted Senator Stortz over the left shoulder of Tuckett, across the room, deep in conversation with a sharply dressed man. The visual prompted Lee to break free from the clasp of his medical team and burst forward towards the Senator. He bumped a waitress carrying a tray of champagne, almost causing the tray to upend. While walking away he heard Tuckett telling the women beside him that a fall earlier in the day caused the facial trauma. Within seconds his quick pace brought him directly into the personal space of the Senator, causing a burly bodyguard to take a cautionary step forward after recognizing the man who was pummeled before him earlier in the day.

"Senator we need to talk," said Lee abruptly with a higher than usual nasal tone due to his facial swelling. "Privately."

The Senator just glanced incredulously at the much shorter Dr. Lee, as did the prominent guest opposite him. The legislator then raised a hand towards his bodyguard, signaling him to keep his distance. The band across the room began playing, a signal to the Senator that his speech was now just ten minutes from start time. The musical signal also prompted a row of cameramen to man their stations in anticipation of the live nationwide event.

"Dr. Lee, as you can see I'm quite preoccupied in conversation with this fine attorney here, and my keynote speech is about to begin. Can it please wait?"

"Absolutely not," barked Lee. "We have to talk. Now!"

The Senator glared at the doctor and an inpatient scowl came across his face. His sharp, analytical mind processed all the variables at hand and he then shook his head slowly while returning his gaze to the attorney.

"Lorenzo, my apologies, but we are going to have to continue this important conversation later this evening, perhaps after the speech?"

"That's quite alright Senator," said the attorney while looking at Dr. Lee with a smile. His suit, smell and semblance screamed power and wealth. "That's quite alright."

The Senator and his bodyguard then moved quickly, grabbing Lee by his left upper arm and driving his body towards a side door. His forward motion propelled Dr. Lee through the door into a side service area, occupied by local teenage girls, working as waitresses that evening. They were restocking their trays when the duo, followed by the thickset guardian entered the room.

"Some privacy ladies," yelled the Senator.

"Clear the room!" shouted the bodyguard with a wide spread wave of his muscled arms. "Please, everyone clear the room."

As the girls scurried away, the Senator turned his cold gaze back upon the face of his host. A muscle below his right eye began to twitch nervously.

"Do you have any idea who that was?" asked the Senator, who glared directly downward upon the battered Lee. "Any idea, doctor?"

"Senator, we…"

"That was Attorney Pellegrini, president of the Half Billion Dollar Roundtable Club. Do you have any idea how long I've been courting that cash cow?

"Senator we have issues at hand that need immediate attention."

"His prominent group of friends are awash with capital and they are thinking of backing my run for the presidency. Imagine that."

The door connecting the holding area to the main hall then opened and in poked the head of the Senator's election campaign saying, "Five minutes to speech Senator, makeup is standing by. All systems are a go."

The senator started to breathe heavily as he nodded in consent to the manager, who vanished back into the crowd. He returned his attention impatiently to Dr. Lee, bringing his face to within inches of the doctor.

"What? What is your pressing problem doctor and please make it quick, the nation is waiting for me to speak."

"Senator I need political asylum to Switzerland, at once," blurted Lee above the band music, which had picked up their tone.

"What the hell are you talking about!" shouted the Senator. "Switzerland! Are you mad?"

"We have no time for details and reason," said Lee. "But you can do it, and I ask you as a personal friend who has backed your cause from the beginning, grant me political asylum immediately."

The Senator just stared at Lee in disbelief.

"You have the capability, your second cousin is the U.S. ambassador to Switzerland. Please Senator I implore you."

"A reason please Dr. Lee," said the impatient Senator with a glance down towards his watch. "A reason as to why I should burden myself with such a public maneuver that will garner scrutiny from all corners of the globe."

"A myriad of reasons," said Lee. "Far too many to discuss within a minute. But please trust me as you always have. The donations will continue to flow into your coffer, ten fold, I promise."

The Senator just gazed downward at the pathetic person before him, seeking solace in his power.

The side door then opened again and in swung the beautiful face of the Senator's wife. She was giddy with excitement in anticipation of her husband's shining moment. "Honey, one minute, come on out, everyone is waiting for you."

"In a minute love," said the Senator. "In a minute."

As the door closed he returned one last look upon the doctor, while contemplating his bizarre request.

"Senator, please, I implore you. For the sake of us all and for the sake of this nation," moaned Lee. "Grant me political asylum, here and now."

"Your nuts in the head," said the Senator as he began to step away from Dr. Lee. "Enjoy the speech."

Dr. Lee then reached out and grabbed the arm of the Senator holding him back. The maneuver prompted the bodyguard to lurch forward.

"Don't ever touch me!" shouted the Senator who turned about to face Lee. A drop of saliva was on his lower lip and his face turned beet red. "Don't ever touch me."

The bodyguard then placed a hold upon Lee's arm with the force of a vice grip, prompting a release. He continued to hold Lee's arm as he brought it down to his side.

"Here's the deal Senator," said Dr. Lee. "Either you grant me political asylum now, immediately, or I release a video onto the internet showing you violating two young women in a manner that disregards all norms of human nature."

"What are you talking about?" said the Senator with a menacing look. Outside the room the music stopped and a speaker could be heard, who was beginning to introduce the Senator.

"A video, actually several videos that documented your little sex romps in my home," said Lee. "Shot in high definition and ready to be uploaded with a touch of my finger."

"You sick little disturbed bastard," said the Senator.

"Asylum, now Senator, for we are both running out of time," said Lee.

"Listen to me," said the Senator with a scowl. "If you ever release such a video I will rain absolute destruction upon your little Center of Excellence, that will bring you to your knees. Understood?"

"Yes or no Senator?" asked Lee.

" I'll have the CIA, FBI and IRS crawl up your warped little ass and die. Do you understand the magnitude of such an event?"

"Political asylum or political Armageddon?" asked Lee.

"Let me be perfectly clear with this last statement Doctor Lee," said the Senator as he adjusted his tie. "If you ever pull such a stunt, I will have your body diced into a thousand morsels and fed to the sharks off the North Atlantic within twenty four hours. I guarantee it."

"Your answer?" said Lee.

"Go to hell," said the Senator as he turned about and burst through the door towards the thunderous roar of the crowd.

"Ladies and Gentlemen," shouted the emcee. "Please welcome your next President of the United States, the great legislator from New England, Senator Ari Stortz!"

As the band and audience broke into a raucous celebration the Senator's body guard held his ground, next to Dr. Lee, who just stared forward, wondering if the body of detective Crackstone had yet been discovered.

"Thank you, thank you my fellow Americans," shouted the Senator to the crowd. "It's so good to be here, among family and good friends!"

The muscled sentry then leaned forward and looked into the beaten face of Doctor Lee. At that moment the group of waitresses burst back into the room, careless with excitement.

"He wasn't kidding, believe me," whispered the guard. "I'll be the first one to break every bone in your body. One by one."

Dr. Lee ignored the comment and slowly walked into the main hall and looked upwards towards the stage, full of dignitaries, wildly applauding.

"Isn't she just beautiful?" said the Senator after introducing his wife. "She has great plans to redecorate a little house we have our eyes on in Washington D.C., on Pennsylvania Avenue."

The crowd roared in appreciation, causing Lee to scan the audience, replete with citizens of the valley, so peculiar in their way. He looked upon the gathering with disdain, noticing that Emily Reyes was staring back at him, aware that something was amiss. The remainder of the crowed was drunk on alcohol and enthusiasm, oblivious to Dr. Lee's meager presence in the shadow of Stortz.

"We've been together thirty five years, " said the Senator to his adoring wife, "But I've got a feeling the next four are going to be the best of all."

The crowd again applauded causing Dr. Lee to slowly lurch his beaten body forward, along a sidewall towards the rear of the venue. He took one last look at the Senator, who despite holding his wife's arm up in the air to a never ending series of camera flashes, glanced towards him, momentarily making eye contact yet maintaining a beaming grin, the consummate politician.

He slowly made his way through the partisan crowd, oblivious to any further roars of devotion. Without looking back he exited the main ballroom of the Brookside and found himself alone, in the ornate lobby of the club. There he sat, among a colorful display of pumpkins and chrysanthemums, pondering his options. On his plate was a dead accountant and detective, a cup with a spy chip missing and the threat of harm from the most powerful Senator in Washington. However, it was the thought of Anastasia being present that disturbed him the most, in a queer way.

He took out his cell phone and queued up the videos documenting the Senator's foul play, realizing the irreversible magnitude of his pending action. Next he single handedly accessed the portal of a popular internet pornography site, following the simple steps to upload a home video. While staring at the flashing "Upload" button, the main door to the ballroom opened and out stepped COO Reynolds with a drink and a smile.

"Got to take a leak," said the rapidly moving head of St. Mike's as he passed by. "Hey did you hear the news?"

Dr. Lee just stared at the drunken buffoon.

Reynolds then stepped back towards Lee and leaned down into his face saying, "The Senator promised to get St. Mike's federal funding to complete the new hospital wing in less than a year! Can you believe it?" His breath reeked of alcohol and cheap tobacco.

Lee just stared ahead. The doors behind him reopened as another drunken guest made her way to the bathroom facility. As the door slowly closed the booming voice of the Senator could be heard saying, "What this country needs is the return of family values. Honor, hard work and integrity, that's what I plan on bringing back...."

"Can you believe it, federal dollars!" shouted Reynolds. "The suits back in Kansas City think I'm a genius, gave me a bonus," cackled the sot. "Screw you and Tuckett, we don't need your money now!" He then slapped Dr. Lee on the top of the right shoulder, causing soaring pain down his right arm, prior to turning about towards the lavatory area. While walking away he mumbled, "Federal money, manna from heaven."

Lee then looked down and without hesitation depressed his cell's "Upload" button and watched his premium ultra G network rapidly send the sex tapes into cyberspace for public consumption. He then departed the building.

It was quiet outside the Brookside that evening as light rain trickled down. A convoy of news trucks presented an obstacle course for the now dishonored guest to traverse. He came upon a local community college news crew sitting in their truck, having been denied access into the inner sanctum of the Brookside because of a late arrival. They were two young college students, perhaps in their early twenties, listening to music with the windows partly rolled down. A hedonistic rampage the prior night caused the duo to oversleep that afternoon, arriving late to miss the big news story. Unknowingly their tardiness was about to be handsomely rewarded. The sudden appearance of Lee's face in their passenger side window didn't alarm them a bit.

"What's up pops?" asked the passenger as he rolled down his window. "Did they get the license of the vehicle that hit you?" He was smoking a cigarette, and a short laugh puffed smoke into the bloated face of Dr. Lee.

"Are you two news reporters?"

"Yes," said the driver, "WWVC, the local community college...."

"I have a directive for the world," said Lee. "Would you be kind enough to broadcast my message?"

The duo just stared at each other and laughed, thinking they would at least get some footage from a crackpot that would be of great interest to their YouTube generation. They had no idea of what was about to occur.

Within two minutes the truck's passenger was holding a microphone in front of both himself and Dr. Lee, under a tarp that protected them from the rain. His junior partner was holding a camera upon his shoulder, which was connected by a series of wires to the truck, humming behind him.

"Oh, before we start, what's your name?" asked the interviewer with a final expulsion of smoke from his lungs.

"Start the tape," said Lee.

"We are here today, outside the Brookside Country Club, speaking to a local dignitary who has something of importance to tell the world," said the young man with a smirk of his face. "Please sir, we hear that you have eye witness account to what is transpiring inside the great halls of the Brookside. What can you tell us is going on inside?"

"I would like to add a final chapter to the sterling resume of the great Senator Stortz," said Dr. Lee with a deadpan look.

"Please sir, tell us more," said the sixth year student.

"In honor of Senator Stortz, I've uploaded a video onto the world wide web summarizing his passion for politics," said Lee. "The nation certainly deserves better insight into his undeniable credentials."

"Can you give us an idea of what the video contains?"

"To the discerning viewer the contents will be self explanatory," said Lee. "I need say no more."

"And where can we find this video sir?" asked the student.

Then, without hesitation the good doctor divulged the web site, upon which he terminated the interview and walked away, confident of the carnage he had laid upon the Senator's legacy, family and future generations.

CHAPTER TWENTY EIGHT
FINAL JUSTICE

THE BLACK MERCEDES SUV driven by Dr. Lee roared through the state park like a freight train in the night. The unforeseen evacuation in progress required a very quick stop at his estate, for the necessary destruction of incriminating documents. A phone call earlier had scrambled his flight crew, which were awaiting his arrival on the airport tarmac. The night sky was pitch black with heavy rain clouds screening the moon and releasing a deluge of precipitation upon the valley. If all went well, lift off would be in thirty minutes.

Despite one hand on the wheel the trip homeward was uneventful until the doctor began crossing the very bridge that John Olson was tossed over. The mist and driving rain obstructed his forward view but an inner instinct caused him to slam on the vehicle's breaks about mid way across the span. Then, while the engine idled, he perceived a shimmering light at the other end of the bridge, which suddenly became brilliant.

On command from Special Agent Flood a series of vehicles blocking the road turned on their headlights, creating an impenetrable and blinding barricade. Dr. Lee immediately threw his vehicle in reverse while looking at the rear view mirror, only to see a lesser series of lights block the road behind. He was trapped on the span. A minute passed before he saw a line of silhouetted men approaching him from the forward end of his vehicle, with weapons drawn. He pondered a few options and then exited his vehicle, with the K5 at his side in his left hand. He then stood still approximately fifteen feet in front of his vehicle, with the engine continuing to run.

"Dr. Lee, my name is Special Agent Flood of the F.B.I., put down your weapon."

There was no movement or response. The cadre of lawmen stood approximately sixty feet in front of Lee, spread across a line, some standing and some squatting, all with weapons drawn.

"You are under arrest for the murders of Anastasia Tuckett and John Olson," said Flood.

Lee did not move. He pondered the option of suicide but the mention of Anastasia perplexed him.

"Again doctor, put down your weapon immediately," said Flood.

Lee was trapped, with no way out. He wondered if his soul mate had made it out of the valley.

"Detective Crackstone is alive," said Flood. "He is going to survive, fully aware of what has happened."

"Anastasia is alive," said Dr. Lee slowly to the lawman. "I need to speak to her immediately."

"Why would you think she is alive?"

"Please, I need to speak to her at once," said Lee, who then inadvertently elevated his left arm towards the horizon.

"Keep your weapon down doctor!" screamed Flood. "Drop your weapon now!"

"I need to speak to Anastasia!" yelled Lee. "Now!"

"To tell her what?"

"That I'm sorry," said Lee. "Sorry for what I did to her." He paused before saying, "She was a good person, and innocent of it all."

"Innocent of what Doctor?"

"Everything, the whole mess that Ian and I got her into. She had no idea what was going on," said Lee.

"What about Ian?" asked Flood, "Was he innocent of it all too?"

"Please, let me talk to Anastasia, then I shall surrender into your custody."

"Anastasia is dead doctor. Lost at sea."

"No, she is alive!" yelled Lee. "Please, ask Tony Crackstone. He received a text message from her earlier today. I need to speak to her at once. She is here, alive and in the valley."

"That was a message from us Doctor," said the lead detective slowly. "We had her cell phone. She mailed it out just prior to her death. I sent that text, as part of a plan to confirm our suspicions." Silence took hold for several seconds before Flood spoke again saying, "Anastasia is dead Dr. Lee."

Lee didn't move upon hearing the news, which now made sense. Panic overtook his thought process. How he failed to consider such a ploy was unthinkable, but all was amiss at that very moment.

"It's over Doctor Lee, please put down your weapon."

"We helped a lot of people, Ian and I," said Lee. "Remember that."

"Please, doctor. There's been enough damage done already. Surrender your firearm at once."

The disgraced doctor then looked upwards at the sky, allowing the cold rain to pelt his face for several seconds, appreciating the texture of the drops. A deep inhalation drew the cool air into his lungs with serene appreciation. He then dropped his weapon and bolted towards the bridge guardrail, fully aware of the abyss below.

"Stop!" screamed Flood who along with his agents began a sprint towards the suspect.

The doctor made it to within one final leap of the rail, upon which he planted his left foot, which slid off the wet gravel upon contact, causing a diversion of his upward momentum. His body still hurled forward but failed to clear the top rail, crashing backwards onto the macadam. He immediately righted himself in a forward attempt to flip over the rail, which he made contact with, but was suddenly overwhelmed by multiple officers who pulled him back to the roadway, alive.

Dr. Aran Lee was then taken into police custody for the alleged murders of Anastasia Tuckett and John Olson.

Due to the magnitude of events a decision was made to fly the prisoner back to Philadelphia that very night. As the jet lifted off from the runway the clouds suddenly parted allowing the doctor an expansive view of the valley below. A deep sense of sorrow gripped his heart as the plane began to bank away from the view. His final visual was the logo of the Tuckett Institute blazing in the dark towards the sky above. The large T.O.I. letters sat atop the facility, allowing all overhead traffic to appreciate the absolute excellence that lay beneath them. Sadly he realized that a return to the pastoral valley would never occur, nor would he appreciate the Center of Excellence that he created, and the beauty of all within it. Upon closing his eyes he wondered if Ian Tuckett had any idea whatsoever of the evil that had so darkly surrounded him.

CHAPTER TWENTY NINE

PHILADELPHIA

THE NEWS FROM the valley spread across the nation like a tidal wave, sparing no one of the sordid details. Senator Stortz immediately withdrew his bid for the White House in order to "bring order to his own house," yet retained his seat in the Senate. An apology to the nation with his wife at his side calmed the waters, thanks to a slick marketing firm and a populace all too familiar with political scandal. The sorrowful portrayal of a repentant husband ultimately salvaged his political career, but never his personal life, which bitterly deteriorated over time.

The magnitude of events prompted the temporary shut down of all resident and nursing programs at St. Michael's Hospital. All trainees were asked to evacuate the dormitories the following morning and return to their respective training programs outside the valley. The newly appointed chairman of surgery at the Philadelphia General Hospital, Frederick Riles II, mandated all house staff back to West Philadelphia immediately. Within twenty-four hours skid row was a ghost town, completely void of youthful personnel.

Phil, Jackie and Rick were asked to remain in the valley the following Saturday afternoon to provide statements to the authorities, specific to the thrashing of Dr. Lee and the events immediately preceding it in the operating room. A concerned pathologist provided the authorities with the discarded Tuckett Cup from Mr. Street, after alerting the hospital COO of a "peculiar device" soldered to its backing. The implant represented the only current spy chip available to authorities, which was sent to FBI headquarters in Washington for detailed examination.

Tony Crackstone was indeed alive, compliments of his bulletproof vest and luck. A single piece of shrapnel had made its way into the base of his skull, measuring only one by two millimeters in size. After being found in the stairwell of the Tuckett Institute, the wounded officer was taken by life flight helicopter back to Philadelphia, where he was emergently admitted to the Philadelphia General Hospital. A series of imaging scans and medical consultations recommended nonoperative management. Peculiar to the case was the final resting place of the bullet fragment, which sat innocently within a portion of his brain called the fusiform gyrus, whose function allows a person to recognize faces in more detail than they do inanimate objects. Soon it become apparent to Detective Crackstone that he suffered from prosopagnosia, or facial blindness, which was an irreversible entity altering his ability to recognize faces. The malady permitted the detective to carry out normal activities of daily living, yet precluded him from identifying the face of the responsible gunslinger, thus pardoning their crime.

Late Saturday night found Phil and Rick Polk roaring down the Schuylkill Expressway into the innards of Philadelphia. They had just heard a recap of the events via a Special News Bulletin from KYX News Radio. The news bulletin mentioned the name of Dr. Lee and the Tuckett Orthopedic Institute, but not that of Ian Tuckett himself. The reporter mentioned that the Institute was being shut down immediately, until further notice, due to an ongoing federal investigation into "listening devices being secretly implanted into unsuspecting patients." A specialist from the FBI was quoted within the report as stating, "such devices are currently available, and if surgically implanted within a human can function as a listening device, although this was the first confirmed episode that the FBI was aware of."

It was eleven thirty P.M as the aging vehicle driven by Polk pulled off the expressway onto the Roosevelt Boulevard exit.

Although late in the evening traffic was still congested on the highway.

"I just can't believe it," said Polk upon completion of the radio broadcast. "Just cannot believe the whole entire thing"

"Neither can I," said Phil. "It's going to take a while to sink in."

"I'm going to miss the valley," said Polk. "Loved the people and their ways, like a portion of the universe set aside for future generations to observe."

"Me too," said Phil. "Kind of a folksy weird, if that makes sense."

"I also cannot believe that Jack is off the hook for slugging Dr. Lee, can you believe...."

"This is the exit," said Phil. "Broad Street."

"I know, I know," said Rick, "I went to school in North Philly, remember? This is my neighborhood."

The vehicle sputtered to a traffic light on north Broad Street, which was alive with activity, not all of it legal. The area was known for an eclectic collection of persons, the polar opposite of the valley just three hours away.

"Her address is three blocks south, and then just two off Broad," said Phil with a nervous intensity. "Do you think I'm doing the right thing?"

"I think so," said Rick. "It's what your heart tells you to do, correct?"

"Yes," said Phil confidently. "Without question."

"Always go with your heart," said Polk with a smile.

The vehicle then turned off Broad Street and rumbled two blocks into a neighborhood that neither man had ever traversed. A series of stark brick apartment complexes, each about three stories tall framed the roadway on each side. Some apartments were lit while others were dark.

"Should be on the left," said Phil squinting ahead, "Number 319."

"There it is," said Rick as he pulled the car over to the curb.

"Well here goes nothing," said Phil as he took a deep breath and opened the car door, stretching his six foot five frame towards the curb. "So long friend."

"Keep the faith!" yelled Polk as he pulled the vehicle away from the curb, leaving his best friend alone, in a foreign neighborhood, with no guarantee of a place to rest that night.

Phil made his way up an indoor apartment stairwell to a small second floor landing, while a dog on the first floor barked wildly. He looked to his right to see the letters 2A nailed to the door and then turned to the left to face the 2B entrance. He inhaled and straightening out his collar, followed by a firm knock on the door. All was quiet until the door opened slowly with a creak.

Kendra Mason stood erect and smiling, as if expecting the man standing outside her apartment at the midnight hour. She waited for his words as they stared into each other's eyes. Three feet separated their bodies. A door opening and closing from the apartment below was then heard, followed by the sound of a dog being walked outside on a leash. Phil loved the way Kendra looked, so beautiful and energetic.

"Kendra, I just had...."

"No Phil, you were right, I'm sorry too," said Kendra while stepping towards him. "It wasn't right, I caught you at a vulnerable time, it was both our fault."

"Kendra I just wanted you to know that I'm sorry if...."

"Enough," said Kendra with a calming smile, "I appreciated the phone call earlier but you didn't have to come down and tell me in person." She stepped closer to him and smiled warmly while shaking her head. "You're a great person and I appreciate it, but no hard feelings. O.K.? I completely understand."

"It's just that everything got out of control up there at Saint Mike's," said Phil. "Events got out of hand and I lost my center of gravity. I'm sorry."

"Apology accepted," said Kendra. "I'm sorry too."

They both stepped forward and hugged each other for some time, providing much needed solace to each other.

"You're going to be a great surgeon," said Kendra as she stepped backwards with a smile. "I can see it."

"And you a great nurse," said Phil. "Keep in touch, let me know where you are headed next month."

"I will Phil, I will."

Another short friendship hug was then exchanged between the two, followed by Phil descending the creaky steps with a final wave. The cool outside air felt good upon his face as he sidestepped a bulldog relieving himself on the curb. In all the excitement Kendra failed to notify him that her new hospital rotation started next week, at the Philadelphia General Hospital.

Phil Drummer knew the route to his next destination well, which sat just ten blocks down Broad Street. Unbridled enthusiasm rocketed his liberated soul across the city mile with ease. The next stop would be completely unexpected, as would be the ultimate outcome, yet the visit was imperative despite the hour. In seemingly no time he arrived at the apartment complex, which sat on Broad Street itself.

The apartment was a three story old brownstone, which still contained a lobby intercom system, permitting occupants to speak to arriving guests. Phil stepped into the lobby and immediately searched the mailbox row for Apartment 3D, which had the name S. Ricketts beneath it. He reached forward and pressed the button that triggered a buzzer in Stacey's apartment, hoping that she was still awake. Silence followed, prompting another press of the button. After several more attempts Phil recalled that it was Saturday night, and perhaps no one was home. A sorrowful angst gripped his heart and thought process. It was only then that he heard a sleepy and somewhat raspy voice over the intercom.

"Hello, who is it?" said the voice slowly.

"Stacey, it's me Phil. I need to come up."

"Phil?"

"Yea, Phil. Phil Drummer. Ring me in."

"Phil, what are you doing here?" said Stacey whose voice was now coming to life. "You've got some nerve coming here."

"Stacey please..."

"Do you know how much pain you caused..."

"Stacey, please, please, I can explain everything. Just ring me in. Please trust me, let me explain."

A long ten seconds of silence passed before the overhead buzzer rang in the lobby, allowing Phil to open the security door, which led to the stairwell. He double timed his frame up the steps and was knocking on the door of Apartment 3D in a flash. The door opened and Stacey Ricketts stood directly in front of him, in her pajamas with a scowl.

"How dare you come here Phil, how dare you!" Her voice was that of a whisper yell, a genetically mutated trait specific to the female species. "The poor girl has been crying for days, not leaving her room."

"Stacey, is she home?"

"She's hurting Phil, all because of you and your cheating ways. You're just like all the others."

"Stacey, please calm down, I just need to see her."

"Don't tell me to calm down Phil!" said Stacey with her voice now starting to rise. "You're the one who couldn't keep your hands off the hottie nurse across the hall. How could you? You're such a creep!"

"Stacey, you don't understand."

"What's wrong?" said a sleepy voice behind Stacey. "Stacey, is everything alright?"

Stacey Ricketts froze while continuing to stare directly at Phil. A menacing look grew upon her face. Phil looked to the right, while reaching his left arm across the body of Stacey, gently shifting her protesting frame aside. It was only then that he laid eyes upon Jennifer, standing in the hallway with a dazed look upon her face. She wore a Philadelphia Love logo tee shirt, which came half way down her legs, to the top of her knees. Her hair was a complete mess and she looked absolutely adorable. Phil felt his heart pounding in his throat and he became somewhat short of breath as their eyes met.

"Phil?" said Jenna in disbelief, thinking it was all a dream. She rubbed the sleep from her eyes slowly with both hands. "What are you doing here?"

"Jenna, I'm sorry," blurted Phil. "I'm so very sorry for what I did."

Jennifer just stared at him, realizing that it was not a dream. She almost became faint and started to breath in a short, deep rapid fashion. Tears immediately welled up in her eyes. She began to shake her head back and forth as a single tear rolled down her left cheek, unabated.

Phil then stepped passed Stacey Ricketts knowing that he had to speak from his heart, now or never. He took two steps forward and stopped, allowing some space between himself and Jenna. He wanted to hug her, but knew he could not.

"Jenna, please I'm so very sorry. I lost my bearings up North, which I know was so wrong, but please, please understand that I'm sorry. I'm so sorry that I hurt you."

Tears now began rolling uncontrollably down her face as her body began to tremble. She slowly lowered her head and began to cry. Short whimpers caused her upper torso to slightly twitch, in unison with her sobs.

Phil took one more step closer saying, "Jennifer, please understand. It's always been you and only you. Please forgive me." He paused before finally saying, "I love you Jennifer. I love you so much."

Phil froze one step away from the woman he truly loved. His heart was pounding and his fervent mea culpa complete. What would happen next was dependent upon the woman before him, who suddenly took a step forward and leaned her beautiful body into his, without saying a word. Emotional union was suddenly complete, sealed by an enchanted embrace.

"O.M.G.!" said Stacey choking back tears. "I knew you two were meant for each other. It's true love!"

Phil and Jenna peered back at the social worker, still holding each other firmly in their arms. Jennifer wiped the tears from her eyes while looking up at Phil with a smile. Their trembling bodies never lost contact with each other for the remainder of the night.

At that very moment the sun was slowly rising over the eastern shores of Lake Geneva. The jagged peaks of the Bernese

Alps fought in vain to conceal the sunshine, but as each minute passed, could not. Chateaus along the western shore welcomed the morning glory first, glistening with glee. Along a central ridge overlooking the widest portion of the lake sat a quaint villa, with a peculiar Asian flair. The view from the expansive deck surrounding the mountain house was considered the best on the western shore. Not surprising, if one knew the owner and his penchant for excellence. Unfortunately the master of the house was not present to see the majestic morn, yet his significant other was, enjoying a strong cup of European coffee on the deck, a bit fatigued from the recent flight across the Atlantic.

James was a bit bemused as to how simple his evacuation was from the United States, considering the magnitude of events. He held a large coffee cup between his hands while gently sipping the warm brew, staring out across the lake. His thoughts were with Aran, whom he had met here in Geneva some fifteen years ago. At that time he was adrift, a struggling waiter in his late twenties, the product of a local orphanage, which up until that point he called home. What followed was a torrid affair that simmered into an emotional union, leaving both parties completely content with each other. Their relationship blossomed in New York City, alive and free among the throngs, enjoying everything that a metropolitan lifestyle offered. Their future was bright, up until the banishment of the Tucketts from the eastern shores of the Hudson River. Reluctantly they followed their dear friends and their crumbling marriage to Pennsylvania, realizing that their outward appearance would have to change in a considerable way. Ian and Anastasia Tuckett were privy to their orientation, yet it was considered wise to conceal their love for each other among the provincial valley masses. This shameful suppression in part served as a catalyst for their twisted plan, which attempted to recoup emotional losses from society as a whole.

Confusion gripped James' mind that earlier morning, fully aware that Detective Crackstone was alive. The authorities would ask questions, yet it would become strangely apparent that Tony Crackstone would never identify him as the accomplice gunman, compliments of bad aim and a lucky ricochet.

James however was confident of two things that beautiful autumn morning, as a flight of geese honked directly above him. One was the need to repent for his sins, perhaps with a donation of criminal riches to a local orphanage that was nearby and dear to his heart. The second was eternal devotion to a man that despite his dastardly scheme was his soul mate for life. A man now imprisoned somewhere in Philadelphia, alone in a cell that was dank, dirty and cold.

THE END

ABOUT THE AUTHOR

DR. MICHAEL BANAS completed his undergraduate studies at the University of Scranton. He then attended the University of Pennsylvania School of Medicine followed by an Orthopedic residency at the University of Rochester. His final year of surgical training took him to Los Angeles where he completed a Sports Medicine Fellowship at the Southern California Orthopedic Institute. Dr. Banas currently resides in Dallas, PA with his wife and six children. He specializes in Orthopedic Surgery and Sports Medicine.

Made in the USA
San Bernardino, CA
31 May 2017